THE CAPTAIN

"THE CAPTAIN"

THE CAPTAIN

STORIES OF THE BLACK BORDER

By
AMBROSE E. GONZALES

The Black Heritage Library Collection

BOOKS FOR LIBRARIES PRESS
FREEPORT, NEW YORK
1972

PS3513
O3895C3

First Published 1924
Reprinted 1972

Reprinted from a copy in the
Fisk University Library Negro Collection

INTERNATIONAL STANDARD BOOK NUMBER:
0-8369-8969-4

LIBRARY OF CONGRESS CATALOG CARD NUMBER:
78-37593

PRINTED IN THE UNITED STATES OF AMERICA
BY
NEW WORLD BOOK MANUFACTURING CO., INC.
HALLANDALE, FLORIDA 33009

TO
RALPH EMMS ELLIOTT
"THE CAPTAIN"

TABLE OF CONTENTS

THE CAPTAIN	1
A RIEVER OF THE BLACK BORDER	17
"RUN, NIGGUH, RUN!"	33
AFTER THE FRUIT THE FLOUR	51
THE GREEN CALABASH	65
DADDY BO'SUN	81
THE UNDER DOG	93
THE QUEST OF THE LAND	111
THE LAND IN SIGHT	125
THE LAND ON PAPER	141
THE LAND SURVEYED	155
THE SURVEY CONTINUED	173
THE SURVEY COMPLETED	187
SETTLING THE LAND	203
THE FIRST CABIN COMPLETED	219
THE LAND SETTLED	235
THE COLONY AT THE FLOOD	251
THE COLONY AT THE EBB	265
THE TIDE RUN LOW	283
HUNTRESS AND THE BUCK	299
THE RIVER AND THE SEA	317
THE TRENCHERMAN AND THE SHARK	333
THE SHARPIE AND THE "TRUS'-ME-GAWD"	349
HOW THE DEVIL LOST HIS TAIL	367

FOREWORD

For nearly two hundred years the institution of slavery bore heavily upon the Southern States.

First, because the wealth that came to them through Negro labor brought upon the slave states the envy—ripening at last into hatred—of the "free" states of the Union, whose unprofitable slaves, sold to the South, had thriven amazingly under genial skies and the kindly discipline of the great plantations, enriching their owners far more through the primitive process of reproduction than by productive labor in the fields.

Second, because the planters' sons, fine as was their culture, high as were the traditions of their race, lacked the ambition, the self-reliance, the incentive to personal effort, that would have been theirs had they depended upon themselves alone and not looked forward to inheriting plantations and Negroes. True, when the supreme trial of war was upon them, they met the test like men, enduring through the tempered steel of their spirits hardships under which men of stronger physical fibre, but weaker spirit, crumpled and broke. What the sons of the plantations could have done, but for the ease of slaveholding, has been demonstrated in countless instances since the Confederate War, by the part that youths of their blood—without means or education—have played in building up, not only their own States, but many great communities of the North and West, carrying into

FOREWORD

their work, at home and abroad, a touch of fineness—putting spiritual above material things—the idealism which, alone, lifts true men above the countless human clods that clutter the earth!

But however slaveholding may have borne upon the slaveholder in denying him knowledge of commercial and industrial life and the mechanic arts—training that would have been worth so much to him in repairing his broken fortunes after the ruin of War, his material loss was his spiritual gain, for while his training was entirely for a planter's life—he could hardly have made a living in any other calling—the planter's, the slaveholder's responsibilities were always before him. The obligation to deal justly, kindly, humanely, with human beings whose bodies he actually owned, appealed to the chivalry, the higher instincts of the slaveholder.

And those whose instincts were not so high, who were disposed to be harsh or exacting taskmasters, were held in check by the strict and wholesome slave code, adopted by the South Carolina planters for their own regulation; a law affording far more protection to the slave (in whom inhered both human and property rights) than the laws of any state afford the poor of any race today. Far stronger, however, than act or code, was a public opinion that scorned and ostracised the hard or cruel master and held him up to public contempt.

And with the responsibility of ownership went the authority, the right to command, and the supreme consciousness of racial superiority that the

FOREWORD

white peasant or the non-slaveholder of the middle class could never attain.

This the Negro slave knew as well as he knew the color of his own skin, and that knowledge went with him into freedom. The once wealthy planter, clad in tawdry, ill-fitting jeans, might walk the dusty road, but the well-dressed freedman on horseback would make his low obeisance as he passed—to character and to "blood." The Negro may have been his own former slave, or another's; the former slaveholder may have been entirely unknown to the Negro who saluted him—it mattered not; the former slave instinctively recognized the master type and "made his manners."

As long as the older Negroes lasted, during the first twenty-five or thirty years of freedom, the *nouveaux-riches*—"the butcher, the baker, the candlestick-maker," and the corner-shopkeeper who had come into the ownership of landed property—while treated with respect, were held rather lightly by the old slaves, as interlopers who, through the fortunes of war, or the misfortunes of Reconstruction, had come into plantations formerly owned by aristocrats, and between the old and the new—whom behind their backs the Negroes referred to as po'-buckruh—the line was sharply drawn.

But with the passing of the old Negroes, who had recognized an aristocracy of blood alone, there came a change, for many "bottom rails" had come on top, and these, having wealth and position, the younger Negroes learned in time to look up to with a com-

FOREWORD

plaisance their fathers would have denounced as snobbery.

Fifty years ago, however, the old order was unchanged, and in the Captain's time and the Captain's country, there was perfect understanding between former master and former slave—save on election day, when former slave went to the polls and voted a red-inked "Union Republican ticket" put into his hands by aliens and renegades, "against the peace and dignity of the State," and the mutual interests of his former master and himself!

But for this biennial gesture—becoming in time only a gesture, and abandoned—there was no break in the perfect understanding. Because of the former relationship, the dispossessed master was supposed to be to his former slave, now freed, "a very present help in time of trouble," and to him he went with the utmost freedom. "Are you not my master? To whom shall I go, if not to you?" And the appeal was seldom resisted.

The obligation of service was not reciprocal, however. It was assumed to rest only upon the former master, never upon the former slave, who expected compensation for the smallest service he was called on to perform for his benefactor, however great may have been the benefaction. This status was recognized and accepted by white and black in perfect amity and understanding. Former master did not expect too much from former slave, and he got what he expected. Sure that he could trust him with his life or his good name, he was exceedingly

FOREWORD

doubtful about his locked corn-crib, and not at all doubtful about his livestock, or anything else that was not locked up!

It is given to few white men to fathom the Negro mind. His former master knows him best, but even he can never get at the bottom of all the Negro is thinking. He may be sure he is lying—he usually is—but what he is trying to conceal, or why, he may not know—he can only suspect, and he always does!

But of one thing the white man of the slaveholding class has always been sure—in war or peace, under slavery or freedom, the good intent of the Negroes toward the persons of those to whom they once belonged. Even during the tense days of Reconstruction, in communities where they swarmed a hundred to one, the white man slept in absolute security with unlocked doors, however securely he nailed up his corn-crib and his smokehouse!

The South has paid high tribute to the loyalty and devotion of the slaves to their masters' families during the Confederate War, when every white man and boy was at the front. Perhaps in time—in God's good time—some Northern man, loving truth, will see, and say that only generations of kindly masters could have commanded such loyalty. It was the consciousness of their own humanity and kindliness toward their slaves, as well as their knowledge of the Negro's innate good nature, that made them willing to leave their families with no other protection. This is true at least of the Low-country plantations of South Carolina and Georgia. Here

FOREWORD

the culture of the slaveholders was generally finer than elsewhere in the slave states, and, "like master, like man," the Negroes benefited by the higher standards set before them.

Under the almost feudal system of the Lowcountry plantations, the devotion of the old family slaves to their masters was comparable to, but even stronger than, that of servant to master in the great English families, wherein for generations the most cordial and confidential relations existed, for if the slave belonged to the master, the master likewise belonged to the slave, who prided himself upon his master's family and upheld its traditions so stoutly that old servants sometimes questioned the fitness of a match under consideration for a son or daughter of the "Big House," objecting to the alliance as unsuitable for a member of "our family."

A lovable old Presbyterian clergyman, a devout and godly militant, who put away his pulpit and his great Bible for the four years of the Confederacy, while—with a pocket testament for his soul's sake, and a long musket for his country's—he fought as a private for the Southern cause, used to tell, with a merry twinkle in his eye, a joke at his own expense.

One Sunday morning before the war, the clergyman, then in early middle life, was driving alone to meet an appointment at a distant church. The road was rough and his harness was light, and as his horse jumped suddenly, to pull the wheels out of a

FOREWORD

deep rut, a trace snapped and brought him to a standstill.

The man of God got out of the buggy, examined the broken trace, and walked around and around in perplexity, trying to think a way out of his trouble—perhaps he prayed, but for half an hour no answer came, and he thought with sinking heart of the little church, yet miles away, and of the expectant congregation slowly gathering, while he for whom they waited was stalled on a lonely road with no help in sight.

At last, a few hundred yards away, a dark spot at the edge of the road, moving slowly nearer, changed to the figure of a man; an old Negro shambled up and, lifting his hat, pulled his forelock in deferential courtesy, giving an extra touch in recognition of the "cloth."

"Maussuh, you dey een trouble?" said the old man, seeing the broken trace. "Kin I fix'um fuh you?"

"Yes, if you can, daddy", said the clergyman, gratefully, "but I don't see how you'll do it."

"Maussuh, you got knife?" The knife was handed over.

"You got string?" and a handful of stout twine was rummaged out of the box under the buggy seat and added to the knife.

The old Negro grunted with satisfaction, and boring with the small blade half a dozen holes in each of the broken ends of the trace, deftly laced the twine through them and spliced them strongly together, wrapping the break with the string that remained

FOREWORD

for additional strength. Then he looked up proudly, and scraped his foot in thankfulness for the half dollar that he clutched in his gnarled old fingers.

"Daddy," said the clergyman, as he gathered up his lines, "I had the knife, and I had the twine, now, why couldn't I do that?"

"Well, you see, Maussuh," said the old darky, with a chuckle, "Gawd, Him ain't gib sense to *ebb'rybody!*"

An old rice-planter, now long dead, used to tell, a generation ago, of an incident in his own experience that showed the absolute freedom of speech old family servants permitted themselves while addressing their masters.

Large families were the rule in the old days, and by the time the war came the planter's quiver was full, but so were his great barns, his stackyards—tented with golden ricks—and the Negro quarters of his great plantation at Rantowles teemed with black children, growing up along with those who would one day be their masters.

But seventy-five years ago the planter's quiver was not yet full. By then, only two or three tiny craft had come to port from the mythical "Babycome Bay." So when, "in the course of human events," news reached the plantation quarters that another young master had arrived, there was great excitement among the black folk, old and young, and they looked forward anxiously to the day, a month or two later, when, according to cus-

FOREWORD

tom, master and mistress would introduce the new arrival to the little Negroes and the old slaves whose infirmities restricted them to the quarters.

"One fine day" in winter, when the sun tempered the soft wind that blew over the marshes from the sea, the planter and his blooming young wife, arm in arm, set out on foot for the distant quarters, followed by an impressive looking mauma, whose headkerchief towered above her like a bishop's mitre. Within her arms she proudly bore, swathed in a "Canton crepe" shawl and cradled upon a soft pillow, the youngster upon whom, for six weeks, the interest of mansion and cabin had centered.

As the triumphal procession neared the quarters, the Negro-house-yard—the long, wide street, flanked by a double row of houses—swarmed with expectant children, faces scrubbed to shininess and kinky heads carefully combed. But these were shoo'd and herded out of the way until the child should first be presented to the old folk who, dressed in their best, sat on their door-steps as the little procession passed, and loyally welcomed the young master with many expressions of admiration and affection. Reaching the far end of the street, they returned on the other side, their progress enlivened by the quaint and graceful compliments the old black folk knew so well how to pay.

At last, having completed the circuit, they paused before leaving the quarters, to receive the greetings of the children, who had been carefully coached by the old plantation nurse. Came up one by one boys

FOREWORD

and girls, to scrape a foot, or drop a curtsy, "each after his kind", and each, as he made his little gesture of fealty, withdrew to the circle of his round-eyed fellows, and gave place to another, until, at last, all had made their devoirs.

Then the plantation nurse, a fine old family servant, stepped up and gazed intently into the pink face and big brown eyes of the wondering child. The planter and his beautiful wife, still arm in arm, paused for the gracious compliment they confidently expected to fall from the old slave's lips—a stirrup-cup to warm them on their way. They waited, but still the old nurse gazed, as though trying to solve a puzzle.

At length she raised her head quickly with a air of great relief, and, with a sly glance at her mistress, gave her master the comforting assurance:

"Maussuh! Missis didn't fool you *dis* time. Dis chile de berry image uh you!"

The first five stories of "The Captain" series were written and published in The State during the winter of 1921-22. The remaining nineteen were written and published in the spring and summer of the present year.

AMBROSE E. GONZALES.

Columbia, S. C.
October, 1924.

THE CAPTAIN AND OTHER STORIES

THE CAPTAIN

For more than twenty years "the Captain," as he was called by the younger men who loved him, has slept his last sleep at Elmwood, on the shoulder of the slope that looks beyond the river, across the wooded hills of Lexington to the far western horizon. The elms that wave their graceful boughs above his grave, the scrub-pines thick-clustered in the woods nearby, are of alien growth, for the sleeper was reared in old Beaufort District, along the Low-Country coasts beside the shimmering waters, where, since the 17th century, his forbears had passed their honorable lives under the moss-draped live-oaks and where at last they rested, each generation handing on to its successor the guiding principle, *noblesse oblige*.

If the Captain could rise from his quiet resting place and look once more with earthly eyes toward the sunset skies as they glowed dull red in the wintry dusk, or lifted glorified thunder-heads in summer, or flamed with the effulgence of autumn, his spirit might yearn for the fields he had roamed as a boy, for the forests he had hunted in his young manhood, for the wide marshes and the broad inlets of the coast, for the flash of the iridescent channel-bass as he leapt in the sunshine, for the

THE CAPTAIN

rush of the antlered deer as he broke cover, and for the dancing white-capped waves as his sailboat sped over them. But with them would mingle memories of the friends—men and women and children—whom he had gained and held in the city of his adoption, for in Columbia the Captain spent the last twenty years of his life, and as he passed along her quiet streets, or sat in the cool of the summer evenings in front of the old News and Courier Bureau, or of The State office, chair tilted back and long pipe in mouth, many paused in kindly greeting or stopped to chat, for those were the days of the Capital City's meditation, and few people hurried on their way.

An ardent Confederate, the Captain loved to foregather with his fellow-veterans of the Lost Cause, and his straight six feet and his beautiful chestnut beard made him a striking figure at every reunion he attended.

Like all Confederates that had encountered only the Eastern armies of the Union, he held "Yankees" lightly, for the hard-fighting Federals, like young Lochinvar, "came out of the West," and at all the meetings of his "Camp" the Captain, an impressive and accomplished raconteur, contributed his full share of reminiscence.

Nor were the veterans his only auditors, for to the end of his days the Captain was a young-man's man. Strange, too, for youth is hopeful, and, in speech, at least, the Captain was a pessimist. Perhaps youth penetrated the verbal disguise in which

THE CAPTAIN

the Captain set forth his thoughts, and realized that, as under the law of averages, ill-luck comes up oftener than its opposite, the Captain was merely playing safe to save his face as a prophet; but certain it is that no crop ever yielded quite so little, no race-horse ever ran quite so far behind, and no political campaign ever brought so deep humiliation upon State and Nation as the Captain predicted!

So, whenever two or three young men gathered about him, the Captain talked slowly, oracularly, convincingly, but always entertainingly; frequently with the sharp edge of his tongue turned toward a friend among those present, for his shrewd and caustic wit was no respecter of persons, and many a wholesome truth was rubbed into one who needed the truth, but in such a jesting, jocular way that he couldn't take offense.

And he hated shams and snobs, and, while recognizing merit, whether under broadcloth or jeans, he held in utter contempt the purse-proud and the *nouveaux-riches*—those who had only their money to commend them.

And what a squire of dames he was! One would walk a mile to see him lift his hat and bend over a lady's hand in courtly Eighteenth-Century fashion, and the swish of a silken petticoat was ever to his ears as the whisper of an angel's wing!

The Captain was early in the war. As a guide he rode his hard-mouthed black "Damphool" across the foot-bridge at Secessionville to show the Louisiana Tigers the way into the fight. Under his gal-

THE CAPTAIN

lant kinsman, Stephen Elliott, he served with the Beaufort artillery in the sand fort at the defense of Port Royal, at another time with the Charleston Light Dragoons, but his title of Captain came from the command of a small company of guides, expert riders, who knew every hunting trail in the forests of the Coast.

As the Captain, from the time his face turned toward the sunset, was a young-man's man, so in early manhood and middle life he was a boy's man, and during the years following the war his young nephews would slip off at night to the one-room log cabin, a hundred yards away from the primitive habitation that sheltered "the family," to hear "Uncle Rafe"—Low-Country (as English) for Ralph—spin his yarns.

"The Shanty," as the Captain called his bachelor bedroom, was built of squared logs, the spaces between stuffed with Spanish moss and plastered with clay. On winter nights fires of oak or hickory logs roared in the wide chimney, and here the Captain, tilted back in a rough plantation rocking-chair of split white-oak, would stretch out his long legs, sometimes crossing his feet upon the low mantel, and then, as the small boys clustered about him on stools or empty soap boxes, he'd light his pipe and, reaching into memory's pigeon-holes, fetch forth such anecdotal treasures as would have gladdened the heart of Sheherezade!

A generation ago the jovial Senator Matt Ransom of North Carolina, known for his "presence"

THE CAPTAIN

as for his great ability, used to tell with much unction a story at his own expense showing how the Tarheels exalted the one and discounted the other of the Senator's distinguishing qualifications.

Upon one occasion Senator Ransom, incognito, was looking through the exhibit of blooded horses at the State Fair at Raleigh. His attention was attracted to a magnificent stallion which a gray-headed black groom was leading proudly around the arena. As the Senator halted the old darky to admire his charge, the stallion veiled his tail, arched his neck, dilated his nostrils, and curveted as proudly as the charger so beautifully described in Shakespere's "Venus and Adonis."

"Fine horse you have there, uncle," said the Senator.

"He yiz dat, suh; he yiz dat."

"What's his name, uncle?"

"Matt Ransom, suh."

"Fine name he has, uncle," said the flattered statesman.

"Yaas, suh; he sho' hab, suh."

"Well, uncle, what can he do? Is he a running horse?"

"Naw, suh, he caint run!"

"Oh, I see, he's a trotter."

"Naw, suh, he caint trot."

"Can't run and can't trot! He's in the stud, then. He must have some fine colts."

"Yaas, suh, but none on 'em ain't no 'count."

THE CAPTAIN

"Well, uncle, if your horse can neither run nor trot, and is a failure in the stud, what has he got to justify his name?"

"Style, suh, style!"

Of his former master, Governor Duncan Clinch Heyward, Joe Fields of Pon Pon asseverates, "You nebbuh see nobody kin cock 'e hat stylish lukkuh Mas' Clinch."

But whatever claims for style may have been advanced by the dusky admirers of these two gentlemen, 'tis certain that none could smoke a pipe with more grace than the Captain. Cigars he held as dudish devices that were liable to burn one's beard unless they were crumbled and rammed into the bowl of a pipe, where those that friends wished upon him soon turned to ashes. Sometimes the bowl was of clay—a deep red Powhatan from Virginia, or a pallid Sally Mikell from North Carolina; and these were smoked with either flexible cane-root stems five feet long, or three-foot reeds from the Ti-Ti. If the long cane roots were used, the bowl of the pipe rested on the bricks of the hearth or on the brass fender; but with the shorter stems the bowl adorned the table. When the Captain went abroad, however, he smoked a briar-root with a wild-cherry stem. There was only cheap tobacco to be had in those days—Blackwell's Durham, flavored with Tonka beans; but the smoke was fragrant, and it rose from his bearded lips like incense as he slowly puffed.

THE CAPTAIN

The Captain would often tell the boys of the fine tobaccoes which he had smoked long ago while a student at the University of Virginia, and "Lone Jack," "Brown Dick," and "Killikinick" became, in time, household words with them.

The Captain seemed to recognize always that the child is father of the man, and he made the boys feel as though they were entirely on the same plane with himself in understanding, and that the same obligation rested upon them as upon himself to live up to the traditions and measure up to the ethical standards of the men of the clan—at least as far as the code of the woods was concerned.

No boy who accepted the Captain as mentor would ever have left his deer-stand in the woods until the horn summoned him to quit the drive; nor would he ever have "cut in" between another stander and the oncoming deer—an unethical practice too often indulged in, and always severely reprobated by the Captain.

The young fisherman whom the Captain coached learned to drop his baited hook upon the bosom of a still pool as softly as a butterfly alighting upon an open flower. And he knew that the big fish lurked on the down-stream side of some old log, where the unvexed waters roiled only with the stir of the big fellows as they neared the surface.

And while the Captain talked always with assurance, with conviction, he was never dogmatic, never vain or boastful of his own exploits; but there had been mighty hunters and fishermen

THE CAPTAIN

among his forbears, and of their prowess afield and afloat, the Captain never wearied of telling. In time we came to know the hunting companions of our grandfather and of our great uncles, the forests they hunted, the horses they rode, the guns they shot, the famous Negro deer-drivers who cared for the equally famous packs and rode with the hounds. And we knew by legend, by word of mouth, the waters that the fishermen of our clan had sailed, the bays and inlets and rivers they had fished, the famous "drops" where the drumfish bit in the month of April, the fallen live-oak at the edge of the tidal river whose barnacle-covered limbs, swept by the salt tides, brought those in quest of sheepshead and black drum from afar, the favored spot where the brackish head-waters of a narrow creek offered at certain seasons the finest run for the beautiful striped bass.

Well for the elder boys that the Captain told them these things in the days of their youth, for, with all their inherited love of nature—sea, field, and forest, and the wild life with which they were peopled—they were never, save in these early memories and in their dreams, to hunt or fish or sail to the end of their days!

Information and admonition flowed from the Captain's lips as smoothly as oil from a cruet, and were absorbed by the boys' minds almost unconsciously. He seldom lectured or scolded. Whenever he pointed a moral, he adorned it with a tale, usually the tale of some incident that happened so long ago that its

THE CAPTAIN

authenticity could not be doubted! If one knew his grandfather to have been a mighty hunter, and that grandfather's son passed on to one the observations of that grandfather on the ways of animals and birds, or on any of the phenomena of nature, the information found lodgment much more firmly than if it had been imparted by way of a lecture or a lesson. Thus the boys early learned the danger of shooting a rifle on the level in a flat wooded country, merely by a recital of the experience of an elder whose ball, striking the side of a pine, had glanced and gone off at right angles disastrously. The boy who carried his gun carelessly soon learned that muzzles should point either toward the heavens above or the earth beneath—never horizontally. And if while riding he thrust his feet too far into the stirrups, he was sure to hear at the next storytelling of some hunter dragged to his death because he could not extricate himself in time from a falling horse!

The Captain often told the boys about the antebellum glories of Charleston's high society: of the St. Cecilia and the Jockey Club balls, of the sumptuous suppers and the rich and sparkling wines; how, at these social reunions, the Captain always drank Hock, or other light, dry wine, and, eschewing the alluring and seductive Champagne, kept his head while others nodded at the board. Thus the boys, to whom molasses and water was a treat, learned the ways of high life in the old times!

THE CAPTAIN

And the races! The Captain sometimes told of the classic events that had made turf history on the famous old Washington race-course at Charleston. And he never tired of telling of the great four-mile race between Tar River and Nina, and we gloried with him in the triumph of the South Carolina mare over the Virginia horse.

The Captain, with his almost uncanny understanding of Negroes, knew the responsiveness of these imaginative people to picturesque and expressive speech, and whenever he found it necessary to stimulate or admonish a gang of lazy or sullen blacks he unlimbered a vocabulary of expletives that would have warmed the heart and moistened the lips of "Uncle Toby" in Flanders! As a rule, they were used jocularly, so they left no sting, and those who received the verbal fire were usually proud of the distinction and always exaggerated the weight of the charge whose impact the target had received.

"Tittuh! Oonuh yeddy me! W'en Mas' Rafe cuss 'e *cuss!* Mas' Rafe, him ent got no kibbuh 'puntop him mout'! En' no use fuh bex 'long Mas' Rafe w'en 'e cuss you, 'cause ef you swell'up w'en 'e cuss you one time, him gwine cuss you *two time,* en' de two-time wuh 'e cuss you gwine wuss mo' den de one-time wuh 'e cuss you, 'cause all de cuss wuh 'e fuhgit fuh t'row 'puntop you de fus' time, him gwine 'membuhr'um befo' him gitt'ru cuss you de las' time; en' w'en him gitt'ru cuss you fuh de two-time, alltwo you yez gwine full'up wid cuss

THE CAPTAIN

same lukkuh stackyaa'd full up wid blackbu'd! Only t'ing fuh do w'en Mas' Rafe cuss you, oonuh haffuh laugh. Soon ez you teet' biggin fuh shine him gwine stop, en' ef oonuh tell'um, 'Ki, Mas' Rafe! you sho' hab uh giftid mout' fuh cuss Nigguh!' him gwine sattify. Mas' Rafe him *done* fuh kin cuss!"

But the Captain's "cussing"—it could hardly have been called cursing—was so picturesque, so apt in its application to the individual addressed, and withal so good-natured, that only those whose consciences pricked them regarded his characterizations as offensive. At all the gatherings around the commissary, or at the noon hour when the field-hands assembled in summer under the shade of some great live-oak, certain of the younger women, secure in the belief that none of their offenses against the plantation had been detected, would say something to touch off Mas' Rafe's always loaded magazine of expletives, in pleasant anticipation of the discomfiture of their companions; but they would not infrequently find that they had caught a tartar, for the Captain's knowledge of Negro nature in general and of certain individuals in particular, would prompt him to sweep the crowd with a gatling-like volley of objurgation, and the general laughter evoked would tell him he had touched up a galled jade or two among those who had started him off. When angered by a real grievance, however, the Captain was a self-starter, and his explosions always carried solid shot to his target!

THE CAPTAIN

However successful these primitive Negroes are in hiding their misdemeanors from "de Buckruh," they know one another too well to concede impeccability to any among their fellow blacks, and the guffaws among the crowd, as the verbal artillerist "shelled the woods," seldom failed to impress upon a shrewd observer like the Captain the truth of the Hibernian observation:

"Manny a shot, at random sint,
Hits the very marrk it was intindid."

The years first following the Confederate War were hard on the elder brothers and the youths and half-grown boys upon whom responsibilities rested, but they were harder far upon the men of gentle birth who had survived, for there was no employment for those who were without the means of planting or conducting a mercantile business of their own. It was very pitiful that men of culture and refinement, university graduates, willing and anxious to work at humble tasks, should be denied employment merely because they were "gentlemen." But so it was. Many of the larger plantations, and practically all the mercantile establishments, from the great stores at the county-seats or the river-landings, to the small shops at the cross-roads, were in the hands of carpet-baggers, or of low-class natives, who, as in all great upheavals, had profited by the wreckage of the strata above them. And these men, commanding well-nigh all the capital in the Low-Country, were indisposed to the employment of "gentlemen" as overseers or clerks—not, it should

THE CAPTAIN

be said to their credit, because of any inherent objection to breeding and culture, but because they were ashamed to employ in subordinate positions and give orders to, the sometime lords of the land. Boys and youths of the same blood, however, having approached manhood under rough and hard conditions, were not supposed to be "gentlemen" —except as to character and deportment—and these the *nouveaux-riches* hired and ordered about with the utmost freedom. Thus it was that a rough, strong young cub of 16 or 17, who had never worn a linen collar in his life, and had but a smattering of education, could often earn twice as much as his highly educated father or uncle, and it cost him just half as much to live.

The wreck of the Confederacy bore heavily upon the Captain's fortunes, as upon those of others of his clan. A few years of precarious planting, on borrowed money at usurious interest and plantation supplies at over-loaded prices, forced him to seek employment of any sort, wherever he could find it.

The Captain found it at a saw mill far from home, where for a long time he worked out of doors willingly, even gladly, measuring lumber, for $25 a month, and keeping bachelor's hall in a rough board shanty.

Throughout the war, men of gentle birth had fought as privates shoulder to shoulder with their rougher comrades, who quit the plow-handles or laid down the tools of the artisan to fight for their

THE CAPTAIN

common country. Brave soldiers in the field, all of them, but the men of culture and refinement, because their spirits were more finely tempered, endured the monotony of the camp with greater fortitude, ate their parched corn more cheerfully, and wore their gray rags more jauntily than did their comrades from the humbler walks of life.

Now the elbow-touch was lost, the fires of combat had burned to the ashes of despair, and even hope was gone! But among the embers of the past the spirit of the South still glowed, and the courage that bore those within whose breasts it flamed through the bloody fields and starving camps of the Confederacy sustained them still, under the yet heavier spiritual strain of Reconstruction! And in the quiet tragedies that were enacted day by day under the live-oaks or along the streams of the ruined Low-Country, the actors played their parts none the less heroically that they wore the garb of the peasant and the slave! For among the trials put upon these men of gentle birth not the least was the lack of decent clothing and the refinements of their former life; the coming down from broadcloth, English cassimere, and fine linen to the coarse plantation jeans and denims worn by the Negro field-hands, was to many more tragic than the loss of prestige and power.

The live-oaks of the Low-Country stretch their protecting arms, as though in prayer, above the unmarked graves of many gallant gentlemen who wore the rough jeans with distinction to the end of

THE CAPTAIN

their lives, putting it off at last only for the homespun wrappings of their shrouds—the coarse though kindly shrouds that brought them rest!

A RIEVER OF THE BLACK BORDER

Monday Parker and his brothers and sisters—a large family—were all intelligent and capable, inheriting these qualities from their mother, Maum Pender—an unusual name, and a Negro of unusual ability, tall and slender, with small and well-shaped hands and feet, high aquiline nose, thin lips, and distinguished carriage. Maum Pender transmitted the shapeliness of her hands and feet, with their tapering fingers and arched insteps, to all her offspring, and the gift of slender fingers made them famous cotton-pickers. But, in respect to husbands, Pender having been as comprehensive as a Smart-Set New Yorker of the present day, her prepotency did not impress her aquiline nose upon more than half her quiver-full, and as Monday had been sired by one of his mother's flatnosed affiliations, no nasal promontory jutted forth to break the broad expanse of his flat, good-natured face.

Monday walked rapidly, with long springy steps, and swung his arms in exaggerated fashion, perhaps through pride in his ancestry, for he claimed descent from an African king—a "Foulah" he said; but as the Foulahs, an intelligent people, are tawny in color, while the members of Monday's clan were all of a rich, shiny, brownish black, it is probable that the Foulah tradition, stuck in the memory of some breech-clouted captive from the West Coast, was no better authenticated than some of the Mayflower pedigrees that have stretched so many mas-

THE CAPTAIN

culine hatbands and swelled so many feminine corsages throughout the North and West!

But whether of Foulah, Gullah, or Mandingo blood, it is certain that Monday's ancestral arms must have borne a boar—a boar not rampant, but quiescent, a boar singed or scalded and hung by the heels, for Monday's instinct for the cloven-footed quadruped forbidden to the children of Israel was as that of the rill for the river, the river for the sea! As he padded noiselessly through the woods forbidden to poachers or prowlers his ears were always pricked for squeal or squeak or grunt —the sweetest music that could come to them—and Monday knew how to interpret their faintest inflection—fear, hope, hunger, satiety, were all expressed as the half-wild shoats foraged through the woods, nosing about under the oaks for the fallen acorns, or rooting in the swampy places for grubs or snails, and if their voices seemed sympathetic, indicating mental serenity, Monday would utter a soft, crooning swineherd's call, *"peeg, peeg, peeg."*

Repeating this at intervals as they neared him with furtive steps and questioning grunts, he would throw wide a handful of corn from his knapsack, then other handfuls nearer and yet nearer, until he had tolled them to his very feet. By now, Monday would have dropped his axe to the ground and his appraising eye would have fixed upon the fattest shoat in the bunch, which by the abundance of his largesse he patiently coaxed into his confidence. When the intended victim had been skilfully ma-

A RIEVER OF THE BLACK BORDER

neuvered into position for vicarious sacrifice, with his tail toward the slaughterer, Monday would stoop as swiftly as a hawk from the blue, seize the animal by a hind leg and throw him, when a blow between the eyes from the ready axe, and the knife slipped into his throat, silenced all but the poor pig's first squeal of protest at the betrayal of his confidence.

As the squeal never reached the ears of "de Buckruh"—for two-legged marauders seldom adventured within a mile of the farmstead—Monday was safe, and slipping his prize into a sack cached it in some convenient thicket near his cabin until nightfall should make its butchery reasonably safe. If the shoat were but a small one, he kept its theft to himself, for its scalding and dressing could be contrived within the privacy of his own cabin, and, needing no help, he took none into his confidence; but for the more ambitious captures, his cronies were called in. If any among these had pigs of his own, and if the weather were cool enough to avert suspicion, the matter was simple, for the pig owner boldly boiled the water on his own premises, and those who passed by believed him to be preparing the product of his own pen; but if none among the Free Companions could thus offer justification for the possession of pork, or if the weather were too warm to make lawful butchery reasonable, the confederates would slip a large iron pot into a sack, build a fire near some woodland branch or spring, scald and dress the porcine carcass, and divide the meat.

THE CAPTAIN

In this brotherhood of the frying-pan his cronies sometimes shared with Monday such spoils as they were able to lift from the pens, the kraals, or the wide pastures of the palefaces, but their contributions to the common good were negligible compared with those of one whose attainments had exalted him among his fellows as Rob Roy was exalted among the cattle-rievers of the Scottish border, or King Arthur among the Knights of the Table Round!

Nor among these lowly jungle folk was a Prophet without honor, nor was a lifter's prowess denied cordial, even generous recognition.

"Paa'kuh, him sho' hab uh giftid han' fuh ketch hog."

"Yaas, man, you talk trute. Him ketch'um en' 'e hol'um alltwo. W'en Gawd mek Buh Monday, Him sho' g'em uh fait'ful han' fuh hol' hog! Ef Buh Monday ebbuh graff hog by 'e hine foot! da' hog done mek up 'e min' fuh dead! 'E nebbuh fuh loose'um 'tel t'unduh roll!"

While Monday, fond of the sound of his own voice, was gregariously inclined during his working hours, and dearly loved the gatherings at the Cross-roads store on pay days or Saturday nights, he was seldom willing to live on a plantation street, preferring the privacy of an isolated cabin some distance away from the "quarters" or "Negro-house-yard." By thus "keeping his distance," Monday not only kept his chickens and his children from mixing too indiscriminately with those of his brothers in black,

A RIEVER OF THE BLACK BORDER

but these brothers in black, together with the sisters thereunto appertaining—all of them inclined to be inquisitive, if not inquisitorial—were prevented from knowing too much about Monday's business; and as long as Monday's business was light, whenever the stolen shoats were small enough to be scalded without help, Monday adhered to a Lodge-like policy of isolation, greasing his own jowls though all those about him were dry, and only when confronted with an animal too heavy to be handled alone, did he impose upon himself entangling alliances, carrying as they did the obligation to divide the spoils!

In a certain autumn, the plantation pig crop had been unusually good, and, as the mast crop, too, was very abundant, there was promise of a full smokehouse by the end of the winter, for in the wild pastures of the Low-Country shoats are turned out in the fall to forage for acorns, pignuts, and haws, and when these are plentiful the porkers need little other food. So, before the first light frost of October, the ground under live-oak, water-oak and Spanish-oak was covered with fallen acorns, while the heavy boughs of white-oak and chestnut-oak were loaded with the big "overcups" that would fall with the coming of the cold nights. Everywhere in the woods there was both promise and fulfilment, and the porkers throve amazingly.

The Captain rode the woods almost daily, and, while looking for deer-tracks, was not unmindful

THE CAPTAIN

of other cloven hoof-prints that mingled with those of wildcat, fox, and raccoon in the soft mud of the swampy places. The Captain was observant, and one day he noticed among the pig-tracks leading into the "seven-acre" field the impression of a plantation brogan—a number six, an extraordinarily small shoe for a Negro—and the Captain knew the shoe for Monday's and knew at once what had become of three or four fine shoats that had, one by one, failed to respond to the far-flung *"whoop-ee"* at the plantation round-up in the forest, whither they were called by the master's voice every two or three days to be counted and inspected, as they squealed and scuffled for the ears of nubbin corn thrown among them.

The Captain rode without pencil or paper, but the Captain was resourceful and, dismounting, he picked up a handful of the richly colored brown needles of the great long-leaf pines. They were of different lengths, but he sorted them over until he found a cluster that exactly measured the length of the footprint. Breaking another off to cover the width of the shoe at its greatest breadth, the Captain carefully put his evidence in his pocket, mounted his horse, and rode away.

The next morning, finding occasion to put Monday at some ditching near the pond, the Captain watched until the ditcher had made plain tracks in the mud, and then, sending him to the lot for a shovel, pulled out the pine needles and proved by

A RIEVER OF THE BLACK BORDER

length and breadth that the pig thief of seven-acre had worn Monday's shoes!

With such convincing evidence against him, Monday, tried by a jury of white men, would have spent two years in the State penitentiary at Columbia; but Monday was a good hand and, if committed to the law, the plantation would lose his labor and, at the same time, be charged with responsibility for the maintenance of his young and dependent family. On the other hand, Monday's absence from the stock-range would undoubtedly result in a large increase in the four-legged population—so, as to economics, 'twas a stand-off whether Monday stayed or went; but the Captain, a kindly man, had withal a sneaking fondness for the former slave, whose frailties he knew so well, and for which he had so often made allowances. Instead of having him arrested, therefore, he resolved upon a punishment so unusual, so subtle in its psychology, so exquisite in its mental torture, that its conception was worthy of Machiavelli himself! The Captain determined to commit the lamb to the watchful care of the wolf, the grunting herd to the custody of the most expert smotherer of grunts in St. Paul's Parish; in short, to make Monday the plantation pig-minder!

"Great Gawd, Mas' Rafe!" Monday groaned, "Wuh de—! yuh de debble now! Mas' Rafe, you duh fun, enty? Put *me* fuh min' *hog!*"

"Yes, Monday, you know every hog-track in the woods and every hog-thief in the Parish. Of course you never stole one, Monday, but if you ever had

THE CAPTAIN

you would know how it was done, and you would be the thief set to catch a thief; but, as you never stole hogs in your life, I know I can trust you to keep others from stealing those under your charge."

"Great Gawd!" and Monday threw his black wool hat on the ground and looked at it long and silently.

"Mas' Rafe, w'en you wan' me fuh tek chaa'ge?"

"Right away, today."

"Great Gawd! Mas' Rafe, enty Chris'mus come een t'ree week?"

"Yes, but what has that to do with it?"

Monday chuckled shamefacedly and looked down with shaking shoulders, while he scratched the thick nap of his woolly head slowly and reflectively. When at last he looked up quickly and cheerfully, his "berrywellden, suh," told the Captain that Monday had bethought him of how to come by his Christmas pork unlawfully without violating the trust but now so rudely imposed upon him!

The news of Monday's elevation, which he had resisted with less success but far more sincerity than Caesar put away the crown upon the Lupercal, bore heavily upon the dusky band whose war-cry was a squeal and whose password was a grunt. Believing that Monday's guardianship would be taken in a Pickwickian sense, they hoped the way would still be open to the herd, and they proceeded to sound the keeper of the portcullis.

"Paa'kuh, Mas' Rafe sho' mek you fuh rich. Him pit de hog een you han'! You jaw gwine greesy fuh true."

A RIEVER OF THE BLACK BORDER

"Rich de debble! Hukkuh Mas' Rafe fuh mek me rich? Him pit de hog een me han' fuh true, but wuh use fuh pit hog een you han' w'en alltwo you han' tie? W'en Mas' Rafe mek me 'sponsubble fuh dem hog him tie me han' en' me foot alltwo sukkuh hog tie! Him count ebb'ry Gawd' hog on de place en' pit'um onduh my 't'oruhty. Him know berrywell suh me, 'self ent able fuh t'ief'um, en' him know same time suh none you t'odduh Nigguh ent fuh t'ief'um. Yuh de debble now! Me haffuh look 'puntop dem hog ebb'ry day, en' shum git mo' fattuh 'tel dem tail quile tight 'puntop dem back sukkuh snake quile. Man! W'en Uh look 'puntop dem barruh en' yeddy'um grunt, me h'aa't hebby en' watuh run out me mout'! Mas' Rafe! Mas' Rafe schemy *tummuch!*"

The Free Companions, convinced that their former chief would be forced, for a time at least, to live up to his responsibilities, exchanged knowing glances and dispersed, intending to meet again and lay plans for the spoliation of some "po'-buckruh'" pasture across the railway toward Caw-Caw Swamp. Realizing that the Captain had hamstrung Monday to the disadvantage of the hunting pack, his compatriots did not take him into their confidence, but decided to leave him to bear, without their spiritual support, his Tantalus task.

For two weeks Monday walked the woods and watched with heavy heart the fattening drove whose every grunt brought anguish to his soul. And as he walked, his busy thoughts pictured every band

THE CAPTAIN

or litter whose range he knew lay beyond the borders of the plantation, for from among these, whether owned by poor-white or thrifty black, his Christmas pork must come, if it came at all.

At last "one fine day," when the holiday to which the Negroes look forward so ardently was almost upon him, Monday recalled having seen early in the fall a bunch of half-grown shoats foraging for new-fallen acorns under the heavy water-oaks that fringed the far side of the Cypress swamp, almost at the boundary of the plantation. Monday remembered them for their rich auburn color and knew them as the property of a well-to-do Negro who rented and maintained a comfortable little farmstead at Moss Hill. So to the belt of oaks Monday made his way, and, as he entered the timber, the rustling of the dead leaves and the low grunts of the feeding pigs told him he had found that for which he was looking. Before they came in sight, however, he uttered softly his coaxing call, hoping to establish an *entente,* but the frightened *"goof, goof,"* and the scurrying feet of the shoats as they hurried away, told him as plainly as sound can tell that the wary creatures had recognized the voice of their hereditary enemy, and, realizing that, as the imminence of Christmas would not allow him time to establish friendly relations and capture his quarry by direct attack, he would have to resort to strategy, he swiftly laid his plans.

Monday resolved to build a trap! As a preliminary, he scattered under the oaks a few handfuls

A RIEVER OF THE BLACK BORDER

of corn from his well-filled knapsack, and laid a thin trail of grain to a point in the thicker woods nearby, where he intended making his capture. The pig-lifters among the Negroes of the Low-Country often catch their game in log traps, simple pens eight or ten feet square and five feet high, made of pine saplings and fitted with a suspended door sliding in grooves and released by a cord when the animals, feeding upon the bait spread within the trap, touch the trigger to which it is attached. Similar devices are often used for taking wild turkeys, and sometimes an entire flock is captured in a single bag.

Had Monday been hunting in company and needed a large haul, he would have built a pen, but as the Knights of the Table Round would assemble at another board at which swineherds would, by the nature of their calling, be unwelcome guests, Monday knew that if he would feast at all he must feast alone; so, to supply his small needs, he determined upon a deadfall as an effective device requiring a minimum of labor. His first concern was to get his intended captives used to the instrument with which he intended to rob them at once of life, liberty, and the pursuit of happiness.

Selecting a comparatively open spot, Monday with ready axe cut two forked hardwood saplings about eight feet long, and sharpened the lower ends which, after first loosening the soil with the blade of his axe, he rammed into the ground as far as he could and packed the earth about their bases. These

THE CAPTAIN

uprights were set about five feet apart and, resting in their forked tops seven feet above the ground, a pole was laid. Having rigged up his rustic horizontal bar that looked like a miniature football goal post, Monday cut near at hand a heavy log twelve feet long, which taxed all his strength and skill to maneuver into position at right angles to the goal post. With the aid of a stout forked pole he raised the heavy end of his log to the top of the bar, upon which it rested securely. The deadfall was now almost complete, lacking only a trigger, and Monday, well pleased with his day's work, scattered corn freely about the little glade and went his ways.

On the following morning and again on the second day, the hunter returned to the Cypress to find that all the scattered corn had been eaten and that the unsuspecting shoats had rooted freely under and around the trap. On successive days, he threw wide his seductive bait under the oaks and laid his train from the oaks to the little glade where the grain was strewn with a heavy hand.

Christmas eve broke clear and cold. The roads were frozen iron hard, the water left by the recent rains in the wheel ruts and in the tracks of horses and cattle had turned to ice, and frost crystals burst from the sides of the damp ditches along the way. Monday, engaged in the preparation of the plantation bacon until a late hour on the preceding night, was not astir until toward noon, and the sun was well in the west before he set out for his private hunting-ground. Here he at once began his preparations to put teeth into the hitherto harmless trap, to which his intended quarry had now become accustomed. First bringing his log to earth with the aid of his forked pole, he beveled with his sharp axe one side of the heavy end, and when this had been smoothed to his satisfaction he rubbed the polished surface with a piece of bacon rind and hoisted it again into position upon the bar, with the beveled side downward, carefully propping it up with his forked pole for additional support until he could adjust his "trigger," a narrow piece of plank, beveled at one end, which he had prepared in advance and brought with him. Scraping out a shallow hole in the ground directly under the heavier end of the log, he filled it with corn, and in the grain he set the lower end of the trigger, while the smooth upper end was fitted snugly against the greased surface of the heavy timber with such nicety that the slightest jar against the lower end would spring the trap and release the lethal log upon the pigs that fed below. Then, once more he laid his trail of corn from the trap to the oaks and, scattering the grain that remained, he returned to his cabin.

An hour after dark, when Venus blazed in the west and the young moon, a golden proa with upturned ends, rode on an even keel nearby, Monday slipped away by woodland paths to his trap, and was rewarded by finding under his deadfall a tawny sixty pound shoat which the heavy log, falling on

THE CAPTAIN

his spine, must have killed instantly. Removing the log, Monday put his pig into a sack and, upon reaching home, came to his cabin from the rear. In response to a stealthy tap, his window was opened from within, and through the narrow aperture he first thrust his sack and then pulled himself. His children were abed, but his trusty wife, Hannah, having implicit faith in the prowess of her lord, had kept the home fires burning under a large caldron of water. The auburn shoat was soon scalded, scraped, and dressed, and the pork was carefully concealed in the cabin loft. Then Monday crept out and threw the handful of red hair far over the fence among the gallberry bushes.

On Christmas day, Monday's jaws, like those of all who called his roof their own, glistened with fatness, and throughout the three-day holiday the comforting sizzling of the frying-pan told those who passed his cabin that Monday's family "fared sumptuously every day."

At last his sometime hunting companions, becoming suspicious, questioned the swineherd, who proudly displayed a pork shoulder that had been given him by the master of the plantation on Christmas eve. From this shoulder only a few slices had been cut, but Monday shrewdly used these as justification for the almost incessant frying within his habitation.

"Paa'kuh, you mout' sho' greesy dis Chris'mus!"

"Yaas, man, me jaw greesy fuh true. Enty you see da' hebby gham wuh Mas' Rafe gimme fuh

A RIEVER OF THE BLACK BORDER

Chris'mus? Him gimme dat 'cause Uh min' him hog so good en' keep oonuh Nigguh' mout' off'um."

"Yaas, Uh yeddy 'bout da' gham, en' Uh yeddy de Lawd' wu'd wuh de sukkus preachuh resplain 'bout how Jedus, Him tek da' string uh fish en' dem t'ree loaf uh bread en' feed 'leb'n t'ous'n' man 'tel dem hongry done gone, but 'e tek Jedus fuh do da' t'ing. *Nigguh* ent fuh do'um!"

A few days later, one of the Free Companions, passing through the gallberry thicket near Monday's cabin, saw a wad of auburn hair and a great light, for he remembered the ruddy band from Moss Hill, and knew that Monday, holding inviolate the plantation drove committed to his care, had deserted his quondam associates and hunted successfully far afield!

"Paa'kuh! Paa'kuh smaa't *tummuch!* W'enebbuh Paa'kuh' jaw greesy, w'edduh de hog red, uh w'edduh 'e black, w'edduh 'e stan' close uh fudduh, *somebody' hog done dead!*"

"RUN, NIGGUH, RUN!"

Although almost all Negroes are free talkers and dearly love the sound of their own voices, they are unusually cautious about giving themselves away in speech, and exceedingly secretive as to their own affairs if there be anything about those affairs to awaken suspicion in the minds higher up. It has been claimed by apologists for the race that the Negro's verbal inexactitude—lying, in short—was learned under slavery and was necessary to protect him from the harshness of his master, but the testimony of all observing men— hunters, explorers, and missionaries—who have known the Negro in Africa under tribal conditions, corroborates the opinion of observers here, that lying is an apparently ineradicable racial characteristic of a people with many fine traits. If the preachers and teachers and editors of the race would concentrate their efforts upon stricter observance of the eighth and ninth commandments—they needn't "scan their fellow man" too closely in respect to the seventh—they would give a pretty good working religion to a people who keep the other seven commandments quite as well as their white neighbors!

In old times, even the fine old house-servants would seldom reveal the rascality of their fellow slaves at the plantation quarters unless the offense was of a serious nature. And under Freedom, as

THE CAPTAIN

under slavery, the Negroes kept the faith, one with another, and "honor among thieves" was strictly observed. But only so long as diplomatic relations were maintained among the wrongdoers. Once these were severed, those who had been held together by the guilty knowledge of their spoliation of "de Buckruh" would fall apart and tell on their former associates, and, once the telling began, the tellers would tell not only all they knew, but add to the tale much that they didn't know, for, as every Southern judge on the Circuit Bench knows, a Negro witness with a grievance against his fellow will swear away that fellow's life or liberty as lightly as he would crack a 'possum's neck under an axe handle!

But under slavery, with few responsibilities or obligations to their black brethren, they seldom quarreled, and so, seldom quarreling, they seldom told on one another. Kindly masters on many plantations were habitually imposed upon by certain shrewd slaves, who, feigning sickness, would dodge their tasks for months or years, cleverly outwitting plantation doctor and plantation nurse by the simple device of scraping a raw place on arm or leg with a bit of broken glass or a shard twisted from a rusty iron barrel hoop; and throughout the daylight hours these smart bucks would mope or drowse around the quarters, but as soon as night fell they made wonderful recoveries and, "taking their feet in their hands," would break bounds with

"RUN, NIGGUH, RUN!"

other venturesome plantation Lotharios and thread the unfrequented byways or woodland paths to some distant plantation, there to dance and frolic until warned by the morning star to make tracks for home, where the scraped shinbone would be bandaged again and the sometime buck-and-wing dancer become once more, for the day, an interesting invalid!

After Freedom, the Negroes revealed many of the tricks with which their fellow slaves had once fooled their unsuspecting masters; in fact there were many instances of self-revelation, where men, who had successfully eluded their master's work for the last ten years of slavery, blossomed out under Freedom into lusty manhood and boasted to the former master himself how they had outwitted him.

One of those who had achieved occasional antebellum vacations was Monday Parker, a lusty brownblack fellow, broad-shouldered, and small-waisted, a fine axeman and a prime hand generally, but noted during slavery for his skill in breaking bounds to frolic at night, and, "attuh Freedom come een," for the more practical accomplishment of slaughtering other people's shoats before they could squeal.

Before and during the Confederate War—perhaps ever since the Negro insurrection or "Gullah War"—it was the custom of the young planters of the Low-Country to take turns at night to "ride patrol" throughout their respective communities, act-

THE CAPTAIN

ing as a "provost guard" in rounding up all the slaves caught abroad without permission.

In the old days, many men among the slaves obtained their master's consent to marry "off the place," and, because it was always thought desirable that man and wife should be under one ownership, those who "would a wooing go" were encouraged—if the flowers blooming on the plantation were thought not worth the picking—to choose wives from other plantations belonging to the same master, rather than to marry girls under alien ownership, involving in most cases either the sale of the husband or the purchase of the wife.

Sometimes, however, slaves were permitted to take wives on neighboring plantations, and, to visit these wives at night, once a week or oftener, they were given written passes by some member of the master's family. With this pass the night-moving darky feared "nae evil," but was ready, like Tam O'Shanter with his usquebae to "face the Devil" —or the patrol—but, caught without it, he was turned over to the plantation to which he belonged, for mild punishment—perhaps an extra task—perhaps restriction for a time to the limits of the plantation.

As passes were easy to get for those who went abroad upon their lawful occasions, he who lacked them was always under suspicion. Sometimes his tongue was so skilful, his story so plausible, that he could impose upon his captors and win free, but woe to the wight who won free thro' deceit, for

"RUN, NIGGUH, RUN!"

he was almost sure to be caught up with at last and get double punishment.

Riding patrol was fun for the young bloods. Always superbly mounted and knowing, through their hunting experience, every bridle-path in the community, they galloped along the highways and neighborhood roads, for upon these they seldom caught anyone, the sound of their horses' hoofs giving warning of their approach in ample time for the truant to slip into the thick woods by the roadside; but, coming to the paths running from plantation to plantation, they slowed down to a walk, let the reins fall upon their horses' necks and rode silently in single file. Sometimes, if these byways threaded forest areas, the riders would leave the path and conceal themselves in thickets a few yards away. Here in the sheltering darkness they could command the track, and see the outlines and hear the voices of all who passed.

Here, too, sitting immovable upon their horses, they could hear the singing, shouting, and stick-beating at whatever dance or other festive entertainment was at the moment going forward on this particular plantation. If the sounds of hilarity indicated that the social function was largely attended, the patrol would quietly surround the dance hall and bide their time, for they knew that within its four walls, breathing joyously its fetid air and shouting madly as they leaped and wriggled in the intricacies of the "Wurrum-Fench" or the "Congo Crawl," would probably be found half the cripples

THE CAPTAIN

and chronic invalids of the nearby plantations. Then, when the revelry was ripe, the riders would close in, guard the doors and windows, and garner the harvest. And what a harvest! Tares, chiefly. A little good grain, for some of them had passes and were where they ought to have been; a little bad grain, for some had passes to other plantations where their wives were, but had come instead to join the merry rout at a plantation where their wives were not; but most of them were usually "lesser breeds without the law," for they had no passes at all.

Then, as the net was shaken out and an inventory made of the catch, the fun began! The fun was not for all, for there was usually a touch or two of tragedy; some smug hypocrite unmasked, some hoary sinner exposed before those whom he had sought to impress with his sanctity; but as most of the revelations were of marital irregularities, the knife of conscience didn't cut very deep. A little fear, but not much, for the penalties imposed would be light, and these were a happy people whose laughter was always near the surface, and soon those but now discomfited would join and even lead the merriment at their own expense. After the round-up, the delinquents would be listed and sent home to the plantation "drivers" or overseers for whatever discipline the plantation chose to impose upon them; and, if the night were yet young enough, the patrol would ride another beat, usually dispersing and going to their homes after midnight.

"RUN, NIGGUH, RUN!"

At times, however, when, under relaxed discipline, breaking bounds became common, and when certain turbulent fellows became runaways, took to the woods, and commenced to kill cattle, sterner measures became necessary. The patrol rode more frequently, stayed out later, and the Negroes caught were subjected to severer punishment, the bad characters among them often coming in for a sound thrashing on the spot, administered under the direction of the patrol by the hand of some always-willing brother in black.

Now and then the patrol castnet caught at one throw all the big fish in the community and yielded a dozen malefactors of great stealth. The dozen thrashings given and received on these epochal occasions would be talked about during the natural lives of the participants, those who received being, strangely enough, quite as proud as those who gave.

"Man! You 'membuh de time w'en me en' Mas' Rafe ketch you da' time to Battlefiel' en' pit da' lick 'puntop you?"

"Ketch who? Lick who? *Me?*"

"Yaas, you."

"W'en you ebbuh ketch me? W'en you ebbuh lick me?"

"Da' same time me en' you en' all dem gal en' t'ing binnuh shout en' beat stick to Battlefiel', w'en Mas' Rafe en' dem patrol ride roun' de dance house en' ketch we."

"Yaas, Uh 'membuh da' time fuh true, but duh Mas' Rafe en' dem wuh ketch we; 'e yent bin you,

THE CAPTAIN

en' same time me git lick, you'self git lick, 'cause w'en Mas' Rafe mek you fuh lick me, same fashi'n him mek me fuh lick you, en' him lub me mo' den 'e lub you, dat de reaz'n de lick wuh you git, hebby mo'nuh de lick wuh I git."

"Hukkuh dat happ'n? Enty Uh bu'n yo' britchiz wid de same lash wuh you hab fuh bu'n my'own? Hukkuh da' lash kin bu'n me mo' wuss den 'e fuh bu'n you?"

"Duh me git de fus' lickin', enty?"

"Yaas, bubbuh, duh you gitt'um fus', en' Uh 'membuh how w'en Uh pit da' lick 'puntop yo' back, Uh mek you fuh cantuh sukkuh buzzut duh dance! Uh laugh w'ile Uh binnuh lick you 'tel de lash mos' drap out me han'!"

"De lick sweet'n me 'tel 'e mek me fuh dance buzzut lope fuh true, but dat de time Uh fool you! Ent you know suh ef you ebbuh graff uh 'ooman en' de 'ooman git bex, you gwine hol'um fas', but ef him smaa't 'nuf fuh mek you fuh laugh, you han' gwine loose, en' fus' t'ing you know de gal git'way? Man' h'aa't en' 'e han' alltwo stan' same fashi'n. Ef 'e h'aa't light, 'e han' gwine light, en' w'en man' h'aa't duh laugh, de lash wuh 'e got een 'e han' gwine laugh, en' w'en lash duh laugh, 'e lick berry light; but w'en man bex, w'en 'e h'aa't hebby! Bubbuh, look out! 'cause de lash gwine hebby 'tel 'e fang cut t'ru you britchiz en' fast'n een you meat! Dat w'ymekso Uh know Mas' Rafe lub me mo'nuh 'e lub you, 'cause 'e mek you fuh gi' me de fus' lickin', en' all de time yo' han' binnuh lick me, my

"RUN, NIGGUH, RUN!"

h'aa't binnuh lick you, en' time Mas' Rafe tell you fuh stop, en' tell me fuh tek de lash en' lick *you,* Uh see 'e yeye biggin fuh shine. Mas' Rafe schemy tummuch! Him know suh w'en bex Nigguh git chance fuh lick anodduh Nigguh, him gwine '*stroy'd-'um!* You 'membuh, enty? W'en Uh staa't fuh lick Uh dat full'up wid bex, I kacely kin see, en' w'en de lash wrop 'round yo' hanch fuh true! Bubbuh, you jump Jim Crow! You gone up een de ele*ment,* en' w'en you light, you seddown flat 'puntop de du't fuh sabe yo' meat! Me! Uh *done* fuh lick you, but you nebbuh see me duh laugh w'en Uh binnuh lick you, enty?"

"You talk trute. You mout' swell'up oagly ez uh catfish all-time you binnuh lick me."

"Berrywellden," and the man who had put in the last lick had the last word.

Under the warming influence of freedom, Monday, taciturn as a slave, unfolded the petals of his speech as a sunflower opens under summer skies. He boasted freely among his dark companions, at times even before his former master, of the skill with which on many occasions he had outwitted the plantation authorities, feigning sickness by day and slipping off at night to frolic at distant plantations. A good sport, too, he boasted freely of the thrashings he had received upon occasions when he had been caught by the patrol.

Monday was especially proud of the success with which, during the entire month of the first winter of the war, he had deceived the doctor, the plantation nurse, and the querulous and suspicious "driver" by the bandaging of a self-inflicted wound upon the shinbone, which, enforcing rest and idleness during the daylight hours, left him free to "ramify" throughout the night.

"Mas' Rafe, great Gawd!" he chuckled, "you ebbuh yeddy 'bout da' time eenjurin' de fus' yeah uh de wah, w'en Uh 'crape me shinbone 'long da' bruk glass en' tie'um up en' fool Ole Maussuh en' Doctuh Smit' en' de dribuh en' ebb'rybody fuh t'ree week? You nebbuh yeddy 'bout'um, suh? Lemme tell you. Dat bin de fus' wintuh w'en de wah staa't, en' you bin een de aa'my! Yaas, suh, Uh know dat, 'cause ef you hadduh bin home Uh woulduh git ketch."

"How did you manage it, you imp of Satan?"

"Great Gawd!" Monday guffawed. "You 'membuh, suh, dat yeah we mek uh hebby crap uh rice to Pon-Pon. Two munt' befo' Chris'mus de rice pile up een baa'nyaa'd high mo'nuh my house. Dem boy wid dem lash haffuh min' bu'd off'um all day. Ef dem ebbuh stop pop dem lash, de blackbu'd' kibbuh de rick 'tel you cyan' shum!

"Soon ez all de rice done haul een en' stack, Ole Maussuh tell 'e dribuh suh 'e wan' all da' rice fuh t'rash befo' Chris'mus come, en' w'en Monday mawnin' come you cyan' see de blackbu'd' fuh de Nigguh'! De pyo' Nigguh' full de baa'nyaa'd. All de man hab flail fuh t'rash de rice, en' de 'ooman en' t'ing hab pitchfawk fuh t'row de sheabe' 'pun

"RUN, NIGGUH, RUN!"

de t'rashin' flo'. Den de boy climb 'puntop de rick en' loose de sheabe' en' t'row'um down."

"What has the Oak Lawn rice crop got to do with your monkey shinbone?"

"Mas' Rafe, lemme tell you. Soon ez dem staa't fuh t'rash, Ole Maussuh pick out de man en' de 'ooman wuh lead all de t'odduh Nigguh' fuh sing, en' 'e tell'um ef dem raise de chune en' keep on sing tell de rice done t'rash, him fuh gi' de 'ooman new frock en' gi' de man uh new britchiz w'en Chris'mus come, en' him fuh full alltwo dem piggin 'long sugar! Mas' Rafe, you nebbuh yeddy Nigguh sing lukkuh dem Nigguh'! Fus' de man raise de sperritual, en' den de 'ooman jine'um. Attuhw'ile ebb'ry Gawd' Nigguh een baa'nyaa'd, eb'nso to de chillun, biggin fuh sing, en' dem mek shishuh hebby woice, 'e roll sukkuh camp-meet'n'! En' alltime dem duh sing you kin yeddy de flail come down, *'blam!'* Me en' all dem t'odduh nyung man wuh duh swing flail, w'en we yeddy de 'ooman' woice rise een de sing', 'e sweet'n' we so 'tel we haffuh fling de flail high een de ele*ment,* en' w'en 'e come down 'e soun' sukkuh dem duh beat stick en' shout. All day da' sing mek we fuh wu'k haa'd. Some uh we boy' tell de man fuh stop sing so we kin tek'um easy, en' de man stop lukkuh we tell'um, but w'enebbuh him jaw shet, da' debble'ub'uh 'ooman him haffuh tek 't'oruhty 'puntop 'eself fuh hice de chune same lukkuh him bin man! Dem boy tell'um: 'Shet you mout', gal! You hab no bidness fuh do da' t'ing. 'Ooman ent fuh hice no

THE CAPTAIN

chune. Man fuh do'um!' But da' 'ooman ent hab de man' wu'd een de back uh 'e head. Him duh study 'pun da' frock en' da' piggin full uh sugar wuh Ole Maussuh prommus'um, en' 'e suck 'e teet' at de man en' 'e op'n' 'e jaw, en' 'e woice shaa'p sukkuh yalluhhammuh w'en 'e holluh *'kee'um! kee'um!'* en' 'e hice 'Roll, Jordan, Roll,' en' all de Nigguh jine-'um, en' dem flail come down, *'flam!'* en' Ole Maussuh' rice git t'rash, en' sametime Ole Maussuh' Nigguh fuh hab pain een dem bone 'cause dem lavuh so hebby. En—"

"Well, you kinky-headed son of darkness, what has all that got to do with your shinbone?"

"Mas' Rafe, lemme tell you. Ef Gawd yeddy me, ebb'ry time da' shaa'p woice gal op'n 'e chuckwilluh mout' fuh sing, 'e tu'n' all uh we man staa't fool. All uh we ten toe biggin fuh eetch fuh dance, but we yent hab uh chance fuh nyuze we foot, so we haffuh dance 'long we han', en' ebb'ry time we han' dance, we t'row da' flail high obuh we back en' fetch'um down hebby, 'tel de rice-sheabe' jump up frum de du't same lukkuh dem duh dance!

"Well, suh, w'en Uh done fling dem flail fuh fo' week, en' stillyet de rick stan' high, Uh git w'ary en' Uh mek up me min' fuh res'. One day Uh gone to baa'nyaa'd-well fuh git watuh fuh drink, en' Uh tek me flail 'cross me shoulduh. W'en Uh git behin' de willuh bush weh none dem Nigguh kin see, Uh tek me knife en' Uh cut da' rawhide wuh fast'n de two pole togedduh half een two. W'en

"RUN, NIGGUH, RUN!"

Uh done cutt'um Uh rub'um een de du't fuh hide de cut, en' Uh gone baa'nyaa'd.

"Uh biggin fuh t'rash 'gen. Uh staa't easy, 'cause Uh know suh soon ez Uh come down hebby 'puntop da' t'ing, 'e gwine bruk. Uh flam me flail light two-t'ree time, den Uh fetch'um down so strong 'tel 'e mek de rice-sheabe fuh hop! W'en Uh t'row'um back obuh me head, Uh g'em uh ju'k, same lukkuh Uh binnuh pop lash, en' de rawhide buss' weh Uh bin cutt'um, en' 'e lef' one half de flail een me han' en' de t'odduh half fly off en' gone 'bout t'irty foot behin' me, en' 'e ketch Ole Wawley, de dribuh, slam een 'e back en' knock'um obuh. Unk' Wawley yeddy dem 'ooman en' t'ing duh laugh, en' w'en 'e git up 'e dat bex 'tel 'e yeye red! Him ready fuh lick Nigguh right off. W'en 'e look 'puntop me en' see half de flail een me han', 'e quizzit me: 'Boy, hukkuh you kin bruk da' rawhide t'ing? You strong to dat, enty?'

"'Uh strong fuh true, Unk' Wawley, but w'en da' gal wuh duh lead de sing squall out lukkuh dem kill-dee, Uh haffuh lam da' rice mo' haa'duh, dat how 'e bruk.'

"'Fetch'um yuh, lemme shum,' 'e say, en' me h'aa't gone down een me shoe, 'cause Uh 'f'aid him gwine ketch me 'bout da' rawhide. Unk' Wawley look 'puntop de knife cut.

"'Boy, w'en you cut dis t'ing?'

"'Who, me? Me nebbuh cutt'um. Da' t'ing stan' same fashi'n ebbuh sence we staa't fuh t'rash las'

THE CAPTAIN

munt', suh. Nutt'n' 'cep' de haa'd wu'k Uh binnuh do mek'um fuh bruk.'

"Unk' Wawley nebbuh crack 'e teet' but Uh know him 'spishun suh me duh lie. 'E tek 'e knife, 'e gone to de big house stable en' w'en 'e come back 'e fetch uh hebby strip uh rawhide, en' w'en 'e gitt'ru tie me flail en' pit'um een me han', Uh know Uh cyan' bruk'um 'gen ef Uh lam rice 'tel Gabrull blow 'e hawn!

"'Now, Buck,' 'e say, ef you man to dat, lemme see hummuch sheaf you, one kin t'rash 'fo' sundown!' En' da' debble'ub'uh ole Nigguh stan' dey wid 'e lash een 'e han', en' 'e hab dem 'ooman pile up de rice sheabe' befo' me 'tel w'en sundown come, me bone ache 'tel Uh fool, but da' same night Uh mek up me min' fuh fool'um.

"Da' night w'en Uh gone Nigguh-house-yaa'd, Uh git uh piece uh bruk glass en' Uh 'crape me shinbone 'tel 'e raw, den Uh git one clawt' en' Uh tie'um up. Uh gone 'sleep. Nex' mawnin' soon, Uh biggin fuh groan. Bumbye, An' Phibby, de plantesshun nuss, come en' ax 'smattuh Uh yent gitt'up fuh eat befo' time come fuh wu'k? Uh tell'um all me bone ache 'tel Uh 'spec' Uh gwine dead, en' Uh ax'um fuh sen' fuh Ole Maussuh.

"Attuh brekwus' gitt'ru to de big house, Ole Maussuh walk. 'E come Nigguh-house-yaa'd fuh see how all him sick Nigguh stan'. W'en Uh yeddy Ole Maussuh' woice Uh biggin fuh groan 'gen, 'cause Uh know him h'aa't saaf' 'tel 'e berry easy fuh

"RUN, NIGGUH, RUN!"

fool'um. Him ent stan' lukkuh you, Mas' Rafe. Great Gawd, no, suh!

"Ole Maussuh come een de do'. 'Wuh 'smattuh boy?' 'e say, 'weh hu't you?' Uh tell'um all me bone hu't me en' Uh tell'um Uh trip up en' fall 'puntop plow de night befo', en' dat how me shinbone git 'crape. Ole Maussuh tell me fuh stay Nigguh-house-yaa'd 'tel da' shin git well, en' ef Uh haffuh walk, Uh fuh hab crotch. Uh tell'um 't'engky, Ole Maussuh,' en' 'e gone! Bumbye, middleday, de dribuh come. Unk' Wawley swell'up, 'e look lukkuh 'e bex, en' 'e quizzit me berry close 'bout de plow, en' 'e try haa'd fuh ketch me, but me Jedus help me fuh fool'um. Den Uh tell'um wuh Ole Maussuh say 'bout de crotch, en' him gone en' cut two bush en' trim'um, en' alltwo hab crotch fuh pit onduh me aa'm, en' ebb'ry day Uh nyam me bittle, en' seddown een de sunhot befo' me do' en' tek me res', en' ef Uh fuh walk, Uh pit me two crotch onduhneet' me two aa'm, en' Uh walk duh Nigguh-house street alltime dem t'odduh Nigguh duh fling flail to baa'nyaa'd. Two time ebb'ry week Ole Maussuh' doctuh come. Dem saa'bint to big house tell me w'en de doctuh fuh come, en' befo' him git Nigguh-house-yaa'd Uh git de bruk glass en' Uh 'crape me bone, en' Uh fool da' doctuh ebb'ry time 'e come.

"Mas' Rafe, you know Unk' Wawley, him duh class-leaduh, en' ebb'ry Sattyday night him git pass frum Ole Maussuh fuh gone Blue House fuh lead him class. Well, suh, soon ez him lef' de street, Uh dey 'pun 'e track! Him alltime gone out t'ru de

THE CAPTAIN

red gate, 'tel 'e git to de big road. Uh trail 'bout half uh acre behine'um 'cause Uh know ef him meet somebody duh paat' dem gwine hail'um fuh 'zammin' 'e pass, en' time 'e do dat, en' Uh yeddy de somebody' woice, Uh kin hab chance fuh dodge een de bush en' git'way. So ebb'ry Sattyday night Uh folluh da' ole Nigguh 'tel 'e gone een Blue House ab'nue, en' den Uh gone Cross-road en' mek fuh Battlefiel'. W'en Uh git dey Uh jine dem boy en' gal en' t'ing fuh dance en' shout 'tel de mawnin' staar rise; den Uh gone home, Uh git een de bed 'tel time fuh eat Sunday, den Uh git up, Uh tek me two crotch, en' Uh git lame 'gen.

"Mas' Rafe, Uh git 'long berrywell 'tel de las' Sattyday night befo' Chris'mus. Uh bin to Battlefiel' to de shout'n', en' all uh we bin knock stick 'tel de flo' shake. All ub'uh'sudd'nt, de do' op'n en' t'ree w'ite man come een. W'en Uh look 'puntop'um me h'aa't *dead*, 'cause all t'ree de man bin po'-buckruh, en dem duh ride patrol! Great Gawd! Po'-buckruh nebbuh hab no nyuse fuh Nigguh nohow, en' Uh know suh we britchiz fuh bu'n!

"Mas' Rafe, you know, suh, w'enebbuh quality Buckruh ride patrol en' dem ketch Nigguh fuh lick, de juntlemun nebbuh hol' de lash, dem mek Nigguh fuh hol'um, en' w'en Nigguh does lick Nigguh, 'scusin' dem bex, dem alltime lick light; but dem t'ree po'-buckruh nebbuh git chance fuh lick Nigguh befo' sence dem bawn, en' w'en dem pick out t'ree uh we man wuh ent hab no papuh fuh show, dem mek all de t'odduh man en' 'ooman line up 'roun'

"RUN, NIGGUH, RUN!"

de wall, en' we t'ree man fuh cantuh 'roun' en' 'roun' da' flo' same lukkuh we bin hawss! Ef one de man bruk 'e cantuh en' slow down fuh trot, dem po'-buckruh lash pop 'round' 'e hanch 'tel him haffuh cantuh 'gen! Mas' Rafe, ebbuh sence den, ebb'ry time Uh seddown 'puntop'uh briah w'en Uh hab on t'in britchiz, Uh t'ink 'pun how da' po'-buckruh' lash fuh do we!

"Bumbye dem op'n de do' en' tell we fuh gone!"

"Did you go?"

"Mas' Rafe, Great Gawd! W'en dem patrol git 'pun dem hawss en' dem lash crack behine we, nutt'n' nebbuh stop we frum run! Ebb'ry man hab fo' foot! All t'ree uh we buss' t'ru dem briah same lukkuh we bin hog!

"Mas' Rafe, Monday mawnin' me duh de fus' man fuh git baa'nyaa'd. W'en Uh ketch me flail Uh fling'um high! W'en Uh fetch'um down, Uh knock'um hebby. 'Uh glad fuh see Buh Monday come back,' Unk' Wawley say. 'Da' plastuh dem po'-buckruh pit 'puntop him shinbone mek'um fuh well.'

"Da' killdee gal stop 'e sing, 'e suck 'e teet', en' 'e laugh.

" 'Dem po'-buckruh mek'um well, fuh true,' 'e say, 'but 'e nebbuh pit plastuh 'puntop no *shinbone!*' De gal talk trute!"

AFTER THE FRUIT THE FLOUR

The Captain's watermelons were ripening in the Orchard field, under the burning suns of a July fifteen years after Freedom, and the five-foot rows of Sea-Island cotton that flanked the melon patch were dotted with happy Negroes, men and women, who were giving the last hoeing and weeding to the beautiful plants, now shoulder-high and well on their way toward the seven-foot growth they would ultimately attain.

The plow-hands, having laid by both corn and cotton for the season, had turned their tired mules into the pasture and, holding awkwardly the unfamiliar hoes, had joined the laughing group of hand-workers who rallied the sometime plowmen upon their want of skill as hoe-hands. Among the disbanded muleteers, now become for the remainder of the crop season "men of their hands," three stood forth prominently as butts for the shrewd and caustic wit of the women, who, having never held a plow-handle, believed they knew far more about how furrows should be laid than those who had watched the switching of a mule's tail through ten thousand miles of corn and cotton rows. So it is, in all walks of life, that Youth and Ignorance constantly admonish Age and Experience, for the laden ass is denied knowledge of his own burden, and those who have walked along smooth and easy ways only are sure there can be no flints beneath the feet

THE CAPTAIN

of the heavy-laden who tread the stony paths of life!

So it is, and so it was that Joe Smashum, Perry Gibbes, and Sike Chisholm were beset by the sharp-tongued women as hawks and crows are harried by kingbirds. Sike was short and fat—so duck-legged, indeed, that he could plow only the slowest mule on the place, one whose phlegmatic attitude toward work was on all-fours with that of Germany toward reparations!

"Joe en' Perry, w'en dem binnuh plow dem schemy sukkuh Buh Rabbit. Dem mule walk fas' out een de op'n weh ebb'rybody kin look 'puntop'um, but soon ez dem git behine de gum bush to de een uh de row weh nobody kin shum, dem fuh stop een de shade fuh talk 'tel Sike en' him slow-foot mule come 'long."

"Yaas," said another tormentor, "en' w'en dem come, you look 'puntop'uh cootuh! Sike en' 'e mule alltwo stan' same fashi'n. Dem alltwo is tarrypin. Ebb'ry time da' mule hice up 'e foot 'e stop fuh study, en' w'enebbuh 'e pit'um down, Great Gawd, 'e stop fuh study befo' him hice'um 'gen! Da' mule walk sedate tummuch!"

"Tittuh! Sike' foot hebby mo'nuh dat, 'cause de mule hab fo' foot en' him only hab two foot, en' w'en dat Nigguh hice 'e foot en' stop fuh study, him haffuh study two-time longuh mo'nuh de mule!"

But this demonstration of feminine mathematics was too much for Sike, who protested ponderously.

AFTER THE FRUIT THE FLOUR

"Gal, you mus'be fool! Da' mule haffuh hice him befo' foot en' him behine foot alltwo fuh tek one step. Hukkuh me kin fuh keep step 'long alltwo? No, suh! Uh keep step wid 'e hine foot. Ebb'ry time him hice him'own, me hice my'own. Ef him stop fuh study, me haffuh stop fuh study. Oonuh gal, oonuh talk trute. Me en' da' mule alltwo stan' same fashi'n."

The three plowmen swung their hoes heavily. This tool is always regarded contemptuously by those who have had to do with horses, and its use is considered something of a degradation by these aristocrats of the field. Now, separated from their four-footed "compagnons de travaille" and thrown among the bourgeoisie, they were despitefully used and reminded of the many occasions upon which they had departed from the straight and narrow way that a plowman must ever tread if he would gain and hold the favor of his fellow workers of the hoe, for crooked furrows, and middles carelessly "knocked out," are not easily forgiven by those who must put the rows in order behind them.

"Look 'puntop dem t'ree man," shouted a feminine critic. "Knock dem grass! *knock dem grass!* You duh kibbuhr'um up, enty? Bumbye w'en Mas' Rafe come, ef him look 'puntop'um, t'ree Nigguh' gwine loss dem job! W'en nex' Sattyday night come, some dem t'odduh man haffuh feed oonuh wife, enty? Berrywellden. *Knock'um! Knock-'um!*"

THE CAPTAIN

"Deseyuh t'ree Nigguh' 'shame fuh hol' hoe een dem han', 'cause dem call demself plow*man*. Bubbuh! de furruh wuh dese Nigguh' mek, crookety ez uh wurrum fench! W'en oonuh folluh dem track t'ru de row 'e stan' sukkuh grummole en' watuhmoccasin binnuh dance. Dese Nigguh' foot done fuh tanglety!"

After nightfall the Captain rode to the Cross-roads, where, in and around the big store, two or three hundred Negroes had gathered from the outlying plantations and from their little homesteads in the neighborhood for their weekly trading and for the interchange of gossip so dear to their hearts. These gatherings on Saturday nights are the general club meetings of the dusky folk, for, as the African denizens of veldt or forest come nightly to the water-hole, so these trading places bring together from time to time, during the early hours of the night, half the Negro population of the community, and here for hours the place resounds with quip and jest and laughter.

All Negroes are gregarious, and flock to church on Sundays and gather during the week at class-meetings, but in the church they are divided into two great bands—Baptists and Methodists—and these, in turn, are sub-divided among several congregations, so it is only at the Cross-roads that the great communal round-ups occur.

In those days of nominal license fees and loose inspection, every cross-roads store and every little way-side shop sold whiskey, and raw white "corn"

AFTER THE FRUIT THE FLOUR

and red and rascally "rye" were everywhere on tap at five cents a drink. Of course these fluids were liberally diluted, for in the flat lands of the Low-Country the water-table is very near the surface, and springs and shallow wells abound; but the limpid flow of the spring was only for the pallid corn; the rye was blended with the waters of the branches, stained a rich wine color by contact with the fallen leaves and the roots of cypress, gum, and juniper, for some of these mixers who worshiped at the shrine of Aquarius were artists, and blended the tawny branch-water so skilfully with the burnt-sugared rye that, whatever it may have fallen short of "proof," its protective coloration, at least, was unimpeachable.

Thus Jew and Gentile—German shop-keeper and native Carolinian—animated solely by acquisitiveness and pretending no altruism, yet served the cause of temperance far more effectively than a hundred anti-saloon leaguers, by the simple expedient of taking the strength out of strong drink, and getting paid for the weakness! (As tho' Delilah had sold Samson's shorn locks to a wig-maker!) But "man can not live by bread alone," nor can alcoholic strength be taken from a Gullah's dram without the substitution of something just as good, or as fiery, for the darky judges the potency of his tipple by the burning in his throat as the drink travels downward, and if the fire reach as far as the diaphragm his spirit is doubly comforted! Physicians testify to the tonic effect of red-pepper in warm cli-

THE CAPTAIN

mates, and the tradesmen who sold the poor freedmen branch-water and red-pepper for alcohol were benefactors of the race, cheats that they were!

The city frauds, who scientifically doctored their whiskey, used to add a few drops of extract of capsicum to each gallon of their watered product, but capsicum was a refinement beyond the blenders of Parker's Ferry Cross-roads, who found the pods of red-pepper grown by every old Negro mauma in the neighborhood quite as effective, and those who had in mind Hamlet's admonition, to have no half dealings with their art, would ram through the bunghole of each doctored barrel a whole string of dried cayenne peppers. At the start, this ruddy rosary was supposed to supply strength if not spirituality to the twenty gallons of branch water customarily added to the barrel of cheap whiskey, but, as the barrel ran low and the few gallons that remained became more strongly impregnated with the wholesome pepper, more water was added, so, whether the alcoholic content was 40 or 20 per cent. it burned the throat just the same, and the dusky tippler was satisfied, and, "day by day in every way" the whiskey grew in grace if it lost in strength, for the cause of temperance was served!

Although drinking was almost universal among the Negro men of the Low-Country forty years ago, there was remarkably little offensive drunkenness—due, in part, to their innate good nature, and in part to the branch-water.

AFTER THE FRUIT THE FLOUR

Whenever a planter rode up to the Cross-roads store on Saturday nights half a dozen Negroes, young and old, would run out to hold his horse, and before he departed the planter usually directed the shop keeper to give the bridle-holder a dram—perhaps two. If the recipient were an old-time Negro the scrape of his foot was long and ceremonious and his grateful grunt deep and sonorous, and, if the pepper burned his throat and brought the water to his eyes, his obeisance was low indeed!

Strychnine was sold at all the country stores and was in universal use among the Negroes for poisoning crows—corn being soaked in a solution of the deadly nightshade. While aware of its all-round efficiency as a lethal agency, it was used only for crows, the Negro adhering to the humane and time-honored method of removing the too-watchful dogs of "de Buckruh" by the administration of powdered glass; while for a woman, who found herself embarrassed by one of the "difficult" husbands that Elinor Glyn writes of so glibly and seems to know so much about, a tablespoonful of the esteemed "consecrate lye," mixed with food or coffee, speedily translated the obnoxious person to a "geographical location" whence only Conan Doyle or Sir Oliver Lodge would ever hear from him again!

As the Captain entered the big store a hundred pairs of eyes followed him. Always a striking figure, some of the Negroes looked upon him with

THE CAPTAIN

awe, others with affection, but all with interest, for his verbal magazine was always loaded and none knew when or upon whom it would be turned loose.

As there were no drug-stores in the Low-Country save at the county-seats, all the general country stores carried, in addition to the painkillers and patent medicine nostrums, a liberal supply of peppermint, ginger, paregoric, and other "plantation" remedies, with whose use all whites and many Negroes needed to be familiar in communities where there were no doctors. The pharmacal department of the big store at the Cross-roads was at the right of the entrance, where, by the light of a big window by day and a great kerosene lamp by night, the busy clerks could distinguish with a fair degree of accuracy the labels on the bottles containing deadly or innocuous drugs. Thus, through the grace of God, His sunlight by day and John D's kerosene by night, strychnine was seldom substituted for quinine, or laudanum for ginger. Perhaps, too, the knowledge that the deadly drugs were the more costly may have helped to minimize errors.

The Captain, exercising a privilege accorded to only a few valued patrons, walked behind the counter and approached the senior clerk, with whom he conferred earnestly. His back was turned to the watching Negroes, whose ears were cocked to catch fragments of the whispered conversation; but they could glean nothing, though their always suspicious minds were apprehensive that something sinister was afoot. From time to time the Captain turned

AFTER THE FRUIT THE FLOUR

and looked behind him as if trying to locate a certain face among the observers at the rear. At last, when he saw the beady eyes of old Simon Jenkins, the "squerril" hunter, watching him intently, he knew the time had come to spring his trap. Turning, he whispered something to the clerk, who moved mysteriously toward the drug department where, with furtive looks over his shoulder to be sure he was being watched, he reached for the quart jar of strychnine, whose poison label flaunted the "raw head and bloody bones"—red symbol of death! The clerk stooped beneath his deep counter, emptied his jar of strychnine into a tin bucket, whence, after hours it would be restored to its rightful receptacle, scooped a quart of flour out of a hidden barrel, put it in a paper bag, and handed it to the Captain with such a show of secrecy that the transfer was seen by everyone in the store! When the empty jar with its grinning death's-head was replaced on the shelf, every watching darky knew that the Captain had bought, and bought surreptitiously, enough strychnine to put golden slippers on half the colored population of St. Paul's Parish! The Captain, still with his back turned, put the flour carefully in an inside pocket. Then he went without, mounted his horse and rode away.

What would he do with it? Crows were out of season, for the corn was now far beyond their reach. Dogs? White men never poisoned them. Only one other guess remained, and, as the old "squerril" hunter followed the Captain into the

THE CAPTAIN

darkness without and joined the group that watched the man of mystery mount and ride away, through his thin lips came the ominous warning "Nigguh!" Yet even Negroes were not poisoned by "de Buckruh" just so, thought old Simon; so he muttered, laconically, *"watuhmilyun,"* shrewdly suspecting that the Captain might extend to the dusky invaders of his melon patch the privilege of committing involuntary harakiri, each quitting himself of the world by falling, not upon his own sword, but upon his own melon!

Simon, a sort of jack-leg witch-doctor or dealer in spells, and withal a wily old sinner, exercised a certain sinister influence among the Negroes who, though quite aware of his occasional depredations upon members of his own race, yet respected the cleverness that prevented the detection of greater offenses against the whites, and in matters involving their relations with the superior race Simon's advice was often sought. Simon knew very well that the Captain had a melon patch, and its exact location in the Orchard field, for the hands that worked at day-labor for the Captain kept him posted, and he intended a discreet invasion on an early night; but now his hopes had fled, for he realized that the assimilation of a quart of strychnine was beyond his powers. So he sent wide a warning by all the Negroes as they returned home that night, cautioning them that the Captain's melon patch was tabu.

AFTER THE FRUIT THE FLOUR

The next morning, as the devout gathered at their little clapboard churches or bush-shelters for Sunday service, the word was passed on and on, until by Sunday night the news had spread through all the dark circles in the community.

At dawn on Monday morning, the Captain walked through his melon patch, and at the dewy end of each big "rattlesnake" whose shriveling tendril showed that 'twas nearly ripe, he put a little dab of flour, until at last he had spotted all the big fellows in the patch.

Soon after sunrise the laughing workers came and were assigned their tasks. They looked askance at the Captain, believing they had penetrated the deadly secret of his quart of strychnine, while the Captain's beard masked his smile of amusement at the lethal properties attributed to his innocent paper-bag of flour.

All through the morning hours, as the hands passed up and down the long cotton field, those working the rows nearest the alluring melon patch cut sharp eyes toward the big fellows, whose white flour spots were plainly visible. And these nearest hands passed the news to those next, who passed it on and on, until long before the noon hour every man and woman in the field knew that the ripening melons were absorbing poison through their stem ends at a dangerous rate!

At last the sun reached his meridian, and as his rays fell vertically upon wool hat and bandanna the horn sounded for the midday knock-off. Laugh-

THE CAPTAIN

ter rang through the field, and, with hoes over their shoulders, all hands trooped to the grateful shade of a big live-oak, whose far-spreading branches could have sheltered half a regiment. Here, since morning, they had left the tin buckets containing their dinners, hanging for safety from the lower branches of the oak to which they were tied by twine or hooked by the handle to snags, and now, seating themselves on wads of Spanish moss pulled from the low boughs of the big oak, they turned from labor to refreshment.

The Negroes of the Low-Country have never become too independent to beg from "de Buckruh" by day whatever they may have failed to lift from "de Buckruh" by night; and, however great their nocturnal prowess, however deep their faith in the watchful care of Divine Providence, God does not always vouchsafe dark nights, and in His moonlight dark shadows are cast by His dusky folk of the Low-Country and, whatever "de Buckruh" may lack in grace, his double-barrel charged with birdshot can usually burn a colored brother's breeches at seventy-five yards. As the Captain's melon patch was doubly guarded by birdshot and strychnine, it was decided to make the safe and easy approach by word of mouth, and beg their way into its treasures.

"Sike," said a young woman as she uncovered her tin bucket and took out her iron spoon, "w'en Mas' Rafe come, baig'um fuh gi' we uh watuhmilyun."

"*Sike, de debble!*" said Joe. "Cuss duh de only t'ing Sike gwine git frum Mas' Rafe. Sike lazy

AFTER THE FRUIT THE FLOUR

tummuch! Mek some dem gal fuh baig'um. Dem debble'ub'uh mout' so 'ceitful, 'ooman kin gitt'um mo' bettuh den we man kin fuh gitt'um."

As the tall figure of the Captain strode under the shade of the live-oak, one of the young women raised the pleading voice of the daughter of the horse-leech.

"Mas' Rafe, please, suh, deseyuh man en' 'ooman ax me fuh baig you fuh gi' we one dem watuhmilyun fuh eat. Alltime we binnuh wu'k een da' fiel' dis mawnin' een da' sunhot, all uh we mout' run watuh ebb'ry time we pass da' patch en' look 'puntop'uh dem watuhmilyun. Please, suh, Mas' Rafe, gi' we."

"All right," said the complaisant Captain. "Go right in the field and help yourself."

"No, suh!" shouted several feminine voices in unison. "You gi' we, you gi' we, please, suh."

"Why, what's the matter?" said the Captain, amused at the concerted outcry that revealed the suspicions they would have concealed. The women chuckled, rather ashamed of having given themselves away; but the Negro is seldom at a loss for words, so with one accord they began to make excuses.

"Mas' Rafe, ef we gone een yo' fiel' fuh git dem t'ing, en' ef we tek de one wuh you pick out fuh de Big House, you gwine bex, Mas' Rafe, en' you fuh cuss we 'tel we yez fuh bu'n."

"You talk trute, tittuh. Nigguh ent fuh pit him han' 'puntop Buckruh watuhmilyun. Buckruh 'self fuh tell we w'ich one fuh tek."

THE CAPTAIN

"Mas' Rafe, ef we 'ooman wuh ent hab no shoe 'puntop we foot walk een da' fiel' en' lef' we track, you gwine medjuhr'um, en' ef some dem t'odduh 'ooman hab foot wuh stan' lukkuh we'own, en' dem t'odduh 'ooman walk een yo' fiel' duh nighttime en' t'ief dem watuhmilyun, you gwine 'spishun suh we tek'um."

The Captain relented, and, walking alone to the far end of the melon patch, stooped and rubbed the protective flour from the stem end of a long 40-pounder, which he severed from the vine. Then he called the clumsy Sike, who clasped it lovingly in his fat arms and, leaving deep barefoot tracks behind him, walked with measured tread to the shade of the oak.

When the big melon was opened "the birds began to sing." "Sike," said a saucy jade, "Mas' Rafe hab yo' track, en' dat watuhmilyun mek you fuh step hebby! Ef you ebbuh walk een da' fiel' duh nighttime you haffuh pit shoe 'puntop yo' foot."

"Yaas," said another, "but eb'nso ef 'e *yiz* hab shoe 'puntop him foot, Sike black mo'nuh all we t'odduh Nigguh, en' ef him nyam dem watuhmilyun en' dead, Mas' Rafe gwine say him pizen dem t'ing fuh kill crow, en' Buh Sike, him duh crow fuh true!"

THE GREEN CALABASH

[*The saying, "to cut the green calabash," sometimes heard in the Low-Country, is equivalent to the expression, "to draw a long bow," in universal use.*]

During the Confederate War a member of the Captain's family, while inspecting picket-posts through the summer months at Tar Bluff and other points along the Combahee River, experimented with quinine as a prophylactic, and was free of fever in a region thought to be deadly during the malarial months. The fruits of these experiences were passed on to others and, after the war, many families, forced to live all the year around on rice plantations, enjoyed complete immunity from malaria; but, as these fevers were almost the only pathological luxuries Low-Country people permitted themselves, without them the doctors were poor indeed!

The Captain's kindred found by intelligent tests that two grains daily for a grown-up and one grain or less for each child, commencing about the beginning of May when the magnolias were in full bloom and continuing until the first ice in November—the dosage for all ages being increased during the more dangerous months of September and October—would insure absolute protection.

Thereafter, neither swamp nor fen held terrors for those who swallowed regularly their nightly

THE CAPTAIN

dose of the protective Jesuits' bark. Men and boys walked waist-deep through the dew-drenched weeds of early morning, hunted or worked under burning suns by day, and, coming home on horseback or afoot at night, passed with impunity through the mists that veiled the long canals, the vapors that hung low over every sodden spot like shrouds in readiness for the stealthy death that lurked beneath. But those who relaxed their vigilance for even a few days and, through forgetfulness or indifference, omitted the nightly protective dose for even a short time, always paid the penalty in severe attacks that yielded only to heavy doses of the bitter drug— so heavy, indeed, that by the time the fever was "broken" the nerves of the patient were shattered as well. A few experiences of bitter mouths and "ringing" ears brought to even thoughtless boys the realization that an ounce (or a grain) of prevention was worth a pound of cure, and thereafter all through the summer, from the time the blooms of magnolia and sweet-bay filled with fragrance the sensuous breath of May to the first "black frosts" of November, the nightly call, "have you had your quinine?" went forth as regularly as the muezzin's sunset cry of "Allah-il-Allah" calls the faithful to prayer throughout the East.

During the Confederate War quinine, the only master to which the deadly malaria yielded, was declared "contraband of war" by the Federal Government, and quinine came into the beleagured states of the South only through the enterprise and daring

THE GREEN CALABASH

of those who slipped through the Federal fleets that were blockading all the seaports of the Confederacy, and ran in contraband cargoes from Nassau.

In the old days the planters of the Low-Country and their families spent the summer months either at the North, where Newport and Saratoga were enriched by their patronage, or at the nearer and equally famous "Virginia Springs;" but with the war the North became an enemy, Virginia a battlefield, and even the mountain resorts of the Southern Appalachians were inaccessible. Who can count the graves of innocent non-combatants—old men, women, and little children—that were filled through this humane decree of a Christian government at war!

Thus, restricted to the malarial regions whence always they had departed at the approach of summer, and deprived of the protective quinine, they were almost decimated in certain communities. Nor in the days of Reconstruction were those in the malarial regions much better off, for, while quinine was available to those who had money to buy, its cost was almost prohibitive to the ruined planters. During the earlier years following the war, the precious sulphate sold by Charleston druggists was of English or French manufacture, but later America entered the market, and a firm of chemists in Philadelphia competed for the custom of the impoverished South. Not, however, to the South's profit, for the American manufacturers exacted the foreign price of seven dollars an ounce! And while

THE CAPTAIN

the Philadelphia ounce may have been as honest as William Penn, the bottles were smaller, the labels less impressive, and the crystals by no means so white and fluffy as the French product. An ounce, seven dollars' worth of quinine, lasted the Captain's household little more than a month, and its cost—small as it seems to those who now pay seven dollars for a few drops of perfumery that make sensitive people turn the other way, or for one leg of an open-work stocking that looks as if the moths had been playing with it—represented the cost of a month's food for a large family; for seven dollars would have bought three bushels of cornmeal and grits, thirty pounds of bacon, and even soda and salt, while, if there were boys strong enough to grind the corn by hand in the heavy plantation mill, enough might have been saved perhaps to have provided a little tea and sugar for the aged or the sick, for seven dollars were seven dollars in the brave days after the war, when men were men and women were women, and many a Low-Country family of gentle birth subsisted for a month on less.

A few years later, when cinchonidia, a coarser and less potent preparation of Peruvian bark, came on the market at one dollar an ounce, it was given hopeful and prayerful consideration, and, as it was found that two grains of the cheaper sulphate were equal to one grain of quinine, cinchonidia came into general use until, under competition, the price of quinine came down.

THE GREEN CALABASH

The ladies and children of the Captain's household took their nightly doses of quinine in the form of pellets, carefully weighed and rolled at home, for gelatine capsules were refinements in taking bitter doses not then invented—at least they had never been heard of on Pon-Pon—but the Captain had a fine scorn for anything that disguised the wholesome bitterness of his prophylactic, and he pretended to like the taste of two or three grains of the powder dissolved in his nightly dram of corn whiskey. How much of this was affectation the boys never knew, for as the bitter draught gurgled slowly down his long throat the Captain's calm blue eyes looked kindly upon the world, and if he ever made wry faces over the martyrdom self-imposed upon his palate his beard completely masked them, and his swallows made his summers healthful!

Although a generous man, the Captain hated to be imposed upon, and held very lightly those companions of the hunting field whose hunting-flasks were usually empty, but who carried always a hunter's thirst. Summer deer-hunts are not infrequent in the Low-Country, for in August and September the blue-skinned bucks with their velveted horns, still leading cloistered, monkish lives, are at their fattest and best, both as to venison and to morals! Before going afield on a summer hunt, the Captain sometimes filled his flask from the bottle of embittered corn whiskey that stood on the low mantel over the "shanty" fireplace, and those

THE CAPTAIN

who on that day tapped the Captain's flask expressed their obligation for the Captain's hospitality through wry and twisted lips!

But 'twas when he treated the dusky folk that the bitterness of the Captain's tipple brought him most amusement. Sometimes on a lonely path through the forest, or as he rode along some unfrequented neighborhood road, he encountered a thirsty wayfarer whose dark face would light up and whose bulging eyes would "pop" as the Captain ostentatiously drew forth his flask and tilted it toward his bearded lips with an air of supreme contentment. When at last it was withdrawn, the pleading look in the eyes of the suppliant would have brought the last drop from a more tightly corked flask than the Captain's, and the darky would be bidden to fetch a big oak leaf and fold it, and into this emerald woodland cup the Captain would pour a generous dram, whose recipient, fearing to spill a single precious drop, would raise the fragile chalice to his mouth and swallow, postponing, until the drink was safely down, the low bow and scrape of the foot with which the darky of the Coast country invariably acknowledges the liquid largesse of "de Buckruh."

"Tengk Gawd, suh! Da' t'ing sweet'n me h'aa't, but 'e twis' me jaw 'tel 'e mek me mout' stan' sukkuh Uh binnuh chaw snakeroot en' wampee alltwo one time!"

Sometimes in summer when the quinine bottle stood on the mantle, hiding its bitter secret from

THE GREEN CALABASH

all the outside world, some plausible old sinner would shuffle up to the shanty door where, under the shade of the great pecan trees, the Captain placidly puffed his long pipe, and, full of lip-service and of flattery, would try to wheedle the Captain out of a dram.

So came Cuffee Scott, the swagger, mouthy foreman of an adjoining plantation.

"Ebenin', Mas' Rafe; huh you do, suh?"

"I'm well, Cuffee. What the devil do you want now?"

"Who, me? Me yent wan' nutt'n', suh. Uh binnuh walk big road gwine Jup'tuh Hill, en' Uh didn' t'ink 'e bin mannusubble fuh pass yo' place bedout stop fuh pass de time uh day."

"What were you going to Jupiter Hill for?"

"Me say Uh binnuh gwine Jup'tuh Hill, Mas' Rafe? Uh done bin Jup'tuh Hill fuh see ole Hamlet Manigo, en' Uh binnuh gwine home w'en Uh stop fuh pass de time uh day."

"Well, what did you go to Jupiter Hill for?"

"Mas' Rafe, you know Mas' Dick him pit me een chaa'ge uh all him Nigguh to Blue House, en' w'en Uh staa't fuh dictate obuh dem Nigguh Uh fin' Uh haffuh hab dog, 'cause w'en de Buckruh mek man 'sponsubble fuh ebb'ryt'ing 'pun de place, you haffuh keep alltwo yo' eye' skin fuh Nigguh' track', 'cause dem man 'puntop Blue House plantesshun lub fuh walk duh nighttime tummuch. Duh summuhtime, w'en dem ent hab no shoe 'puntop dem foot, dem

THE CAPTAIN

walk dat saaf'ly 'roun de smokehouse en' t'ing oonuh cyan' yeddy'um bedout you hab dog."

"I see you need a dog to help you catch up with your fellow blacks, but your Mas' Dick's whole pack of hounds can't keep up with you. But what has a dog to do with old Hamlet Manigo and Jupiter Hill?"

Cuffee guffawed at the Captain's questionable compliment. "Mas' Rafe, you know, suh, Uh loss de dog wuh Uh bin hab, 'cause alligettuh ketch'um week befo' las', so Uh haffuh git anodduh one, en' Uh gone 'cross Caw-Caw swamp t'odduh day en' peruse 'roun' 'mong dem po'-buckruh wuh lib een dem flat pinelan', 'tel Uh git one fuh suit."

"Well, did you get one?"

"Yaas, suh, Uh git one."

"Whom did you get if from?"

"Uh yent know de po'-buckruh' name, suh. Him ent bin to 'e house w'en Uh buy de dog frum'um."

"How did you buy him, then? What did you pay for him?"

"Suh?"

"How could you buy him if the man wasn't at home? How could you pay for him?"

"Mas' Rafe, me tell you suh Uh pay fuhr'um? Uh buy'um fuh true, 'cause Uh nebbuh git ketch een no t'ief, but Uh nebbuh pay fuhr'um 'cause, een de fus' place, ef de man *iz* bin home, me yent hab no money fuh pay fuhr'um. Wuh use fuh pay fuhr'um w'en man kin gitt'um bedout? W'en Uh gone to de

THE GREEN CALABASH

man' house two dog run out, one duh my dog en' t'odduh one duh my dog' maamy."

"Your dog?"

"Yaas, suh, enty Uh tell you Uh buy'um? W'en de two dog come out, my dog' maamy try fuh bite me, but my dog seem lukkuh him wan' me fuh him maussuh, en' soon ez 'e come close 'e biggin fuh wag 'e tail, den Uh know him duh my'own, en' Uh bruk off piece uh cawn bread wuh Uh bin hab een me pocket, en' Uh g'em fuh eat. W'en 'e done nyam'um, 'e wag 'e tail gen, en' w'en Uh talk saaf'ly to'um and walk off slow wid de bittle een me han', my dog folluh me *spang* Blue House, en' Uh nebbuh hab no trouble, no mo'."

"Your trouble will come, you coffee-colored old sinner, when that Caw-Caw swamp cracker sends you to Walterboro' jail for dog-stealing."

"Mas' Rafe, him ent fuh ketch me, 'cause dem po'-buckruh frum obuh de swamp nebbuh come yuh een we country, 'scuzin' dem try fuh ketch cow, eeduhso hog wuh blonx to some uh we quality Buckruh, en' eb'nso ef 'e yiz ketch me, enty Gawd full Nigguh' jaw teet' wid lie fuh fool Buckruh? 'Speshly po'-buckruh, 'cause dem ent know nutt'n' 'tall 'bout Nigguh, en' Nigguh *done* fuh fool'um, but quality Buckruh! W'en dem stan' lukkuh you, Mas' Rafe, dem berry haa'd fuh fool!"

"You don't fool me because I never believe a word any one of you says."

"Ki! Mas' Rafe, enty you duh we Maussuh? You know we fuh true! Enty you know suh Gawd

THE CAPTAIN

gi' we uh good ecknowledge fuh tell lie fuh puhtek weself? Een slabery time, w'en Nigguh tell lie to 'e Maussuh, him eeduh know de Nigguh lie, elseso 'e s'pishun'um; but de Maussuh say to 'eself, 'wuh use fuh onkibbuh dis Nigguh? Wuh use fuh 'cuze-'um? Ef Uh lick'um, him gwine lie 'gen, 'cause de debble 'self ent fuh stop'um! En' wuh use fuh lick me own Nigguh? Him duh me proputty, enty? Berrywell.' En' de Maussuh mek de Nigguh t'ink him b'leebe'um, en' de Nigguh keep on fuh trus' 'e blin' Gawd, 'tel bumbye 'e git ketch een uh hebby lie en' de dribuh tie'um up en' bu'n 'e britchiz fuh true! But now, sence Freedom come een, de old Maussuh dem ent fuh b'leebe Nigguh no mo'. Ebb'ry time dem study 'pun hummuch lie Nigguh tell'um een slabery time, dem git bex. Dem say, 'de debble! Deseyuh Nigguh ent blonx to we no mo'. Ef dem ent blonx to de Nyankee, dem blonx to demself, en' free Nigguh iz uh t'ing wuh haffuh git lick.' Dat w'ymekso summuch Nigguh git lick sence dem free, wuh nebbuh lick befo' sence dem bawn. Dem ent hab no Maussuh, en' dem Jedus stan' fudduh. So w'enebbuh dem kill cow, eeduhso t'ief hog en' git ketch, de Buckruh ax'um, 'Nigguh, w'ich one you redduh, fuh gone Walterburruh jail fuh six munt', eeduhso fuh tek fifty lash'?' De Nigguh 'f'aid de lick fuh true, but him study 'bout da' cawn-hom'ny en' dem t'odduh dry bittle him fuh nyam een da' jail, en' 'e t'ink 'pun how him fuh lef' him fowl en' 'e wife en' t'ing fuh six munt', en' 'e study 'bout all dem t'odduh man duh ramify 'roun' t'ru Nigguh-

THE GREEN CALABASH

house-yaa'd ebb'ry night Gawd sen', en' 'e mek up 'e min' fuh tek de lick. De Buckruh mek'um fuh leddown 'cross one flour barrel wid 'e face down, den 'e mek anodduh Nigguh fuh pull one stabe out de barrel, en' de Nigguh come down 'pun 'e britchiz 'tel 'e mek'um fuh wabble sukkuh watuh-moccasin wabble w'en 'e duh swim! Ebb'ry time 'e come down 'puntop de Nigguh' britchiz de barrel jump off de groun'! Bumbye, de Nigguh mek shishuh hebby cumplain, en' 'e woice soun' so mo'nful, de Buckruh sorry fuhr'um, en' attuh 'e done git t'irty lick', 'e tell de man fuh stop. Mas' Rafe, Gawd sho' bin good to Nigguh' mout'! W'en 'e hongry, 'e mout' feed'um; en' w'en him git ketch, 'e mout' sabe'um!"

"If God gives so much to you kinky-headed Ethiopians, what does he give 'de Buckruh?'"

"Mas' Rafe, Gawd gi' we 'ceitful mout', fuh true, en' Him full'um up wid lie fuh fool de Buckruh; but, sametime, enty Him gi' de Buckruh yez fuh yeddy'um, en' fait' fuh b'leebe'um?"

The Captain puffed slowly, and watched the smoke rings, the spirits of the weed, drift gracefully upward and dissolve into the air. So, mused the Captain, the souls of the blest troop like ghostly ships across the bar out into eternity!

"Cuffee!"

"Suh."

"You see that smoke?"

"Yaas, suh, Uh shum."

"Where is it now?"

THE CAPTAIN

" 'E done gone."

"Very well. So long as that smoke ring floats, the white man's faith lasts in anything Cuffee says, and those lies that slip out of a darky's mouth like molasses running out of a bunghole, go in one ear and out the other."

"Yaas, Mas' Rafe, but da' duh you. En' all uh oonuh quality Buckruh stan' same fashi'n, 'cause oonuh bin had Nigguh een Slabery Time, en' de Nigguh fool 'e Maussuh some de time, but 'e yent fuh fool'um all de time, 'cause attuhw'ile de Nigguh tell 'e Maussuh summuch lie 'tel de Maussuh nebbuh b'leebe'um no mo'; da' duh you, Mas' Rafe! You yeddy but you ent haa'kee; but deseyuh rich po'-buckruh wuh keep sto' een town en' to de Crossroad, en' deseyuh po' po'-buckruh wuh keep dem cow en' hog en' t'ing 'puntop groun' wuh blonx to quality Buckruh, dem ent know uh Cryce t'ing 'bout Nigguh, en' de lie wuh de Nigguh tell'um fast'n een dem yez sukkuh cucklebuhr ketch een mule' yez! Dem yeddy en' dem haa'kee alltwo! En' ef da' Caw-Caw swamp po'-buckruh bin ketch me wid my dog wuh Uh buy frum'um, Uh woulduh tell'um, 'yaas, man, dishyuh duh yo' dog fuh true. Uh yeddy 'bout you bin hab dog, en' Uh gone to you house fuh buy'um, en' Uh berry sorry you ent bin home. Dishyuh dog mus'be know wuh dey een me min', en' 'e know suh Uh gone to you house fuh buy'um, 'cause 'e folluh me foot w'en Uh lef' yo' house, en' alldo' Uh bruk stick en' beat'um fuh dribe'um back home, stillyet Uh cyan' mek'um fuh gone'way.' Mas'

THE GREEN CALABASH

Rafe, ef da' po'-buckruh ebbuh wet 'e foot fuh cross Caw-Caw en' come obuh yuh to we side en' ketch me wid da' dog, w'en Uh done gitt'ru talk, ef me Jedus help me, da' po'-buckruh gwine b'leebe suh me buy de dog fuh true. Him nebbuh s'pishun suh me t'ief'um! But eb'nso ef 'e *yiz* come, ef 'e foot slow en' 'e yent come fuh two-t'ree week, w'en 'e look 'puntop da' dog 'gen him nebbuh fuh ruckuhnize'um."

"What rascally trick are you up to now?"

"Mas' Rafe, you know ebb'ry day Uh haffuh mek cawn bread, eeduhso bile uh hebby pot full'uh tu'n-flour en' 'tettuh fuh Mas' Dick' pack uh beagle, en', you know suh, when Nigguh haffuh cook bittle fuh Buckruh, eeduhso fuh Buckruh' dog, dem han' berry hebby en' dem h'aa't light, 'cause dem know suh 'nuf gwine lef' fuh de Nigguh en' de Nigguh dog alltwo. Berrywellden, suh, w'en Uh buy da' dog 'e bin po' ez uh snake, en' now Mas' Dick' tu'nflour mek'um dat fat 'tel 'e roll w'en 'e walk, sukkuh barruh. Den, w'en Uh buy da' dog 'e bin red, but t'oddul day Uh tek da' t'ing wuh Mas' Dick hab fuh clip him mule' tail', en' Uh shabe da' red dog 'tel now 'e stan' blue sukkuh ashish!"

"Well, you swapped a lean red dog for a fat blue one, but when his 'po'-buckruh' owner comes for him he'll know him by his ears, and his tail will wag for his master, whether it's red or blue."

"Mas' Rafe, lemme tell you. Da' dog ent hab no tail fuh wag, en' 'e yent fuh hab no yez. Him done loss 'e tail, en' ef Jedus yeddy me, him gwine loss

THE CAPTAIN

alltwo 'e yez befo' sundown tomorruh. Mas' Rafe, wuh use dog hab fuh yez? Rokkoon too easy fuh ketch'um. Eb'nso hog ent hab no use fuh yez 'cause dog kin hol'um too good. Da' w'ymekso summuch Nigguh' hog en' po'-buckruh' hog nebbuh hab no yez."

"Yes, you make way with the ears to get rid of the Buckruh's earmarks."

"Great Gawd, Mas' Rafe! You know Nigguh *tummuch!* 'E stan' so fuh true. Well, suh, w'en Uh buy my dog him hab long yez lukkuh beagle, en' 'e tail long. W'en Uh study 'pun 'e yez en' t'ing Uh mek up me min' fuh cutt'um off, 'cause de time' too haa'd fuh buy bittle fuh feed dog' yez en' 'e tail, so Uh tek'um to ole Unk' Hamlet Manigo wuh lib to Jup'tuh Hill fuh gitt'um fuh bob 'e tail en' fice 'e yez."

"Fice his ears!"

"Yaas, suh, roach'um fuh mek'um stan'up shaa'p lukkuh fox' yez en' fice dog. Ole Hamlet him hab uh smaa't han' fuh hol' knife, en' w'en him trim dog yez, 'e cutt'um clean sukkuh 'ooman cut dem patch fuh mek quilt. Uh tell da' Nigguh fuh trim my dog yez en' 'e tail so ef 'e ebbuh git 'cross Caw-Caw Swamp 'gen, dem po'-buckruh shoot'um fuh wil'cat!

"Well, suh, w'en Uh tek me dog Jup'tuh Hill w'ile ago, old Hamlet him binnuh mek fench en' 'e hab 'e hatchitch een 'e han'. Uh tell'um wuh Uh want'um fuh do, en' 'e say 'berrywell,' but him haffuh gone to 'e house fuh git knife fuh cut de dog yez;

THE GREEN CALABASH

but him say suh 'e hab 'e hatchitch een 'e han' en' him kin bob 'e tail fus', so Uh ketch de dog by 'e yez en' tell ole Hamlet fuh chop! Da' ole Nigguh pull de dog' tail 'cross one log, en' 'e come down 'pun'um close to 'e hanch! Mas' Rafe, ebbuh sence Uh shabe da' dog 'e skin slick ez ottuh, en' w'en da' hatchitch knock 'pun 'e tail, please Gawd 'e buss' t'ru me han' en' lick out down de big road gwine Blue House, en' ebb'ry time 'e jump 'e holluh! 'E tail stan' sukkuh rabbit, en' 'e foot stan' sukkuh rabbit. Him nebbuh fuh ketch flea out'uh 'e tail 'gen, no mo'!"

"Well, you old humbug, you came in just to pass the time of day, did you? What the devil are you grinning for?"

"Well, suh, w'en Uh study 'bout da' dram you gimme las' time Uh bin yuh, me jaw haffuh grin. Da' t'ing sweet'n' me tummuch!"

"So that's what you were spelling for, you prince of hypocrites! Go to the well and bring that calabash."

Cuffee swaggered over to the well and lifted from its hook the long-handled drinking gourd used by the Negroes. "Yuh him, Mas' Rafe, t'engk-gawd," and he bowed low and scraped an elaborate foot as the "glug-glug" of the Captain's bitter bottle filled his ears and his soul with ecstasy! He drained the gourd at one gulp. Then his face writhed in a monkey-like grimace, and he spat on the ground furiously. "Dem debble'ub'uh 'ooman cut da' killybash befo' 'e ripe! 'E full me mout' wid gall!"

"Yes, Cuffee, you've been cutting the green calabash all the evening. The fool is answered according to his folly, and the mouth of him that cheweth green gourds shall be filled with bitterness!"

"DADDY BO'SUN"

"Daddy Bo'sun," as the old Negro was known to the younger generation of white people and to black folk of all ages, was one of the characters of the Pon-Pon community and a man of strong will and sound principles, marred only by his love of strong drink, but when tipsy, as he often was, old Bo'sun was as weak and undependable as tipsy men, white and black, usually are. A former slave of Major Hawkins King, the Captain's nearest neighbor, the master had christened the black boy Boatswain Smashum, and although plantation and community, thinking the nautical "Bo'sun," quite sufficient for the runty little fellow, quickly adopted the shorter appellation, Major King, to the day of his death, held on to the mouth-filling syllables, and morning and evening his high-pitched voice carried his call of "Boat-swain! Boat-swain!" even over to the adjoining plantation half a mile away!

Growing to young manhood, Bo'sun became an expert horseman, and as he was quick and intelligent, and never weighed more than a hundred and twenty-five pounds, Major King made him his huntsman, or deer-driver, whose duties were, throughout the year, the care of hounds and saddle-horses, while in the hunting season he became at once master of hounds and whipper-in, putting the pack in the "drive," following the hounds through, wherever the cry might lead, whipping them off the trails of bay-lynx or gray fox—outlawed by all Low-Country

THE CAPTAIN

deer-hunters—and, at last, stopping them at the river's brink, whenever the deer should take the water. Bo'sun's bow-legs, curved like the prongs of a wishbone, clasped the ribs of his mount as closely as if they had been fashioned to order and, crouched over the withers of his horse, like a circus monkey on a trick mule, he threaded the hazardous mazes of the forest, slipping between the trunks of thick-set pines, leaping giant logs, swerving swiftly around dangerous stump-holes, floundering through the treacherous bogs of old canals, and throwing himself backward, flat upon his horse's crupper, to avoid the swoop of low-swung grape vines—all the tricks of Low-Country woods-riding that fox-hunting horsemen of the open country know nothing about—these Bo'sun had mastered in the days of his youth, and, long before the breaking out of the war set the hard-riding planters of the Confederacy more serious tasks, the Major's pack and the Major's huntsman were known throughout the countryside.

Freedom brought no comfort to old Bo'sun's spirit, and to his body it brought hardship, for Sherman's army had passed that way and had written its story in the ashes of a day that was dead! And with that army passed every four-footed creature that could furnish its own means of locomotion, horses, mules, and cattle. Stables and pastures were swept bare, while army wagons groaned under the spoils of smokehouse and granary.

"DADDY BO'SUN"

Freedom, the great leveler, had put all freedmen on the same footing. The field-hands—the peasantry of the plantations—were exalted, for, as their state under slavery had been the lowliest, their uplift was now the greatest. But for many of the upper house-servants, the drivers, the coachmen, the huntsmen—all who had been in authority in their masters' households—the leveling process was almost tragic. The artisans—carpenters, wheelwrights, and blacksmiths—were well enough, for even in a wasted region there were at least cabins and shacks to be built and primitive wagons and carts to be put together; but for those who were without mechanical trades a Freedom that debased them to the level of those over whom they sometime lorded it made them poor, indeed. As their former masters were mostly unable to pay or feed house-servants, these were forced to earn their bread in the fields, and, entirely unaccustomed to hard labor, or to exposure to the sun, they were able to earn very little, too little to supply them with more than the coarsest food and clothing. Similar and greater hardships were imposed upon the gentlewomen and gentlemen to whom these aristocratic house-servants once belonged, yet those who had lost everything except themselves—their own indomitable spirit—bore their trials jauntily, while those to whom, out of the womb of war, a Caesarian lancet of exigency had brought the boon of freedom, still yearned for the fleshpots of their former masters' kitchens, and would not be comforted because the

THE CAPTAIN

authority they once exercised in the "big house" was, like the house itself, now gone forever!

A few years after the war, Bo'sun's old master gave him a strip of land, five or six acres, lying between the railway and the old King's highway— the "big road" of the Negroes. Leaving a few sentinel pines, Bo'sun cleared the rest and planted his little patches of corn, cotton, peas, sweet potatoes, and upland rice. The small stumps were taken up, the larger were left for odd times in the winter season when other work was slack and fuel most in demand. Then the old man built a comfortable cabin, small though adequate outbuildings and, with his fine old wife, moved into the home of their declining years, where, at last, their eyes should close upon a changing world that for them, at least, had not changed for the better.

Maum Anne was a woman of high principles and strong character, respected and esteemed by both races. A home keeper, she seldom went abroad, and her home was beautifully kept. The broad, coarse planks of her pine floor were scoured almost to whiteness. The fluted longcloth curtains that hung at the tiny windows of the cabin were spotless, and everywhere about the house the touch of a competent hand was evident. An excellent gardener, Maum Anne had a fine "hand" for simples, and always in winter bunches of dried sage and thyme hung from the rafters, while long strings of red peppers fell in graceful festoons. The front yard, swept alternately with home made brooms of split

"DADDY BO'SUN"

white-oak and "bullhead" broomgrass, was always immaculate, and upon the wattled palings of the enclosing fence there grew every summer, until nipped by November frosts, a luxuriant crop of the little "See-wee" Lima beans.

Like many another fine couple in other walks of life, Maum Anne and old Bo'sun were not blessed in their children. The son, while not vicious, drank, and was generally trifling, while their two married daughters brought them no credit. In time, all of them came to live close under the shelter of the parental wing, for the old man allowed them to build cabins on a part of his little landed estate. And, whatever freedom of deportment these children permitted themselves while they lived abroad, once within the sound of Bo'sun's admonitory voice, Joe and Silvia and Rose walked the proverbial chalk-line, for they knew that, grown men and women as they were, the slightest deviation from the law laid down for their guidance would bring across their backs the curl of the buckskin "cracker" at the end of old Bo'sun's dog whip. When the time came for punishment, Bo'sun attended to Joe, but Maum Anne applied the rod unsparingly to her daughters, and the wholesome discipline of Maum Anne's day took no account of raps over the knuckles, or slaps upon the wrist! Weak old woman as she was, her spiritual and physical mastery over her lusty daughters, full of freedom as they were, was a fine example at once of the lasting effects of early training and the triumph of moral over physical force.

THE CAPTAIN

A stout cord, almost as thick as a plow-line, hung in a neat coil upon a convenient peg in the living-room of the cabin, and one end of the cord was looped into a hangman's noose. Whenever a daughter was ripe for discipline, Maum Anne quietly called her into the house and pointed to the cord upon the wall. Although the girl might utter a whimpering plea for mercy, she obeyed the pantomimic order promptly. Uncoiling the cord, she threw the free end across a beam overhead, and as it fell, she placed it in her mother's hand, then, putting her own hands within the noose at the other end, she awaited whatever fate might have in store for her. Fate usually had a plenty. Pulling upon her end of the cord, Maum Anne drew the loop close about her daughter's wrists and triced up her hands over her head, thus preserving them from possible injury during chastisement, and leaving a fair field below the waistline to receive the full sweep of the plaited buckskin. Then, taking down the heavy huntsman's whip, Maum Anne cultivated the field so assiduously that the clumsy girl jumped as lightly as a child skipping rope. When it was all over, daughter dropped a dutiful curtsey, and went her ways, with chastened spirit and tingling body, while Maum Anne, conscious of duty well done, resumed her household tasks with the dignity and serenity of one who would always be "mistress of herself, tho' china fall!"

Always respectful to white people, old and young —those, at least, who merited respect—Bo'sun, as

"DADDY BO'SUN"

he grew older, became almost truculent toward the young of his own race. White boys were exceedingly fond of him, as he was devoted to them, answering with infinite patience—often with quizzical humor and philosophy—their endless questions, storing their minds with wood-lore, and recounting many stirring incidents of the old hunting days. Between the former slave, and the young sons of former slaveholders, however, there was mutual respect and esteem, courtesy and consideration, and perfect understanding. But Negro youths and boys he held in utter contempt, having no patience with their indolence and lack of manners. His warning "B-o-y!" was as sharp as the scream of a red-tailed hawk. "B-o-y! Weh you mannus! Ent you know mannus cya' you t'ru w'en nutt'n' else will? Mek you mannus! Mek you mannus! Pull you wool! 'Crape you foot! B-o-y!—Gimme de lash!"

But the younger Negroes, coached as they were by the low whites who affiliated with them and the blacks who had served in the Federal army, found it hard enough to treat the members of former slave-holding families with civility, and they had no respect at all for the old servants of slavery, while they looked upon the deferential observances of pulling wool and scraping the foot much as the cigareted cuttysark of today would regard the flounces and furbelows of the mid-Victorian days, when, if people didn't condone their sins, at least they covered them up!

THE CAPTAIN

When, a few years after the war, Major King changed his residence to a plantation near the coast, old Bo'sun attached himself to the Captain's family, coming over every day, morning and evening, to milk the cows, while in winter he cured and smoked whatever bacon—having run the gauntlet of the dusky rievers who infested the woods pastures —came to the plantation pens. In all these arts the old man was a past master. Full of nervous energy, he was quick as he was competent. His red eyes were sharp as a hawk's and his gnarled and swiftly moving fingers were deft as a woman's. And if the Negro boys who came under his hand showed any disposition to learn he was always willing to teach them, though they found him a hard taskmaster who administered frequent tongue-lashings and dealt them as many thwacks of an imaginary stick as Sancho Panza, with a very real cudgel, bestowed upon his sleek tho' sluggish ass! "B-o-y! Step fas'! Step fas'! Slow walkin' mek quick lickin', you know! Enty I tell you 'tek care bettuh mo'nuh baig paa'don!' Attuh I done lick you, who gwine tek'um off? You jacket kin come off, you shu't kin come off, you britchiz kin come off, you skin kin come off, but da' lickin' cyan' come off, enty? Berrywell!"

But while Bo'sun's bark was usually worse than his bite, he sometimes bit. Like many of the older Negroes, he had become in his youth expert in the use of the singlestick, and, whirling a four-foot hickory sprout, or a light hoe-handle before him, he

THE "OAK LAWN" AVENUE, FROM THE KING'S HIGHWAY

"DADDY BO'SUN"

could whack you a head as lustily as a Donnybrook Hibernian! Knowing nothing of boxing, he would crumple up his knotty old knuckles into an impossible fist and shove it threateningly under the noses of the younger Negroes with the warning, "Ole bone haa'd, you know!" But, small as he was, none of the youngsters cared to test the hardness of his old bones, and, as he feared nothing that wore wool, he was seldom molested.

And his skull was of iron hardness. One day as he was repairing his garden fence a rude hail from the road, caused him to look up. A cart had stopped in front of his door, and from the high vantage of the driver's seat Ephraim, a middle-aged yellow Negro, insolently commanded his presence in the "big road"—the King's highway—common ground, upon which the Negroes usually composed such differences as were submitted to the arbitrament of foot, fist, and skull.

Bo'sun dropped his hatchet, and went without.

"Ole man," Ephraim demanded, "wuh dat Uh yeddy you bin say 'bout me?"

"You yeddy Uh bin say sump'n', enty?"

"Yaas, Uh yiz. Uh yeddy suh you tell Mas' Rafe suh you s'pishun me duh de man wuh t'ief him hog, en' Uh come yuh fuh mek you talk'um straight."

"You yeddy wrong. Uh nebbuh say nutt'n' 'bout s'pishun. Uh tell Mas' Rafe you *t'ief* de hog, en' you *eat* de hog. Uh see de shoat' tail duh stick out you mout' now!"

THE CAPTAIN

Ephraim drew his hand quickly across his mouth, and, at old Bo'sun's unctuous chuckle and grunt: "You shum, enty? Berrywell," fairly writhed at the old man's shrewd trick and, sputtering angrily, "Ef you bin man lukkuh me, Uh wouluh ride you frame right yuh een dishyuh road, but ef Uh knock ole man lukkuh you Uh fuh hab sin," pulled his lines and started to drive off.

Bo'sun's hand shot out, and seizing the mule by the bridle, jerked him to a standstill. "Come down, son, come down," he said gently, still holding the bridle in an iron grip. "Ef you haffuh hab sin, Gawd will tek'um off, enty? Come down, son!"

The boastful Ephraim for very shame could not decline the challenge, and, jumping down from the cart, drew back his right arm threateningly, after the fashion of all untutored boxers who think it desirable to apprise their adversaries when and where they intend to strike.

But Ephraim never struck! Before he could unleash his tawny fist, old Bo'sun sprang at him like a wildcat, grabbed him by the ears with both hands and, pulling his head down, butted him full in the forehead. The impact was as of a mallet upon a wedge. Ephraim fell as if he had been pole-axed, and crumpled up in the road. Calling to Maum Anne, who stood in the doorway, to fetch water, Bo'sun splashed the contents of the calabash in the yellow face at his feet, and the dazed Ephraim regained consciousness. "Son," said the old man, pityingly, "Son, you head hu't you, enty? Yaas,

"DADDY BO'SUN"

Uh t'aw't so. Berrywell," and turning his back, he picked up his hatchet and resumed his work, while the astonished Ephraim climbed in his cart and took the road without a word.

In her last days Maum Anne became a great sufferer, but, in one white family, at least, she was not forgotten, and there often came to her the comfort of warm flannels and such little delicacies as the straitened circumstances of her benefactors permitted.

But she went away, and Daddy Bo'sun was never the same again. After a few years of solitude, he took another wife, an unworthy woman with whom he had little in common. The association only deepened his spiritual loneliness, and more and more he turned to the white friends who understood him so well. And when, at last, he went to join his faithful old wife, he left, in the hearts of those friends who survive, memories—still bright after fifty years—of a lowly couple who carried through their simple lives loyalty, gratitude, and courtesy— coinage of the heart that there's none too poor to pay, nor any too rich to need.

THE UNDER DOG

On a late Saturday afternoon in early summer the Captain rode to the Cross-roads. The day had been showery, but as the sun dipped the skies cleared and all the opulent leafage of June shone forth in green and gold and crystal. Here, overarching live-oaks—graybeard patriarchs of the forest—stretched their limbs above the road, the graceful Spanish moss swaying in the light air; there, the thick, damp foliage of the sweet-gum exhaled a faint breath of spice; while at intervals along the way the rain-washed tangles of wild-grape in bloom drenched the dusk with fragrance.

Cantering past "King's Gate," the entrance to the long lane that led to "Blue House" plantation (once called "Encampment" from the Gullah war), the Captain ascended a gentle slope from the branch to the high pineland, and drew rein at the gate of a little homestead by the roadside, for a word with its occupant.

Daddy Bo'sun was abroad, but Maum Anne, the dignified chatelaine of the humble castle, promised to give him, upon his return, the Captain's message to report to the Cross-roads store, where, on Saturday evenings, the few white employers in the community—planters and timber-cutters—went to pay off their hands.

For many years after the Confederate War, men of gentle birth—planters and others—were forced to keep country stores in order to keep their heads

THE CAPTAIN

above water. As a rule, the planters not only had no aptitude for commercial life, but actually despised "trade." But "needs must, when the devil drives," and, as the devil drove rough-shod over the coast country during "Reconstruction" and for a long time thereafter, certain gentlemen, obliged to support their families, pocketed their scruples in the hope of pocketing a few dollars, and became shop-keepers; but most of this country trade was in the hands of wandering Jews, cheap Germans from the cities, and native whites of the lower strata, and these last—still "po'-buckruh" to the Negroes, however fat their pocketbooks—would tear off a 33-inch yard, or weigh you a fourteen-ounce pound, as unctuously as any Hans or Isaac that ever grunted gutterals, or rubbed together oily palms!

The benefits of these weekly settlements at the Cross-roads were three-fold. First, to the merchant, who got the trade, second, to the laborer, who was paid off at the source of his weekly supplies of food and clothing, and third, to the planter, who settled once a month, or at even longer intervals, for the orders given weekly on the merchant.

During the earlier years after the war, money was exceedingly scarce on the plantations, and labor was paid for almost exclusively in such supplies as were carried in the "commissaries" of the planters, or by orders on the more pretentious stocks of the stores in the vicinity. But, later on, money became easier, and the Negroes, scorning the commissary stores, demanded cash from the planter or

THE UNDER DOG

from the merchant upon whom the planter's orders were drawn. To the demand for cash, the merchant, thoroughly versed in Negro psychology, readily yielded, for he knew that as soon as Cuffee had smoothed out the greasy shin-plasters, or jingled the small silver in his horny hands, he would proceed to get rid of it as speedily as possible. Most of it, indeed, was spent over the counter, and passed quickly back into the canny merchant's hands. If any, by chance, reached the Negro's pocket, it soon gnawed its way out, to come into the hands of one of the laughing, chattering women who waited without.

So much for the money of the men. The women were more thrifty with theirs, for upon them rested the keeping up the dues of the church society and of tithing the always exacting clergy, provision having to be made for the feeing and feeding of both the local pastor, who, like the poor, they had with them alway, and the peripatetic circuit-rider whose periodic visits, tho' looked forward to with exaltation, lured the last coin from the tin cup cache in the chimney corner and the last spare rooster from the roost!

"Ef fox, eeduhso wil'cat ketch da' roostuh wuh Uh got, wuh me fuh do? Uh cyan' do nutt'n'! 'Cause Uh yent got no money, none'tall, fuh buy 'nodduh one. 'Ooman sho' hab uh haa'd time fuh feed two preachuh! Uh yent study summuch 'bout Buh Paul, we locus Pastuh, 'cause, alldo' him fuhrebbuh hongry, ef 'e come to me house en' Uh g'em roas' 'tettuh

THE CAPTAIN

fuh eat out de ashish, him sattify, en' ef you pit uh fibe cent een 'e han', 'e t'engkful 'tel 'e mos' ready fuh 'crape 'e foot, but w'en de sukkus-preachuh come! Ki! You cyan' do him no shishuh way lukkuh dat. No, suh! Him call 'eself de Lawd' renointed, en' him ent fuh ren'int wid no roas' 'tettuh, needuhso no fibe cent! You haffuh feed'um, tittuh, en' you haffuh feed'um high! W'en Pa Manigo come een you house en' stan'up befo' you fiah, en' spraddle 'e two foot wide, en' fol' 'e two han' befor'um 'puntop da' w'ite weskit 'e hab on, en' lick out 'e tongue en' leek'um obuh 'e mout', Bubbuh! Den Uh know berry well da' weskit haffuh 'tretch 'tel de button done buss'off, en' da' mout' haffuh greese 'tel 'e shine! En' you ent fuh greese'um wid no bakin skin! You haffuh fry fowl fuhr'um, enty? En' da' stylish weskit ent fuh swell 'long no 'tettuh, needuhso no cawn-hom'ny! Uh haffuh gone een me yaa'd fuh beat rice, 'cause him haffuh hab hopp'n'john, enty? Pa Manigo t'ink suh nutt'n' else fuh 'tretch'um digni*fy* lukkuh dat! En', attuhw'ile, w'en 'e gone, please Gawd, 'e done nyam all de bittle een me house, 'e tek ebb'ry Cryce ten-cent wuh Uh got, en' 'e yent lef' nutt'n' behin'um 'cep' fedduh!"

So every woman took home with her part, at least, of her weekly earnings in cash, securely knotted in a corner of her apron.

The Saturday evening gatherings at the Crossroads forty or fifty years ago were lively occasions, far more full of fun than they were a few

THE UNDER DOG

years later, for the Negroes reared under slavery were more natural, more humorous, and more spontaneous than those of later years. Sophistication had developed self-consciousness in the younger generations and, however great the mirth they provoke in others, the self-conscious, the self-contemplative, are necessarily without a sense of humor. Then, too, the old Negroes had the background that the younger Negroes lacked. Their memories of slavery were still vivid, and they could weigh the merits and faults of the two systems under which they had lived with surprising understanding. Naturally, the point of view varied with certain groups or classifications. Those who had been known as "bad" Negroes before the war—cattle-thieves, burglars, wife-beaters, and turbulent, quarrelsome fellows, who had tasted the driver's lash for such offenses as have since put freedmen in the penitentiary—these found freedom all to the good, for to such men, liberty means license. And the smarter and more competent of the good Negroes, who had no harsh memories of slavery, were also happy under freedom, for, as their energy, ability, and thrift enabled them to get more and hold more than their fellows, they became in time the substantial men of their black communities and were respected accordingly. But, upon the old, the feeble, and the inefficient, freedom bore heavily, for, under slavery, whose days they were always lamenting, their tasks were fitted to their strength, while clothing, food, and medicines were fitted to their needs. Under

THE CAPTAIN

freedom, such humanitarian adjustments were impossible, for, in the intra-racial relations of the freedmen, *lex talionis* was the rule, and those who were without claws could get very little. How many lives of enfeebled old Negroes, cast aside by their kindred, have been prolonged by the kindly ministrations of former slaveholders, will never be known, but there were countless thousands to be set against the South's share of the responsibility for slavery.

But, however the older Negroes regarded past slavery and present freedom, they were of one mind as to the advantage, to themselves, of having been taught to work and made to work, and this superiority they were always proclaiming to the younger Negroes, whose laziness and inefficiency they denounced daily. They were agreed, too, that, however bad, however undeserved, the whippings of the old days had been for them, no moral medicine whatsoever could have so beneficent effects upon those growing up under Freedom as a dose of the driver's lash.

Freedmen in the Low-Country have always been hard on their women—wives and daughters—and their young children. For a few years after the war, they also disciplined severely their half-grown sons, and thus saved from the law many youths who were ripe for the chain-gang; but, as far back as the Reconstruction period, these fellows learned to appeal to magistrate or trial justice for protection, and a decent father, who had thrashed a fifteen year old boy for theft, would

THE UNDER DOG

often be haled to court, fined, and admonished to keep hands off his son. And many unscrupulous magistrates under succeeding Democratic administrations, have added to the criminal Negro population by similarly staying the parental hand that sought to bend the twig in the way it should grow.

"Wuh you know?" an old fellow would demand of a group of adolescent idlers. "Wuh de debble you know? Nutt'n'! You know w'ymekso wunnuh ent know nutt'n'? You ent know'um 'cause you nebbuh bin git no lick sence you bawn. Ef you hadduh bin raise een slabery time, en' you farruh, eeduhso de dribuh, bin t'row da' hebby lash 'cross you hanch w'enebbuh you sassy'um, you wouldduh bin mannusubble, 'stead'uh stick'out da' oagly mout' at me lukkuh catfish! Enty you know suh nyung Nigguh cyan' raise deestunt bedout lick? Nigguh duh de groun', lash duh de plow, no-mannus duh de grass. Wunnuh nyung Nigguh wuh grow'up sence freedom, wunnuh full'up wid grass. Ef da' lash ent fuh plow'um up, him fuh 'stroy'd you, enty? Berry-well. Don' suck you teet' at me, Nigguh! Git out me way! Git out me way, 'fo' Uh trompe you! Uh yent count you no mo'nuh you bin limus-cootuh een me paat'! You swell'up, enty? You swell'up sukkuh toad-frog! You bex? Wuh you duh blow 'bout? Mus'be you t'ink you is pawpuss, enty? Wunnuh nutt'n'tall but finguh mullet! Ef Uh bin hab me cyas'net Uh coulduh ketch wunnuh all one time. Git out me way! Git out me way! *Wunnuh yent wu't'!*"

THE CAPTAIN

The Captain's visits to the crowded Cross-roads store were eagerly looked forward to by the assembled darkies, for not only was he liberal with his always ample store of smoking tobacco, but he was a fun-maker, constantly pitting the younger Negroes against one-another in friendly "skylarking" adventures. And his insight into Negro character was so keen that a shrewd remark would sometimes set an entire group by the ears, each one suspecting his fellow of having revealed secrets that the Captain had come at through his observation alone.

"Mas' Rafe so spo'ty. Uh glad 'e come."

"Yaas, tittuh, 'e spo'ty, fuh true. En' 'e so free-han'!"

"'E freehan' fuh sowl. Wuhebbuh him hab een 'e han', ef you ax'um, him gwine gi' you."

"You talk trute, but him fuh cuss you fus', enty? En' 'e mout' free mo'nuh 'e han', 'cause 'e han' nebbuh op'n 'tel you ax'um, but him mout' ent stan' so. Mas' Rafe fuh t'row da' cuss 'puntop you befo' you hab chance fuh baig fuhr'um!"

"Dat so, but Uh nebbuh bodduh 'bout de cuss, 'cause Uh know de han' fuh folluh de mout', en' w'enebbuh Mas' Rafe crack 'e teet' fuh cuss, Uh know him tubackuh bag fuh gyaap 'e mout' een de same time, en' me pipe fuh full'up 'tel 'e choke. Mas' Rafe' mout' en' 'e han' stan' sukkuh chinky-*pen*. You 'f'aid'um at de fus', 'cause da' buhr shaa'p en' 'e sting you fuh true, but, bumbye, w'en de buhr crack op'n en' da' meat sweet'n you mout', you chaw'um en' you nebbuh 'membuh *nutt'n'* 'bout

THE UNDER DOG

da' sting. Duh so Mas' Rafe stan'! De buhr duh 'e mout', de meat duh 'e han'! Me, Uh lub fuh yeddy-'um cuss, 'cause w'enebbuh 'e do'um de smoke rise out me pipe fuh tell'um t'engky!"

Soon after the Captain rode up, night fell, and the Negroes gathered lightwood knots and made a blazing fire on a "jack" or fire-stand that stood nearby. The drifting smoke abated somewhat the annoyance of sandflies and mosquitoes, the resinous fumes were thought to neutralize the poisonous vapors of a malarial region, and the leaping flames illumined the spacious yard in front of the big store, through whose open door, back and forth, the Negroes streamed like ants. The Captain, having hitched his horse to a swinging limb, sat on a log, notebook in hand, computing the last of his weekly labor accounts, for whose settlement he handed the waiting Negroes penciled orders on the store. He was not too absorbed in his work, however, to miss the marrow of a conversation between old Bo'sun Smashum, who had just arrived, and another aged and respectable Negro, Scipio Drayton, formerly driver on a great plantation, but now as out of tune with Negro life in St. Paul's Parish as a member of the old French noblesse under the upheaval of the great Revolution.

"Ebenin', Smashum. Huh you do?" asked Scipio.

"W-e-l-l," Bo'sun drawled, "jis' betwix' en' between. Uh cyan' brag, en' Uh cyan' cumplain. Nutt'n' ent stan' like 'e nyuse to be, but 'e cyan' be

THE CAPTAIN

help', en' no use fuh 'spute wuh Gawd pit 'puntop you.''

"Dat so. You cyan' 'spute Him, en' wuhebbuh Him pit 'puntop we, Uh dunkyuh how hebby de load stan', we haffuh tote'um, en' tek dat fuh we share. Uh know dat, 'cause Uh bin git relijun w'en Uh bin nyung man. Uh know dat berry well, but, sometime, w'en Uh study 'bout how de time done change fuh man lukkuh you en' me, wuh bin raise en' fetch'up onduhneet' we ole Maussuh' han', Uh mos' t'ink Gawd load we too hebby. Wuh we got fuh lib fuh now? All de w'ite people wuh we nyuse to blonx to stan' po' lukkuh we, en' ef *dem* ent got nutt'n', *we* ent got nutt'n'. De po'-buckruh en' de common Nigguh got all de money wuh iz fuh git, en' de common Nigguh haffuh t'row'way all wuh *dem* git, so, bumbye, po'-buckruh fuh hab all! W'en man binnuh eat frum de big house kitchen een ole Maussuh' day, en' hab deestunt jacket en' britchiz fuh pit on duh Sunday, en' hab shoe 'pun 'e foot, 'e berry haa'd fuh haffuh nyam dry cawn-hom'ny, en' haffuh gone chu'ch een dem raggety britchiz wuh Uh got. Uh lub da' britchiz 'cause 'e nyuse to blonx to ole Maussuh, en' him gimme'um befo' 'e dead. De britchiz bin black at de fus', but da' sun wuh Gawd sen' fuh shine 'puntop'um ebb'ry Sunday fuh de las' ten yeah tu'n'um kind'uh green, but de clawt' so feeble now, 'tel you kacely kin shum, me wife haffuh patch'um summuch. Ebb'ry scrap uh clawt' de po' 'ooman kin git, seem lukkuh him haffuh tek'um fuh mek patch fuh da' Sunday

THE UNDER DOG

britchiz. Now, w'en you shum, 'e hab summuch colluh 'tel 'e stan' sukkuh gum tree een de fall attuh 'e leaf tu'n! En' me shoe! Uh pay de po'-buckruh dolluh en' uh quawtuh fuh dem debble-'ub'uh brogan las' munt', en' now alltwo de shoe gyap op'n sukkuh alligettuh mout', en' me big toe stick out'um sukkuh cootuh snout! 'E mek me shame!"

"Yaas, man, 'e haa'd, fuh true, but man haffuh tek'um ez 'e come, enty?"

"Uh tek'um ez 'e come, yaas, but de t'ing wuh hu't me feelin's mo'nuh cawn-hom'ny en' raggety britchiz, de t'ing wuh mek me bex 'tel me yeye tu'n red en' me han' eetch fuh graff da' lash, is deseyuh Satan'ub'uh no-mannus boy wuh Freedom tu'n loose 'puntop we! Dem britchiz cry out fuh lick ebb'ry day Gawd sen', but, ef you lick'um fuh ease you h'aa't en' filfil Gawd' wu'd lukkuh Him tell you fuh do, da' boy, eb'nso ef 'e duh you own chile, fuh tek you to de Trial Jestuss fuh pay fine, en' ef you ent got de money fuh pit een 'e han' you haffuh mawgidge you cow, you fowl, eb'nso you bed, 'cep' you wan' go Walterburruh jail. Shishuh law lukkuh dat ent wu't'! Nyung Nigguh haffuh lick, 'cep' dem spile. Ef Gawd only gimme chance fuh lick t'ree uh fo' befo' me time come, Uh fuh say t'engky Maussuh, en' Uh fuh dead happy!"

Old Scipio's prayer was about to be answered, for the dream ship of his hopes, now hovering in the offing, would soon come to port—piloted by the Captain!

THE CAPTAIN

Those who have loved and played with children will recall the ecstasy of delight with which a child will often receive a self-invited, playful spanking, whose sting, if given punitively, would bring a flood of resentful tears. And the young buck Negroes, youths of fifteen to eighteen, who would have run hot-foot to a magistrate in resentment of paternal discipline, seemed never so happy as when, in playful moments, they would make play upon one-another's quarters with their long birdminder's whips of plaited hickory bark. So, the Captain, knowing this characteristic, and overhearing old Scipio's passionate prayer, was minded to see to it that 'twas answered forthwith. A couple of youths, surrounded by a group of young women, were tussling playfully in the full glare of the firelight. Calling them to him, the Captain suggested a game in which they would be the central figures and, at once, active and passive participants. They saw the humor of the proposition, and, welcoming a chance to show off before the women, promptly agreed. The Captain entered the store, selected a serviceable buggy whip from the shopkeeper's rack, and, giving the boys a dram to tune them up, called to Bo'sun and Scipio, and approached the fire, followed by half the Negroes in the store who, scenting fun, postponed their purchases until it should be over.

As the Captain stalked among them swishing the supple whalebone, the women, full of curiosity and suppressed excitement, whispered, one to another, "Oh Gawd, britchiz fuh bu'n! britchiz fuh bu'n!"

THE UNDER DOG

But the youths paid no attention to them, and the master of ceremonies quickly explained the philosophy of a contest in which the victor would be the under-dog, he who could stay at the bottom, not the top!

The young bucks closed in an awkward wrestler's grip, and went to earth. Old Scipio's eyes followed the whip with the pleading look of a chained setter, as his master takes his gun out of the corner and walks away; but Bo'sun, long a faithful servitor, had claims upon the Captain's consideration, and into his hands he placed the precious tool which the old Negro grasped as proudly as a king his scepter!

"Gimme room, gal, gimme room!" he cried, stepping within a pace of the scuffling pair on the ground. For a moment, Bo'sun waited for the presentation of the target he wanted, but only for a moment, for a quick flirt of the under-dog brought the top man fairly to the surface, and, for a second, the tightly stretched seat of his thin cotton trousers lay invitingly before him. In that second, as swiftly as a hawk, old Bo'sun struck, and the frenzied yell of the writhing victim was drowned in the delighted laughter of a hundred darkies, men and women. Among those who laughed, was the under-dog, who, safe in sanctuary, with his back upon the friendly earth, chuckled gleefully over his rival's discomfiture. But his joy was short-lived, for, caught off his guard while he laughed, a sudden wrench from the other fellow brought the under-dog to the top of the pile, to hear, in turn, the wicked swish of

THE CAPTAIN

the whalebone, and feel its waspish sting. And he got a double dose, for, before he could turn his antagonist, who, having tasted wormwood at the top, now clung to earth as ardently as any Antæus, the whip came down once more, and, out of a grateful heart old Bo'sun grunted his deep delight. "Umh! 'E sweet'n you, enty? Uh bin hab dis physic fuh you een me h'aa't long time, en' now Gawd pit'um een me han'! Wuh dat you say? Uh por'um too fas'! You duh git mo'nuh yo' share? Berrywell. Tu'n obuh, son, tu'n obuh. Leh de t'odduh man hab him'own! Gawd tell me fuh freehan'. Nobody fuh stint! Ebb'ry man fuh hab wuh blonx to'um!"

Back and forth the youths, interlocked in each other's arms, floundered like seined fish upon the shore, and always he who was uppermost received old Bo'sun's close attention. And whatever welts there were were pretty evenly divided, for the convulsive spasm of the recipient of the attentions was usually strong enough to enable him to reverse his position and twist his antagonist out of his bomb-proof into the line of fire. So honors were easy when, after each had received about a dozen cuts, the Captain called the game for the first two, and summoned another pair to the playful adventure. And did the first couple rub the seats of their trousers or otherwise show they had been stung? They did not. They were too proud of their exploit, and, like the fox who had lost his tail, too anxious that the others should lose theirs also! So, in high spirits,

THE UNDER DOG

they joined the laughing women, and another pair of young bucks fell squirming to earth.

Bo'sun exaltation was that of one who has beheld a vision, and with a "fate cannot harm me, I have dined today" expression of deep contentment, he prepared to continue his labors in what he believed to be the vineyard of the Lord!

But not so. Old Scipio's eyes devoured the whip avidly and, pulling Bo'sun by the sleeve, he cried, "Gimme da' t'ing, Smashum, gimme da' t'ing! You too greedy!"

At a nod from the Captain, Bo'sun passed the whip to Scipio, who, before taking it, spat on his hands impressively, as if to assure the bystanders of his purpose to take a hold that could in no wise be loosened. Grasping the whip handle, Scipio threw his battered old hat on the ground and, raising his eyes to heaven, pulled his kinky forelock and scraped his foot in thankfulness to his Maker, as one who reverently says grace before meat! The meat lay before him, and Scipio proceeded to dress it to his taste, and his taste inclined to Tartar sauce! Nor could he forbear a dash of the Tabasco of the tongue! "Haw! Buck!" as the whip, whistling through the air like a blue-wing teal, alighted on a tender spot. "You yeddy me song, enty? Dishyuh duh de day Uh binnuh seek fuh de longes'! De lash tas'e you meat dat time, enty? Me en' da' lash bin hongry fuh Nigguh' meat ebbuh sence freedom. T'engk-gawd, we tas'e'um at las'!"

THE CAPTAIN

And Scipio was a fast worker. Long experience as plantation disciplinarian, had taught him enough rough-and-tumble physiology to know just where he could sting without injury, and he stung all along the line. He was no respecter of persons, nor of any part of any person's person whatsoever. All dark meat that wore breeches looked the same to him. The uppermost man was uppermost in his mind, and upon him the whalebone fell with the rhythmic regularity of a flail! Bo'sun was what Stewart Edward White calls a "choicy" marksman, preferring to "place" his shots. Not so old Scipio! No pent-up Utica restrained his pow'rs. The boundless continent was his—at least from hip to hock —"Wuh use fuh bodduh 'bout weh you knock'um, Smashum? Uh duh bu'n britchiz, enty? Enty 'e hab feelin's een 'e knee same lukkuh 'e hab'um een 'e hanch? Gawd pit dis t'ing een me han' en' tell me fuh lick Nigguh yuh tenight, fuh filfil Him wu'd. 'E tell me de shu't ent fuh tetch, de jacket ent fuh tetch, but de britchiz fuh bu'n. Berrywellden." But, however fast he talked, the punitive piston of his arm never missed a stroke, and, catching them sometimes as they were turning, he stung the two with a single cut. "Flapjack een de pan. Tu'n'um obuh! Hoecake 'puntop de hoe, tu'n'um obuh! Ef 'e yent tu'n obuh, 'e fuh bu'n, enty? Yaas, en' ef 'e *yiz* tu'n obuh 'e fuh bu'n, same fashi'n, 'cause Gawd' wu'd haffuh filfil en' Nigguh haffuh lick! Wawss duh sing. Yeddy'um! Bee duh hum. Yeddy'um! *Yeddy'um, yeddy'um, yeddy'um!*" And in

THE UNDER DOG

a frenzy of delight the old Negro leaped in the air to give greater force to his blows. The pace was too hot for his victims who, lathered from ankle to hip, had received twice the punishment of Bo'sun's team, and, yelling lustily, they sprang to their feet and made off, rubbing themselves in the rear, with many loud lamentations.

Old Scipio's prowess, upon which the older Negroes congratulated him warmly, uplifted the old fellow tremendously. Approaching the Captain furtively, he asked, "Mas' Rafe, you gwine be yuh nex' Sattyday night? Uh bin prommus Gawd ef Him lemme lick t'ree-fo' Nigguh one mo' time, Uh woulduh ready fuh dead, but w'en Uh say dat, Uh bin t'aw't Uh done loss me han' fuh lick Nigguh, en' Uh nebbuh know weh any Nigguh iz fuh lick, but, attuh tenight, Uh know suh you got de Nigguh en' me got de han'. Uh yent loss me han', Mas' Rafe. Enty Uh gott'um? Berrywell. So now, Uh yent ready fuh dead no mo', Mas' Rafe, 'cause Uh lub fuh lick Nigguh tummuch. Uh lub fuh lick'um *tummuch!*"

THE QUEST OF THE LAND

Up to fifty years ago, very little land in the Pon-Pon neighborhood had been acquired by Negroes. Altho' most of the planters were "land poor" and burdened by the heavy taxes of "Reconstruction," and altho' many Negroes, having abandoned hope of "forty acres and a mule" from the Federal Government, were now ready to buy ten acres and an ox, the sale of land to Negroes was generally reprobated, for it not only demoralized labor on the plantations but created little plague-spots in the community where cattle-riever and pig-thief—each in the fancied security of his own "castle"—could ply his trade safe from the white man's eye.

In those days the two-day contract system was in general use in the Low-Country, and it was usually possible to fill with such hands all the houses at the planter's command. Some of the plantations lost only the "big house" during the March to the Sea, and these, having saved the comfortable double-houses of the old slave-quarters, were able to fill them with freedmen and command all the labor they required, but upon other plantations the torch of the invader—knowing no brother—had made a clean sweep, and the salted ashes of mansion and hovel mingled in the common dust of desolation. Upon these holdings log cabins with clay chimneys were built for such contract hands as could be secured.

The two-day plan required the householder to work two days—Monday and Tuesday—each week

THE CAPTAIN

throughout the year, as consideration for house, fuel, and four acres of arable land. And the householder could, upon occasion, send his wife or a grown son or daughter to work his contract days; or two members of the family could work one day and acquit the household of the obligation for the week, so the arrangement was flexible. As field labor was worth fifty cents a day, the tenant paid for house, land, and fuel fifty dollars a year, not an excessive price for families where there were always two, sometimes half a dozen, workers. The advantage to the planter was his command, throughout the year, of a certain number of hands who—wages being equal—were obliged to give the owner of the plantation first call on their labor, whenever there was any work to be done. The advantage to the laborer was the assurance of a home and a few acres of land, to be paid for in labor in small instalments, and abundant work for his family close at hand. Of course, the regular plowmen were paid monthly wages and were rationed and housed.

In view of the scarcity of land offered to Negro purchasers, there was great excitement in the community when it was announced in the autumn of 1873 that the Mitchell plantation, which had several years earlier come into the possession of a Charleston factor under foreclosure of mortgage, was to be divided into small tracts and sold to Negroes at three dollars an acre. The plantation, lying between Oak Lawn and Penny Creek, a tributary of

THE QUEST OF THE LAND

the Edisto, had belonged at one time to the Bulloch family, maternal ancestors of Theodore Roosevelt.

As his agent for the sale of the Mitchell place the Charleston factor had chosen the Reverend Lester Flood, the finest-looking Negro in the Parish and one of the most reliable, commanding the respect of both races. A former slave of Mr. Baring's, whose slaves, trained under their English-born master, were of an unusually fine type, Lester was a carpenter by profession, but went into the ministry after the war. His charge was a church on the "big-road," between King's Gate and the Crossroads. The congregation numbered many fine voices, and on summer nights the stirring old hymns and haunting spirituals echoed thro' the forests and reached outlying plantations a mile or more away. And sometimes, on still moonlight nights, a "Buckruh" youth, lured by the poignant sweetness of the melody, would saddle-up, and ride to within a hundred yards of the church and, halting his horse among the pines, would fill his spirit with music and listen to the fervent prayers that alternated with the song services. And then followed Lester's common-sense sermons, full of sound advice. He never ranted, but was always impressive, his deep, sonorous voice booming like slow billows on the beach. Thus, during the years of Reconstruction and for some time thereafter in the Low-Country, solitary watchers of the white race often sat their horses in the shadows near the Negro churches on prayer-meeting nights and

THE CAPTAIN

listened—but not to the music—for many Negro preachers were dangerous firebrands, whose congregations were hotbeds of radical politics, and these it was necessary to watch, and to know. But never a word fell from Lester's lips that did not promote amity between the races; and he lived the life he preached.

And this preacher was a magnificent man physically, six feet one, and of massive proportions, with fine features and so luxuriant a beard that, but for his dark pigmentation, he might have passed for an Arab sheik or a father in Israel. "Pa Lester" graced his pulpit, but no ruined planter could look upon the dignified priest without realizing what a splendid butler he would have made, and feeling regret that he could never grace a gentleman's livery and, with a great silver waiter before him and shining cut-glass decanters of Madeira, Port, and Sherry, offer the hospitality of a gentleman's home to a gentleman's guests! But these were but the dreams of those who, living on sweet potatoes and corn bread, could yet recognize the eternal fitness of things. So, Lester, preaching on Sundays and at night, worked at his trade by day, and found many small jobs among the friendly planters of the neighborhood. Between whiles, he found time to build a comfortable home for his small family on his little holding near the church—a modest house of two stories and four rooms, but very imposing in the eyes of his people, as well because of the sanctity of its occupant, as for its two stories and piazza,

THE QUEST OF THE LAND

in a community of one-story cabins. The pathway from the front gate to the house, was flanked by euonymus hedges and sentineled by clumps of tall Spanish bayonets. And around house and lot and garden Lester had built a tall, close fence of split yellow-pine clapboards, giving the whole place the reserve and detachment of the high-walled garden of an old English rectory.

When news of the sale of Mitchell's came to Pon-Pon, the agent was flooded with applications from would-be purchasers, and many tentative reservations were made, most of them from the "Savage," or Kinzie King place, which, having been without white occupancy since the war, and rented to Negro tenants and share-croppers by its non-resident owners, now harbored the most lawless and undisciplined Negroes in the community, tho', withal, some of the best workers, men and women whose labor was always in demand on neighboring plantations.

There was no land surveyor nearer than Walterboro, and as there were thirty or forty intending purchasers, and as many separate plats to be made, the surveyor's bill at the regular rates charged by the gentlemen of the compass and chain, would have absorbed the reverend agent's commissions and swamped the enterprise. So Lester scratched his head in perplexity, and went to his neighbor and best friend for advice. The Captain was able to give it, for his 16-year old nephew had just returned from the Valley of Virginia, where, in his brief

THE CAPTAIN

term at school, he had gorged himself on Davies' Legendre and Davies' Surveying, hoping somehow, some day, to take a course in engineering. This hope the necessity of going immediately to work put "up the spout," and, having applied unsuccessfully for a job as brakeman on the Charleston & Savannah Railroad (Negro brakemen were preferred in those days), the youth was eager for any work he could find for hand or foot or head. The Mitchell survey called for the exercise of all three, and, altho' entirely without field practice, he applied for the work, and got it, hoping, through luck or ingenuity, to overcome his professional limitations. Then, too, he counted upon the Captain's help, for the Captain had hunted throughout the Parish and was familiar with the lines of the three plantations surrounding the Mitchell tract.

When the engagement was announced, there was excitement in one white and forty black households, and the embryo surveyor, full of his responsibilities, set about securing the tools of his trade. From a friend of the family, Sup't. C. S. Gadsden, of the C. & S. Railroad, he borrowed a compass and chain. From Charleston, drawing materials for plat-making were obtained, and he was ready for work.

On the morning of the first of December, a bright, frosty day, the Captain and the surveyor met "Pa Lester" and forty or fifty very important Negroes, all very full of themselves as prospective land-owners, and each man determined he would, through his own merit or his own cunning, secure

THE QUEST OF THE LAND

the most fertile and best drained part of the tract for himself. The place of meeting was in the pineland in front of Lester's house, and the Captain and the surveyor, seating themselves on a log, were soon surrounded by the excited Negroes, anxious for an interpretation of the plat, and to see how the land lay. Lester produced the plat, made in 1835, and beautifully lettered and tinted in the manner dear to the hearts of the old surveyors. It was spread upon the log, and, taking turns, the Negroes in little groups inspected it critically and made their comments. All of them were more or less familiar with the tract, having hunted or roamed over it by day and night, and since its division and sale had been talked about many of them had paid furtive visits to the place and cast wistful eyes at certain choice portions they had marked for their own. So it was that, when apportionment was discussed, Lester found the minds of many men met upon the same spot of ground, and with the meeting of minds, came also the clash of tempers—and, almost, the clash of skulls—and when the surveyor had explained that the areas on the plot dotted with little toy trees meant forests, and that certain other marks or shadings indicated swamps or ricefields or arable uplands, poor Lester was beset by many tongues, each clamoring for ricefield or arable upland, and each having potent reasons for the allotment of swamps and uncleared forests to his fellows. The Captain sought to compose their differences, and cited the law of the deer-hunters of the Low-Coun-

THE CAPTAIN

try, who, at the close of a successful hunt, divided the venison into so many parts and then drew lots for the selection of the choice pieces. "So," said the Captain, "One man may get a haunch, another a loin, and another a rack, but even the rack is good, if you know how to cook it, and every man has his chance to get the best; so why don't you get Lester to fix up some little papers with numbers on them and put them in a hat? Then each man draws out a slip. If he gets number one, he has first choice, and so on down the line to numbers thirty-nine and forty."

"Yaas, Mas' Rafe. Da' plan stan' berry good fuh de fus' man, en' de two man, en' de t'ree man, but w'en Pa Lester git down to de t'irty-nine man en' de fawty man, wuh him fuh hab? Nutt'n'! W'en you cut up hog, en' de fus' man tek de ham, en' de two man tek de gham, en' de t'ree man tek de flitch, dem 'wide'um up, 'tel, bumbye, w'en t'irty-nine en' fawty come 'long, nutt'n' ent fuh lef' 'cep' de yez en' de tail! En' da' duh wuh me fuh git ef we tek plan lukkuh dat, 'cause, ebbuh sence Uh bin step 'cross da' dry toad-frog wrop'up een da' blacksnake skin, wuh da' somebody pit een me paat' fuh t'row spell 'puntop me, Uh nebbuh fuh hab no good luck no mo', en' ef Uh gone een da' t'ing fuh pull papuh out de hat, me fuh be de fawty man, eeduhso de t'irty-nine man, sho' ez Gawd, 'cause bad luck ketch een me britchiz en' stick to'um sukkuh cucklebuhr ketch cowtail! En' da' rack you duh talk 'bout, Mas' Rafe, ef Uh draw da' rack een da' t'ick 'ood

THE QUEST OF THE LAND

en' da' hebby swamp, befo' Uh done gitt'ru t'row down dem tree en' root up dem 'tump, me bone fuh racktify, fuh true. Uh yent hab no appetite fuh da' rack."

The Captain's plan met with no favor, for each man feared his fate too much to "put it to the touch to gain or lose it all." And the babel of voices started again, each man urging upon Pa Lester his special claims for consideration.

Up spoke Ben Summers, a mouthy old sinner, jackleg carpenter and jackleg preacher, a man of many wives and many children, at home and abroad; for old Ben was no Lodge-like isolationist, and foreign entanglements had no terrors for him—if only they wore petticoats! Altho' insolent and boisterous with his own race, he took no chances with the whites, and always approached the Captain—his former master—with exceeding humility. Affecting infinite piety, his Maker's name was ever on his lips by day, but the Negroes said that after dark they were otherwise anointed, and under the friendly mask of night, when the dew had softened the dead leaves into silence, the wily old reprobate would slip stealthily through the forest to the kraal of a planter or, if more convenient, to the pen of a lowly brother in black, and smother the squeals of a shoat as skilfully as his kinsman, Monday Parker, the smartest pig-lifter in a pig-lifting community! So, Ben, coveting a fertile corner of the Mitchell tract, lying next to the Captain's land, put in a plausible plea for its possession. "Reb'ren'," he

THE CAPTAIN

said, to Lester. "All we man wuh use to blonx to Oak Lawn plantesshun oughtuh hab chance fuh buy we groun' 'longside'um, 'cause, een de fus' place, all we fambly bury een Nigguh-buryin'-groun' onduhneet' dem oak tree, en' Uh wan' buy me groun' en' buil' me house so Uh kin lib close'um, w'ile Uh duh lib, en' attuh Uh done dead de bredduh wuh haffuh tote me cawpse to da' grabeyaa'd would'n' hab fudduh fuh go; en', een de two place—"
"Nemmin' 'bout de two place, man," interrupted a knowing brother, "All uh we man yuh know berrywell de reaz'n mekso you hankuh attuh hab you house close da' Nigguh-buryin'-groun', en' Mas' Rafe —you shum duh laugh—him know'um, too. Da' grabeyaa'd kibbuh wid hebby libe-oak tree, en', een de fall uh de yeah, en' duh wintuhtime, dem tree full'up wid acu'n, en', t'odduh side de grabeyaa'd, de dam betwix' him en' de ole ricefiel' t'ick wid dem high swamp-w'iteoak, en' de swamp-w'iteoak full'uh dem big obuhcup acu'n, en' de Buckruh' hog lub fuh use een da' Nigguh-buryin'-groun' 'cause dem bittle dey dey, en' de hog kin leddown duh night-time fuh sleep 'mong dem Nigguh grabe, en' nutt'n' ent fuh bodduhr'um. De only t'ing dainjus fuh hog, iz wil'cat, alligettuh, en' Nigguh. All de wil'cat kin do iz fuh ketch dem leely pig out de bed w'en de maamy ent dey dey, 'cause him nebbuh fuh tek chance wid no sow. En', 'cep' hog go close de watuh, alligettuh yent fuh bodduhr'um; but hog 'f'aid Nigguh mo'nuh all de res', 'cause Nigguh ketch'um w'edduh 'e big uh w'edduh 'e leetle, en'

THE QUEST OF THE LAND

Nigguh, him dey ebb'ryweh—ebb'ryweh, 'cep' een Nigguh-buryin'-groun'! Nutt'n' 'cep' *dead* Nigguh fuh dey dey, 'cause libe Nigguh 'f'aid da' place tummuch! Hog know suh Nigguh yent fuh tek chance wid dem sperrit en' t'ing duh night, en' 'e yent fuh gone da' place een de daytime, 'cep' 'e got cump'ny, en' eb'nso ef 'e got cump'ny, him en' 'e cump'ny haffuh talk strong, so dem h'aa't kin fawti*fy*, en' ef hog yeddy da' strong talk out de Nigguh' mout', him fuh tek 'e foot een 'e han' en' gone! De Nigguh nebbuh shum, 'e nebbuh yeddy'um grunt! Dat mekso hog peruse t'ru da' Nigguh-buryin'-groun' duh daytime en' root obuh you gran'daddy' grabe, en' crack acu'n 'tel night come, en' den 'e 'crape'up de dead leaf en' mek bed fuh him en' 'e fambly 'mong de grabe, en' 'e leddown fuh sleep, jis' ez sattify ez ef him binnuh heng up een de Buckruh' smokehouse, 'cause 'e say to 'eself: 'Deseyuh Nigguh dead, enty? T'engk-gawd fuh dead Nigguh, 'cause dead Nigguh ent dainjus, en' dem sperrit watch obuh me, fuh keep off de libe Nigguh'; en' 'e shet 'e yeye, en' 'e drap 'sleep, en' 'e nebbuh dream 'bout no Nigguh!"

The laughter that greeted this shrewd analysis of Ben's reason for wishing to build a home near the ashes of his fathers roused the old Negro to instant and sputtering wrath. "Who! Me! Wuh me got fuh do wid hog? Enty Uh sancti*fy*? Uh binnuh preach Gawd' wu'd ebbuh sence freedom come een, en' you talk to me 'bout hog! Wuh me know 'bout hog?"

THE CAPTAIN

"Wuh you know 'bout hog? Budduh, you know-'um frum 'e snout spang to 'e tail; en' w'en you talk 'bout sancti*fy*, lemme tell you dis, ef all hunnuh Nigguh-preachuh wuh bin sancti*fy* sence freedom, so you kin nyam 'ooman' fowl en' 'queeze money out'uh 'ooman' ap'un, ef Gawd tek notion fuh knock hunnuh een de head, eeduhso pit hoe een you han' fuh knock grass, hog nebbuh haffuh squeal no mo', en' fowl nebbuh haffuh roos' 'puntop no tree! Dat hummuch you know 'bout hog!"

Old Ben rallied. "Lookyuh, Nigguh!" he demanded of his tormentor. "Uh fuh ketch you een you own trap. Ef Uh so 'f'aid fuh go close me gran'-daddy' grabe, lukkuh you say, en' Uh 'f'aid'um fuh true, how me fuh ketch dem hog wuh feed een Nigguh-buryin'-groun'? Ansuh me dat!"

"Yaas, Uh fuh ansuh you; Uh know berry well you ent fuh walk close da' grabe, Uh dunkyuh how fat de hog stan', but dem swamp-w'iteoak 'pun de dam, stan' outside de grabeyaa'd, en' 'e dey close'um too, enty? En' ef you buy da' piece'uh groun' wuh you duh hankuh attuh, enty you kin pit two-t'ree quawt uh cawn een you knabsack, en' cross Mas' Rafe' pinelan' to Cotton Hill, en' gone down by de Redtrunk, en' sneak down de ole dam to de w'iteoak tree, en' mek you pen onduhneet'um, en' trail some de cawn fuh toll de hog to de trap, en' t'row de t'odduh cawn een de pen? Den, all you got fuh do iz fuh set you deadfall, en' tek you two foot en' gone back home fuh hab da' praise-meetin' wid you chu'ch sistuh en' t'ing. Duh mawnin', soon,

THE QUEST OF THE LAND

you fuh tek you axe—axe bettuh mo'nuh gun, 'cause him ent hab no woice—en' gone back to you trap. Ef Gawd bin yeddy you pray, en' ansuhr'um, you fuh fin' de Buckruh' hog een you pen, enty? Berrywell. Knock'um een 'e head, pit'um een you bag, en' gone 'bout you bidness. No use fuh git ketch. Rain fuh wash'out you track, 'cause Gawd duh watch obuh you, enty? You duh Him man, you know. En', ef Mas' Rafe chance fuh come 'cross you trap, him fuh s'pishun some dem po'-buckruh wuh lib to Beech, eeduhso to Moss Hill, mek'um fuh ketch tuckrey."

There was both laughter and surprise among the Negroes at this frank revelation of the technique of the dusky brotherhood of rievers, but the Captain, knowing every cow-path cn the plantation, and every twisting pig-path in the Negro mind, was confirmed only in what he already knew, and jokingly urged Lester to yield to Ben's entreaties and establish him near the Oak Lawn line, where, with certain other known pig-thieves, he would be under the Captain's eye. Old Ben grunted, "Ki! Mas' Rafe, you too commikil," and subsided.

Then, other claimants for special consideration put forth special pleas for the allotment of the tracts their eyes had looked upon and found good. Some asked to be near the church; others looked to the fatness of the land alone. Some, gregariously inclined, wished to group with friends or kindred; others sought isolated situations where their chickens and their children would not be interfered with

THE CAPTAIN

by those of near neighbors. About two-thirds of the Mitchell tract was wooded, the remainder arable upland and abandoned ricefields. As each of the forty Negroes wished both arable upland and rice land, with an allotment of timbered land sufficient for building material, fencing, and fuel, and wanted them all together in one body, while a distance of a mile separated the heavily timbered area from the ricefield, the Reverend Flood was confronted with a situation demanding the Loaves and Fishes of the Lord! So, having reached an impasse after several hours of profitless discussion of differences that could in no way be composed, Lester adjourned the meeting until the following morning, admonishing the men that unless, in a spirit of give and take, they could get together, the plat would be returned to the factor in Charleston, and the sale of the Mitchell place abandoned. And the forty—"so many men, so many minds"—went their ways. Their minds met upon the following day—but that's another story.

THE LAND IN SIGHT

The Captain's nephew, who, without field experience and but limited knowledge of surveying, had undertaken the sub-division of the Mitchell plantation into forty-odd tracts for forty-odd Negroes, in December, 1873, took the plat home with many misgivings. His own professional limitations, tho' great, could in some way be overcome, but Negro psychology had to be reckoned with. Forty land-hungry Negroes were buying land. Each of the forty had looked covetously upon certain choice portions of the tract which, with entire disregard of the equally strong claims of the thirty-nine, he demanded for himself. The Rev. Lester Flood, agent of the Charleston factor, having sought in vain to bring the men to a reasonable state of mind, had, after hours of wrangling, adjourned the meeting until the following morning, promising that, if they could not then modify their individual aspirations and find a common ground for compromise, the land would be withdrawn from sale and their hopes of presently acquiring real estate would vanish.

So the young surveyor, realizing that whatever light should illumine the forty minds upon the morrow would have to come from the Captain and himself, began seriously to think a way thro' the darkest Africa that encompassed him. Out of the darkness came, like a flash, an inspiration that solved his own problem and gave hope of lining up the

THE CAPTAIN

Negroes along rectangular lines. A close examination of the plat, over which he quickly ran his instruments, showed that, save for a sharp triangle of pineland adjoining the Oak Lawn plantation, the Mitchell tract was an almost perfect square, with a wave line only where it followed the winding course of Penny Creek, its Western boundary. The youth, who had dreaded the task of measuring and fitting together the irregular patchwork of forty territorial conceptions, saw how beautifully the plat would lend itself to checkerboard treatment. Why shouldn't the tract be run off in ten-acre squares, each of them numbered? The Negroes were buying in parcels of ten to thirty acres. Why couldn't they be induced to select one, two, or three lots by numbers from the checkerboard, before actually entering upon the land itself? It was worth trying, and with compass, square and ruler, he platted a checkerboard of generous proportions, whose squares were numbered from one to eighty, inclusive, the seventy-five-acre triangle being left for separate treatment. Having made his plan and made his plat, the young surveyor took thought how to synchronize the forty minds into their acceptance. Knowing Negro nature—human nature, after all—he believed they needed, like hesitant children, to have their minds made up for them, and, once brought to regard the numbered squares of the checkerboard plat as a writ irrevocable, they would accept its benefits gratefully, and its hardships philosophically, as the will of the Lord. Upon

THE LAND IN SIGHT

that acceptance depended not only the simplified survey, but the sale of the plantation, for the two were inextricably tied together, and, with the Captain's assistance, he hoped to reach the mind of Africa upon the following morning.

When the Captain and the surveyor reached the rendezvous the Negroes had already assembled, and Lester's troubles were augmented by the presence of several women, some of the men having brought their wives along to strengthen their claims upon the Reverend's consideration.

The most intelligent and energetic of the "Savage" Negroes were the two Chisholm brothers, Sam and John, and, having been the most active in organizing the colonization of the Mitchell tract from the Kinzie King plantation, they spoke with authority in directing the migration. Through the exercise of this authority, the Captain and the Surveyor hoped to put through the checkerboard project, and before coming to the meeting, they had mapped out a plan of campaign.

Sam Chisholm, the elder brother, was a fluent and convincing talker, and a slight stammer made his speech more effective. Something of a sea-lawyer on the plantation, he was always ready for argument, tho' talk never interfered with his work. John, the younger, was a quiet, dignified man, and the two brothers were among the most expert axemen and ditchers in the community.

Sam and John had married, during slavery, two sisters, capable, self-respecting women, fine hands, and noted cotton-pickers. A third brother had taken a third sister to wife, but in the spring of 1865, while Sherman was yet on his way to the sea, this brother, believing imitation to be "the sincerest flattery," burned a few barns and smokehouses, as a practical expression of his gratitude for freedom; but when the spoilers left the neighborhood—all they did leave—the barn-burner was promptly caught by the "Po'-Buckruh" Regulators and hanged, for a great General—now long entrenched "on Fame's eternal camping ground"—could take liberties with the torch that would never be permitted a lowly freedman! The departed brother left a plump, even-tempered widow, Emma, who in time became the spouse of old Cato Giles, and a son, Sike, a fat, black boy who grew to manhood slowly and slothfully under old Cato's roof, and under many reminders of his worthlessness. Sam took his brother's ignominious death much to heart, and to the end of his days, the name "Po'-Buckruh" was as poison to his soul.

The wives of the Chisholm brothers had another sister, Margaret, the eldest of the four, whom, long before the war, Simon Jenkins, slave on the same plantation, had married. Simon was slippery—the freedmen in the neighborhood called him "Okra"—and his light-fingered propensities were known to his fellows under slavery but were held lightly against him, for slaves had little to lose, and he who helped himself from his master's store was held as free from fault as the mule that, "laying by" his

THE LAND IN SIGHT

master's corn, bites a few mouthfuls of blades as he threads the rustling rows. But Simon's status changed with freedom, for, much or little, freedmen had property, and property had rights, and Simon, the "squerril"-hunter was, all the days of him, a menace to the property rights of others; so, altho' a good worker, when he worked, he was regarded on the Savage plantation as a liability rather than an asset, while as to the Mitchell colony presently under consideration, not even his brothers-in-law cared to locate too near him. "Uh yent hab no fau't to fin' wid Maa'gret. Him en' my wife is two sistuh, but Buh Simon' eye too keen, en' 'e foot walk too saaf', fuh me fuh lib close'um. Bredduh-law iz bredduh-law, fuh true, but fowl iz fowl, en' hog is hog, enty? Berrywell."

So, when the Chisholm brothers were called aside for consultation with the white men, the "squerril"-hunter was not among the conferees.

"Now, Sam," said the Captain, "you and John are both sensible, level-headed men, aren't you?"

"Yaas, Mas' Rafe, I believe so, suh."

"Very good. Now, you know very well that if you turn these fellows loose on the Mitchell place and let each man pick and choose for himself, at the end of the month each man would have his hands full of the other fellow's wool, and that'd be all he would have."

"You're right, suh. You're egzac'ly right. Ef you tu'n'um loose fuh pick en' choose, nobody fuh sattify."

THE CAPTAIN

"Well, then, Lester has told you that if you don't get together today he'll send the plat back to town and you'll lose your chance to buy the place. Now, you and John are the leaders among your people and whatever you tell them to do they'll do. You know, only a few of you have learned how to think for yourselves since freedom, and the others need somebody to help them make up their minds, and the responsibility for that help rests upon men like John and yourself. The Surveyor has worked out a plan which seems to me the only plan for dividing the Mitchell place. Let him explain it to you, and remember to make them understand that none of you is going to get just what he wants. Each man will have to give up something, or he will end by getting nothing."

"Dat's so, suh," the brothers promptly agreed.

The Surveyor, full of his scheme, spread the plat on a big stump, weighted down the corners with chips, and, with the help of the old plat, indicated approximately, the area and location of the three classes—arable upland, timbered land, and ricefields—and set forth to the attentive listeners the merits of his plan, explaining the great advantage for Negroes—now owning land for the first time—of having straight and clearly defined boundary lines, thus minimizing the inevitable squabbles and disputes. Then, too, the rectangular tracts would simplify the fencing problems, by permitting the construction of party fences by the land-owners and their nearest neighbors. Those who wished to buy ten, twenty,

THE LAND IN SIGHT

or thirty acres had only to select one, two, or three of the ten-acre squares lying together. Those who wished fifteen, twenty-five, or thirty-five acres, could take one and a half, two and a half, or three and a half squares, but the squares, if divided at all, must be halved, for five acres had been arbitrarily fixed by the Surveyor as the unit of measurement. It was all very simple, and its simplicity appealed to the intelligent Negroes, who, knowing their own people, realized the advantage of putting before them a definite plan, saying: "Your line runs there, your corner post goes here. Take it or leave it," and forthwith cutting off all debate. So, the Chisholms promptly accepted the checkerboard conception as scientifically sound and psychologically astute. They were concerned, however, about how to satisfy each man's desire for rice-land, upland, and timbered land. Of rice-land there was little enough, sufficient only for an allotment of five acres each to ten or fifteen families, and this, as the Surveyor advised, should be assigned to those who had no swampy spots in their wooded tracts upon which upland-rice could be grown. It was further recommended that the rice-lands should be taken over by those who were well disposed toward one another, for the planting, the cultivation, and the flooding of the fields, at least as far as each "square" was concerned, was a matter of communal agreement, as the keeping up of dams and "trunks" was one for communal effort, for if one man elected to plant in March or April, and a brother in the same square

THE CAPTAIN

chose for his seed-time "the leafy month of June," an opened sluice-gate might turn the wine-colored waters of Penny Creek into a harvest-flow for the early planter, while the midsummer laggard would hardly be ready for the stretch-flow.

These points the brothers quickly saw and, the rice-fields out of the way, the youth, full of enthusiasm, laid before the shrewd tho' "untutored mind" of Sam, a plan for the equitable apportionment of the upland.

"To begin with, there's only enough open land, counting broomgrass fields, myrtle thickets, and all, to supply eight or ten of you. The others will have to take wooded land and clear whatever is needed for planting. Some of the squares on this plat have both open land and wooded land, and those who get these plots will have all they want; but a few others will have only open land, with no timber for house or fencing, and no wood to burn. Now, by dividing that long wedge of pineland next to Oak Lawn into five or ten acre lots, the 75 acres will give the open-land men all the timber they want. Of course, the open-land man will have the trouble of going some distance away for his house material, fencing, and firewood, but he will have plenty of time to do that, for he will have no woods to cut down, and, all his land being open, he can plant twice as much as the man who has to clear new ground, and can afford to keep a horse, or mule, or ox, to do his own plowing and help out his neighbors who have none. So much for the man who

THE LAND IN SIGHT

gets the cleared land. What does the other fellow get? Most of you will be the other fellow, because there's more wooded land on the Mitchell tract than anything else.

"First of all, he gets, right at his door, poles and sills and joists and rafters and shingles for his house, and clapboards for his yard fence, and firewood. Of course, he has to cut down trees and clean up his land, but at the same time he is providing himself with fencing and building material. He need only clear his land a little at a time, as he finds it most convenient, and every acre of new ground that he clears is worth two acres of the old worn-out land that darkies have been abusing ever since the War, and in two or three years the man with the timber land will have cleared all he needs for planting, and his little farm will be laid out just to suit him, because he will have done it all himself. He will have so many acres in woods, so many acres cleared for corn and cotton and peas and potatoes, and maybe a piece of low-ground for a patch of upland rice, and all in one body, right under hand. So, you see, things are pretty evenly balanced between the man who gets the open land and the man who gets the wood land, but if either of them has the advantage, it's the fellow that takes the woods."

"Dat's so, dat's so, suh! I see de p'int. De man wuh 'f'aid fuh tek de woods lan' ent know wuh 'e duh talk 'bout. I see de p'int."

THE CAPTAIN

"Well, then, Sam, it's up to you two to tell them what to do. Make them understand that this thing is settled. The plat has been made and all the lots are numbered. A man can take whole lots or half lots—nothing else. As soon as you agree among yourselves which numbers each man will take, the land will be surveyed by this plat, and wherever the corner falls each man will put down his own corner post, which the surveyor will mark for him, and that will be the law."

"Yaas, suh, we onduhstan', suh," and the four benevolent conspirators—conspiring only that they might more efficiently serve their fellowman—returned to the buzzing group around Lester, a group whose hum was now pitched a tone or two higher up the treble clef since the inclusion of the women's voices.

Those who have listened to the arguments of intelligent Negroes in their political conventions or club meetings—even in the rough-and-tumble discussions at the railway station or the Cross-roads—have marveled at their aptitude for quickly catching up the thoughts or expressions of influential or prominent white men, changing them to serve their turn, and putting them forth as the improvisations of the moment. So, Sam, in whose eyes the young Surveyor had risen tremendously since his presentation of a practical plan, quickly adopted the plan as his own and, without ceremony, proceeded forthwith to ram it down the throats of his compatriots. And, from time to time, as is the way of Negro ora-

THE LAND IN SIGHT

tors when there is a white man about, he turned to the receptive pair upon the log for a nod of approval of the plan, which, with much elaboration, he unfolded before his auditors, white and black. "Mens," he said, "all you mens, liss'n good. Dis mek de two day we bin t'row'way de Reb'ren' time, de suhweyuh' time, en' we own time, en' none uh we hab time fuh t'row'way. We iz free now, en' free man haffuh wu'k fuh 'eself."

"Yaas, man we free fuh true, en' free man haffuh wu'k fuh 'eself."

"Berrywell. Now, befo' de suhweyuh come, en' befo' de Reb'ren' git de plat frum town, all we man wuh know how de Mitchell place stan' binnuh pick en' choose een we min' 'bout weh we lan' fuh fall w'en we gitt'um, but pick en' choose een we min', en' pick en' choose wid we han', stan' diff'unt, enty?"

" 'E stan' diff'unt, fuh true."

"En' you know w'y 'e diff'unt? Lemme tell you. 'E diff'unt 'cause ebb'rybody kin pick wid 'e min', but only one somebody kin pick wid 'e han'. You see uh smaa't lookin' gal gwine down de big road. De gal look so keen, ef you ent got wife you fuh say 'Uh lub da' gal. Uh gwine hab'um fuh wife.' But da' duh you min' duh talk, enty? En' t'ree-fo' odduh man shum duh big road, en' dem all lub'um same fashi'n lukkuh you—een dem min'—. Bumbye, one de man fuh ketch de gal een 'e han' en' tek'um een 'e house fuh wife. Plenty man kin hab de gal een 'e min', but only one kin hab'um een 'e house, enty?"

THE CAPTAIN

"Yaas, bubbuh! Only one kin hab'um een 'e house."

"Berrywell. 'E stan' same way 'bout dis Mitchell place. Ebb'ry man pick out 'e own piece uh groun' een 'e min', en' nebbuh study 'bout nobody else, but ef dat groun' 'e min' pick out stan' lukkuh da' keen lookin' gal een de big road, you kin mek sho' t'ree-fo' odduh man done pitch dem min' 'pun da' same spot wuh you bin choose. Now, w'en you fetch you money en' ax de Reb'ren' fuh cut off da' groun' en' pit'um een you han', an' all dem t'odduh man fetch dem money en' ax'um fuh pit de same groun' een dem'own, wuh him fuh do? You know de parable 'bout de loave en' de fish, 'cause Uh bin yeddy Pa Lester preach 'bout'um; how our Mastuh tek da' leely bit uh bittle een His han' en' feed de multichude so dey shall not be hongry no mo', but de Reb'ren' iz only de saa'bunt ub our Mastuh, en' 'e haffuh tek de lan' jis' ez 'e come frum de han' uh de Lawd wuh mek de sea en' de dry lan', alltwo. En' de sea en' de dry lan' wuh de Mastuh mek, 'e yent fuh change, enty?"

"No, man! 'E yent fuh change! Gawd mek'um. Le'm stay dey."

Berrywell. Now, Penny Crik en' da' rice lan' wuh dey close'um, duh de sea, enty? En' da' high pinelan' duh de dry lan'?"

"Now you duh talk'um!"

"Well, same way Gawd mek'um en' leff'um, dat same way man haffuh tek'um, 'cep' him gwine leff'um, en', oonuh mens, ef you fool 'nuf fuh

THE LAND IN SIGHT

leff'um dis time, you chance nebbuh come no mo'. En' all uh we wuh yent sattify fuh tek'um ez 'e come—ricefiel', broomgrass, eeduhso pinelan'—we duh 'spute de Lawd, enty? En' man ent fuh do dat."

"No, me Jedus! Man ent fuh do dat!"

The chorus of approval from men and women showed that Sam was having things his own way; too much so to please old Ben Summers, who broke in with a surly interruption. "Hol' on, Chizzum! Wuh dat you duh say 'bout Gawd ent fuh 'spute? You duh tek Him 't'oruhty 'puntop yo'self, enty? Him tell you fuh talk fuh Him 'bout pinelan' en' ricefiel'? Him tell you fuh pick out my groun'? Enty Uh got me two eye fuh choose'um fuh meself?"

"You got eye fuh true, budduh. You got berry good eye fuh see hog' track en' 'ooman' track, alltwo. All oonuh sancti*fy* man wuh staa't fuh preach sence freedom stan' same fashi'n. De Lawd' name fuhrebbuh dey 'puntop you mout', but ef you look eenside'um, de holluh een you jaw teet' full'up wid de po' sinnuh' hog meat! Duh so 'e yiz. Sinnuh fuhrebbuh haffuh wu'k haa'd fuh feed de sancti*fy* man."

"Ai-ai, Buh Ben! 'E git you dat time!"

"Who, me? Shuh! 'E nebbuh git nutt'n'! 'E git me bex, da' all 'e git, en' Uh bex 'cause all oonuh man stan' dey duh gaze 'puntop Chizzum jis' 'cause 'e lub fuh talk. En' all wuh 'e say oonuh swalluhr'um sukkuh nyung mockin'bu'd swalluh wurrum! En' nobody nebbuh say nutt'n', 'cep' fuh

THE CAPTAIN

praise'um, en' nobody nebbuh 'spute'um, 'cep' me, one! You yeddy'um talk 'bout how Gawd mek de sea en' de dry lan', en' pit'um een shish en' shish uh place, en' w'en Him pit'um dey 'e fuh stay dey. Den, fus' t'ing you know, 'e tek da' sea en' 'e fetch'um down yuh en' 'e t'row'um een Penny Crik en' Mitchell ricefiel', en' da' dry lan', 'e pit him 'puntop da' high groun' close Mas' Rafe' line. Uh know berrywell Gawd mek'um, en' leff'um dey, but w'en Him do dat, 'E *done!*

"Wuh Him got fuh do wid'um now? Him fuh buy groun' fuh gimme? No, suh! Uh haffuh run me han' een me *own* britchiz pocket, eeduhso een de 'ooman' killybash, fuh git money fuh buy'um fuh meself. Uh bin yeddy 'bout da' fawty acre en' da' mule, wuh de Nyankee en' de Freedmun Bruro bin prommus we, but Uh yent shum yet, en' Uh 'spec' Uh nebbuh yiz fuh shum! Man haffuh 'pen' 'pun 'eself en', w'en 'e do dat, nobody kin pick en' choose fuhr'um. Uh gwine een da' 'ood, en' Uh gwine pick out me t'irty acre. Uh fuh pick lan' wuh hab hick'ry tree en' dogwood 'pun'um, 'cause da' duh strong groun', enty? Den, Uh fuh git de Suhweyuh fuh run'um off fuh suit, en' w'en him gimme de fo' cawnuh, Uh fuh cut me stake en' tek me axe en' dribe'um down, en' dem stake fuh stay dey 'tel Jedg*ment* day—'cep' fiah bu'n'um off. No Nigguh nebbuh fuh root'um up!"

"Yaas, Nigguh yiz fuh root'um up! Me duh de man fuh root'um up out you skull, en' Uh fuh do'um now! En' same time Uh fuh root'um out'uh

THE LAND IN SIGHT

all de t'odduh man' skull wuh hab 'pick en' choose' een dem min'. Dishyuh plat wuh Uh got een me han' done mek. You yeddy? *'E done mek!* 'Stead-'uh run out de groun' fus', en' mek de plat fuh folluh de groun', lukkuh dem befo'-de-wah Suhweyuh bin do, we Suhweyuh mek de plat fus', en' now him fuh run out de groun' fuh suit de plat, enty? Dat 'cause Pa Lester pick we uh smaa't Suhweyuh, enty? Now, ebb'ry one uh deseyuh plot wuh him pit 'pun de plat hab ten acre; ef you cutt'um een half, him fuh hab fibe. You cyan' gitt'um no odduh way. So, now, all we mens haffuh do iz fuh leh de Suhweyuh show we how de number stan' 'pun ebb'ry one de plot, den, attuh ebb'ry man pick out him'own, de Suhweyuh fuh pit de man' name 'puntop'um, en' den, attuh 'e done pit 'e money fuh de groun' een de Reb'ren' han', de Suhweyuh fuh tek 'e chain en' t'ing, en' gone duh 'ood en' run out ebb'ry man' groun' fuh match de man' number 'puntop de plat. Onduhstan'?"

Everybody—even old Ben—understood Sam's vehement ultimatum, and his novel plan was accepted enthusiastically, for the poor darkies were glad to be relieved of the trouble of making up their own minds. The meeting adjourned until the next day. How well the plan worked will be told in another story.

THE LAND ON PAPER

Early next morning the Captain and the young Surveyor met the prospective Negro colonists of the Mitchell tract at the corner of the "Landing Road," the thoroughfare running from the ante-bellum "Public Landing" on Penny Creek to the King's Highway, which it entered at the corner of the "orchard field," a point midway between the Oak Lawn avenue and King's Gate. Altho' this road for the greater part of its two miles traversed the Mitchell tract, and altho' the landing was on Mitchell land, it was, as its name implies, public—free to all comers, by sloop or barge or flat.

Here in the old days planters who were within easy hauling distance brought their plantation supplies from Charleston in small sailing vessels, which took return cargoes of rice and Sea-Island cotton. Here, too, came before, even during the first year or two of, the Confederate War, the fine sloop Cheeha, built by the author of Carolina Sports to carry his crops to market, and for intercommunication among his plantations lying along the tidal waters of the coast country—a great convenience, for along these waterways the sloop could supply the deficiencies of one plantation from the surplus of another, fifty miles away. If a drought cut short the corn crop on Hilton Head, or Parris Island, a thousand bushels could be quickly and cheaply transferred from the full granaries of "Social Hall" or "the Bluff." Perhaps "The Yankees"—or the Confed-

THE CAPTAIN

erate government—got the sloop later in the war, but her last voyage to Pon-Pon was during the second year of the Confederacy, when, with a cargo of brick from the brick-kiln at Social Hall Landing on the Cheeha river, she came to the Public Landing on Penny Creek, and Edward, her stout brown skipper, came to Oak Lawn to report her arrival to his old master.

Edward and his crew of three sleek, lusty fellows were always pampered, their fellow slaves averred, because their master loved the sea, and they swaggered mightily whenever they came among the black folk of the inland plantation. What Conrad tales they must have told at the quarters! Tales of the salt seas that lay between the Stono and Dawfuskie Island! Of Wappoo Cut and the Dawhoo, of Brickyard and Skull Creek, and of the rough waters of Port Royal! Of the snaky course of the Cheeha—winding, like the brook Meander, the treacherous sands and perilous cross-currents of St. Helena sound and the dreaded Calibogue!—bogy of all mariners who essayed the Inland Passage! But, however large big Edward loomed in the eyes of his fellow slaves, he seemed indeed a mighty man of his hands to the little Confederates of four and five years, who "stood by" to hear the sailorman spin the yarn of his last voyage. They had not then heard of "Blackbeard," nor even of Stede Bonnet, and they hung upon Edward's words as, cap in hand, he stood, sailor-fashion, feet wide apart as if steadying himself

THE LAND ON PAPER

on a slanting deck, and made his report. How the old master's pulses must have throbbed as he heard once more of the flowing waters where lurked channel bass and drum, of the broad sweep of the inlet where, undisturbed save by the thunders of the blockading squadron, the mighty devil-fish still leapt! The old master was soon to cross the bar on "such a tide as, moving, seems asleep," and "put out to sea," but in the memory of one little Confederate, upon whose tides of thought countless dream-ships have come up out of the mist, and into the mists have vanished, big Edward still walks the gently heaving deck, and watches the swelling sails of the sloop Cheeha as she stands forth bravely among them!

At a point on the Landing Road, where, nearby in the high pineland, the Oak Lawn and the Mitchell tracts "cornered," Lester and his crowd had gathered when the white men came up. Here, with the Mitchell land actually under foot, the checkerboard plat was spread once more on a big stump, and the would-be landholders—like the little peoples—gathered 'round to express "self-determination" upon what had largely been determined for them in advance! The first three ten-acre plots in the high pineland, desirable because they touched the Oak Lawn land, and were near the "big road" and the church, were, at their request, awarded to Dick Pinckney and his smart wife Nancy, the best disposed and least contentious Negroes in the colony. Not until the Surveyor had penciled Dick's name upon the chosen sections, did the greedier Negroes seem to realize that the mildest-mannered and least assertive among them had secured a very choice allotment. "Lookyuh, Pinckney! Hukkuh you chance fuh git shishuh good groun' lukkuh dat? You nebbuh quawl 'bout'um, you nebbuh 'spute, nuh nutt'n'! You jis' pick'um out, en' ax fuhr'um, en' gitt'um. Nobody nebbuh crack 'e teet', 'cep' fuh say: 'Berrywell, Buh Dick, tek'um ef you want'um, tek'um.' W'en my time come fuh pick groun', Uh fuh do same fashi'n, en' w'en de Suhweyuh pit my name 'puntop de plat, Uh yent fuh yeddy no Nigguh gyaap 'e mout' fuh say 'tek'um off.' Ebb'rybody fuh say 'tek'um, man, tek'um.' All you Nigguh fuh 'membuh dat!"

"Uh git me groun'," said the quiet Dick, "Uh git me groun' 'cawd'n' to me mannus. Ef man hab mannus, en' nebbuh bodduh nobody, den nobody fuh bodduh him, en' 'e mannus fuh cya'um t'ru, enty?"

"Dat's so," and there was general verbal acquiescence in the efficacy of the "suaviter in modo," whatever may have been in the back of their heads in respect to the "fortiter in re."

As the head-men of the tribe—now on foot and moving into the land of Egypt—the Chisholm brothers, Sam and John, were conceded the right to locate wherever they pleased, and it pleased them to take up between them six sections lying on both sides of the Willtown Road—rich land, having both open and wooded areas. The ricefield was not very far

THE LAND ON PAPER

away, and here they each bespoke five acres. There were other rich squares of high land lying next to the Chisholms, and upon some of these Slippery Simon, asserting the rights of a brother-in-law, sought to locate, but the other Negroes, willing enough to give way to the leaders, drew the line at old Okra, for not only did they begrudge him fat land but they knew his propinquity would be perilous to the livestock of his in-laws. So there was prompt and vehement protest. "Wuffuh you haffuh lib close Chizzum?" he was asked. "You eat een him house? You wu'k een him fiel'? Wuh you got fuh do wid'um?"

"Enty we is bredduh-law? Chizzum' wife en' Maa'gret is two tittuh, enty?"

"Tittuh fuh true. But Uh dunkyuh ef 'e yiz. Ef uh man' wife hab ten tittuh, en' ebb'ry one de tittuh hab man, en' ebb'ry one de man hab house, him fuh lib close'um all, 'cause him iz bredduh-law, enty? Hukkuh you happ'n fuh pick Chizzum fuh bredduh-law?"

"Who, me? Me nebbuh pick'um, him pick me! Enty you know Uh bin hab Maa'gret fuh wife spang back een slabery time? W'en Uh bin hab'um fus', him tittuh, wuh Chizzum en' dem hab fuh wife, bin leely gal; dem head quile up wid plait, 'tel 'e stan' sukkuh deseyuh black wurrum! En' dem bin leely chillun-gal w'en my daa'tuh Riah bin bawn, en' Uh 'membuh berry well w'en de gal bawn, 'cause da' same yeah Maussuh cut down new-groun', en' w'en de man tek axe en' t'row down dem hebby loblolly

THE CAPTAIN

pine wuh grow close de bay-gall, mos' ebb'ry one de tree hab fox-squerril nes' een'um. All-time de axe duh knock de tree, de squerril nebbuh moobe. Ef 'e yent quile up close een 'e nes', him fuh leddown flat een de crotch, en' 'e nebbuh study 'bout de axe, 'cause 'e t'ink de man duh knock de tree fuh mek'um jump off, en' de mo' strong de axe knock de tree, de mo' tight de squerril' toenail fuh jam een de baa'k. Da' squerril fuh hol' 'e holt fuh who las' de longes'! Bumbye, de loblolly biggin fuh groan, en' 'e lean fuh drap. Da' de time squerril git oneasy. 'E say to 'eself, 'Eh, eh! Uh lub fuh ride, but dishyuh t'ing ride me too fas', enty?' En' 'e look fuh place fuh jump, but de groun' rise fuh meet'um so swif', 'e 'f'aid fuh leggo de tree, en' 'e claw dig een'um mo' tightuh, en' 'e nebbuh loose'um 'tel de tree hit de groun' 'brim!' en' ef squerril ent dead, 'e tek 'e foot een 'e han', en' gone, 'tel him fin' annoduh tree. But, sometime, 'e dead, 'cause de tree kill'um, en' w'en 'e yiz, we man tek'um home en' eat'um. Uh lub fuh eat'um, too, but de only chance we bin hab fuh gitt'um den iz w'en tree drap 'puntop'um, 'cause een dem time Nigguh yent fuh tote no gun. But now, sence Uh free, t'engkgawd, Uh got me muskick een me han' w'enebbuh Uh gone duh paat', eeduhso duh 'ood, en' ef any fox-squerril wabe 'e tail befo' me, w'en ole Betsy speak, Uh dunkyuh how high de tree stan', da' squerril fuh drap!"

"Yaas, Buh Okra, da' ole muskick wuh you got,

THE LAND ON PAPER

shoot strong, fuh true, but dem squerril wuh you shoot wid'um lib 'puntop de groun', enty?"

"Some time Uh shoot'um 'pun de groun' befo' 'e git chance fuh climb tree, but 'nodduh time Uh fuh drap'um out de berry tree-top."

"Hukkuh hog fuh climb tree? Uh bin yeddy 'bout da' gang uh hog een de Scriptuh, wuh git de debble een'um, en' run spang Willtown bluff en' jump off een de sea, but Uh nebbuh yeddy 'bout none fuh climb no loblolly tree! En' dem squerril wuh ole Betsy drap hab snout fuh root een de du't, enty? En' 'e tail shawt, en' 'e quile tight, en' w'en you shoot'um 'e yent hab fudduh fuh fall, 'e jis' tu'n obuh 'pun de du't fuh dead. En' you nebbuh fuh skin da' squerril wuh ole Betsy drap! No, man! Ef 'e leetle, you fuh swinge'um, sukkuh 'possum, en' ef 'e stan' big, you fuh git hot watuh en' scal'um fuh git de bristle off da' squerril, enty? En' w'en you done clean'um en' cutt'um up, you fuh git ham en gham en' flitch out da' squerril, enty? 'Cause dem squerril wuh ole Betsy fetch you, dem done fuh fat!"

"Who, me? Wuh dat you say 'bout hog? W'en you ebbuh see me shoot hog? You ebbuh ketch me?"

"No, Budduh, nobody nebbuh ketch you. You too slipp'ry fuh git ketch. Da' mekso dem fuh call you Okra. But w'en somebody yeddy you gun shoot duh 'ood, ef de somebody walk close you house duh night time w'en you wife duh cook, him fuh yeddy da' fat meat sing een de pan, en' de t'ing call hog' name same ez ef you bin yeddy'um squeal! But, ef you

THE CAPTAIN

yiz bin ketch dead squerril een slabery time, en' ef you wife' daa'tuh yiz bin big gal befo' de Nyankee come, hukkuh dat fuh gi' you prib'lidge fuh buy groun' close Chizzum? Fus' t'ing you know, you fuh say you haffuh lib close'um 'cause ti' Maa'gret hab teet'ache duh night time!"

"Hukkuh you know dat? Maa'gret hab teet'ache fuh true! Enty Uh haffuh gone Chizzum' house middlenight t'odduh night fuh baig 'e tittuh fuh gimme some painkilluh fuh pit een'um? Da' duh one de reaz'n Uh wan' lib close'um." But his arguments availed him nothing, and as the Captain remembered a group of tall shortleaf pines on the Landing Road, where wild turkeys sometimes roosted, and jocularly suggested them as equally good for fox squirrels, Simon agreed, and got a far better piece of land than he deserved.

All through the day the reverend agent, the Captain, and the young "Suhweyuh," knowing better than the Negroes themselves the needs of each individual or family, strove to fit the men to the land best suited to them. It was not easy to do. As a small man will not infrequently fix his affections and his hopes upon the largest woman in sight, so certain ambitious colonists, weak themselves and with aged or sickly wives, aspired to take up heavily wooded sections that they could not have cleared in a decade, while the heads of other households, rich in lusty sons and daughters, asked for worn-out open land, upon which they would have starved in idleness. Sometimes a timely joke—a bit of

THE LAND ON PAPER

homely philosophy from the Captain, or a word of sound advice from the level-headed Lester—would smooth the way to an adjustment, and there were surprisingly few serious disputes. Now and then these arose, however, and they were always aggravated by the participation of the gentler sex, for altho' nearly fifty years ahead of the 19th Amendment, there were advanced feminists even in those days, ladies in whose competent hands the hoe handle was quite as efficacious as the ballot, and whenever these gentle disputants entered the lists—arms akimbo and lethal tongues unleashed—the skeletons rattled in many a cabin closet and volumes of hitherto unspoken history came to light!

Out of a feminine group on the fringe of the crowd flared up, without warning, a dispute between two young women, who—years before Reno—had achieved an "off agin, on agin" facility in respect to marital relations that would have done no discredit to a Smart-Set New Yorker of today.

"You talk me?"

"Yaas, Uh talk you."

"Wuffuh you talk me?"

"Uh hab mout', enty?"

"You hab mout' fuh nyam da' haa'd hoecake you juntlemun gi' you fuh eat. You ent hab'um fuh call me out me name."

"Me call you out you name?"

"Yaas, you iz."

"Wuh me call you? Uh call you Mis' Manigo. Da' duh you name, enty?"

THE CAPTAIN

"No, 'e yent me name."

"W'ymekso 'e yent you name?"

"'E yent me name, 'cause Uh done t'row'way Manigo, en' Uh hab anodduh juntlemun."

"You t'row'um'way attuh him done t'row you 'way fus', enty?"

"Who tell you him bin t'row me 'way fus'?"

"Me tell you suh somebody susso?"

"Ef nobody nebbuh susso, den you, 'self mus' be susso?"

"Ef Uh yiz susso, wuh you gwine do 'bout'um?"

"Wuh me gwine do 'bout'um?"

"Yaas, wuh you gwine do 'bout'um?"

"Me haffuh tell you wuh Uh gwine do 'bout'um?"

"You ent haffuh tell me, 'cause Uh know berrywell wuh you gwine do 'bout'um?"

"Wuh me gwine do 'bout'um?"

"You ent gwine do nutt'n' 'bout'um."

"Wuffuh you say me yent gwine do nutt'n' 'bout'um?"

"'Cause you ent, enty?"

"Who say Uh yent?"

"Me haffuh tell you who say you ent?"

"Yaas, 'cep' Uh fuh ride you frame."

"Ride who' frame? My'own?"

"Yaas, you'own. You t'ink Uh 'f'aid fuh ride Nigguh' frame?"

"Who you call Nigguh? Me?"

"Yaas, you! Enty you iz Nigguh?"

"Ef Uh yiz, no Nigguh got prib'lidge fuh susso."

THE LAND ON PAPER

"W'en Gawd mek you, Him pit da' black taar 'puntop you so hebby 'tel ebb'ryt'ing wuh stan' black hab prib'lidge fuh call you Nigguh—crow, blackbu'd, eb'nso buzzut—'cause you black mo'nuh all!"

"'Ooman! Gimme you two eyeball! Gimme'um! Gimme'um!" and Judy Pringle flew in the face of "Mis' Manigo" as recklessly as a Fundamentalist flies in the face of a protoplasm! Only the prompt intervention of a couple of laughing men, saved the coveted eyeballs from Judy's "ten commandments."

The gust of sudden heat and passion swept the dusky disputants like the sirocco's breath, but swiftly passed away before the laughter that rocked the crowd, for laughter, the solvent of so many hard situations, is always on tap in the hearts of these lowly Negroes. And men whose ears sometime had burned under tart tongues, whose skins had been gridironed by the sharp nails of wives and lady friends, were very willing spectators of a "Ladies' Day" event that promised to wound the hearts and scarify the complexions of even two of the fiercer sex! So, as the combatants were torn asunder and put a safe distance apart, the men began to chaff. "Ki!" said one: "Ti' Judy hab uh swif' foot, enty? Him moobe fas' sukkuh bullet-hawk! Ef da' man didn' bin ketch'um, him woulduh hab Liz'bet' two eyeball out 'e head en' gone!"

"Yaas, man, 'ooman' claw duh de debble! 'E yent hab no sense, en' 'e yent hab no mannus. W'en de 'ooman bex, him fuh clabbuhclaw 'e sweethaa't same

THE CAPTAIN

lukkuh 'e clabbuhclaw 'e own husbun'! 'E chupid tummuch!"

"Yaas, en' w'en 'ooman fight 'bout man, de mo' no-count 'e yiz, de mo' 'ooman fuh fight obuhr'um. Ef you see uh man wuh yent wu't' 'tel 'e yent hab no shu't, da' man fuh hab two-t'ree 'ooman fuh folluhr'um. Ef de man hab britchiz, da' duh all de 'ooman bodduh 'bout!"

"Yaas, en' sometime de 'ooman lub de no-'count man w'en 'e yent got no britchiz. De 'ooman lub'um jis' 'cause 'e no-'count. 'Ooman duh we maamy, you know, en' w'enebbuh 'e see uh po'-creetuh kind'uh man wuh yent wu't', de 'ooman haffuh maamy'um. 'Ooman iz uh cu'yus t'ing, sho' ez Gawd!"

"'Ooman haffuh lub all de man, den," said ole Minda Giles—mother of many sons and daughters—"'cause wunnuh ebb'ry drat one iz po'-creetuh!"

With this shrewd observation from one who knew men as the goldfish knows its globe, the sportive intermission ended, and the business of taking up lots was resumed.

An hour before sundown the allotment was finished, and the colonists, who at first regarded the checkerboard plat doubtfully, now, without exception, accepted it with enthusiasm, for the India-inked lines on the fair white sheet, marked plots that stood four-square to all the winds that blew, and—on paper—represented a perfect democracy, promising—like all other democracies on paper—"Equal rights to all, special privileges to none." But, as in life, tomorrow, when their feet should

THE LAND ON PAPER

touch the ground, some lines would fall in pleasant places, others among thorns, some would traverse gently rolling uplands, others, dank and noisome fens. But that was for tomorrow. For today, at least, they were all brothers on paper; and, as the sun dipped, they started for their homes, promising an early start next morning and full of excitement over what the unrolling of the scroll would reveal.

THE LAND SURVEYED

And now commenced ten days of interesting and strenuous experiences for the Captain, the Reverend Lester Flood, agent for the Charleston factor, the forty-odd Negroes who were buying the Mitchell place through the Reverend Agent, and the 16-year-old Surveyor, who, having drawn a checkerboard plat of the square tract and secured its acceptance by his patrons, was eager to try out his novel plan—reversing the regular order—of fitting the land to the paper, rather than the paper to the land. And it worked; worked beautifully, for these poor Negroes, however they jarred and quarreled among themselves, kept faith with the young surveyor and stuck, with singular fidelity, to the promises they had made, before seeing the land, to take the plots marked with their names upon the plat. It was a lottery, a gamble, but an adventure whose hazards were accepted in a sportsmanlike spirit. If the land that fell to them was fat, they chuckled; if lean, they laughed. Happy the man who can laugh at himself. Philosophy is not very far away! But, fat or lean, they kept their word, as many men in far higher circles have not yet learned to do.

And, before he was through, the youth was to gain, through the reactions of these primitive minds to the varied emotions of men, an insight into character that has since needed only a raising of the sights to reach the manifestations of minds higher up. For the cowardly—petulant under disappoint-

THE CAPTAIN

ment, crumpling under adversity or defeat; the selfish, the boastful, the exacting, the assertive, the vain—wear black skins as well as white, as do their opposites.

As the Surveyor's fees for the services of his " 'prentice han' " were very small, he required the Negroes to furnish chain-carriers and pioneers—axemen—to cut away the underbrush, and "blaze" the trees along the way; and he chose these relays, day by day, with respect to the ownership of the sections to be surveyed, so that each purchaser should be "among those present," either as pioneer or chain-carrier, while his own land was being run out. Thus he learned the lines and the corners of his tract, and could amplify the Surveyor's marks upon the line-trees for the exaltation of his own spirit and the warning away of contiguous neighbors who might be tempted to encroach upon him. "Dishyuh side de tree duh my'own, t'odduh side duh him'own. Me fuh maa'k my'own, en' him fuh maa'k him'own. Me yent fuh bodduh him'own, en' him ent fuh bodduh my'own. En' da' tree ent fuh cut down, 'cause him iz line-tree, en' 'e fuh stan' dey 'tel attuh we all done dead—'cep' Gawd want-'um. Ef 'E yiz, en' sen' Him lightnin' fuh 'trike'um, berrywell. Him kin hab'um. But man fuh le'm-'lone. 'E yent fuh tetch'um!" And they never did! Not only their own, but every one else's line-trees were tabu, for the ante-bellum surveyors had impressed upon the woodsmen who accompanied them the importance of holding line-trees

THE LAND SURVEYED

inviolate, and the warning had been passed, from mouth to mouth, through the plantations. Almost equally sacrosanct to many Negroes were trees that had been struck by lightning. In clearing new ground, or cutting firewood, the more superstitious axemen looked with awe upon the boles of forest giants gashed and riven by thunderbolts, and gave them a wide berth. "No, suh! Da' tree ent fuh knock wid axe! Ef Uh cutt'um down, Uh fuh hab sin, 'cause, attuh Gawd pit Him han' 'puntop'um, man ent fuh tetch'um!"

The young "Suhweyuh," treated with great respect by the Negroes who had employed him, looked very grave and felt very important as he set his compass at the starting point, where Mitchell's "cornered" with the Oak Lawn and Encampment plantations. The corner-tree, a great long-leaf pine, had kept the faith and, tho' swept by forest fires and blown upon by fierce autumnal gales, still bore the slowly healing wounds of the last survey, thirty-nine years ago! The old surveyor, who etched the legend on the parchment plat, the stout slave who swung the axe that bit through the bark and gashed the bleeding pine, had long been gone, their spirits freed from the dust that held them here. And the axe had long been rust; but the towering "palustris" still bore the symbols that proclaimed a landmark!

For the first day there were many volunteer chain-carriers, and, as almost every Negro carried his axe, there was no lack of pioneers. All of them

THE CAPTAIN

were anxious to take a hand, and those who were chosen from their fellows seemed to regard their gratuitous service as a distinction. Among the crowd were two or three old Negroes who had carried chains, or at least had accompanied surveyors, before the War, and these thrust the other Negroes aside contemptuously and laid possessive hands on the chain, which they would by no means relinquish, until, late in the day, sheer exhaustion forced them to entrust the linked steel to others. Even then, the novitiates were vigorously admonished. "Tek care, boy! Wuh you duh do? Da' t'ing ent fuh hol' *so,* you mus' hol'um *so!* You shum, enty? Berrywell. Now, 'membuh wuh Uh tell you 'bout'um. Da' t'ing ent fuh hol' lukkuh you hol' hoe. 'Membuh, now, 'membuh! Ef you ebbuh fuhgit, de suhweyuh fuh mek me tek'um out you han', 'cause da' duh 'sponsubble t'ing, sho' ez Gawd!"

The Captain, with a squad of axemen, led the way, and when the Surveyor, by the compass, gave him a tall tree far ahead, the Captain, an expert woodsman, went straight to his objective, the pioneers cutting away the underbrush before the chain-carriers that followed in their wake. There was no lost motion, and, greenhorns though they were, earnestness and enthusiasm made up for lack of experience, and the survey moved with perfect precision.

From the starting point, the Captain and the Surveyor ran, first, the long line almost due south, dividing Mitchell's from Oak Lawn. The Negroes

THE LAND SURVEYED

looked with awe upon the compass which brought them thro' a forest wilderness to the corner of the Allston plantation a mile and a quarter away. "Great Gawd! Da' t'ing hab sperrit een'um, you shum stan' so! Him fetch we spang from Landin'-Road yuh to Allstun, en' run we smack up to de cawnuh tree, straight, sukkuh 'ooman' money run to de preachuh' han'!"

Running down the Allston line toward Penny Creek, temporary stakes were set at ten-acre intervals, and then, about half-way through the tract, the party turned at right angles and followed the needle toward the pole, setting ten-acre stakes as they went. When the northern boundary had been reached at the Encampment line, the surveyors turned their faces to the big pine at the Oak Lawn corner, from which they had started in the morning—driving down, on their way, stakes at the ten-acre corners. Thus, when the starting point had been reached, a parallelogram of five hundred acres had been outlined, with the stakes so set that its subdivision into ten-acre squares and the setting of permanent corner-posts would be a very simple matter. As the weather was cold, the survey of the bad-lands—rice-fields and canebrakes lying between the "Mitchell Bridges" on the Willtown road and Penny Creek—were reserved for a later day, until a change of the moon should bring milder weather. For, as the Mussulman, in things spiritual, rests upon the Koran, so the Captain, in

THE CAPTAIN

matters meteorological, clasped the moon to his bosom, in a beautiful and abiding faith!

At the close of the day there was general satisfaction with its work, for three boundary lines had been established, many markers set for the subdivisions to follow, and, through his luck in running straight to the corners, the young Surveyor had gained the complete confidence of the Negroes and had established a needed confidence in himself.

Next morning, when the men assembled (the women, as on the previous day, had been bidden at home, for there was serious work afoot) there was much bustling around about lightwood posts for the corners of the sections presently to be surveyed. A few of the more forehanded had brought carefully hewn posts of "fat" lightwood on their shoulders; others were scouting about the pineland, thumping the dead logs with their axes, in quest of suitable material. There was no need for haste, of course, for the Surveyor's stakes would serve to mark their corners until replaced by permanent posts, but they would take no chances with their fellows, whom they regarded as none too good to pull up stakes marking a neighbor's boundaries and, by moving them back, enlarge their own.

"No, suh! Uh yent fuh tek no chance wid no Nigguh 'bout me groun'. Nigguh too mischeebus, en' stake too easy fuh pull up. Uh fuh tek me spade en' dig hole two foot deep, en' den, w'en de Suhweyuh maa'k'um fuh me, Uh fuh sink me cawnuhpos' een de hole en' tamp de du't 'roun'um close,

THE LAND SURVEYED

en' den Uh fuh tek me axe en' chop all de bresh en' t'ing wuh grow close'um, en' t'row'um 'way. En' den, bumbye, Uh fuh fetch me hoe en' rake off all de pine straw, en' 'crape'way all de dead grass en' de leaf, so fiah yent fuh bu'n'um, 'cause da' cawnuhpos' duh my'own, him fuh tell ebb'rybody weh my groun' stan', en' him fuh dey dey attuh Uh done dead —eb'nso attuh me chillun, en' me gran' done dead! So, Uh fuh treat dis pos' right, en' g'em all wuh blonx to'um, enty? Uh haffuh stan'up to'um, long ez Uh lib, 'cause, attuh Uh dead him fuh stan'up fuh me, enty? Berrywell." And all through the survey, the older Negroes would set their cornerposts in a sort of spiritual exaltation, tamping the earth around them as reverently as one presses down the clods upon the coffin of a beloved child.

An agricultural people, the yearning of these poor Negroes for the land, and their pride in its possession, were touching, and the Captain and the young Surveyor, loving land themselves, understood the sentiment and tried to advise them how to care for and improve their little bits of Mother Earth. Some of the older Negroes accepted the advice gratefully and acted upon it, but the younger ones were indifferent, for to them land meant property—little more—while, to those who had worked long years under slavery, and had been knocked about under freedom, without even the comfort and security of the old slave-quarters, the promise of a cabin and a few acres of land, to work and tend

THE CAPTAIN

and pass on to those who would come after them, was a promise of freedom, indeed!

The Captain gave the hunter's whoop—the view-halloo of the Low-Country deer-driver when a buck "jumps"—and recalled the post-hunters, who had been tapping logs as lustily as so many great pileated woodpeckers!

Chain-carriers and axemen were chosen from among those whose land, on paper, would, by grace of compass and chain, be transmuted into tangible real estate before the close of day, but so great was the interest in the proceedings that full half the colony, impelled by curiosity, joined the surveying party to see how their neighbors fared in the lottery. And in their comments upon the prizes drawn, and the blanks, they were as vocal, and expressed themselves as freely, as a tree-full of African parrots! "Ki! Buh John sho' git uh good groun'! 'E hab hick'ry tree, en' dogwood, alltwo! W'en you shum stan' so, 'e strong; 'e done fuh strong!"

"Yaas, man! 'E strong fuh true. 'E strong sukkuh Buh John' wife. Buh John say suh him ent haffuh buy no oxin fuh plow, 'long ez 'e got Phibby fuh wife. Da' 'ooman hab double-j'int, en' w'en 'e ketch da' hebby hoe een 'e han', en' swing 'e swing fuh knock dem tough pine-root, de groun' haffuh groan, de 'ooman lam'um so haa'd! En' Buh John plow'um! Enty you know dat? Yaas, 'e yiz. 'E plow'um! De 'ooman pit de haa'ness obuh 'e shoulduh, en' 'cross 'e buzzum, en' Buh John tek de plow-handle, en' Phibby pull da' bulltongue t'ru de

THE LAND SURVEYED

root, en' 'e tayre'up de blackberry wine sukkuh him bin cow! Da' 'ooman wallyubble tummuch!"

"Yaas, 'e too debble'ub'uh wallyubble fuh suit man lukkuh me, bubbuh! Uh too lub fuh look 'puntop'uh 'ooman! But man wuh hab Phibby fuh wife, him nebbuh fuh t'row 'e yeye 'puntop no odduh 'ooman 'cep' him. Ef 'e yiz, him fuh hab acksi*dent*, sho' ez Gawd! Ef 'e yent hab'um wid axe, him fuh hab'um wid hoe! Buh John bin hab uh acksi*dent* lukkuh dat one time, en' 'e yent hab no appetite fuh hab shishuh acksi*dent* 'gen, no mo'!"

"Hukkuh dat? Me nebbuh yeddy 'bout'um."

"You nebbuh yeddy? Lemme tell you. 'E bin een de summuh, een Augus' munt', en' 'e bin on Sattyday. W'en ebenin' come, Phibby, him hab wu'k fuh do een 'e house, en' 'bout de yaa'd, en' 'e tell Buh John fuh gone to de Cross-road fuh buy bittle. De 'ooman g'em de bucket fuh fetch de muhlassis, en' de bag fuh de gritch en' t'ing, en' tell'um fuh mekace en' git back home, 'cause 'e hongry en' 'e yent got nutt'n' een 'e house fuh cook 'tel de man git back. So Buh John gone. 'E buy 'e rashi'n, en' 'e tubackuh, 'e light 'e pipe, 'e t'row 'e bag obuh 'e shoulduh, en' 'e staa't fuh home. De we'dduh bin hot, but, attuh de sun drap, en' fus' dus' come, 'e git mo' cooluh, en' Buh John' h'aa't light, 'tel him haffuh sing sperritual. Buh John nebbuh bin study 'bout no gal. Him h'aa't bin 'pun 'e Jedus, en' him nebbuh 'spishun suh de debble gwine t'row da' skittish gal frum Kinzie King een 'e paat'! But de debble do'um, bubbuh, de debble

THE CAPTAIN

do'um! Buh John binnuh drag 'e foot ez 'e sing, en' shamble 'long kind'uh ca'less like, w'en 'e 'tump 'e toe 'pun uh hebby root, en' 'e stagguh 'tel 'e mos' fall. W'en 'e ketch 'eself, en' hice 'e yeye, please Gawd, de debble en' da' skittish gal dey *smack* befor'um! De gal bin come out de Kinzie King place, en' Buh John nebbuh shum 'tel 'e mos' butt'um een 'e mout'! De debble him dey dey too, but Buh John nebbuh shum. 'E yent see nutt'n' but de gal! En' w'en da' 'ceitful Satan roll 'e yeye 'tel 'e yeyeball shine, en' 'e drap 'e cutchey, en' say 'ebenin', suh!' wuh Buh John fuh do? 'Cause him is mannusubble man, you know, en' de night binnuh git daa'k 'tel de jew biggin fuh fall, en' de gum-bush bin berry t'ick, en' Buh John nebbuh 'spishun *nutt'n'* 'bout de debble! Berrywell.

"Attuhw'ile, de staar come out. 'Bout two hour attuh daa'k, some man binnuh gwine 'long de road en' dem come 'cross Buh John en' cya'm home. Dem tell Phibby 'e seem lukkuh somebody mus'be knock'um een 'e head wid hoe, 'cause dem see weh de hoe' eye mek hole een 'e head sukkuh woodpeckuh' hole. De 'ooman nebbuh say nutt'n', but 'e pit pinegum plastuh 'puntop de hole. En' Uh yeddy suh da' skittish gal bin hab acksi*dent* too, 'cause 'e jaw tie'up fuh t'ree week!

"Attuh dat, w'enebbuh Buh John meet gal duh paat', him pass de time uh day, but him pass de gal same time, enty? Buh John, him 'f'aid acksi*dent* tummuch!"

THE LAND SURVEYED

But all the land didn't have the dogwood and hickory growth that promised fruitfulness, for there were high pinelands, whose soil, though warm and generous, was light. Two of these sections fell to Cassius Brown, a wizened but wiry old darky, so full of the pride of ownership that, as soon as his lines had been determined, he fell upon the linetrees with his axe and proceeded to mark a blazed trail that could be seen half a mile away. As he slashed the bark of a noble long-leaf, the Captain admonished him: "That's not a blaze, Cassius, that's a conflagration!"

"Suh!"

"That's a conflagration. That blaze is broad enough for the devil's shirt-tail!"

"Ki! Mas' Rafe! De debble kin hab shu't-tail? Uh know 'e hab tail, en' de tail hab fawk een'um, but Uh nebbuh yeddy 'bout no shu't, needuhso no britchiz. Ef 'e yiz bin hab'um at de fus', 'e mus'be bu'n off now, 'cause da' place weh him lib, 'e too hot, enty? Uh yeddy suh 'e *done* fuh hot!"

"Hot enough, but 'twill be hotter still when you and Ben Summers and Simon Jenkins all get there together!"

"Great Gawd, Mas' Rafe! Gawd fuh pit me een da' place wid dem two man! No, suh! Him nebbuh fuh do dat! Uh hab sin, fuh true, Mas' Rafe. Uh bin sinnuh all me life, but Uh nebbuh ketch nobody' hog, en' ef Gawd sen' Buh Simon en' Buh Ben to da' place you duh talk 'bout, me yent fuh dey dey, en' soon ez de debble yeddy 'bout'um him

THE CAPTAIN

fuh lock'up all 'e hog *tight* een 'e pen, 'cep' him fuh loss'um, 'cause dem two Nigguh too smaa't fuh nyam dry cawn-hom'ny een da' place 'long ez hog dey dey, en' de fiah stan' so cunweenyunt fuh swinge'um en' fry de meat, enty?"

This sally convulsed the crowd with laughter, and brought very dry grins to the cunning countenance of the "squerril"-hunter, and the brutal face of old Ben.

Cassius set his corner-posts carefully, and the survey left him looking lovingly over the land that meant much to him materially, but so much more spiritually! How many generations of men had these virgin pines and their predecessors looked down upon? For ages the red men, lords of the soil, had roamed these forests, had followed deer and bear and buffalo over the high ridges and through the tangled paths that threaded thick places—bays and swamps and canebrakes! Eight generations of the all-conquering whites had followed. Wrested from the last of these by the ruthless hand of War, it was presently come to yet another race, whose forbears were savages in the Dark continent when the whites took the land from the red men. And, through a curious twirl in the whirligig of time, this virgin-soil of the New World would be broken for the first time by the rude hoe of the sometime jungle-man, who, but for his falling captive to his African brothers in tribal wars; but for his having been driven to the slave coast and swapped off by his captors for rum and red

THE LAND SURVEYED

flannel; but for his having been thriftily transported across the Atlantic by New England slavers and sold for gold to the Southern plantations, where he was civilized and Christianized; but for his labor having been so profitable to these plantations as to arouse the envy of those who had once used him for the profitable transmutation of "old Medford" into gold; but for the growth of envy into the germ of a fratricidal war; but for the freedom that came to the slaves as a war measure, and a war measure only; but for the malignity of the victors, who crushed and despoiled the vanquished; but for the passing of the land into alien hands through this spoliation—but for this, and all this, old Cassius, a professed Christian, a Baptist at that, and wearing breeches every day, might have been a very Gorilla-of-the-Gaboon, wearing a grass string for a breech-clout and, armed with spear and knobkerrie, leading the chase of his fellow-man with the view of "benevolent assimilation!" He would never have heard of God, he would never have caught and "swinged" and eaten a Pon-Pon 'possum, and he would never have worn one of the honorable Roman names the classical Low-Country planters loved to bestow upon their slaves! But the whirligig whirled on, and so it came that, as in the nursery jingle:

"The black began to hunt the black,
The black began to catch the black,
The black began to sell the black,"

until, at last, under God's mysterious providence,

THE CAPTAIN

the rats of Reconstruction began to gnaw the rope that held up the South's economic structure, when the black "jumped over the stile," and came at last to the ownership of land!

But Cassius was eight generations away from breech-clout and knobkerrie. He knew that God was in His heaven, and was sure that if all was not presently "right with the world," it would be, as soon as he could clear part of his land, plant a little winter garden, and begin to get out material for building and fencing. So, as the Survey passed on and left him, like Robinson Crusoe, alone on his island, he began, like Robinson Crusoe, to explore the domain, the twenty acres, whose boundaries, like those of Crusoe's Island, held at the moment all the world for him, and, axe on shoulder, he began to quarter the ground like a trained pointer and take stock of his possessions. His land lay beautifully, at the crown of a gentle rise or "cooterback," with just fall enough on two sides to insure perfect drainage. The growth was almost entirely long-leaf pine, virgin growth, tall, fine trees, with, here and there, clumps of straight saplings of just the right size for house poles. These, Cassius appraised with great satisfaction, for straight longleaf poles, carefully peeled and notched, and cut square at the ends, insure a sightly, a lasting, and a comfortable cabin. There was little undergrowth on the tract, so its clearing up, save for the big pines, would be an easy task. And Cassius noted with satisfaction some large post-oaks, the only

THE LAND SURVEYED

oaks on the land, that would furnish his cabin chimney with back-logs for many a winter's night to come.

An experienced axeman, old Cassius ran his eye over the brown boles as he walked through the pines, and chipped with his axe those he knew to be straight-grained, and suitable for splitting into shingles, rails, or clapboards. Others, whose whorls and twists he noted, would do only for blocks or for firewood. Upon the ground lay many logs of heart lightwood, thrown long ago by storms or forest fires, and from these, in time, the old Negro would get posts for his yard and garden. There would never be lack of firewood, he knew, for the odds and ends of the logs from which he hewed his lightwood posts, and the stumps upon which these logs sometime had stood, would kindle fires for a generation, while the tops and limbs of the trees to be split for rails and shingles would furnish a bountiful store of wood for the kindling. So all was well with the old man, and, as he "cruised" his timber over and over again, his gratitude for the fortune that had come to him was expressed in fervent thanks to the spiritual and temporal agencies that had watched over his interests. "Uh t'engkful to me Gawd," he said. "Uh t'engkful to me Gawd, 'cause Him tell Mas' Rafe en' de Suhweyuh fuh pit me 'puntop shishuh good groun' lukkuh dis, en' Uh t'engkful to alltwo de Buckruh 'cause dem tell me so 'sponsubble en' 'splain'um so good, 'cause, w'en Uh bin back me yez sukkuh mule, en' balk

THE CAPTAIN

'bout'um, de Buckruh obuhrule me, en' mek me tek'um. Dem *mek* me tek'um! T'engk-gawd."

Toward evening, the old man, full of nervous energy and eager to begin work, "threw" a dozen straight saplings, measured nine lengths of his axe-handle and cut them off, thus providing, when they should be "peeled," almost poles enough for one of the long sides of his cabin. When he was through, though tired, he returned to the spot he had selected as the site of his little homestead, chiefly because of three fine post-oaks that stood close together in what would become his front yard. Tho' leafless now, their thick branches held promise of grateful shade from summer suns, and their owner once more grunted an earnest "t'engk-gawd." Now with his heavy hoe, he raked away the pine straw and chopped the sparse patches of pineland grass that grew beneath, clearing the spot where his house would stand. Wearied at last, he stopped to rest, and, Negro-like, his spirit yearned for fire.

He found a match, and with splinters from a lightwood stump started a small blaze on a spot that he had raked clear of pine straw and, sitting on the ground with his back against the stump, he watched the flickering flames in deep contentment. Gradually his head slumped between his shoulders. His chin rested upon his chest. The old man drowsed, then slept.

The sun sank lower, and over beyond the river hung at last, a clot of blood, at the rim of the horizon. There was a tang of frost in the air, and the

THE LAND SURVEYED

chill that creeps along the earth as the sun goes down was on its way. Softly, from a distant clump of hickories, came the plaintive sunset bark of a cat-squirrel—the yearning cry sent out on winter evenings to tell the woods good night. Faintly first, from far away, then louder and nearer, came the voices of the surveying party on their way home. Passing near, the Captain's whoop aroused old Cassius, crouched over the now smouldering altar-fire he had kindled on the open hearth of "God's Green Inn." Jumping up, he rubbed his eyes, and then raked out the embers. "Mas' Rafe," he said. "Uh drap 'sleep, en'—Uh binnuh dream!"

THE SURVEY CONTINUED

The Survey moved on smoothly and rapidly. Day by day, additional settlers came into their own, set their lightwood corner-posts, blazed their line-trees, and reacted to the ownership of the land according to their respective temperaments. All of them were pleased with the straight lines that bounded their tracts, and all of them were at last pleased with the land that fell to their share. Once irrevocably in their hands, if every goose did not forthwith become a swan, at least the cygnet quills straightway began to sprout! There were no stones on the Mitchell tract from which to furnish forth sermons; the "running brooks" were both sluggish and snaky, and the songs they sang were dirges; but, as far as his land went, each settler was prepared to find "good in everything!"

"Wuh you duh laugh 'bout, Nigguh? You laugh at me briahpatch 'cause 'e tayre me britchiz, enty? Wait 'tel dem blackberry ripe duh summuhtime! Uh fuh eat dem t'ing 'tel me bellyban' ready fuh buss'! En' da' canebrake! You t'ink Uh fuh strain me back fuh chop up dem tough root wid pickaxe, enty? Uh yent fuh dig'um up. Da' canebrake fuh stay right weh 'e yiz! Enty. you know da' place full'up wid rokkoon? Een de wintuhtime all Uh haffuh do iz fuh split me light-'ood, light me tawch, call me dog, en' gone een me

THE CAPTAIN

canebrake en' ketch me rokkoon 'pun me own groun'!

"Den, een de Spring, w'en de we'dduh git wawm, en' de bee duh swawm, en' de blackbu'd mek dem nes' een de willuh bush, en' de yalluh-belly cootuh string out 'puntop de log, en' de alli-gettuh' eye rise out de watuh, en' de watuh-snake quile up 'pun de tree limb fuh sleep een de sunhot—w'en da' time come, Uh know suh fish duh bite een Penny Crik! So, Uh fuh gone een me canebrake, en' cut me aa'm full uh de longes' cane Uh kin fin'. Dem duh me fishin' pole. W'en 'e done trim, Uh fix me line en' me hook en' t'ing 'pun'um, Uh fuh gone Penny Crik, Uh git een me bateau, en' Uh paddle 'tel Uh git to uh smood place 'roun', de ben' weh de watuh stan' kind'uh still; den Uh t'row obuh da' t'ing wuh Uh hab fuh hol' me boat to de bottom, Uh bait all me hook, en' Uh cyas' me line. Uh fuh hab fo' line, one to de boat' front, one to 'e back, en' two obuh de side. Den, w'en Uh gitt'um all set, en' attuh Uh done tie down me pole so de fish cyan' cya'um 'way, Uh fuh leddown een de bateau fuh tek me res'. Uh yent bodduh fuh watch de cawk w'en de fel-luh bob. No, man! wuh use fuh wu'k w'en you hab somebody fuh wu'k fuh you? Uh fuh mek da' fish ketch 'eself, enty? So, Uh wait 'tel Uh see de cane biggin fuh trimble, sukkuh man shake w'en 'e hab chill en' febuh. W'en Uh shum do dat, Uh know de fish done hook 'eself, en' Uh pick up me pole en' haul'um een. Den, Uh bait me hook

THE SURVEY CONTINUED

en' t'row'um out 'gen, 'tel, bumbye, w'en sun ready fuh down, Uh hab 'nuf catfish 'pun me string fuh full bushel tub, 'cause Uh ketch'um wid all fo' me line. Den, w'en Uh tek'um home, de 'ooman en' t'ing fuh fry fish 'tel middlenight. En' w'en all wunnuh boy smell da' fish duh fry, wunnuh jaw fuh leak 'tel you haffuh come to me house fuh eat, enty?

"So da' canebrake nebbuh yiz fuh dig up! Him fuh dey dey, same lukkuh you shum, long ez Uh lib, en' den, attuh Uh done dead, sperrit fuh walk t'ru'um ebb'ry night fuh keep Nigguh off de rokkoon wuh Uh lef' behine me!"

And as one Colonist found happiness in briar patches and canebrakes, another's spirit was solaced by long-leaf saplings for house-poles, by the possession of a clay-hole from which to dig material for the clay chimneys appurtenant to all the log cabins in the neighborhood, or by a fine spring, found under the roots of a great white-oak. Each had something to be thankful for—some little distinction to set him apart from his fellows, if 'twere but a clump of persimmon trees to tempt the 'possum, or a patch of "bullhead" broomgrass for making the brooms in universal use for keeping house and yard clean. And, as compass and chain discovered day by day the treasures of forest and field and determined their ownership, the possessors laughed and chaffed and compared their fortunes and, like the happy peo-

THE CAPTAIN

ple they still were, eight years after freedom, made the best of whatever fell to their lot.

As the lines of the Survey criscrossed the tract at intervals of only a few hundred yards, the ground was covered almost as thoroughly as English coverts are beaten for grouse by the gamekeepers on the great estates, and much game of sorts was flushed. Rabbits bounced out of every briar patch, gray fox-squirrels, making for their tall pines, ran jerkily over the ground, bobbing their plumy tails, and, full-cry after rabbits and squirrels, ran futilely and noisily the whole pack of nondescript curs that followed the Negroes everywhere. Coveys of partridge rose from the bunches of petticoat grass that fringed the thickets at the edge of the woods, and whirred away over the broomgrass like brown leaves blown before the wind. Sometimes a bay-lynx skulking along a canebrake path, or a gray fox, trotting contemptuously across the way, led the yelping mongrels away after a quarry that, fortunately for them, they never overtook. In the swamps, barred-owls blinked at the intruders from high branches and then slipped away on silent wing to the thicker places.

Now and then flocks of wild turkeys feeding in the dogwood thickets, disturbed by the voices of the Surveying party, took wing while they were yet a quarter of a mile distant, and broke the forest silence with great beating of wings, as they rose above the pines on their way to the

THE SURVEY CONTINUED

swamp. But these wary birds were not always so alert, for one day, crossing a beautiful pineland ridge, the Survey entered a thicket of low chinquapin bushes, hardly shoulder high. The young surveyor was in the lead and, for the moment, empty-handed, for the compass, having picked up a line tree far ahead, had been committed to the hands of a Negro "gun-bearer" following close at heel. As the dry burs rattled in the first bush, there was a tremendous flutter midway of the thicket, and a magnificent gobbler, surprised at his solitary meal, burst through the scrub at top speed! One look at his burnished back was enough, and the youth, fleet of foot and full of the confidence of 16, set out to run him down, followed by the full cry of the pygmy pack. The turkey had ten to fifteen yards start of his fellow-biped, but the bird was overweight, the boy was not, and at the end of a fifty yard chase the gobbler lifted his heavy body and "took the air," just in time to save his tail feathers! The turkey got away from the boy, but the boy didn't get away from the Captain for many a day, for he was to hear often and lightly of the cock-sureness of one who thought he could run down a wild turkey!

At last the Survey of the first five hundred acres was completed, and the rougher country to the west of the Willtown road was entered upon. Here long-leaf pines gave way to loblolly and rosemary, but even these were but sparsely scattered through heavy hardwood growths of oak

THE CAPTAIN

and beech, hickory and yellow poplar. Between these forest areas and the swamps of tupelo and cypress that skirted Penny Creek lay wide broomgrass fields, thick set with myrtle thickets and briar patches—beautiful coverts for deer and partridge. At the old settlement lived an ancient darky, Friday Giles, sometime manager of the plantation, and here the Charleston factor reserved for himself fifty acres of arable land.

Besides the forests and the broomgrass, the long-abandoned ricefields, overgrown with cattails and intersected by half-filled canals, were yet to be traversed. The Captain's moon proved inconstant and brought colder, not milder weather, but the adventure of the low-lands had to be essayed, and on a bright tho' frosty morning the Surveyor, leaving the Captain on dry land, took with his chain-carriers half a dozen axemen with long stakes, and bogged his way through mud and water—often knee-deep, sometimes waist-deep—until, at sunset, when the tough job had been finished, he was as black as his companions. "Well, you *are* a sight!" was the Captain's cheerful greeting, as the outfit came up on the high dam where the critical gentleman was placidly smoking his pipe, "and in your good clothes, too!"

The Captain was jocular, for there were no "good clothes" in those days—the best—of coarse plantation jeans, put together, grievously and cruelly, by the hands of some sewing-woman in the neighborhood—were bad enough, God knows! In these

THE SURVEY CONTINUED

days, when patent neckbands are to be had at the ten-cent stores, women doubtless contrive Christian shirts, for during the negligee months of Spring and Summer a man will often throw back his coat and thump himself proudly on a percale or madras covered bosom with a "See! my wife made this!" and you see! And, seeing that the man is able to breathe and his Adam's apple functions normally, the sophisticated eye of remembrance detects at his throat a narrow line of the white neckband, and credits the bands of the ten-cent store with doing more to hold couples in the holy bonds of wedlock than the combined influence of "Kirk an' State"—even with the State's anti-divorce law thrown in! For whatever comfort woman's arms about man's neck may bring, when, thro' her needlework, she clasps his throat, the iron collar of the Spanish *garrote* is hardly more restrictive, more repressive of the Adam's apple, which, once given, she now seeks, perhaps, to take away! In the old days many a poor fellow, with a fifteen inch rural neckband riding up to his chin, would, after tearing at his throat in agony, open the thing, fold the corners of the shirt down to the second button, buy a box of paper collars with long points, size 17 or 18, and, buttoning them down over his breastbone, achieve not only great comfort, but a low-cut Byronic effect that, if he had read Don Juan, made him feel very wicked and very dangerous to the opposite sex!

THE CAPTAIN

But whatever the country seamstresses—sometimes gentlewomen, sometimes "crackers," or Negroes—did to the shirts of men, they did far worse to their coats and trousers, for the shirt, in part at least, could hide its shame, but the country trousers, however charitably they covered up the tails of shirts, must themselves stand forth before the world in all their hideous deformity!

Of course the jeans of the country stores and commissaries was not altogether without fault, for 'twas an erratic and undependable cloth—shrinking one way, like a suffragette before a mouse, while as uncompromising on the bias as the same suffragette before a man! But often the feminine artist that tailored the Jeans, indisposed, perhaps, to interfere with the ways of Providence, didn't shrink the cloth, but left that process for the rain and the dew, so when the wearer, "all unwary," walked through tall weeds at night, or under showers by day, there was no telling where his clothes would go when they dried out, for in some places they'd be as baggy as an elephant's breeches, and in others as skin-tight as an eel's! And the cloth was narrow—narrow as the path of propriety—tho' of a convenient width, withal, for trouser legs; the practice being to cut two pieces of the required length, fold them the long way, sew up the seams, and you had two perfectly good trouser legs, suitable for a man of any height between five and six feet, and ready for attachment to waist and seat and hips by whatever

THE SURVEY CONTINUED

method the ingenuity of the artist suggested. This, of course, was the cruder method, for certain Pon-Pon mantuamakers were more sartorially sophisticated in respect to men, but, at the best, the men always felt like clothes-horses upon which women had hung things out to dry!

And the pockets! The pockets! They ought to have shrunk, for—save barlow knives and nails and bits of twine—there was nothing to put in them; but, tho' generous in size, and the cotton drill of which they were made was strong enough, the maker's thread, or something—perhaps her patience, poor soul!—almost invariably gave out before the pocket was completed, leaving a hole in the bottom. Until the boy or man had tied up this hole with twine, the thing was as unretentive as a plaquet-hole! And as an absent-minded woman sometimes drops her purse carefully into her plaquet-hole, sometimes a forgetful man would drop his precious knife or nails into a pocket that had not been tied, and then, unless by chance his boots were outside his trousers, his loss would give him a lesson in caution. So, about the "good clothes" the Captain was jocular!

'Twas a hard day's work—the adventure of the ricefields—but full of fun, for the Negroes, old and young, were always responsive to any humorous suggestion and were always laughing at one another and at themselves. If a man floundered into an alligator hole, and was muddied up to his chin, or slipped off into the water while "cooning" his way over a canal on a slippery pine pole, he was

THE CAPTAIN

as ready to laugh at his own discomfiture as his fellows were to laugh at him.

"Ai-ai! Buh Quash! You drap hebby dat time, enty? Hukkuh you slip off da' log? Uh t'aw't you bin smaa't ez rokkoon! Ef him fuh coon da' pole, mekso you cyan' do'um?"

"Uh coon'um fuh true, budduh, Uh coon'um sukkuh rokkoon, but Uh bin hab acksi*dent*. You know man hebby mo'nuh rokkoon, en' w'en Uh git 'pun da' pole 'e buckle onduh me en' tu'n obuh. W'en 'e do dat, Uh haffuh loss me holt. Ef Uh hadduh hab tail lukkuh 'possum, w'en da' t'ing staa't fuh roll, Uh coulduh t'row me tail obuhr'um en' hice meself back 'puntop'um, jis' ez easy ez dat, but no annimel fuh do'um 'cep' 'e hab claw een 'e tail, lukkuh 'possum. Rokkoon 'eself, cyan' do'um!"

"Dat so. You talk trute. Rokkoon 'self, cyan' do'um! But, enty Mas' Rafe bin tell we suh one time all we gran'daddy en' t'ing een Aff'iky bin hab tail? Him say suh een de ole time' dem Aff'iky Nigguh *done* fuh hab tail, en' dem fuh climb tree sukkuh mongkey, en' ef dem foot slip 'pun de branch, da' tail fuh wrop obuhr'um en' hol' 'e holt 'tel t'unduh roll, sukkuh 'possum, 'cause da' tail hab claw een'um, enty?"

"Shuh! Man! Mas' Rafe duh mek fun. Nigguh nebbuh bin hab no tail! Enty you know Mas' Rafe? Him done fuh spo'ty!"

" 'E spo'ty fuh true, but him tell we 'sponsubble. Him *b'leebe'um!*"

THE SURVEY CONTINUED

"Ef Nigguh bin hab tail one time, hukkuh 'e loss'um? Weh 'e dey now?"

"Uh 'spec' 'e mus'be breed off, sukkuh butt-head cow t'row'way 'e hawn, en' wil' hog t'row'way 'e tush. Ef you ketch wil' hog en' shet'um up een you pen, en' feed'um hebby so 'e yent haffuh root fuh 'e bittle, attuhw'ile da' hog' chillun en' 'e gran' fuh hab shawt snout, en' dem ent fuh hab long snout no mo'. En' Mas' Rafe say suh ef you ketch all de calf w'en 'e bawn, en' cut off 'e tail, en' saw off 'e hawn soon ez 'e biggin fuh grow, en' ef you 'stroy'd all de cowfly, so nutt'n' ent fuh bodduhr'um fuh mek'um hankuh attuh switch de tail wuh 'e done loss, bumbye, attuh long time done pass, all da' breed uh cow fuh t'row'way dem hawn en' dem tail, alltwo. 'Cause, Mas' Rafe say suh Gawd Him ent mek nutt'n' fuh was'e, en' ef you ent nyuze wuh Him gi' you, 'E gwine bex, en', bumbye, 'E tek'um'way. Ef Him pit marruh een you head, en' you nebbuh nyuze'um, nuh nutt'n', Him gwine tek'um out, enty? Da' de reaz'n da' marruh een Buh Quash' head staa't fuh dry up, 'cause him nebbuh t'ink, him nebbuh study 'bout nutt'n'. Da' mekso him fall off da' log."

"Who, me? Wuffuh you say me head duh dry up 'cause Uh fall off da' log? Uh yent fall 'cause me head ent wu't', Uh fall 'cause Uh yent got da' tail you en' Mas' Rafe say me gran'daddy bin hab. But you bin tell we 'bout how hog loss 'e tush, en' how cow loss 'e hawn, but you nebbuh tell we how Nigguh loss 'e tail."

THE CAPTAIN

" 'E loss'um 'cause 'e lazy. At de fus', de Nigguh bin lub fuh climb tree fuh git 'e bittle, en' 'e blan quile da' tail 'roun' de limb obuh weh de cokynot stan', en' 'e swing down 'tel 'e git de cokynot een 'e han', den 'e drap'um en' gone down to de groun' fuh nyam'um; but, bumbye, 'e git lazy, en' 'e say to 'eself, 'Eh, eh! dishyuh tail wuh Uh got stan' too stylish fuh 'buze'um lukkuh dis. Uh strain'um tummuch w'en Uh swing attuh dem cokynot. En' wuh use fuh wu'k w'en you got somebody fuh do'um fuh you? Dem t'ing haffuh drap, enty? Uh fuh leddown onduhneet' de tree, en' Gawd gwine t'row'um down fuh me'. En' de Nigguh nebbuh climb no mo'! 'E leddown een de sunhot, close de tree, en' ebb'ry time da' t'ing drap, de Nigguh crack'um op'n en' nyam wuh dey eenside'um.

"At de fus', w'en de Nigguh sleep, 'e too lazy fuh quile up 'e tail onduhneet'um en' 'e 'tretch'um out een de sunhot. Some leely bush bin kibbuh up de half uh de tail wuh stan' close to de Nigguh, but de half wuh stan' fudduh frum de Nigguh 'tretch'out sukkuh blacksnake duh sleep! Buzzut duh sail up high. Dem ride de ele*ment,* en' sukkle 'roun' en' 'roun' en' t'row dem eye 'puntop de du't fuh see wuh dey dey fuh eat. Bumbye, one de buzzut ketch da' piece uh de Nigguh' tail een 'e yeye, en' 'e say, 'Eh, eh! Lookuh da' dead snake duh leddown close da' Nigguh! Dem alltwo duh sleep, but de snake sleep hebby mo'nuh de Nigguh, 'cause 'e dead, enty? Uh fuh hab'um fuh me bittle', en' de buzzut stoop out de sky, 'e drap 'puntop da' blacksnake, 'e clamp-

THE SURVEY CONTINUED

'um een 'e jaw, en' 'e mos' pull'um off de Nigguh. But de Nigguh holluh so strong, buzzut shame fuh nyaw'um no mo', so 'e drap de snake out 'e jaw, 'e tell de Nigguh, 'So long, bubbuh! You haffuh 'scuze me ef Uh hu't you feelin's, but you bin fool me dat time, sho's you bawn', en' buzzut 'tretch'out 'e wing, 'e jump off de du't, en' 'e gone!

"Attuh dat, de Nigguh git mo' en' mo' lazy, 'e tail biggin fuh dry'up, 'cause him nebbuh nyuze'um fuh heng frum tree limb no mo'. W'en Gawd shum, en' see how 'e stan', 'E say 'No use fuh t'row'way shishuh good tail lukkuh dat 'pun no lazy Nigguh. Ef 'e yent nyuze'um, Uh fuh tek'um off,' en' de tail staa't fuh gone. Ebb'ry day 'e dry up leetle mo', 'tel, bumbye, de t'ing gone, clean! Ebbuh sence dat time, nutt'n' 'cep' 'possum en' mongkey en' snake fuh wrop dem tail 'roun' tree limb, 'cause no odduh creetuh hab claw een 'e tail. Gawd Him nebbuh mek nutt'n' fuh t'row'way, en' ef you ent nyuze wuh Him pit 'puntop you, you gwine loss'um! Now, sence Nigguh t'row'way de exwantidge wuh Gawd bin g'em at de fus', him haffuh coon log wid 'e han' en' 'e foot, same lukkuh rokkoon en' dem t'odduh annimel, 'cause Nigguh ent got no tail fuh 'pen' 'pun no mo'! Duh so Mas' Rafe tell we, en' him tell we *'sponsubble.*"

Quash, a Fundamentalist fallen—for lack of the tail of his fathers—realizing that such an appendage might have proved a very present help in time of trouble, was almost ready to accept the Captain's theory of the Descent of Man—the black man, at

THE CAPTAIN

least.—"Uh sorry me gran'daddy bin so ca'less wid da' tail him bin hab. Ef Gawd didn' haffuh tek'um 'way, da' pole nebbuh woulduh twis' out me han', en' me back nebbuh woulduh wet. Uh done fuh sorry!" But he was indisposed to pursue the argument further, for the water into which he had fallen was shallow, while the subject under discussion was deep! So, with the other muddied-men, white and black, Quash joined the Captain and his dry-shod fellows, and stepped forth as one who, with the heavy, tho' metrical feet of Mr. Gray's plowman, "homeward plods his weary way."

THE SURVEY COMPLETED

And now, as the work drew toward its close, the Surveyor neared the river swamp, now almost dry although periodically overflowed by the flood waters of river and creek. The old plat showed but a narrow strip of swamp bordering the broad serpentine indicated as "Penny Creek," but when the Surveyor had run the number of chains specified, instead of coming to the river's brink he found, where there should have been water, the edge of a heavily wooded swamp, lying but little below the upland level and now perfectly dry under foot. The Surveyor was puzzled, but kept his course until he reached the river, full five hundred yards away! Then the light broke upon him, and he read the story of the last survey as clearly as if it lay in print before him.

In the summer of 1835 the Master of the Mitchell plantation determined to have the place surveyed —perhaps to settle a dispute with a neighbor, perhaps only to re-establish his own boundary lines, as Low-Country land-holders, out of abundant caution, did from time to time. The planter was away at the Virginia Springs, at Saratoga, or at Newport, but he wrote his factor in Charleston to engage the best surveyor in the district, and see that all arrangements were made at the plantation for his comfort and for the facilitation of his work. So the easy-going, tho' accomplished, old Surveyor was engaged and a day settled upon for his arrival

THE CAPTAIN

at the plantation. Then the factor's servant rode 33 miles from Charleston to apprise the "driver" at Mitchell's of the Surveyor's coming, and bearing explicit oral instructions to have all in readiness for his entertainment in a manner befitting the traditions of the place. House servants bestirred themselves, cleaning silver, polishing furniture, airing beds, and sunning linen. Stock was taken of the resources of fold and farmyard, orchard and garden, fishermen and "trunk-minders" were questioned about trout and bream and terrapin—all things done in advance of the Surveyor's coming that a master's well-trained servants could do to insure the comfort of the master's guest.

At last when all was ready, came on an August day from Charleston, Walterboro, or McPhersonville, the seasoned old Surveyor, tanned and weatherbeaten by summer's suns and winter's winds, but hale, withal, from his outdoor life. Perhaps he rode, for surveyors, so constantly on foot, love the rest the saddle affords. But if he journeyed from a distance, almost certainly he drove a sulky—one of those high-wheeled, single-seated affairs, whose long, springy shafts and leather-strap suspension, made them the easiest and safest vehicles for rough country roads, and the lightest draft. The Surveyor's compass and chain and carpet-bag were, of course, in the net of the sulky, and the tripod was strapped to the seat.

In the sunset cool of the evening the Surveyor drove up to Mitchell's, and the expectant house-ser-

THE SURVEY COMPLETED

vants were on hand to welcome him. The sashes had been down and the shutters closed all day to exclude the heat, but now, as the sun had paled his fire, they were thrown wide and the fresh air of evening, laden with the fragrance of honeysuckle, mingled with the cloistered coolness within doors. The guest's room was sweet with vases of late roses and the wholesome freshness of sun-dried linen. The tin bathtub, filled with cool spring water, awaited the refreshment of the dusty traveler.

In an easy chair on the broad veranda, the old Surveyor smoked his pipe after supper, while the plantation "driver"—the master's trusted representative—sat on the steps and told of the arrangements he had made for chain-carriers and axemen. And, at the Surveyor's elbow, a small table held a silver waiter with decanter and wine glasses—perhaps a tall goblet with a cooler and more potent drink. Virginia, mother of Presidents and mother of mint, had conferred the Julep upon South Carolina before 1835, but the seductive interloper from the Old Dominion never seriously challenged the supremacy of the Santa Cruz or Jamaica rum-punch, introduced with the first colonists, and steadfastly supported as an institution—almost as a sacrament—by their Low-Country descendants. Some of these early settlers, from Antigua and the Barbados, possessed the art of combining exquisitely the juices of oranges, pineapples, and limes with the potent spirit of the cane, and this knowledge passed from father to son through the generations

THE CAPTAIN

of masters and servants, until the war-wracked region was thrown upon the crude and uncouth corn and the "rectified" rye of iniquity!

On the more remote plantations tropical fruits were seldom to be had, but the colonists who had come to Carolina from the British West-Indies brought with them a very thorough British appreciation of limejuice as an ingredient of all hot weather drinks, and, as bottled limejuice was almost certainly in the storeroom at Mitchell's, the tall glass at the Surveyor's elbow almost as certainly exhaled the fragrance of mellow old Santa Cruz! Mellow and mellowing, for, as the weary man alternately sipped and puffed, the peace of the quiet night, the low, respectful voice of the old slave at his feet, brought him almost to the brink of sleep, but before the drowsy imps could push him over into oblivion, a bittern boomed from the ricefields, a heron, flying high up in the night, uttered at intervals a harsh and eerie cry, and the great frogs in the canal groaned rhythmically.

Roused by these sounds, the guest began to talk, and for hours the driver hung upon his words, for surveyors were traveled men, and brought news from one plantation to another, as, in England in the old days peddlers brought to ladies in the country homes both garters and gossip. When, at last, the house-servants came to remind him that the hour was late, and next morning's start would be early, the driver had added to his store of wood-lore, had heard many interesting stories of forest and

THE SURVEY COMPLETED

field, and knew something about the crops and the management of two score plantations. And the essentials of what the old slave heard would be remembered as long as he lived, for if "reading maketh a full man," so, also, does listening, and the information imparted orally to those before whom the printed page has never been opened is impressed more accurately upon the memory and held more tenaciously—as the legends of unlettered peoples bear witness—than any knowledge acquired through casual reading. So for many a night the tales of the old Surveyor would pass by word of mouth from the driver through the plantation quarters, filling the ears of the listening Negroes, old and young, for ninety years ago the art of storytelling—a lost art today, with the passing of the old slaves—was in high favor on the plantations and from old family servants the young boys at the "big house" heard many interesting things of their forbears, things their kindred seldom took the trouble to talk about.

Next morning an early start was made, for, while a starlight night had drenched the world with dew, the starting point at the Oak Lawn corner was to be reached on horseback, and in the open pine-lands, almost free from underbrush, dews, however heavy, were of little account. For three or four days the survey moved on in leisurely fashion. There was no hurry. Why should there have been? Corn and cotton had been laid by, the harvest-flow was on the ricefields, and labor without stint was avail-

THE CAPTAIN

able for chain-carriers and axemen. The kitchen-garden was full of summer vegetables, there were pears and clingstone peaches in the orchard, cantaloupes cooling in the shade of the broad veranda, while, in the cold depths of the well, ten fathoms down, watermelons, tied in a bag and weighted with iron plowshares, awaited resurrection at the appointed hour. And in the cellar—whose key the old butler kept as the Crusader kept his vow—the bins held, under waxen seals inviolate, old wines laid down long, long ago. And there was still an anker or two of old Santa Cruz, ripening in solitude year by year, as some men ripen with their thoughts!

Every day they went forth, "for to admire and for to see"—and, incidentally, to run the lines. There was much to see. The pinelands were dotted with the lovely yellow orchis and the rarer white, and many flat meadow-like places were covered with the crimson-throated Sarracenia—painted wantons of the field, luring many tiny winged things to destruction. The brownish-purple boles of the great pines, always beautiful, were lovelier still under the slanting rays of the evening sun, and the forest floor at their feet showed here and there the first yellow and purple blooms—the advance guard—of the autumn flowers, the coarse tho' brilliant bourgeoisie of the woods, before whose onset the fragile orchis would presently vanish as the French noblesse before the canaille of the great Revolution!

THE SURVEY COMPLETED

But, with all their beauty, the woods didn't hold the old Surveyor and his companions too constantly afield. Three hours in the morning and two more in the late afternoon the old driver considered quite enough for hot-weather work, and the Surveyor, loving his ease and the good things of life, found himself in ready agreement.

"Maussuh," said the voice of the tempter: "No use fuh strain weself fuh wu'k too fas' een shishuh hot we'dduh lukkuh dis! Maussuh ent 'spec' we fuh do'um! Dishyuh groun' ent gwine run'way! Ef 'e tek notion fuh run, 'e yent got no foot fuh cya'um, enty, suh? Berrywell. Ef my Maussuh bin yuh, 'eself, Uh know puhzac'ly wuh him fuh say, 'cause him fuh tell me 'e no use fuh 'buze weself een de sunhot w'en de we'dduh stan' lukkuh dis. Him woulduh tell me fuh fetch you out fuh two hour een de mawnin', en' cya' you home long time befo' middleday, so you kin hab chance fuh 'fresh you'self een da' tub en' da' spring watuh, en' hab time fuh you nap 'fo' time come fuh eat. En', den, long time attuh dinnuh, w'en de shadduh biggin fuh git long, en' de ebenin' staa't fuh cool, Uh fuh saddle you hawss en' fetch you out 'gen, fuh anodduh two hour; but we fuh gone home time de sun down, so you foot ent fuh wet een da' hebby jew, 'cause Maussuh ent wan' you fuh git no febuh, no, suh. Da' wuh him woulduh say ef him bin yuh, but w'en him ent dey een place him lef' me yuh fuh dictate sukkuh him; en' t'odduh day Maussuh' factuh een town sen' uh ansuh by 'e saa'bunt fuh tell me 'sponsubble suh de

THE CAPTAIN

Suhweyuh fuh come dis week fuh run out Maussuh' groun', en' 'e tell me fuh ketch fish en' tarrypin en' t'ing, en' mek de house-saa'bunt treat'um berry mannusubble w'en 'e come, en' feed'um high. So, Uh try fuh filfil Maussuh' wu'd same lukkuh de metsidge come out de factuh' mout'. En' now, suh, ez Uh stan' een Maussuh' place, Uh haffuh tell you 'bout da' cootuh soup en' da' trout en' da' summuhduck wuh An' Jane hab fuh you dinnuh. En' da' t'ing fuh drink out da' kyag een de sto'room! Yaas, suh, dat' so, suh, 'e *yiz* time fuh gone, 'cause de sun berry hot. Yuh you hawss, suh—Mekace wunnuh boy! Fetch da' chain en' t'ing. Time fuh gone!"

Then came the first day of the "cool week in August," eagerly looked forward to in the Low-Country as a break in the sustained heat of the long summer. Heavy rains had fallen in the Up-Country, and lower temperatures and precipitation moved down toward the Coast. First, cloudiness, and a spit of rain on a northeast wind. Then the clouds opened and it poured. Followed a day or two of slowly clearing weather, with a flying wrack of ragged clouds, but the clearing was reluctant. As a tempestuous woman, after an indulgence in storm, relinquishes her passion as grudgingly as tho' 'twere her dearest possession, the storm passed at last, leaving the outdoor world clean and sweet and fresh, as is the way with summer partnerships of wind and rain.

THE SURVEY COMPLETED

Weatherbound while the spell lasted, the old Surveyor took his ease, finding a library well stored with books, and no distracting newspapers, withal, to divert a man's mind from the serious consideration of the English classics. To dispel the dampness and remove the chill, fires of oak logs were built every day in the big fireplace of the hall, and upon these, from time to time, dry cedar branches were thrown, for their cheerful crackle as the flames leapt among them and for the fragrant incense they breathed. And the guest "fared sumptuously every day," served with the prodigal hospitality that Low-Country servants could extend so graciously at their masters' expense. Garden and orchard and farmyard yielded their stores lavishly, terrapin were abundant, and, although the waters were too high for fishing in the creek, the resourceful old trunk-minder had, at the first coming of his master's guest, dammed off a section of a water-filled ditch, and put away "for a rainy day" a store of fine trout and bream. So every day, in the all but empty house, the table was spread with snowy napery and silver and cut-glass for the solitary guest the household had been bidden to welcome.

And the solitary guest did himself exceedingly well! So well, indeed, that when bright skies summoned him to complete his unfinished task his spirit dragged like the feet of a Monday schoolboy!

Meanwhile, in the middle-country, every rill and creek in Lexington, Barnwell, and Orangeburg districts, brimming from the August rains, poured

THE CAPTAIN

its flood waters down the gentle slope of the watershed into the Edisto. The river swelled and rose to its banks, then, impatient of restraint, swept over them and flooded the river swamps far back to the up-lands, driving deer and turkeys and rabbits out of these summer fastnesses to the safety of dry land. Down through Colleton district the dark flood swept on its way to the sea, upon whose broad and compassionate bosom all the rivers of the world throw themselves and come to rest. The clean, the foul, the placid, the turbulent, the swift, the sluggish, all find surcease at last!

As a willing and dutiful child helping her mother at a household task comes lovingly with her little laden hands, so, from the first day rivers began to run down the coastal plain of what men now call Carolina, Penny Creek had brought all her narrow watershed would yield to pour into the Edisto. Not very much, perhaps, but a steady, dependable flow and— all she had! In time of flood, however, the bosom of the Edisto swelled for her tributaries, and, as the Lord sometime showered horses, asses, camels, and kine upon the faithful servant who had been stripped of all his livestock, save his wife, so the river, having presently more water than she knew what to do with, poured her largesse into Penny Creek, overflowing her banks and backing water far up to the highlands in all her tributary swamps.

Before the coming of the stormy week, the old Surveyor had run all the lines save the line of the

THE SURVEY COMPLETED

swamp, and on the bright morning after the storm, when he came to the edge of the wooded swamp, he found a flowing river, whose current, swirling among the trunks of the trees, would have made navigation even in a stout bateau extremely hazardous. Even had it been possible to reach the river bank by boat, a straight course by compass could not have been laid, nor could the distance have been measured.

"Maussuh, you cyan' go een da' place. 'E too dainjus!" The creek was five or six hundred yards distant but, asked how far it was, the driver, with the Negro's uncertainty about distance, made light of it and, pointing to a spot a hundred yards away, said, "Oh, 'e yent fudduh. 'E close. Shum dey, suh! Shum? 'E dey dey, right weh you shum! No use fuh gone een da' place! Leh we call dis de ribbuh. 'E yiz ribbuh teday, enty?"

They called it the river; the edge of the swamp was the river's brim, and the old Surveyor's plat bore the legend "Penny Creek."

Because, in the month of August, 1835, heavy rains fell over the mid-country water-shed of the Edisto, swelling the river into flood; because, out of her abundance, the brimming river filled Penny Creek to the banks and overflowed her tributary swamps far out to the contiguous highlands; because the old Surveyor listened to the voice of the hospitable driver, tempting him to shorten his hours afield that he might devote himself more assiduously to trout and terrapin and rum-shrub; because the

THE CAPTAIN

old Surveyor's addiction to the pleasures of the table lost him a precious day upon which he could have run the river line before the waters rose; and because, in December, 1873, the water was low, and the young Surveyor walked dry-shod through the swamp to the river's brink, the Charleston factor came into the ownership of two hundred acres of swamp that his old plat didn't call for, and whose existence he had not suspected.

The youth's theory of the old survey, was conceded, even by the cynical Captain, to be as good as another's, and the darkies—less critical—thought it plausible enough.

But before the Survey came to the end of the upland it was to run into an exciting adventure, and the Captain was to have another laugh at the expense of his "niece."

Nearing the swamp the land became richer, and the growth of broomgrass, briars, and myrtles taller and thicker. More than once the Captain—an old hunter—recalled occasions upon which, on windy days in winter, he had ridden up old bucks basking in the sun on the sheltered side of similar thickets. But the Negro curs, although they poked inquisitive noses into every briarpatch along the way, put up nothing larger than rabbits, woodrats, and "such small deer." And then, almost at the edge of the swamp, the last thicket was reached.

A more sheltered spot could not have been found in a day's journey. It was protected from the cold winds of the west by the wooded swamp at the back,

THE SURVEY COMPLETED

and the morning sun poured upon the open side that faced the field a flood of warmth. On this sheltered side, broomsedge, briars, and soft "petticoat" grass grew close up to the myrtles, and as the Captain neared the beautiful covert he shouted with enthusiasm: "If there isn't an old buck in that thicket, I'll eat my hat!"

The Captain didn't eat his hat! The course of the survey lay to the right of the thicket, and, as the leaders of the party came abreast of the first bushes, there was a tremendous flutter in the myrtles, a panicky outcry from the nondescripts, and a beautiful doe with her two yearlings broke cover and made for the river, clearing the bushes in long bounds, their white flags flying and the frenzied pack hot-foot in pursuit. There was not a gun in the party, but the Captain's farflung whoop sped them on their way.

The white tails vanished through the trees. The deer reached the river and crossed. Their baffled pursuers came straggling back with looks of mingled pride for having put to flight so noble a quarry, and shame for the futility of the pursuit. Several minutes passed in discussing the incident.

"I shouldn't be surprised if the old buck were there now," said the Captain. "I've known them to do that—hang back and let the does and yearlings jump and run off, then, when all the guns had been emptied, and the pack was out of hearing, the sly old rascal would get up quietly and sneak off. Let's look at their beds."

THE CAPTAIN

The Captain and the Surveyor entered the thicket, the Negroes at their heels. There, deeply impressed in the petticoat grass, were the beds in which the three fugitives had lain since dawn, when they had come from their nocturnal feeding, and there, ten feet away, in a deeper and more luxurious bed, lay the big brown body of the cunning old buck, whose "ladies-and-children-first" trick had doubtless saved his selfish skin on many occasions. With perfect composure and marvelous self-restraint he had listened for ten minutes to the voices of a dozen men within twenty yards of where he lay, and when at last they invaded the privacy of his sequestered chamber, "whence all but he had fled," his self-control did not desert him, and he lay absolutely motionless, long neck outstretched before him, and wide, unwinking eyes. Not until the eye of man met his did he move an eyelash, but, then, he jumped!

And the young Surveyor jumped with him. The compass and the heavy tripod were in his hands, and, too excited to lay them down, he plunged in the wake of the buck, cantering leisurely through the thicket to the wooded swamp beyond. But the pursuer was to lose his handicap, for just beyond the thicket lay a narrow ditch, long disused and overgrown with vines and tangled grass. Running high, his eyes upon the deer and taking no thought for his feet, he caught the blind ditch in his stride and came a cropper that sent compass and tripod flying, and measured his length—such as it was— upon the

THE SURVEY COMPLETED

forest floor. But he was quickly on his feet, and, running lighter now, followed the chase for another hundred yards, when the big buck, flirting his outspread tail contemptuously, put on a burst of speed that quickly turned his pursuer upon the back track. Picking up compass and tripod, the youth limped back to his work, not at all abashed by the enthusiasm that, for the moment, had led him away.

"Well!" said the Captain, consolingly: "There's no fool like a young fool!" And there isn't, really!

Another day or two and the adventure of the Mitchell survey would end, for there remained only the long triangle of high pineland adjoining Oak Lawn, and this was quickly apportioned in five-and-ten-acre plots to the colonists who had drawn land upon which there was little or no timber. When this had been finished, a new checkerboard plat was delivered to the Reverend Lester Flood, and a very explicit chart was put into his hands, setting forth each colonist's lines so clearly that the simplest could understand.

The adventure of the Mitchell survey was over. The ten days of hard work had been full of fun, and had brought to whites and blacks the mutual respect that comes from perfect understanding. The Captain and the Surveyor went their ways, while the Negro colonists addressed themselves to Settling the Land.

SETTLING THE LAND

The survey of the Mitchell land was completed a few days before Christmas, and the Negroes began, with one accord, to enter upon their possessions, to get out building material, and clear up "new-ground." Some of them were so eager to commence work that they denied themselves even the three-day rest at Christmas—a holiday claimed on all Low-Country plantations, under slavery and freedom.

The young Surveyor, soon to go away to work on the railroad, was not to see the Mitchell place again for several years, but the Captain was at hand, and to him the older Negroes often came for "exwice" in respect to building operations and the cultivation of their land—sometimes, too, as to domestic relations. The Captain's counsel, always sound, always disinterested, was frequently seasoned with "cussing" thrown in for good measure. This they took laughingly, tho' they didn't always take the "exwice."

Among the first to build was old Cassius, who had commenced to cut poles for his cabin on the day his corner-posts were set. Almost every plantation Negro of the period immediately following the War knew how to build a log cabin, for these were the Negro habitations in almost universal use in the regions that had been swept by fire—where the plantation slave-quarters, as well as the "big house," had been put to the torch. And not freedmen alone,

THE CAPTAIN

but many former slaveholders, were glad of the shelter of such primitive cabins as their ancestors had built two centuries earlier, when they wrested the soil from the Indians.

While all Negroes could build log cabins after a fashion, the popular fashion was as "lame and unfashionable" as Richard, Duke of Gloster, himself! Poles, of either long-leaf or short-leaf, were cut of varying lengths and diverse diameters. Sometimes they were "peeled," but often the lazier brethren notched and set them up with the bark on, leaving the stripping process to Nature, which, operating through her wood-borers or "sawyers," Nature proceeded to do very thoroughly, tho' very untidily, the poles shedding the bark in "shreds and patches," bit by bit. By the time 'twas all off, the logs, rotting from the rain-water that had entered the tunnels of the wood-borers, were falling to pieces. Then the householder would set up another pen of unpeeled poles, to which, when the clapboard roof was on, he would transfer the flooring and the doors and windows, with their frames, from the old house, and move in.

A few of the older Negroes, however, had the patience, the industry, and the skill to build cabins which, tho' small, might have been models for the famous log-camps of the Adirondacks. Cassius, at once architect and builder, now set about the construction of a cabin that would not only shelter his old wife and himself comfortably for the rest of their days, but would set before

SETTLING THE LAND

the younger of the Mitchell colonists the superiority of craftsmen trained under slavery over those who had learned their trade haphazard after the war. And the greater efficiency of the older Negroes was so marked that it was generally conceded, even by those with whose new craft it was contemptuously compared.

"Enty ole-time Nigguh wu't' mo'nuh new Nigguh? Co'se 'e yiz! Ole-time Nigguh *haffuh* l'aa'n! Ef you dey een de fiel', en' you slight you wu'k en' dribuh tell you wuh fuh do, you bettuh do'um, enty? Ef you sassy'um, 'e knock you, sho' ez Gawd! Ef you dey onduh cya'p'ntuh fuh l'aa'n you trade, en' you stubbunt en' haa'dhead, de flat side uh da' hatchitch wuh cya'p'ntuh hab een 'e han' gwine mek da' head saaf', enty? En' ef you lazy en' drap 'sleep w'ile you duh blow da' hebby bellus fuh de blacksmit', ef you seddown 'puntop da' hot tongs een you dream, enty you fuh wake up fas'? Berrywell. Da' w'ymekso all de new Nigguh yent wu't'!"

So old Cassius, single-handed, began to prove his faith by his works. "Uh fuh buil' dis house me, one—me en' Gawd—'cause Gawd fuh gimme de sperrit fuh cya'um t'ru. Him got de sperrit, en' me got de han' en' foot, enty? Berrywell."

Cassius had already cut his straight, smooth long-leaf poles;—in two lengths, 28 feet for the long side and 16 for the short side or gable. Next he proceeded to "peel" them. There are two methods of stripping the bark: the quicker and easier being to "skin" it with a sharp spade, the

THE CAPTAIN

other to shave it off slowly and cleanly with a drawing-knife. Cassius chose the drawing-knife, for the skinned poles, flecked as they were with strips of bark, could never look clean enough to satisfy a critical eye. So, when the poles had been hauled or dragged up to the building site, one at a time, tied to the rear axle of a little wagon, a wooden "horse" was made and brought close to the pile. Resting upon this support, one end of a pole would be raised to a convenient height for the drawing-knife operator and when that had been shaved clean; the "horse" would be slipped toward the middle, until the stripped end would go down and the bark end tilt up and come under the hand of the workman. When all had been peeled, Cassius borrowed a cross-cut saw and the helping hand of a neighbor's boy, and sawed them square at the ends, and exactly to length. Then he carefully notched each pole a foot from the end, so that, when set in place, the poles, tho' seven or eight inches in diameter, would be separated by spaces of only two or three inches.

Sills, plates, joists, and rafters for the model cabin, all laboriously hewn out of long-leaf pines of varying sizes, while lacking somewhat in symmetry, would be more lasting, where exposed to moisture, than the rough-surfaced product of the sawmills. Flat "puncheons," two inches thick by four inches wide, for flooring the loft, were hewn in similar fashion, and the same small timber from which these were cut yielded, as a by-product,

SETTLING THE LAND

thin slats to nail across the rafters to support the shingled roof.

The log cabins of the Low-Country were seldom covered with the short shingles in general use for more pretentious dwellings, for they were more costly in themselves, and required more nails, more time to lay, and better craftsmanship for the laying, than clapboards, so clapboards were in almost universal use. These, split out of long-leaf pine, were usually five to six feet long and four to six inches wide, depending on the "splitting" qualities of the log from which they were riven. If the log proved responsive to the advances of "frow" and mallet, the boards were cut to the maximum widths and lengths desired; but if stubborn or resistant, the workman had to content himself with narrower and shorter cuts. The clapboards were commonly laid in three rows, and the process was far simpler than the putting on of shingles, for the artisan simply set the first clapboard of the lower layer or "course" to the overhang desired at the eaves, nailed it down, and carried the course through to the other gable. Then the joints were "lapped," and the shingler went on to the next course. As even the errant eye of an untrained freedman could achieve a reasonably straight alignment of three rows of clapboards, these roofs were well enough to look at and, if split out of straight-grained logs and nailed down at both ends, were fairly weather-proof—save when it rained hard—but if split from twisted trees, or thriftily nailed only in the middle, exposure to sun

THE CAPTAIN

and rain would cause them to warp and curl up as kinkily as the thatch with which Nature had covered the heads of their builders!

Cassius scorned such slipshod work, however, and, having decided that shingles were too expensive and long clapboards both unsightly and unserviceable, proceeded to compromise upon three-foot clapboards to be laid in six courses. The short boards would never warp or buckle, and his roof would be as tight, and almost as good to look at, as one of shingles. So, having long selected and thrown a suitable pine, he borrowed again the boy and the long cross-cut, and sawed the tree into three-foot blocks. These, with maul and wedges, were first divided into slabs six inches thick, and then, with frow and mallet, he split them into beautiful boards. The product of each day's work he built up at evening into little pens or racks to air-dry until he should be ready to lay them on the roof. All the wide heart-boards were reserved for the house; the narrower ones, and those that showed streaks of sapwood, were put apart for covering the little barn—perhaps a tiny stable for an ox—to be built later.

Then, with saw and boy still in hand, he cut from a heart-lightwood log six blocks, each two feet long, upon which, as piers, his cabin would rest—brick supports or foundations being unknown for such structures.

At last, after several weeks' hard work, old Cassius, having made ready all his building material

SETTLING THE LAND

and brought it conveniently near the site, sent out a call to some of his neighbors to come and help him raise his house. On a bright day in early February they came. Very willingly, for Cassius stood well in the community, and they knew, too, that whenever their cry for similar help should go forth the old darky would be the first to respond. Fifty years ago the older Negroes observed such amenities far more freely among themselves than they have done in later years, for the courtesy of their old masters was still fresh in their impressionable minds. It was a fine thing to watch, during the earlier years following the Confederate War, the meeting of two butlers or coachmen of the old regime. Their dignity was impressive, their deferential courtesy toward each other beautiful, and their unconscious aping of the mannerisms of their old masters, very amusing.

The weather since the new-year had been mild and the season was as far advanced as it sometimes is on the first of March. In sheltered spots the yellow jessamines were slowly coming into bloom —here and there, over-night, one among a string of golden beads would open its fragrant chalice, timidly, hesitantly, as tho' afraid to "waste its sweetness on the desert air." In the swamps, the buds of the poplars swelled, and the maples lit their signal fires to rouse the slumberous earth to its promise of resurrection! The wind among the pine tops seemed softer, more caressing, and blue-birds—harbingers of the Northern spring—that had

THE CAPTAIN

wintered in these forests, now sounded their plaintive little notes more sweetly, while, in the quiet dawns, the cardinals fluted their reveilles with all the ardor of May.

The old men came—among them a young man or two—but they were unmoved by bluebird, or cardinal, or the South wind among the pines.

"Mawnin', Buh Cassius. Huh you do? De we'dduh stan' fine."

"De we'dduh stan' good, fuh true, en' Uh do de bes' Uh kin, t'engk-gawd! You see wuh Uh bin do, enty? Shum yuh! Shum dey! Shum yanduh! Me pole all done peel, me block all done saw, me shingle all done split, en' me sill, en' me plate, en' me jice, en' me puncheon en' me raftuh, all done git out. Dem all dey dey, en' dem all pass t'ru deseyuh ten finguh wuh Gawd bin gimme, en' ole Maussuh show me how fuh nyuze. Nobody nebbuh help me 'cep' da' chupit boy Uh bin borruh fuh pull one side de cross-cut saw. En' 'e nebbuh pull-'um! 'E jis' hol'um, en' me, 'self, haffuh pull en' shub, alltwo! Stillyet, Uh haffuh hab'um fuh hol' de t'odduh handle, but de boy ent wu't'. 'E bin yuh t'ree day, 'e nyam t'ree peck uh me roas' 'tettuh, en' 'e drap 'sleep 'puntop de saw, en' me haffuh pull him en' 'e dream, alltwo! En' da' Nigguh dream *hebby!* 'E yent wu't'!

In this opinion the supreme court of elders—sitting in judgment upon Youth—concurred without dissent. Then they set to work. The first step was to place the six lightwood blocks in the posi-

SETTLING THE LAND

tions old Cassius had carefully marked out for them —four at the corners, and the others midway of the two long sides. These blocks, two feet long and eighteen inches in diameter, were set on end in slight excavations in the sandy soil, the lower ends having first been given a coat of pitch to make them impervious to moisture. Upon these the first poles were laid, extra heavy ones having been selected. The notches fell directly over the lightwood blocks, to which the poles were bolted with iron spikes, cabbaged from the railroad. Then followed the slow and careful raising of the house—the up-building, pole by pole, of the pen of alternately long and short members. The heaviest poles were laid at the bottom, the diameters gradually decreasing, until the very lightest lay at the top. The poles cut by old Cassius had been so carefully chosen that they were almost cylindrical, but, even with these, the old Negroes were careful to lay them with butt-ends and upper ends alternating, so that the four sides of the house would rise uniformly together. And from time to time a spirit-level, borrowed from the Reverend Lester Flood, carpenter, would be run over the poles, and any marked deviation from the horizontal would be overcome by chipping the notch, on one or the other side, a little deeper. By noon, with the help of willing hands, the last poles were in place, twelve feet above the ground, and the workers stopped for dinner, before putting on the plates, joists, and rafters.

The dinner-pail of the Low-Country plantation

THE CAPTAIN

hand of fifty years ago—not always a full dinner-pail, poor fellow—was invariably a two-quart tin bucket, carried by men and women to the fields, to the woods, wherever they went to work. In this was packed for the mid-day meal whatever the family larder afforded, the food prepared by firelight at dawn by the women of the household—often by the man himself. The basis of the daily ration was always coarse hominy or corn bread, tho' sometimes, for a change, heavy wheat bread was substituted—a flat, unleavened bread, of the common flour of the commissaries, baked crudely and hurriedly in a deep frying pan or spider. If the tin bucket contained meat, it was always coarse, fat bacon, but often the ration was meatless, and then the hominy would be omitted, for dry corn bread, however coarse and short of shortening, can be choked down far more successfully than the Negro's dietetic abomination, "dry cawn-hom'ny." Sometimes a bit of bacon and a handful of cowpeas boiled with rice would fill the bucket with "hopp'n'john"—a toothsome and a sustaining ration. If rice were not available, the peas and bacon would be boiled with grist, a fairly satisfactory substitute. On meatless days, sweet potatoes, baked or roasted, helped out the bread; often the ration consisted of sweet potatoes alone. And if the food were only bread, a little flask of molasses would be added. But, on the darkest dietary days, the poor freedman would have to his dinner but dry hominy—cold, coarse, "dry cawn-hom'ny"!—with black mo-

SETTLING THE LAND

lasses, the worst food that black man—or white boy—ever tried to eat!

The tired Negroes, turning "from labor to refreshment," gathered around the fire, from whose deep ashes Cassius began to rake with a forked stick the sweet potatoes that had been roasting for hours. One at a time, he tossed each hot tuber from hand to hand and blew upon it vigorously, until, rid of the ashes that clung to the candied skin, it was laid upon the clean pine straw to cool, when he addressed himself to another. When they were all dusted, the tin buckets that had been warming around the fire were uncovered, and—on this day, at least—none contained a meatless ration. Most of them, indeed, were packed with hopp'n'-john," for peas and rice and bacon had happened to come their way, and, each ingredient having a strong affinity for the other two, they had been combined, as only the older Negroes knew how to combine them, into the most satisfactory "balanced ration" ever set before a dusky gourmet of the Coast-country. "Um-umh," as the iron spoons commenced to rattle against the tin: "Dishyuh t'ing good!"

"Yaas, man, 'e good fuh true! En' 'e strong! Ef man nyam strong bittle lukkuh dis, de man, 'self, haffuh strong, enty?"

"You talk trute, 'e yiz strong. En' 'e hab shishuh good ralish! You nebbuh see no bittle fuh ralish Nigguh' mout' lukkuh dis, duh wintuh-time, 'cep' ham-en'-rice! Dem eegnunt Nigguh een town,

THE CAPTAIN

talk 'bout how Nigguh fuh lub chickin, but, shuh! Dem town-Nigguh ent know nutt'n'! Nigguh lub fuh raise'um, eb'nso 'e lub fuh t'ief'um, but, w'edduh 'e raise'um, uh w'edduh 'e t'ief'um, him nebbuh bodduh 'bout eat'um, 'cause da' fowl en' dem aig haffuh sell, en' de 'ooman tek de money fuh buy hog meat, enty? Berrywell."

" 'E stan' so, bubbuh, same lukkuh you say, 'cause Uh 'membuh een slabery time, w'en Chris'mus come, en' Maussuh hab uh hebby beef kill' fuh de plantesshun, sometime 'e call some uh we fait'ful man wuh him hab fuh 'pen' 'pun, en' 'e say, 'Wunnuh boy, Uh pick out you t'irty man, 'cause you iz good Nigguh, en' wuhebbuh you wan' fuh you Chris'mus dinnuh you kin hab'um. Maum Phibby hab fowl, en' goose, en' tuckrey en' t'ing, een baa'nyaa'd, sheep dey een de fiel', cow dey duh 'ood, hog duh grunt een de pen, en' de smokehouse full 'tel 'e duh groan. Now, wuh you wan' fuh eat?"

"All time Maussuh duh tell we 'bout dem ralishin' bittle, we belly hankuh attuhr'um 'tel de watuh leak out we mout'! Ebb'ry man pull 'e wool, 'crape 'e foot, en' crack 'e teet' fuh talk, one time, but de dribuh step out to de front, 'e hice 'e han', en' all uh we man shet we mout' tight, sukkuh alligettuhcootuh snap 'e jaw w'en you poke'um wid stick. Nobody nebbuh say nutt'n'."

"No, wuh use fuh t'irty man fuh talk one time, w'en dribuh dey dey fuh talk'um fuh you?"

"Yaas, 'cause ebb'ry man know puhzac'ly wuh

SETTLING THE LAND

de dribuh gwine say, 'cause da' dribuh' belly duh hankuh attuh hog, sukkuh we'own."

"You shum, enty?"

"So, dribuh clear 'e t'roat, 'e 'crape 'e foot, en' 'e say, 'My Maussuh, all dem t'ing wuh you call 'e name, stan' berry good, en' 'e mek Nigguh' mout' leak fuh yeddy 'bout'um, but, you know, my Maussuh, hog iz Nigguh meat, so, please suh, gi' we hog. All kind'uh hog stan' good een Nigguh' mout', en' da' hopp'n'john, him done fuh good, but him kin mek out'uh side meat en' shoulduh, but Nigguh nebbuh git chance fuh nyam ham out'uh 'e Maussuh' smokehouse 'cep' Chris'mus come, so do, my Maussuh, gi' we ham en' rice.' En' all de man holluh, 'Yaas, Maussuh, dribuh talk'um 'traight!' Maussuh laugh, 'e say, 'Berrywell,' en' 'e tell dribuh wuh fuh do.

"W'en Chris'mus mawnin' come, dribuh git da' hebby b'iluh dem hab fuh b'ile watuh fuh scal' hog. 'E mek fiah een Nigguh-house-yaa'd, en' 'e tell de leely Nigguh fuh pick up chip en' keep fiah onduhr'um all day. Den' 'e gone to de smoke-house, en' Da' Ben g'em ten ham, en' Da' Ben cutt'um up fuhr'um wid 'e hatchitch en' saw, so 'e fuh b'ile easy. Den, dribuh gone to de big house en' 'e baig fuh some black peppuh. Ole Missis gone een 'e sto'room en' 'e g'em 'bout uh quawt. Dribuh tek 'e meat en' 'e peppuh, en' 'e gone Nigguh-house-yaa'd. Time him git dey, pot duh b'ile. 'E t'row een de ham en' de peppuh, en' 'e tell de 'ooman fuh watch de pot 'sponsubble, en' skim'um off w'enebbuh

THE CAPTAIN

de scum rise. Attuh de meat done b'ile 'bout t'ree hour, dribuh t'row een bushel uh clean rice, en' 'e tell de 'ooman fuh skim'um 'gen. Attuh one mo' hour done gone, dribuh stan' close da' pot, 'eself, en' 'e stuhr'um wid 'e hebby i'un spoon 'bout two foot long. W'en all de watuh mos' dry out, dribuh rake'out de fiah frum onduhneet' de pot en' lef' da' rice fuh soak. At de fus', steam bubble out'um fas', sukkuh 'ooman w'en 'e bex fuh true-true; den, bumbye, 'e jis' sputtuh leetle bit, lukkuh de bex staa't fuh gone out de 'ooman w'en you nebbuh ansuhr'um back, en' 'e fiah gone out 'cause nobody nebbuh blow'um up!

"W'en dribuh shum stan' so, 'e holluh, en' 'e holluh loud! 'E yent haffuh holluh long, 'cause, by dat time all de t'odduh Nigguh ready fuh eat de cow en' t'ing Maussuh g'em, en' we'self iz hongry, en', budduh! Lemme tell you! W'en de Nigguh smell da' t'ing, en' look 'puntop de steam duh come out'um en' staa't fuh rise to de sky, ebb'ry Nigguh feel lukkuh him sperrit dey een da' steam, gwine to 'e Jedus! Dribuh tek 'e long fawk, en' da' big i'un spoon, en' 'e shubble out de bittle. Ebb'ry man fetch de bigges' bucket 'e kin git, en' dribuh full'um wid rice en' ham. Ebb'rybody git big piece'uh ham, en' ebb'rybody hankuh attuh de hock, 'cause da' ham' hock sweet tummuch, enty? Now en' den, one de man git one de hock, but dribuh smaa't, en' 'e schemy, en' w'enebbuh 'e see one de hock biggin fuh rise out de rice, 'e shub'um back, en' push'um down; den, bumbye, w'en all de t'odduh

SETTLING THE LAND

man done git dem'own, en' dribuh ready fuh help 'eself, 'e got all de sweet hock meat, en' da' rice-cake, down to de bottom uh de pot—"

"'Top man! 'Top talk 'bout da' t'ing! Uh jis' done eat en' you mek me hongry 'gen, jis' fuh yeddy 'bout'um! Time fuh wu'k, enty?"

Refreshed with food and invigorated by talk, the Negroes returned to work with renewed energy and, by night, plates, joists, rafters, laths, and ridge-pole, had all been set, and the sills were laid for the down-stairs flooring. The house was not yet half finished, but it had been "raised," and could be completed by the old man himself with very little help. So, with profuse thanks from Cassius for their aid, and polite assurances from the helpers that he was entirely welcome, they went their several ways.

THE FIRST CABIN COMPLETED

Cassius, early at work next morning, decided to cover his house first, so that if bad weather came he could work indoors—laying the puncheons to floor the loft and the sawmill flooring downstairs, and nail the clapboard lining over the openings between the logs. Needing some one, however trifling, to hand him the shingles on the roof, he borrowed again the "ent wu't'" boy from the obliging neighbor, who was glad enough to have him fed for his work. Nor was Cassius unaware of the cost of his maintenance. "Da' boy sho' hab uh 'ceib'in' belly! You shum stan' so, 'e look narruh, but w'en 'e eat, da' belly fuh 'tretch sukkuh kingfishuh' t'roat w'en 'e swalluh fish! W'en da' boy git ready fuh nyam 'tettuh, ef you full you peck medjuh 'e gwine empty'um befo' de day done! Him done fuh eat!"

For four days the boy handed up shingles, first from a rude scaffold, and then from the roof, and old Cassius hammered them down in workmanlike manner. He was unsparing in the use of nails. "Uh yent fuh stingy wid me nail. Ef Uh treat me roof right, en' g'em all wuh blonx to'um, bumbye, w'en de rain fall 'puntop'um, him fuh treat me right, enty? Some dese new Nigguh wuh duh mek house, dem dat triflin', w'en dem nail de clapboa'd down dem too stingy fuh pit mo'nuh one nail een'um, en' dem nail *him* een de middle. Attuhw'ile, rain come. 'E wet'um. Sunhot come attuh de rain. 'E dry'um. En', w'ile 'e duh dry, 'e wawp'um, 'tel ebb'ry Gawd'

THE CAPTAIN

clapboa'd 'puntop de roof quile en' twis'up 'tel 'e stan' sukkuh fedduh 'puntop frizzle fowl! W'en de we'dduh shum stan' so, 'e bex. 'E say, 'Eh, eh, da' Nigguh duh fix fuh git wet, enty? Da' roof duh gyap all dem mout' sukkuh nyung bu'd gyap dem mout' fuh de wurrum dem maamy fetch! Uh wunduh ef da' roof duh laugh 'cause 'e yent count me? Ef 'e yiz, Uh fuh wet da' Nigguh soon ez Gawd en' de moon lemme do'um!' 'E do'um, too. Soon ez de moon change, en' Gawd tu'n'um loose, de we'dduh gone een da' house en' 'e wet'um, 'tel de Nigguh haffuh creep onduhneet' 'e bed fuh sleep! Uh yent wan' no frizzle'hen roof, en' Uh yent want'um fuh gyap 'e mout' at de we'dduh fuh mek'um bex. So Uh fuh nail'um tight!"

And he did. When his incessant woodpecker-tapping ceased, and he came down from the top to inspect his completed roof, he saw, on each side, six smoothly laid courses in perfect alignment—good to look at, and tight enough, he was sure, to withstand even the slanting floods of the equinoctial gales.

On another day he fitted, and nailed down lightly, his rough 12-inch boards from the saw-mill. There was no dressed tongued-and-grooved flooring for Negro cabins in those days, nor, indeed, for the log cabins of whites—in Saint Paul's Parish. Cassius knew that the green boards would shrink and show ever-widening cracks until they were thoroughly seasoned. He knew, too, that the air-drying process would be hastened by the fires that the Ne-

THE FIRST CABIN COMPLETED

groes burn in their living-room kitchens summer and winter. By the following winter, then, his boards would be seasoned enough to nail down permanently, and, meantime, he might even borrow a fore-plane in the summer, after his crop was laid by, and dress them off. But the crop to be laid by was not yet planted, nor was the forest cleared upon which it would be grown! So, as the old man's ultimate objective of a smooth, tight floor could not be attained before the coming autumn, he consoled himself with the thought that the cracks would give his house better ventilation in summer, and the cool air that would creep up at night from the porous pineland soil, would temper the heat of many a torrid spell.

Many Negro log cabins have no lining whatever, being merely "chinked" with clay—mixed, when wet, with the fibrous, hair-like "black" moss—Spanish moss—from which the softer parts have been rotted away. This is found in limited quantities under the live-oak trees, but if the supply thus gathered is not sufficient to meet the demand, piles of green moss are covered with wet sand and left to rot until only the springy black fibres remain. These, first washed and dried, are mixed with wet clay, and the mortar is packed by handfuls into the crevices—from two to four inches wide—between the logs. The moss holds the clay together until it hardens. Once hard, if properly packed, it is fairly weatherproof.

THE CAPTAIN

But the cabin old Cassius was presently building was no ordinary cabin, and the crude methods in common use were rejected as unworthy of consideration by one trained under slavery. So, with saw and hatchet and nails, Cassius set to work to cover the spaces between the logs with smooth 6-inch clapboards, fitting them together in so workmanlike a manner that when, at the end of two days, his task was finished, he had given his house an inner lining that would be proof against ordinary storms, even should the "chinking" with clay be delayed. But the "chinking" was not delayed, for the old man's helpful wife had found time from her work on the Kinzie King place to gather, from under the live-oaks, a store of black moss quite sufficient to hold the plastic clay firmly in the bond of economic wedlock in which, by the custom of the community, it had been joined in the chinks of a thousand cabins!

The loamy soils of the Pon-Pon area, whether of the sandy type of the pinelands, or the dark, heavy land of the plantations, are underlaid with red clay at no great depth below the surface, and, here and there along the highways and neighborhood roads, "clay-holes" are found, wherein the rain-water lies throughout the year, save in periods of excessive drought. From these, builders who have no clay of their own, freely help themselves. Certain roadside clay-holes, whose locations Cassius recalled, were within easy hauling distance of his cabin, but, a resourceful old fellow, he remembered

THE FIRST CABIN COMPLETED

that, while setting his lightwood corner-posts at the beginning of the survey, he had struck stiff red clay of very fine quality within three feet of the surface. An idea struck him—a single stone of thought—and brought down, forthwith, two birds of difficulty. "Wuh use fuh borruh oxin-cyaa't, en' trabble spang t'odduh side Willtown road, fuh dig clay out da' clay-hole en' haul'um yuh, w'en Uh got clay right yuh een me own yaa'd, onduh me han'—en' onduh me foot, 'cause Uh yent dig'um yet. Uh haffuh hab well, enty?" He had to have a well, for, upon his elevated land there were no springs, nor were there any upon the holdings of his nearest neighbors.

Perhaps it is a survival from their Eastern origin, when, at desert water-holes, even the primitive savage would share the fetid moisture of his muddy pool with those who passed that way athirst, but Negroes controlling wells or springs dispense their waters more generously; those having none make freer use of those of their neighbors than do the whites.

Water, to the Negro, is as free as air, and to none is it ever forbidden; so, to the deep wells, the cool, sequestered springs, of those that have, their neighbors come or send their children with the utmost freedom, as a matter of course. And the chance meetings of women and children at the pools are as friendly as those of the lesser ruminants at African water-holes.

THE CAPTAIN

If a spring had bubbled from among the roots of beech or oak on any one else's land within easy reach of old Cassius, its waters—dipped by gourd, or pail, or piggin—would have been his, without the ceremony of a "by-your-leave," but upon this pineland ridge there were no springs, and his nearest neighbors, like himself, would have to dig down for the waters under the earth.

Cassius lost no time in beginning, and the knowledge that, while going after water, he would be throwing out clay for his chimney and the chinks in his walls, spurred him to extra effort. A few of the older Negroes believed in the willow wand as an effective instrument for detecting the presence of subterranean waters, but Cassius had little faith in water-witches, or willow switches, and, knowing that the water-table of his ridge lay but fifteen feet below the surface, he was concerned only with locating his well in the most convenient place. "De watuh dey dey. No use fuh bodduh 'bout *him*, 'cause, wehebbuh me spade drap, ef Uh dig down, de watuh dey dey duh wait fuh me." He took thought for a moment—tho' only for a moment—whether to place his well at the back, where it would be more convenient for him, or at the front, where its cool waters might better offer refreshment to passing friends or casual wayfarers. Like the considerate old fellow he was, his decision was for his friends, not himself.

" 'E mo' cunweenyunt fuh me fuh hab'um to de back uh me house, but ef man come een me yaa'd

THE FIRST CABIN COMPLETED

t'us'ty, Uh cyan' tell'um fuh gone 'roun' me house fuh drink. Uh cyan' treat'um lukkuh him bin cow! So, Uh gwine dig da' well een front, close dem oak-tree; den, w'en summuh come, ef somebody come een me yaa'd fuh drink, him kin full de killybash wid de watuh out me well, en' seddown onduh me tree fuh 'fresh 'eself een me shade, enty?"

So, warming his heart with the thought of the simple hospitality he would some day offer to friends and neighbors—even to the stranger within his gates—he drove his sharp spade into the loam and commenced to dig near his clump of post-oaks, whose summer shade would shelter those who drank or rested at the well. The old man dug rapidly, for the loam was soft, and he threw each spadeful as far as he could, casting first to one side and then to another, until, when he got down to the clay, three feet below the surface, he had scattered the top soil uniformly around the well, but the clay— the precious mortar that would plaster both walls and chimney—could not thus lightly be cast aside, so Cassius set about its conservation. And again he needed the boy his spirit spurned.

"Da' boy bex me tummuch, but Gawd nebbuh gimme but two han' en' two foot, en' Uh nyuze dem all Uh kin, en' nebbuh call on nobody fuh help me, 'cep' Uh need mo' han' en' mo' foot den wuh Uh got. Now, Uh need fo' han' en' fo' foot fuh moobe dis clay, so Uh haffuh git da' boy 'gen; but attuh Uh done git all de han' en' foot wuh 'e got, en' t'row'um een wid my'own, Uh yent got but t'ree han' en' t'ree

THE CAPTAIN

foot—me nuh him, alltwo! Uh count'um fo', my Mastuh, but 'e yent but t'ree!"

With three hands and three feet at his command, Cassius faced the task of digging a hole four feet square, through twelve feet of stubborn clay down to the gravel bed that held the cool and limpid waters of his hope, and the even harder job of hauling up the clay and moving it away from the mouth of the well. Besides his spade, he had patched up a dilapidated mattock, and picked up an old shovel, whose handle he had shortened to permit its use within the narrow walls of his well. So his tools were adequate. Lacking a wheelbarrow, he was not without a wheeled contrivance for removing the clay, once he got it above ground. While sawing out the blocks from which he had split his clapboards, the old man had cut four solid wheels, three inches thick and sixteen inches in diameter, and put them aside until he should need them. Needing them now, he selected two, bored large auger holes through their centers, and fitted into them a short axle cut from a small hickory sapling. Upon this primitive running gear he mounted an old box, attached a stout handle, and was forthwith possessed of a serviceable hand-cart that would serve his turn quite as well as a wheelbarrow.

For the first six feet of his downward progress, Cassius dug with spade and mattock, and threw out the loosened clay, which the boy shoveled into the cart and hauled to the spot where the mortar bed had already been laid; but, as he went deeper,

THE FIRST CABIN COMPLETED

the up-throw was beyond the power of his arm, so he built a rude crane over the deepening well, and rigged up, with an ante-bellum pulley from some coastwise craft long gone and a new plow-line, a block-and-fall to bring the clay to the surface. To this an iron bucket was attached, and, first slipping down a rough ladder to assure himself a means of egress independently of the good offices of the boy, the old man climbed down once more, with many admonitions to his youthful helper as to his manipulation of the bucket.

"Tek care how you handle da' bucket, boy! Ef you hol'um loose w'en 'e full'up wid da' hebby clay, en' 'e slip'out you han' en' drap 'puntop me head en' kill me, Uh fuh lick you, enty? Uh lick you sho' ez Gawd, soon ez Uh git out dis well, Uh dunkyuh wuh you maamy say, so you bettuh min'!"

The boy hauled slowly and carefully, and the team work was perfect. Cassius would dig up a foot or two at a time, and when it got in his way the boy was summoned to lower the bucket and haul it up, piling the clay by the side of the well; then, while the old man dug for another spell, the boy would be moving the last pile to the mortar-bed. So they worked for two days, when, in the gravel bed under foot, Cassius came upon the living waters that welled up to meet him. "T'engk-gawd! but dish-yuh t'ing come strong! Uh haffuh git out 'e way!" He climbed out, hauled up his ladder after him, and dismissed the boy with a word of praise that his heart begrudged to any one of his race born since the days of nullification! "Uh bin call you no'count, en' you bin no'count, fuh true, 'pun all da' t'odduh wu'k, but dishyuh job, you do'um berry well. En' now you kin gone!"

On another day his friends helped him put in his curb and rig up a permanent windlass, and his well was known thereafter as the source of the clearest and coolest water in the Mitchell community.

Now that both clay and water were at hand, Cassius made ready to build his chimney. He had already prepared the material for his wooden framework, and again he called on his helpful friends to join him in putting together and building up the pen—broad and square at the bottom to enclose the wide, deep fireplace, then sloping from the shoulders to the throat that narrowed gradually to the top. The more primitive clay-chimney-builders construct their framework with no more regard for symmetry than an osprey shows in putting together its nest; but Cassius was building a chimney to match his cabin, and his cabin was already a model, so his uprights were set with precision and on their four sides the crosspieces were nailed as closely and evenly as a plasterer's laths. The stiff clay was then mixed with water and kneaded to the right consistency, and his friends helped him plaster it heavily over the framework of the chimney, inside and out. Then, when the clay hearth, built up two feet above the ground, had been carefully leveled, Cassius gathered chips

THE FIRST CABIN COMPLETED

and kindled a little blaze. As the firelight flickered over the cabin walls, his tired old eyes, for a moment, reflected its glow. But for a moment only. Going outside, he watched the blue smoke rising straight up into the dusk. And, baring his head, he whispered a fervent "t'engk-gawd!"

Another day he mixed black moss and wet clay, and chinked from the outside all the crevices between the logs, packing them so tightly as to make his walls almost air-tight. He smoothed the clay with a trowel, and—all ship-shape now—the home he had yearned for, the home he had striven for, had come to him at last!

With two or three turns of a neighbor's ox-cart, Cassius brought his poor household belongings and bestowed them in the cabin. With them came his wife, and the few fowls, so important a part of every country Negro's establishment. For these a latticed house had been built, and, shut in for the first night, they were turned out at daylight each morning thereafter to forage the woods for pine-mast, grass seeds, and such bugs and other creeping things as the early season had tempted to forsake their hibernation.

Next, Cassius put up a little barn, or storehouse. There was nothing to put into it yet, nor would there be for many months to come, but the old man thought it well to be forehanded, and, with a heart full of hope for the harvest of the autumn, still so far away, he had provided a capacious crib for his

THE CAPTAIN

corn, a smaller bin for peas, and a loft for his seed cotton.

"Uh cyan' wait fuh mek house fuh hol' me crap 'tel attuh de crap done mek. No, suh! Ef da' crap ready fuh ripe, en' Uh yent hab house fuh pit'um een, da' crap fuh shame me, enty? 'E shame me sho' ez Gawd, 'cause de cawn fuh say: 'Wuh kind'uh man dis? 'E plant me, en' hoe me, 'e plow me en' all, en' now, attuh Uh done mek, 'e lef' me yuh fuh crow en' bluejay en' all dem debble'ub'uh fambly fuh bodduh me en' pull out me grain, en' de rokkoon en' 'possum fuh 'stroy'd me wuss mo'nuh de bluejay en' de crow.' Den, attuh cawn done talk, cotton him haffuh crack 'e teet'! De boll gyap dem mout' wide op'n, en' 'e fluff'out w'ite, sukkuh boy' mout' w'en 'e binnuh chaw soap! En' da' cotton fuh say: 'Uh wunduh weh da' man iz wuh Uh blonx to? Uh binnuh agguhnize wid grass en' hebby rain en' cattuhpilluh en' t'ing all t'ru de summuh, en' now, w'en Uh ready fuh pick, nobody come fuh pick me.' Da' wuh dem gwine say, enty? Uh cyan' 'low me crap fuh shame me lukkuh dat, so befo' de crap plant Uh mek house fuh pit'um een."

Before undertaking the arduous task of felling timber and grubbing up new ground for the crop, whose seed, as yet, had sprouted only in his mind, Cassius enclosed his yard and garden with a six-foot fence of "wattled" palings, and when he had swung his front gate between two great lightwood posts, imposing enough to have flanked the lodge

THE FIRST CABIN COMPLETED

entrance of an English park, his bones were weary, but his heart was full of honest pride at having built, with his own capable hands, the first homestead set up on the Mitchell land.

While traversing the long-leaf areas of the Mitchell tract, the Captain, the Surveyor, and the older Negroes were impressed with the lasting properties of the lightwood corner-posts they came across. Even in damp places, where the water-table lay very near the surface, the posts were as sound as they had been when set in 1835!

The durability of red-cedar posts is common knowledge wherever the cedar grows; the Virginia squire would rather a vandal steal his feather-bed or even up-root his mint-bed, than cut a walking stick or a riding switch from his thicket of black locust; but it is doubtful if either of these lasting woods is comparable with "fat" lightwood for use in the moister regions of the South.

In 1885 there stood in the "Garris neighborhood" of upper Colleton County a substantial farm-house whose occupant, then an old man, was the grandson of the builder. Proud of his grandfather's house, he was prouder still of his grandfather's wide farm-gate, hung eighty-five years earlier, and of the great lightwood posts upon which it swung, for these had been standing for 110 years! The posts, twelve inches square, had been hewn from lightwood logs with the broadaxe, their sides and corners smoothed and rounded with adze and drawing-knife. The four

THE CAPTAIN

feet of their length below ground had been charred and pitched before they were set, the old man said, and, impervious to moisture, the rains of more than five score winters had made no impression upon them. What earlier gates had hung between these posts, the old man couldn't tell. He only knew that the "new" gate was 85 years old!

And a beautiful gate it was. First roughly split from ten-foot lightwood logs, the square pieces had then been riven with frow and mallet, and "drawn" and smoothed with the drawing-knife, into slats four inches wide and three-quarters of an inch thick. These, mortised and tenoned, were so perfectly fitted together that only the closest scrutiny could detect the little lightwood pins that fastened them. The hinges, slowly hammered out at the primitive forge of a country blacksmith, were in perfect artistic keeping with the gate they upheld, and had withstood, withal, the rusts of nearly a century, for in the old days work, however beautiful, was made to last, and men wrought for the sake of the work —for the honor of their hands—not alone for what the work brought into them! Weathered by sun and wind and rain, posts and gate were a soft and beautiful gray—the surface slightly roughened, where driving rains, from time to time, had worn away the softer parts of the wood. But a sliver shaved from the gray surface with a penknife showed beneath the rich yellow wood, charged to saturation with a spirit that would preserve it for centuries!

THE FIRST CABIN COMPLETED

How many sermons lie in those old posts, set firm in Mother Earth a century and a half ago! The Declaration of Independence had not then been written, and the germ of the great republic was yet in the keeping of a handful of feeble colonies. From the date of their setting, fifty years had passed before the forests echoed the shriek of the first locomotive; seventy-five, before Morse's momentous "what hath God wrought!" bound the world together with a wire!

For lightwood comes by fire. As gold is freed from dross in the furnace, and comes out pure and bright, so in the fires that sweep the long-leaf forests the sapwood burns away from the fallen log, and the heart, tho' seared and bruised and darkened becomes richer and stronger for the ordeal through which it has passed—its character fixed, immutable. But for the fires that swept the forests and turned into lightwood the fallen log from which the old posts were cut, the wood, as common yellow pine, would have rotted away a hundred years ago!

Swept by the fires of sorrow—dross and sapwood burned away—the hearts of men, if only the hearts be sound, are strengthened and enriched—standing at last like the old lightwood posts, "steadfast, unmovable," and holding within themselves the will to withstand all the adverse winds that blow!

THE LAND SETTLED

One by one, the Mitchell colonists, following the lead of old Cassius, entered upon their land, built cabins, storehouses, and fences, and began to make ready for the coming crop. As there were forty odd settlers, there were full two-score different styles of architecture. The taste of some inclined to solid structures, with simple lines; that of others—contrary to the advice of old Polonius—was "express'd in fancy"—lurid, flagrant fancy, at that! Lacking livestock, however, none among them built "a cottage with a double coach-house," so none could be charged with the "pride that apes humility!" Indeed, to the contrary, for the Negro is none too considerate of his work animals, and a clapboard shed with one side boarded up against the north wind, was regarded by most of them as adequate shelter for horse or mule or ox. If boarded on two sides, the man was a humanitarian, while he that sheltered his "creetuh" on three sides was held as one "who loveth well both man and bird and beast."

"Wuh use fuh pampuhr'um? Ef you feed'um too high, ef you mek 'e house too wawm, 'e gwine git dat skittish, fus' t'ing you know, 'e t'row you, enty? Da' t'ing stan' sukkuh 'ooman! Ef you sp'il'um; ef you fetch'um een you house en' feed'um high, da' 'ooman gwine mischeebus en' dainjus, alltwo! Soon ez 'e git fat fuh true-true, ef you trus'um, 'e fling you, sho' ez Gawd!"

THE CAPTAIN

So, out of abundant caution, neither woman, nor any other "creetuh" appurtenant to a freedman's establishment, was unduly pampered in Saint Paul's Parish in the year of our Lord eighteen hundred and seventy-four!

The Chisholm brothers, Sam and John, built substantial cabins, as became substantial men, and their fencing and outbuildings were in perfect keeping with their houses. Their slippery brother-in-law, Simon Jenkins, the "squerril"-hunter, constructed, in a sequestered corner of the woods, a weird habitation, whose indifference to right lines was in accord with the character of its builder.

"Buh Simon, w'ymekso you duh mek shishuh crookety house?"

"Who, me?"

"Yaas, you."

"Wuffuh you call'um crookety?"

" 'E yiz crookety, enty? En' wuffuh you hab all dem leely do' en' winduh en' t'ing to de side en' to de back? W'en man git one do' to de front uh 'e house, 'e oughtuh sattify. Wuffuh you haffuh hab summuch?"

"Who, me? Uh haffuh hab'um! Ef fiah bruk'-out een me house duh night-time, enty Uh fuh hab place fuh git out? Ef rat en' squerril en' rokkoon hab two-t'ree hole, mekso man cyan' hab'um? Me fuh bu'n'up een me own house? No, suh!"

"Yaas, y-a-a-s! Uh yeddy wuh you say, Buh Simon. Uh yeddy wuh you say, but de fiah wuh fuh bu'n you, ent dey een you chimbly. De Deb-

THE LAND SETTLED

ble gott'um een da' place weh him lib, en' you bettuh 'f'aid'um, 'cause 'e done mek, en' 'e stan' hot, en' da' fiah dey dey fuh ebb'rybody wuh nyam hog wuh blonx to somebody else. Soon ez you git da' place weh him lib, de Debble gwine s'aa'ch you. Ef you got somebody' hog meat een you jaw teet', eb'nso ef you mout' greesy, him fuh say, 'Come'yuh, Buh Simon, Uh binnuh wait fuh you, enty? You see, me griddle done hot!' En' 'e jab da' pitchfawk een you britchiz, 'e hice you up, en' 'e pitch you 'puntop da' hot gridi'un fuh brile. *Dat* wuh 'e gwine do!"

"Brile who? Me! Wuffuh me haffuh brile? No man nebbuh ketch me wid hog!"

"Man nebbuh ketch you, 'cause you too schemy, en' ef de Buckruh ebbuh come to you do' duh night time, attuh you done mek dishyuh new house, time you yeddy'um knock 'bram! bram!', ef hog dey dey, you fuh slip'um een you bag en' pitch'um out one dem leely winduh to de back, befo' you wife kin op'n de do'. Da' de reaz'n man nebbuh ketch you, but de Debble ketch you, 'cause him dey dey, budduh, him dey dey! Da' Debble quile'up een you h'aa't sukkuh wurrum quile up een de Buckruh' peach!"

But Simon was concerned only with the ills he had, and took no thought for those he knew not of. He was sure, too, that if he could but outwit the very real "Buckruh," the mythical Devil's scalp would also be added unto him. So he put in all the little doors and windows, agreeing with the Wife of Bath that

"The mouse that trusts himself to one poor hole,
Can never be a mouse of any soul."

And, however he subsequently fared with the Devil, old Simon outwitted "de Buckruh" to the end of his days. He was never caught!

Old Cato Giles, also a brother-in-law of the Chisholms, but a man of far different type from Simon, settled directly on the Willtown road, near its intersection with the "Landing road." He built his cabin on a beautiful site, near a great magnolia tree standing alone in an open field of eight or ten acres. Some ante-bellum settlement must have stood here, for Cato found old bricks enough to build his chimney, and a deep well, long unused, that, when cleaned out, yielded excellent water. A few hundred yards away were "the Mitchell bridges," narrow, and shaky structures—the Scylla and Charybdis of all who rode or drove along the Willtown road fifty years ago. Rough puncheons, split pine saplings nine or ten feet long, were laid, unfastened, across trembling sleepers, supported upon unsteady pilings. Almost invariably, man or boy, adventuring these bridges while riding or driving, would first tie his horse and hazard the crossing on foot, shoving closer together the loose puncheons, and noting carefully the gaps that were large enough for a horse's foot to slip through. Then, having "joggled" the bridge to test its strength, he would go back to his horse and lead him carefully

THE LAND SETTLED

over on a loose rein, so that with lowered head he could watch his step and feel his way. If the horse got over without "skinning" a leg, or other painful injury, the boy or man breathed a prayer of thankfulness, and his faith in a watchful Providence was strengthened!

The creek or "run" that flowed under the Mitchell bridges carried into Penny Creek, in the old days, the waters of "the Cypress" run draining the Oak Lawn ricefields and those of several other "inland-swamp" plantations whose waters flowed through the Oak Lawn canals, into the Cypress. These fields, like those of all inland swamps, were "flowed" or irrigated by waters impounded in reservoirs, or "backwaters," lying at higher levels. The water that had flowed the ricefields higher up, passed, in turn, into the reservoirs and over the ricefields of all the plantations lying along the waterway, until, through the common outlet, it flowed into the river.

While the inland-swamp plantations were immune from many vicissitudes that befel the tidewater plantations lying along the rivers, and suffered neither from brackish water, bad "breaks," "blown" trunks, nor the 'whelming waters of the autumnal storms, they were not without troubles of their own, for, during periods of protracted drought, the backwaters seldom yielded enough water, while at other times, when the rainfall was excessive, the fall to the distant outlet at the river was insufficient to carry off the surplus water at critical periods, and the crop suffered. And, lacking the independence of a river supply, there were many disputes, and occasional law-suits between planters who found it difficult to synchronize the flowing of their respective fields.

Some of these inland-swamp plantations were among the most productive in the State. Because of occasional dearth of water, "white" rice was usually planted, but the author of "Carolina Sports," one year harvested on certain squares of his Social Hall plantation, on Cheeha, eighty-seven bushels of "gold" rice to the acre—said to have been a record yield at the time.

But after the Confederate War little rice was grown on the inland swamp plantations, and none at all along the waters that flowed, at last, under the Mitchell bridges into Penny Creek, for the long neglected dams of backwaters needed rebuilding, trunks had rotted away through neglect, canals, clogged and overgrown with rushes, refusing to carry off the sluggish waters, gradually absorbed them, and rose, at last, almost to the level of the land they had once drained, in the common fellowship of mud!

In the higher spots of the old backwaters pine saplings sprang up almost in a night. Thickset growths of gum and maple and tangles of bamboo and briars, harbored bay-lynx, fox, and rabbit, while along the lower levels of backwaters and ricefields, cattails and rushes struggled for possession.

THE LAND SETTLED

The filling up of canals was gradual, however, and for many years after the War, the main waterways flowed freely. In those days they were full of fish, and afforded many a summer afternoon's sport to the white boys of the plantations, who sometimes took home heavy strings of very respectable perch and bream, while the Negroes of all ages and both sexes fished at every hour of the day, with gear and bait that must have made Izaak Walton's spirit groan! But they caught what they fished for, which is more than most men do, and they would not have swapped a basket of mudfish and "cats" for a creel of rainbow trout!

And when the fish were there, the cranes were there—cranes without number—from the little green heron to the tall "Po'-Joe;" beautiful white cranes, great and small; at times lovely snowy egrets, at other times great flocks of curlews—all of them unafraid, for there were neither breech-loaders nor "pump-guns" then. Few Negroes had learned to shoot, and those that had, leveled their pieces and took aim with such deliberation that, by the time the whole-arm movement of cocking the rusty Enfield musket was completed, even the sluggish "Po'-Joe," warned by the lethal gesture that mischief was afoot, would be in the air and several flaps away, before the thunders of the dreadful artillery broke the brooding silence of the backwater!

In the days of the fish, alligators, too, were plentiful; but, as the freedman attained greater profi-

THE CAPTAIN

ciency in the use of firearms, they shared the fate of many other forms of wild life, and have almost disappeared.

The freedman's growing proficiency in the use of firearms was, however, only partly responsible for the passing of the alligators, for the filling up of the canals and the absorption of the waters they once carried by the sodden soil of the old ricefields deprived them of both fish and water, so, in time, they moved to more favored localities. And, for lack of water, the terrapins, once so plentiful, gradually disappeared, for in the half-dry pools to which they were restricted they were easily captured by the ever-questing Negroes.

Before the waters subsided, the long central canals in these old ricefields were lovely at certain times in late spring or early summer, when their bosoms were jeweled with the fragrant white pond-lilies and the yellow blooms of the lotus—necklaces of pearls and topazes—in the jade-setting of their broad leaves. Between them the water, gently ruffled by the wind, sparkled in the sun. At intervals along their length, white cranes—yet larger pearls—stood motionless, with here and there among them the dull amethyst of a great blue heron!

So, year by year, the beauty of the lagoons and the long canals passed away, but at the time old Cato came into his land near the rickety Mitchell bridges, the waters they spanned still flowed freely,

THE LAND SETTLED

and still held fish enough to tempt the sluggish Sike, old Cato's step-son, now come to young manhood, having brought with him through adolescence the angler's temperament and the ability to sit motionless for hours on a log by the waterside, with a fishing-pole in his hands, watching, with slowly blinking eyes, a huge cork, roughly fashioned out of a hunk of tupelo wood—a float so large, so buoyant, that its complete submergence assured the angler that a heavy fish had taken the bait. Silver-fish and perch nibbled at it from time to time, often nibbling it away to the angler's intense disgust, but their mouths were too small to encompass the rusty iron hook, stout enough to have taken a forty-pound channel-bass! But Sike knew exactly what he was after, for, tho' he fished from sun to sun, he never had time, he thought, to be bothered with taking small fish off his hook; so, to minimize the interruption of his drowsing reverie, he baited a hook so large that it could be taken only by the heavier "cats" and mudfish—clumsy, unwary creatures that would hook themselves and save him the trouble of angling for them. When his float curtseyed to the advances of the nibblers, therefore, Sike merely blinked contemptuously; his interest was aroused only when the pole vibrated in his hands, and the great cork was carried entirely below the surface; then, a violent jerk landed his catch on the bank behind him, or lodged the fish in the vines and boughs

THE CAPTAIN

overhead, whence, by dint of poking and climbing, it was dislodged and brought to earth.

"Uh yent hab time fuh bodduh wid deseyuh putch en' silbuhfish. Ef me hook bin leetle 'nuf fuh dem narruh mout', dem bite so fas' 'e woulduh tek all me time fuh ketch'um, en' w'en Uh *yiz* ketch'um 'e yent wu't'! So, Uh fuh nyuze hebby hook, en' da' bakin skin fuh bait, den, attuh me cawk done folluh de fish spang to de bottom, Uh know da' fish duh big fish, en' Uh know 'e done ketch 'eself, so all Uh haffuh do is fuh haul'um een."

Before the fishing season was far advanced, however, old Cato, one of the most forehanded among the colonists, had squeezed out of Sike's reluctant hands enough labor, of a sort, to enable him to build his cabin and "pitch" his crop. Other settlers followed the leaders, until, by early summer, the colony was settled and at work upon its economic salvation in its own way, as free from the white man's interference as Haiti or Liberia. Some of them—trained workers and intelligent men who valued the blessing of independence—built well, worked hard, diversified their crops, and raised pigs and poultry, determined to "live at home" and make the land support them. These men worked out only when they could be spared from their own crops, and while they were abroad their wives and children "carried on" at home.

Many of the better workers among the Negroes owned horses, mules, or oxen. Such ownership was not only a distinction but a great economic advan-

THE LAND SETTLED

tage, for the man with a "creetuh" could cultivate double the acreage of a man without, and when not at work upon his own crop he could plow for his horseless neighbors, taking payment in money, provisions, or day labor—a day's plowing of a man with his horse or mule being held equivalent to three days' work of a hand with the hoe. A plowman who "gee'd" and "haw'd" an ox, received an exchange commensurate with the slower speed of his beast.

The less thrifty colonists, without work animals of their own, and without the training to enable them to use the power of their own hands to advantage, did the best they could, but—like the morals east of Suez—the best was like the worst, and many of the poor cabins they built, bad enough to look at, were even worse to live in. And their agricultural methods were as primitive as their habitations. Girdling the great pines with a "ring" through the bark, they were left to die, while the landholder cut and grubbed up, with axe and mattock, the scrub that grew between. These, with the larger pine roots, were piled and burned on the land.

In this virgin soil, yet too rough for plowing, the Negro chopped, at intervals, deep holes with his heavy hoe, into which he dropped seeds of corn, peas, and watermelons. The holes were often far out of line, but for hand culture that made little difference. And the cultivation was comparatively easy, for there was little grass during the first year,

THE CAPTAIN

and scrub-oak sprouts and pineland weeds were the only things to be cut away from the growing plants. The sweet potato patch was more carefully prepared, of course, and in damp spots little plots for upland rice were prepared with equal care. The yields of all the Negro's food crops were surprisingly good on the "new-ground" of the pineland, however roughly treated. He failed only when he attempted Sea-island cotton, for the humus in the virgin soil sent up a seven-foot stalk, as striking to look at, but as chary of fruiting, withal, as a Smart-Set New Yorker! All in all, the Man with the Hoe, who took up new-ground, did well enough the first year, if he worked hard, and his land, properly treated, would retain its fertility for years, and become easier to work with each successive season.

Among the last of the Mitchell settlers to complete his building program and build a fire on his own hearth, was old Ben Summers, Jack-leg carpenter, and Jack-leg preacher; with strong predilections for wives—wed or unwed, and swine—marked or unmarked. A former slave of the Captain's, he sought, when the land was being divided, an allotment next the Oak Lawn plantation, upon the plea that he wished to be near the old Negro burying-ground, where his fathers slept, but his compatriots said scoffingly, that his interest was more in the Captain's shoats that cracked acorns under the live-oaks of the graveyard, than in any ancestral bones whatsoever! Ben got the land he

THE LAND SETTLED

wanted, and, within ten years—caught with one of the Captain's shoats in his cupboard—he was sent to the penitentiary for two years, returned fat and in high feather, resumed his place in the pulpit—and triumphantly vindicated the prescience of his brothers in black!

But, in the summer of 1874, Ben had not been caught—by the whites, at least—and, whatever his brothers knew, or suspected, of his depredations upon the live stock of "de Buckruh," was, with true racial secretiveness, hidden as securely in their hearts, as tho' "in the deep bosom of the ocean buried!"

Ben was late about his house, not because of laziness for, when working for himself, he was energetic enough, but because, tho' an indifferent carpenter, his vanity prompted him to out-build everyone else in the settlement. He had determined upon a two-story house, whose design had long bubbled in his brain until it simmered down at last into a more or less definite plan. "Dishyuh house binnuh schew een me head long time, but Uh bin wait fuhr'um fuh bile down. Now, all de watuh done steam off, en' nutt'n' but de nakity meat lef'. Uh ready fuh mek me house, enty?" But the "meat" of his plan, naked as the architect saw it, was garnished with many a sprig of parsley, with many a florid fancy, as it came out of his mind to be put into execution.

Logs were not good enough for Ben. A carpenter, he must have things to nail, or be shamed. So

THE CAPTAIN

he contrived to get rough boards enough for the weatherboarding, although he hewed most of his framing from long-leaf saplings on his own land. When he was ready to "raise" his house, the neighbors were summoned to help, tho' not much help was needed, for the framing was light and the combined height of the two stories was but 13½ feet! Ben, himself falling several inches short of six feet, could see no reason for giving his guest-room, upstairs, a high ceiling.

"Uh fuh mek da' top story two-yaa'd high, enty? Ef dat high 'nuf fuh me, 'e haffuh high 'nuf fuh ebb'rybody wuh come fuh wisit me. Ef man come een me house, en' 'e gone een me top story fuh sleep, ef 'e stan' mo'nuh two yaa'd high, him head haffuh bump, enty? Berrywell."

So, with his carpenter's square, he measured meticulously a first story of two and a half, and a second story of two yards in the clear, and thought he had leaned toward liberality in respect to fresh air. To the lower floor Ben attached two grotesque looking porches, while from the upper hung—like Mahomet's coffin—a little barnacle of a Romeo-and-Juliet balcony. For the ornamentation of porches and balcony Ben had conceived an elaborate jig-saw pattern, but, as there were no jig-saws in the neighborhood, he had to say it with clapboards, and these, with hand-saw and hatchet, he gnawed until they said it—and said it outrageously!

THE LAND SETTLED

When this, the last house in the Mitchell Colony and the most pretentious, was completed, Ben, one of its most important members because of his carpenter's trade and his position in the church, gave a house-warming.

In the summer pork was not to be had, but the old backwaters were full of fish, which the Negroes took with fish-baskets, or "jam-pots." So the house-warming guests feasted on fish, of several sorts —most of it fried—most offensively fried—with highly questionable commissary bacon. For a few favored epicures, however, the women of the establishment had prepared a "catfish-schew."

When the feast was over, the older Negroes, men and women, pulled out their clay pipes, crumbled up strong plug-tobacco in their hands, and began to smoke. Under the soothing influence of the weed they discussed, with unction, the relative gastronomic merits of fish, flesh, and fowl as food for the African; the elders agreeing that, however bad for the children of Israel, the flesh of the cloven-footed creature that "cheweth not the cud" was the most delectable food that could be set before the plantation Negro; and the minstrel songs brought from Charleston by the younger freedmen, lauding the Negro's love for chicken, they held to be sacrilegious.

"No, man! 'E mek me bex fuh yeddy deseyuh new Nigguh talk 'bout fowl. Fowl stan' berry well fuh Buckruh en' wil'cat en' fox—en' town-Nigguh, but fuh man lukkuh we, hog duh we meat! Enty

THE CAPTAIN

Gawd show de Nigguh de hog track en' tell'um fuh folluhr'um?"

"No, man! Gawd nebbuh do'um! De Debble do'um! *Him* duh de man! Debble meet Nigguh duh paat', en' de Nigguh dey een uh hebby trouble. 'E 'cratch 'e head fuh study, but 'e head ent tell'um nutt'n', 'cause nutt'n' dey dey. 'Wuh you trouble, budduh?' de Debble ax'um, 'wuh you trouble?'

" 'Deseyuh track bodduh me,' de Nigguh say. 'Uh cyan' suffuhrate de sheep' track frum de hog' track, en' Uh yent got no time fuh t'row'way fuh folluh no sheep' track, 'cause Uh hongry now.' Debble suck 'e teet'. 'Shum yuh,' 'e say. Him en' de Nigguh alltwo squat down 'pun de du't, en' de Debble tek 'e tail een 'e han' en' nyuze'um fuh p'int de Nigguh to de two track. 'Shum yuh.' En' 'e show'um how de sheep' toe roun' mo'nuh de hog' toe, en' de hog' toe shaa'p mo'nuh de sheep' toe, en' 'e tell'um suh sheep hab shawt heel 'pun 'e foot, sukkuh Buckruh, en' hog hab long heel, lukkuh Nigguh. W'en de Debble done 'splain'um 'sponsubble, Nigguh tell'um t'engky, en' 'e pick'up 'e foot en' 'e folluh de hog' track. De Debble grin. 'Da' Nigguh duh my'own,' 'e say. 'Uh gott'um hog-tie, enty? 'E same ez ef him bin een me pan duh fry!' En' Nigguh, en' hog, en' Debble, bin tie'up *tight* togedduh, ebbuh sence!"

"Uh wunduh who dat bin show we 'ooman' track?"

"De same man wuh show we hog' track, enty? Berrywell."

THE COLONY AT THE FLOOD

"Bluejay died uh whoopin'-cough,
    Sparruh died uh colic,
Meet Bull-frog wid 'e fiddle on 'e back,
    Gwine down to de frolic.
Big-eye Buh Rabbit, who dey?
Big-eye Buh Rabbit, who dey?
Big-eye Buh Rabbit, who dey?
Oh, Maria, po' gal!"

"Weh you gwine, gal?"

"Enty you see w'ich way me toe duh p'int? Uh gwine Cross-road!" and the slim black girl never shortened her stride, as she swung along the Willtown road on her way from the newly settled Mitchell colony to the Parker's Ferry Cross-roads. "Oh, M-a-r-i-a! p-o' g-a-l!"

"Ef Maria shishuh po' gal, stop, en' Uh fuh mek'um rich!"

"Wuh you got fuh mek 'ooman rich?" Tossing her head saucily, she paused long enough to allow the adventuring male to come up, while she dug an inquiring big toe in the sand.

"Uh got credik to de sto', en' Uh got money een me pocket."

"Me, 'self, got credik to de sto'. Lemme see you money!"

"You cyan' shum."

"W'ymekso Uh cyan' shum?"

"You cyan' shum 'cause 'e dey een me pocket, enty?"

THE CAPTAIN

"Mekso you cyan' gitt'um out you pocket? Enty you hab han'?"

"Uh got han', fuh true, but w'en da' han' pit'um dey, 'e prommus me h'aa't 'e nebbuh gwine pull'um out da' pocket fuh no 'ooman!"

"Wuh you stop me fuh, Nigguh? Uh binnuh gwine 'bout me bidness, en' you haffuh holluh at me wid you big-mout' talk 'bout mek me rich. Rich! You nutt'n' but uh fifty-cent Nigguh! Me, 'self, kin tek me hoe een me han' en' mek me fifty cent! Hukkuh fifty-cent man fuh mek 'ooman rich? 'E yent wu't'!" And with a contemptuous flirt of her short homespun skirt, she was gone!

The Low-Country plantation laborer of fifty years ago, who plowed or hoed or spaded for fifty cents a day, was—considering the relation of living costs to earnings—better off economically than he has been since, for at that time he was still content with an approximation to the simple life he had lived as a slave—the coarse, wholesome food, the plain, serviceable clothing. Nor had he then forgotten the industry imposed upon him by slavery. The men habitually worked six days a week; the women five—stopping on Saturdays to wash clothes and clean house. A man and wife, then, earned $5.50 a week, and paid nothing for fuel or shelter. Food was cheap—corn fifty cents a bushel, cowpeas and "rough" rice, sixty to seventy-five, while common bacon was sold in the country stores at six to ten cents a pound. Half a bushel of corn,

THE COLONY AT THE FLOOD

ground by hand in the plantation mill and separated with sifter and "fanner" into grist and meal, five pounds of bacon, and a few quarts each of peas and rice, costing a dollar or less, would furnish ample sustenance for a small family. Only young children cost anything to maintain, for those over ten years of age paid their own way, doing light tasks as "half-hands" on the plantations, or working their own gardens and patches at home.

Clothing, too, was cheap enough, for during the early years of Freedom the plantation Negroes, remembering the comfortable clothing they had worn as slaves, were content to dress plainly and sensibly, as became their station. While bright calicoes were often worn on Sundays, the women's everyday frocks—sometimes their holiday frocks—were of gingham, in bright plaids and checks, and their petticoats were of heavy unbleached drills or sheetings. For greater warmth in winter, they added cheap, tho' heavy, imitations of the Balmoral skirts of mid-Victorian days. The men wore in winter suits of rough jeans, in summer of the blue denim now in universal use for overalls. Their shirts were of either striped "hickory" shirting or unbleached drills.

The shoes worn by men and women were broad, plain, low-heeled "brogans," whose wooden pegs withstood the water thro' which the Negroes constantly walked, far better than the thread fastenings of sewn footwear. These brogans, commonly sold at a dollar a pair, were sometimes made of

THE CAPTAIN

honest cowhide, with solid soles, but often the unwary freedman was tricked into buying wretched frauds of split leather, whose surface, as soon as the heavily-plastered blacking came off, was as fuzzy as fur, and this flimsy material was fastened to "Yankee" soles—several layers of hard brown paper cunningly pasted together and covered with a thin skin of split leather. One walk in the rain was all the wearer of such shoes ever took. Thereafter, until he could find the price of an honest pair, his horny feet, unshod, left their impress upon the bosom of Mother Earth, unhampered by the brownpaper soles of Freedom's friends!

The wool hats of the men cost 75 cents or a dollar, and were durable enough, tho' they soon lost shape and hung down over eyes, ears, and the nape of the neck as dejectedly as the trench-helmets worn by French soldiers in the World War! And these flop-eared hats were also used by the women, who sometimes bought them but more often sported those belonging to their husbands, or other men with whom they were for the moment affiliated. When they "dressed up," the younger women wore cheap, plain straw hats, but the middle-aged and the elderly still held fast to the bandana handkerchiefs of the old days—not the tawdry red-and-white spotted things known as bandanas today, but large and handsome cambric squares, a yard wide, woven in plaids of lilac and pink and blue, sometimes gray and brown, but the shades were so delicate that at a little distance they seemed to be white.

THE COLONY AT THE FLOOD

These kerchiefs, stiffly starched, the elder women would pile up and pin upon their heads in the towering shape of a Bishop's mitre—a skilful feat accomplished without a mirror, or the help of other hands, which, in arranging her own "hengkitchuh," any self-respecting old-timer would have scorned. Certainly no head-covering could have been more dignified, more striking, or more effective in affording protection from the burning sun, and when the wearer pinned a broad kerchief of the same sort across her bosom, she stood out in a motley group of church-goers like a deep-sea ship under full sail among a fleet of coastwise craft!

Fifty years ago, then, a Negro man and his wife, working as common field hands on the Low-Country plantations, could earn between them $5.50 a week, and would pay nothing for cabin or fuel, or garden patch. At the low cost of food and clothing, the family could live on less than half its income, saving, if it would, a hundred and fifty dollars a year —sufficient to have bought thirty to fifty acres of good land, which, properly tended, would support them comfortably for life. The savings of another year would have built a cabin and bought a horse or mule, adding to the earning capacity of the family and to its comfort. To those Negroes, therefore, who had the will to work and the will to save, the way was open to economic independence through the ownership of land, as it has never been open to the peasantry of any other country. Nowhere else could a farm, a home, and a horse have been

THE CAPTAIN

bought and paid for out of the savings of a peasant family for two years. It may be said his work was hard, and his food poor. Not so. None save the plowmen worked from "sun to sun," and these were rationed and better paid. Hoe hands worked almost entirely by the task, and as a day's task was usually finished in the early afternoon, the laborer could either add to his day's earnings by working longer hours, or put in the time on his own crops or gardens at home. As to his food, tho' coarse, it was abundant, and quite as varied as the fare of the Spanish, Italian, or Balkan peasantry, to say nothing of that of China and Japan. And it was what the Negro wanted.

And the Negro who came into land had a great advantage over the white landholder, in that he controlled his own labor, while the white planter, of large or small areas, was, in a measure, subject to the whims of a very unreliable work-people. Another great advantage possessed by the Negro landholder in the Low-Country lay in the proximity of the large plantations, where a certain amount of day-labor was in demand throughout the year. In other countries, and almost everywhere else in the United States, the small landholder must dig his livelihood out of his own soil, or perish, for he leans solely upon his land. The Low-Country Negro, on the other hand, could sell his labor to himself or to the plantations, as he chose. If cotton and rice were high, he could plant maximum crops on his own land, and work out only when these were laid

THE COLONY AT THE FLOOD

by. If prices for money crops were low, he need plant food-stuffs only, and work out for the greater part of the year. Even tho', through floods or drought, he lost his crop, wholly or in part, his day-labor could sustain him until the coming of another harvest; and always there was work on the plantations between seasons, when his own crop didn't need his labor. The landholding freedman, therefore, could accept with equanimity, all the hazards of agriculture, sure that, at the worst, he could not starve.

In such a strong economic position, it was not surprising that every acre of cheap land the whites were forced to sell was quickly taken up by Negroes. Of the many who bought, however, only a few had the industry and intelligence to utilize their advantages and establish themselves as substantial members of the community. Nor were many able even to hold on to the land, once the importance of ownership, the pride of possession, had worn off; and the weaker and more shiftless among them soon wearied of re-shingling roofs, repairing fences, and other obligations imposed upon property-holders, and their little holdings gradually reverted to the bush from which they had sometime been cleared.

Perhaps if the Pon-Pon community had remained entirely agricultural, and there had been change neither in the normal scale of wages nor in the normal standards of living, most of the Mitchell colonists, plain plantation people, content and happy

THE CAPTAIN

in their simple life, their wholesome food, and sensible clothing, might have held and improved their land and passed it on to their children, for certain progressive colonists quickly made good and set an example before their fellows, which many of them sought to emulate.

They were making decided progress when, a few years after the founding of the colony, its whole plan of life was disrupted by the discovery of phosphate rock on the Baring plantation on the Edisto river three miles away.

Students of economics, or at least gentlemen who write very glibly on the subject, assume that higher wages inevitably bring about higher standards of living, and, reciprocally, that higher standards of living demand and exact higher wages. And, of course, these higher standards are assumed to mean better, cleaner, and more comfortably furnished homes, better clothes and more of them, better and more wholesome food, more books, and better schooling for their children. Theoretically alluring, and economically sound, if it meant that, for industry could better bear the load of high wages if it brought about the permanent betterment of the laborer, and, through him, strengthened the community, and, too, if the stability of the higher wage could be assured through the ability of industry to stand it. But temporary inflations of wage scales, or those that affect only certain workers in a community, have a demoralizing effect, for, when the reaction comes and wages fall,

THE COLONY AT THE FLOOD

the spenders—who have acquired nothing lasting but expensive tastes—find economic readjustment difficult. Through the building of the World-War training camps, easy money came to thousands of Southern Negroes. Where one built a home or made a permanent investment, ten bought flivvers or indulged in riotous raiment. When it was all over, the waster had acquired tastes that to the end of his days could never be gratified, and a dollar would never look the same to him again.

During the World-War wage-inflation in the steel mills, Slovak workers at Gary, Indiana, bought twelve-dollar silk shirts by the dozen in Chicago, and put thousand-dollar pianos in the company's shacks in which they lived. They had the right to buy these things, of course, as the homeless Negro had a right to his Ford and his flashy clothes, but the theorist will find it hard to see higher standards of living in the expenditures of either wastrel Negro, or spendthrift Slovak!

The news of the discovery of phosphate at Baring's excited the Negroes tremendously. There was certain to be a heavy demand for the labor of the men at high prices, for the mouths of the Pon-Pon black people had long watered at the stories that had reached them, from time to time. of the rich earnings of those who worked at the "Pinckney" and other mines near Charleston. Now, this wealth was to be brought to their very doors, filling the pockets of the men and lightening the

THE CAPTAIN

labors of the women whose heaviest task would now be to lighten the pockets of their men, it being axiomatic among ladies of color that the wives and sweethearts of well-paid men should do no work.

Surveys were made of the Baring lands, and every acre was sounded with steel rods to determine the depth of the fossil-bed below the surface, and areas that soundings indicated could be mined profitably were staked out for exploitation. The Charleston & Savannah Railway was tapped, Pon-Pon station, with switches and sidetracks, established, and a spur-line run to the Edisto, half a mile away, where a great "washer" and a huge steam plant were erected for washing and drying the rock.

Industry began to hum. Trees were felled and the logs cut into cord-wood for firing the great boilers. Houses were built for foremen and the higher employes, and long rows of cabins for Negro laborers sprang up. From the first pits the diggers brought home huge heart-shaped teeth of monster sharks, bits of bone and fossil fragments of the vertebrae of strange amphibians, and the splintered knuckle-joints of fearful creatures that lived and died long eons, perhaps, after the dinosaur that laid her eggs in the Gobi Desert of Mongolia a million years ago, but whose antiquity was, nathless, sufficiently authenticated to establish them, with entire independence of Mr. Salley's genealogical charts, as among the very first families of the Great Coastal Plain!

And through it all, money, unwonted money,

THE COLONY AT THE FLOOD

began to flow into the pockets of the Negroes, and, almost as fast as it flowed in, it flowed out again. Few men have the resolution to hold easy money very firmly, and 'twas quite beyond the incontinent freedman of forty-five or fifty years ago.

"Bluejay died uh whoopin'-cough,
   Sparruh died uh colic,
Meet Bull-frog wid 'e fiddle on 'e back,
   Gwine down to de frolic.
Big-eye Buh Rabbit, who dey?
Big-eye Buh Rabbit, who dey?
Big-eye Buh Rabbit, who dey?
   Oh, Maria! po' gal!"

"Weh you gwine, gal!"
"Uh gwine weh Uh duh gwine, enty?"
"Don' sassy me, gal! Weh you gwine?"
"Uh gwine da' same place Uh binnuh gwine da' time w'en Uh bin meet you duh paat', en' Uh binnuh sing 'bout Maria, po' gal, en' you bin quizzit me, en' tell me ef Uh stop, you gwine mek de po' gal rich, en' w'en Uh bin stop en' quizzit you fuh see wuh you got een you han', you han' empty ez uh las' yeah bu'd-nes', nutt'n' dey dey, en' w'en Uh ax you wuh you got een you pocket, you bin brag 'bout how you got uh fifty cent een'um, en' w'en Uh tell you fuh pull'um out en' lemme look 'puntop de fifty cent, you nebbuh pull'um out, en' Uh nebbuh look 'puntop de fifty cent frum dat day, 'tel now, en' Uh bin tell you suh money wuh man hab' een 'e pocket ent wu't' 'cep' 'ooman hab'um een

THE CAPTAIN

'e han', en', fudduhmo', Uh bin tell you suh man' pocket hab bidness fuh strong mo'nuh 'ooman' pocket, so de 'ooman kin hab place fuh reach 'e han', w'en him pocket run low, en', ef de man, w'en 'e wu'k, cyan' mek mo'nuh de 'ooman, w'en *him* wu'k, de man' pocket nebbuh hab chance fuh fawti*fy*, en' Uh bin tell you suh ef man' pocket ent wu't', de man wuh de pocket blonx to, *him* ent wu't'."

"Iz you done? You gitt'ru?"

"No, Uh yent done! Wuffuh me haffuh stop? You ebbuh yeddy 'bout 'ooman haffuh gitt'ru talk? No, Uh yent gitt'ru. Uh jis' git fix good fuh talk, now! Uh bin staa't fuh tell you 'gen, wuh Uh bin tell you de las' time you bin quizzit me, suh ef man too stingy fuh pull out 'e money fuh treat de 'ooman, de 'ooman nebbuh count'um! 'E yent count'um nohow ef 'e yent got but fifty cent, 'cause uh fifty-cent Nigguh yent wu't'!"

"Who you call fifty-cent Nigguh? Me! Enty you know suh wu'k staa't to de Rock? Da' las' time me en' you bin talk Uh bin hab hoe een me han' duh knock grass fuh fifty cent uh day. Now, de hoe done t'row'way, en' all las' week Uh binnuh wu'k to de phoskit. All day Uh hab da' w'eelbar-ruh een me han', en' roll rock obuh dem long plank fuh load box-cyaar. De wu'k haa'd, fuh sowl, but w'en Sattyday ebenin' come, de Buckruh pit six dolluh een me han'. Shum yuh! Shum! 'E mek you grin, enty? You nebbuh fuh suck yo' teet' at me 'gen, no mo'! Come yuh, gal! Come yuh!

THE COLONY AT THE FLOOD

De dolluh Nigguh done come! De fifty-cent Nigguh done dead!" And into his grave, went with him, the hopes of the once promising Mitchell colony!

THE COLONY AT THE EBB

The Baring mines were opened before the days of steam-shovel phosphate mining. The overburden had to be removed by hand, and if more than three or four feet of earth lay above the precious strata of rock, its removal was unprofitable at the market prices of the day.

The Negro miner received a certain fixed price for the excavation of a pit, so many feet square and so many feet deep, or, rather, deep enough to remove the layer of rock that might be one to two feet thick. If the rock lay near the surface, the miner was in luck, for as soon as it was broken up and thrown out, his task was ended; but sometimes the "dip" of the fossil bed would force the digger into unprofitable depths, for he had to follow its dive to the maximum depth prescribed for his pit, however far it might take him.

The pits were all measured in advance and marked with stakes by the foreman. It was simple enough where the land was open, for single pits could be allotted to individual miners, but in wooded areas, where the trees had first to be cut and their stumps uprooted, the cost of removal was lumped in with the mining, and several contiguous pits would be awarded to one man. If the surface of his pit was smooth and free from stumps, the miner first dug away the overburden with his sharp spade, throwing the earth to one side in the empty pits from which the rock had already been removed. When

THE CAPTAIN

he reached the rock, it was broken with a pickaxe into lumps small enough to be thrown out with a shovel, and the miner pitched it out on the opposite side from where he had thrown the earth, whence it was hauled by tram to the "washer" at the edge of the river. When the miner was assigned pits in the forest, he added axe and mattock to his everyday tools of spade, shovel, and pick.

Among the workers at the Baring mines were many Negroes who, under slavery, had been expert ditchers, and these, of course, were the better workers and the larger wage-earners. When the rock was not too deep, a good hand could dig a pit in a short day, and earn a dollar and a quarter. If the luck ran with him, he might even dig two pits between sun and sun, but when he did, he was almost sure to lay off next day—the African, not unlike some of his Aryan brethren, even of the Nordic strain, feeling it necessary to apologize to himself for any extra exertion his spirit may impose upon his body!

While the men who dug were the best paid workers at the Baring mines, there were many other employes engaged upon miscellaneous tasks who earned higher wages than the plantations could afford to pay. So the nearer plantations lost not only their ditchers but their plowmen, who now drove the trams at the mines, and the common laborers, who loaded cars, or shoveled rock, and rolled wheelbarrows around the big washer.

THE COLONY AT THE EBB

Among the earliest of the Mitchell colonists to follow the lure of high wages at the Baring mines were the Chisholm brothers, Sam and John. Strong men, both of them, and expert in the use of spade and pick, they soon gained the distinction of being among the best workers and largest wage-earners at the mines. Even their slippery brother-in-law, Simon Jenkins, sometime "squerril"-hunter and weaver of spells, now became a digger of profitable pits. Tho' not very strong, he was wiry and would stick to piece-work well enough, tho' none was more successful in killing time while working by the day.

About this time the Captain, who had been absent from Oak Lawn for a year or two, returned to the old plantation to engage in stock-raising on a small scale. There was no barbed wire in those days—in the South, at least—so a thousand acres of the tract were enclosed in a tight rail fence, built after the most approved Low-Country fashion, "ten rails high, staked and ridered." In this pasture the plantation flocks and herds, such as they were, would, the Captain hoped, be safe from the black rievers who levied upon the cattle, sheep, and swine of all "de Buckruh." The Captain's pasture contained pinelands, thick swamps, and abandoned ricefields. These swamps and overgrown ricefields, swarming with raccoons, had long been the nocturnal hunting-grounds of the freedmen, whose smart coon-dogs were entirely competent to catch and hold any of the "Buckruh's" shoats that happened to cross a raccoon's trail. Such captures

THE CAPTAIN

were usually made with impunity in the more remote parts of the plantation, and even if the pig were caught near enough for his squeals to be heard at the settlement, his captors, under cover of darkness, could be half a mile away before the owner of the stolen pig could saddle a horse and reach the place whence the squeal had come.

When the pasture fence was completed, the Captain sent word far and wide that the area enclosed, over which the freedmen of the community had been wont to roam so freely, would be their happy hunting-ground no more; that those who trespassed would be dealt with severely, and depredating dogs would be shot.

While the Negroes had a very wholesome respect for the Captain, they knew that the kindliness of his heart restrained him from carrying his direst threats into execution, so his bark was generally held as somewhat worse than his bite. As with the poacher, the spice of danger to the cattle-riever added to the zest of the adventure, and, as the woods were wide and "de Buckruh" few and far between, they were always willing to take a chance. Their depredations were small, however, for their hunting-dogs, caught among the pigs or sheep, were promptly shot, which chilled their masters' ardor. Still, they sometimes climbed the fences in going 'cross-country, as their tracks in the muddy soil showed, and, as their disregard of his far-flung warnings irked the Captain, he resolved to have done with open diplomacy and re-

THE COLONY AT THE EBB

sort to secrecy and strategem. So he sent for Simon.

Simon came on Sunday. The Captain's urgent message reached him at the Cross-roads on Saturday night, and, having attended half the morning service at "Pa Lester's" church, he cut the rest and was soon shambling up the Oak Lawn avenue, turning his head furtively from side to side as tho' he were being shadowed. The Captain knew his "Nigger"—knew Simon in particular—so he kept him waiting, and, when he came out at last, smoking his long pipe and, with an air of great mystery, called Simon behind the biggest live-oak in the avenue, he puffed very slowly, very deliberately, before he spoke.

"Simon," he said, "I've sent for you because you're the biggest rascal on Pon-Pon, and because you know how to keep your mouth shut."

Simon grinned at the double compliment.

"Mas' Rafe, Uh got close-mout', fuh true. Anyt'ing wuh you tell me, me yez tek'um een, en' cya'um to me h'aa't; me h'aa't lock'um up, en' me mout' nebbuh know nutt'n' 'bout'um!"

"Very good. That's why I sent for you. Now, I have a very particular piece of work in hand, but it must be done very secretly, for if the secret ever gets out it will spoil everything."

Simon's eyes brightened, and with characteristic cunning he looked about him to see if he were being watched. This he would have done had he been in the midst of an open field at high noon dis-

THE CAPTAIN

cussing with his pastor a possible change in the weather, for Simon took no chances, and one could as easily have sneaked up behind a watching hawk on the top of a dead tree as have taken the "Squerril"-hunter unawares.

"Wuh 'e yiz, Mas' Rafe?" he asked in a stage whisper. "Wuh 'e yiz?"

"You know about the warning I sent out when the Oak Lawn pasture fence was finished, don't you?"

"Yaas, suh, Uh yeddy 'bout'um to de Cross-road en' de chu'ch, alltwo."

"What did you hear?"

"Uh yeddy suh you sen' out de news fuh say ef dog cross de fench, de dog haffuh dead, en' ef Nigguh cross'um, de Nigguh fuh hab acksi*dent*."

"Very good. You've heard about the dogs?"

"Uh yeddy suh de dog done dead."

"But you haven't heard anything about accidents to Niggers?"

"No, suh, Uh nebbuh yeddy nutt'n' 'bout no Nigguh."

"Now, Simon, you know the corners of the pasture fence, because you helped to build it."

"Yaas, suh, Uh know puhzac'ly weh de fo' cawnuh stan'. One dey to Jup'tuh Hill, one dey yonduh weh de Landin'-road jine de big-road, 'nodduh one dey spang to de Mitchell cawnuh mos' to de Cypruss, en' t'odduh one stan' nex' to de Beech place ez you gwine Adam' Run."

THE COLONY AT THE EBB

"Very good. This job I want you to do has to be kept very quiet. If the news gets out it will throw the fat in the fire and spoil my plan. So it will have to be done at night. You will need light to work by, but I'm afraid if you carry a torch in the woods at night somebody will catch up with you; but the moon will be high enough by the end of the week for you to dig the graves by moonlight, so—"

"*Grabe*, Mas' Rafe! *Grabe?*"

"Yes, I want one dug at each of the four corners of the pasture, just inside the fence, but they must be dug in the thick bushes, so the dirt you throw out of the graves can't be seen by anyone passing near."

"Yaas, suh," Simon gasped, but his face was as blank as if he had been turned into stone.

"And you must dig them six feet long, three feet wide, and six feet deep."

"Six-foot long, Mas' Rafe?"

"Yes. Isn't that long enough for any hog-thief in the neighborhood?"

"'E long 'nuf! Mas' Rafe, dem grabe fuh Nigguh?"

"Never mind whom they're for. They may be for cows, or hogs."

"Ef hog fuh bury een da' place, de hog mus'be bury een de Nigguh fus'! Six-foot long, t'ree-foot wide, en' six-foot deep!" And, as he mumbled over the gruesome specifications, Simon's eyeballs rolled!

THE CAPTAIN

"When you are through, I'll pay you two dollars for each grave. That's more than you get for a pit at the phosphate works, and you won't have any rock to throw out. I expect you to keep your mouth shut. If you ever say a word, you know what will happen to you! Now, when will you start?"

"Lemme see. Mas' Rafe, de moon fuh suit 'bout nex' Friday night. Uh staa't fuh dig'um den, sho' ez Gawd! En' ez fuh me mout'! nobody nebbuh yeddy 'bout dem grabe long ez Uh lib. Me jaw lock tight!" He pulled his wool, scraped his foot, and took his leave, but the Captain knew that, despite his promises and protestations, the graves would never be dug on Friday night, or any other night, and on that very evening, before the silver shallop of the young moon should drift down the West to the dark horizon, the pregnant hinges of Simon's jaws would release the Captain's lethal secret to a hundred friends and acquaintances, through whom, by the mysterious grapevine-telegraph, five hundred black people would know by midnight that four huge graves had been ordered dug at the four corners of the Oak Lawn pasture to offer decent sepulture to the mortal remains of the first four rievers that jumped the fence! Which was, of course, exactly what the Captain knew would happen, and precisely what he had planned.

"Ebenin', Joe."

"Ebenin', gal. You yeddy de news?"

THE COLONY AT THE EBB

"Obsco'se Uh yeddy'um. Uh yeddy'um two time. One de time, Minda bin tell me, en' Uh jis' yeddy'um 'gen fuh de two time frum Hacklus, da' boy wuh lib to Battlefiel', en' him ketch'um ez 'e bin gwine t'ru Nigguh-house-yaa'd to Blue House, jis' befo' sundown. Ebb'rybody know'um by dis time."

"Wuh you bin yeddy?"

"Uh yeddy suh Mas' Rafe bin sen' uh ansuh to de Cross-road las' night fuh tell Buh Simon fuh come fuh shum dis mawnin', sho', 'cause 'e got some berry 'pawtun' bidness fuh talk 'bout. W'en Buh Simon come, Mas' Rafe hide'um behin' one dem hebby oaktree, 'e so 'f'aid somebody gwine yeddy wuh 'e say. En' w'en Mas' Rafe look 'roun' behin'um en' see suh nobody 'cep' him en' Buh Simon dey dey, 'e tell Buh Simon 'sponsubble suh him haffuh dig fo' hebby grabe to de fo' cawnuh uh Mas' Rafe' pastuh, jis' eenside de fench, so w'en him ketch de Nigguh 'pun 'e hog, en' 'e shoot de Nigguh, him kin hab cunweenyunt place fuh pit de Nigguh bedout leff'um fuh buzzut fuh tell ebb'rybody weh 'e dey. En' 'e tell Buh Simon fuh mek ebb'ry one de grabe nine foot long en' t'irteen foot deep, so him fuh hab room fuh all de Nigguh wuh binnuh bodduh 'e cow en' hog en' t'ing!"

"Buh Simon prommus fuh dig'um, enty?"

"You *know* 'e prommus'um! Buh Simon ent name 'Okra' fuh nutt'n'! Him prommus'um fait'ful fuh dig'um Friday night, soon ez de moon stan' high 'nuf een de ele*ment* so him kin see fuh dig bedout mek no fiah!"

THE CAPTAIN

So the story went the rounds, and the Captain helped it along, for whenever he rode to the Crossroads on Saturday evenings and saw Simon, he would call the "Squerril"-hunter to his stirrup, and, with an air of mystery for the benefit of the hundred eyes that were watching him, would upbraid him for his broken promise. But Simon was full of specious excuses. Once, as he told it, he had just entered the edge of the woods at Jupiter Hill, when a Negro who had come up behind him, hailed him from the road, and he was forced to hide his spade and give up the adventure. On another night, at the far-away corner at the edge of the Cypress swamp, just as he dug his spade into the ground a "hant" or "sperrit" rose out of the bushes before him and, wraithlike, floated away in the silver-spangled, moon-lit forest! As he told the Captain his fairy tale, old Simon shuddered with the terror of his own story, for tho' he had not been within a mile of the Cypress for a month, he believed every word of it.

"Uh bin jis' jam me spade een de du't, Mas' Rafe, Uh pit me foot 'pun'um, en' Uh shub'um down to de eye. Befo' Uh kin hice me han' fuh t'row de du't obuh me shoulduh, please my Mastuh! da' sperrit rise out de bush right befo' me yeye, en' 'e wabe 'e han' berry slow, en' 'e float, float, een de moonlight, 'tel 'e gone, obuh de bush, en' up t'ru de tree 'tel 'e git to de top; en' soon ez 'e ride de tree top, Gawd reach 'E han' down en' ketch'um up en' gone! 'E stan' sukkuh 'ooman w'en 'e chile run out de house, 'e maamy ketch'um up en' cya'um back. En' Uh 'spec' da' sperrit git'way frum Gawd, en' come down fuh peruse 'roun' t'ru da' Cypruss swamp fuh see wuh Nigguh duh do."

"Well, there's one Nigger he didn't see do anything."

"Yaas, Mas' Rafe, 'e see me run! Attuh Uh shum, Uh nebbuh hab no appetite fuh wu'k me han', but Uh wu'k alltwo me foot! Uh nebbuh know how Uh git home. Uh yent 'membuh nutt'n'tall 'bout no road, needuhso no paat'. Uh nebbuh see none. Uh nebbuh bodduh 'bout none. Uh nebbuh had no nyuse fuh none, 'cause, Mas' Rafe, Uh tell you de trute, frum de time da' t'ing float obuh de tree-top, en' Gawd ketch'um up een 'E han', me sperrit nebbuh study 'bout nutt'n', 'cause me sperrit *dead*. 'E jis' lef' me body en' tu'n'um obuh to me foot! En' me foot cya' me t'ru dem bush same lukkuh da' t'ing float obuhr'um. Uh nebbuh tell me foot *nutt'n'*. Uh jis' yeddy'um duh beat du't, en' de win' wuh Uh mek sing een me yez ez Uh gwine! Fus' t'ing Uh know, Uh dey een me house! En', ef dem grabe haffuh dig, Mas' Rafe, 'e haffuh dig een de day, 'cause da' place too dainjus duh nighttime!"

How much the Negroes believed of the Captain's fell purpose the Captain never knew, but it is certain that the sinister suggestiveness of the order given old Simon had a wholesome effect in holding the Oak Lawn pasture inviolate; for its

THE CAPTAIN

sanctity was not invaded for more than a year, and if at night a Negro's coon-dog, hunting on his own account, crossed the fence and "treed" within the danger zone, his master's voice, from without, would send a poignant recall thro' the darkness: "Yuh, Ring! Yuh, Ring! Yuh! Yuh!" And many a Negro traveling the King's Highway for many a year thereafter would cut his eye furtively at the Landing-road and Jupiter Hill corners of the Oak Lawn fence and wonder just where the graves would have been dug, had Simon dug them; so well did the old "Squerril"-hunter guard the Captain's secret!

The opening of the Baring phosphate mines three miles away spurred the hitherto easy-going merchants at the Cross-roads into unwonted activity. Knowing that if the Negroes continued to live simply they could never spend half their increased earnings for food and clothing, these merchants, as forward-looking men—to make sure that none of the Negroes' earnings could be invested in betterments—forthwith began to lay in stocks of tempting trifles that they hoped would lure the last never-very-reluctant dollar from the pocket of the poor freedman. And, as they depended largely upon the hand of woman to pull out that dollar, the canny merchants set about the capture of the feminine hand and the feminine heart!

Thereafter the old maumas, the plain black folk, who went to the Cross-roads to buy ginghams or checked homespun or unbleached drills, had to

THE COLONY AT THE EBB

wait their turn, and their turn came last, for the plain and serviceable stuffs that at one time everybody wore, were now on the top shelves, or in out-of-the-way places, among the half-forgotten things of the past, while the counter and the nearer shelves were piled with bolts of flimsy fabrics, bright prints, and gauzy muslins that seemed hardly able to bear the strong colors they carried.

Through their manual labor in the fields, the arms of the plantation women of fifty years ago were rounded and well-developed, and, when untrammeled by sleeves, shone like black marble in the sun, but, spurred to emulation of the city fashions, shrewdly hinted at by the country shopkeepers, the fine arms were soon disfigured on Sundays by the sleeves of thin and gaudy waists, whose vivid reds and blues and greens contrasted horribly with the black skin beneath; a chromatic combination that never failed to arouse the elder women to wrathful expression. "Eh, eh! Wuh dis t'ing? Lookuh da' sleebe da' gal got 'puntop 'e aa'm! 'E stan' sukkuh blacksnake bin git ketch een spiduh' web! Da' phoskit *done* fuh tu'n dese nyung she-Nigguh fool!"

"You talk trute, tittuh. En' de she-Nigguh tu'n all de man fool, wid'um! De man wu'k haa'd to de rock fuh dig dem pit, en' roll dem w'eelbarruh, en' de man come home Sattyday wid de money een 'e han', en' befo' de po' creetuh hab time fuh seddown fuh ease 'e w'ary bone, dem nyung she-Nigguh mek'um drap da' money sukkuh eagle mek fish-hawk drap 'e fish down on de Salt! W'en

THE CAPTAIN

de eagle tek'way de fish frum fish-hawk, him kin nyam de fish, but weh de money dem gal mek de man fuh drap? Weh 'e yiz? De po'-buckruh to de sto' gott'um, enty? Wuh de man got? Nutt'n'! En' de 'ooman! Wuh him got? 'E mek me shame fuh shum!"

Yet other shelves in the Cross-roads shops bloomed forth in flowered and feathered hats like hollyhocks in a summer garden! Poppies, peonies, and other flashy flowers, crudely imitated in cloth and paper, flaunted their riotous colors atop straw hats of many shapes and shades. Other straws that showed how the winds of African fancy blew were trimmed with the feathers of barnyard fowls, dyed in orange and red and purple! Not even Aesop's jackdaw sported gayer borrowed feathers than presently sprouted upon a hundred poor, foolish, topsy-turvy heads!

The broad and common sense brogans of the past were left for the level-headed and the old. Youth would have none of them, for Youth strode forth, or, rather, limped along with Youth's ten toes "cabined, cribbed, confined" within two narrow, toothpick-pointed boots, with high laced tops and gaudy red linings of split sheepskin! And red stockings—very red stockings—began to appear, and, concomitantly, garters! Garters at the Cross-roads! But worse than that! Far worse than that! For the shopkeepers, having set "the glass of fashion," now essayed to take liberties with "the mould of form," and every last member of the

THE COLONY AT THE EBB

dusky smart-set burgeoned forth in a lumpy, bumpy bustle! Horrible things of straw, or cotton, or woven wire, oft set awry, and as evil to look at as a laden ship that, having shifted her cargo, lists heavily to starboard or port!

So much, sartorially, the Cross-roads shopkeepers did to the hard-worked men of the Baring mines, or, rather, so much they did to their women, for the poor, plucked men had little left for self-adornment. Now and then, however, some young buck, holding his feminine affiliations lightly, would spend his earnings on himself, and buy store-clothes, as well as fancy hats and shoes.

In the seventies and early eighties two extreme styles of trousers reached Charleston and Savannah, and some time later crawled or wormed their way into the hinterlands. Men laugh at woman's extremes in dress, but nothing funnier was ever seen than these, and the women who once saw them must be laughing still! The trousers known as "peg-top"—made popular by the elder Sothern, who wore them in the character of "Lord Dundreary"—were as full as bloomers above the ankle, but there they were pinched in to the narrowness of the shoe-top. These peg-tops, exposing the entire shoe, of course exaggerated tremendously the size of the masculine foot, and, by a queer quirk of fashion, the shoes worn contemporaneously were extremely long, with hard, sharp-pointed toes, so when the Baring buck—"proud man"—set forth, before high Heaven to make the angels weep, if he

THE CAPTAIN

wore number elevens or twelves, as was the custom of the country, his feet protruded from the bottoms of his "peg-tops" like the heads of twin 5-foot alligators running a neck and neck race! At another period, the buck would follow the fashion into a pair of the "spring-bottom" trousers, an even more reprehensible extreme. These, skin-tight about the seat and thighs, began to swell at the knee, and kept on swelling, until, by the time the ankle was reached, they yawned like the bell-mouthed muzzle of a Puritan blunderbuss! As the mouths of the spring-bottoms swallowed up even the alligator-head feet of the buck who wore them, the offense of the fashion was somewhat mitigated. Bad as both types of "britchiz" were, however, the sartorial sins of the men were sporadic. Those of the women the Cross-roads community had with them alway.

"Oh! Satan you needn't fuh to wink attuh me!
Oh! Satan you needn't fuh to wink attuh me!
Oh! Satan you needn't fuh to wink attuh me!
Fuh Juhruz'lum iz my home!"

"Satan duh wink at you, enty? Uh t'aw't so, 'cause de debble got good eye." And the old woman, without taking her clay pipe out of her mouth, appraised contemptuously a girl who sailed by, with diaphanous sleeves, flowered hat, sharp-toed shoes, a red parasol, and a huge bustle, piled—Pelion upon Ossa—where no bustle in the world need ever have been!

THE COLONY AT THE EBB

"Great Gawd! Lookuh da' she-Nigguh! 'E yent sattify wid de meat wuh de Mastuh g'em, en' 'e haffuh pile da' t'ing 'puntop'um! Satan ent duh wink at you, tittuh! Him duh cock 'e yeye!"

THE TIDE RUN LOW

As the tide of easier money rose higher at the Baring mines and the Cross-roads, the fortunes of the little Mitchell colony ran low. The nice adjustment of agricultural communities to mining and manufacturing industries that spring up suddenly nearby is always difficult, even among enlightened peoples, for the mines and factories draw the more efficient workers from the farms, and those who remain upon the land often struggle along, trying, with decreased man-power, to raise low-priced staple crops, instead of growing fruits, vegetables, and other products that could be sold profitably to the well-paid industrial workers at their doors.

As an economic problem so difficult of solution by intelligent whites could not be satisfactorily worked out by the untutored black people of the plantations, it is not surprising that the sudden wealth brought to Pon-Pon by the phosphate industry changed in a day the whole plan of life at Mitchell's. When the able men went away to dig or roll rock at the mines, leaving behind them only women and children and old men, if these feebler hands had had the wit and the will, they might have raised pigs, and grown the coarser vegetables that are always in demand among the Negroes, and thus brought to their households some of the ready money of the miners; they could at least have grown their own food and sustained themselves, leaving the earnings of the head of the

THE CAPTAIN

family for clothing, shoes, and luxuries. This they could have done, had the wife of the miner's bosom been minded to "keep the home fires burning."

But when Adam shouldered pick and spade and shovel and went away to delve, did Eve spin? She did not! "No, suh! W'en my juntlemun mek dolluh en' uh quawtuh uh day, *me* yent haffuh wu'k. W'en de man binnuh wu'k fuh fifty cent uh day, befo' de phoskit come, de 'ooman haffuh hol' hoe fuh he'p'um out; dem alltwo haffuh wu'k, but now, attuh de man' han' stan' so rich ebb'ry Sattyday night, de 'ooman' hoe haffuh lean'up een de cawnuh, enty? Berrywell."

And, with the putting away of her hoe, the woman put away many of her old habits of economy and thrift. She still made her own clothes and her children's, but they were of thinner, less durable material. Still a good cook, as most Low-Country Negro women were fifty years ago, she cooked less at home, for the shopkeepers at the Cross-roads had lured the poor Negroes away from their simple food, with sardines, salmon, lobster, and all sorts of, then, abominable canned things. And oysters! With the oyster banks of Toogoodoo only six or seven miles away! And even in spring and summer, when the thickets were full of blackberries, huckleberries, and plums, the poor creatures frittered away their money on canned peaches! The downward path was easy. For the Negro's wife—formerly a fellow worker, a helpmate indeed—was now become a parasite, a very daughter of the horse-

THE KING'S HIGHWAY—THE "BIG ROAD"—LOOKING TOWARD "JUPITER HILL"

leech whose insistent "give! give!" kept her man constantly at work. Even tho' he never stopped, save for sickness, his unremitting labor brought in little more than the combined efforts of his wife and himself, when they had worked together in the fields, while it cost far more to maintain an idle woman, than one who worked, Satan still finding extravagance, as well as mischief, for the hands of the unemployed!

The disintegration of the Mitchell colony was gradual, of course, and the picture here drawn is a composite in which there are more shadows than lights, because, at last, the shadows swallowed up the lights. There were exceptions, too, for a few of the workers at the mines were wise enough to save, and strong enough to restrain their women, and these put some of their surplus earnings into betterments, and held, more nearly than their fellows, to the simplicity of their former lives. A few others, older men, resisted the call of the mines and remained on the land to dig a living out of it as best they could, but the good example of the conservative handful had little effect in checking the downward course of the spenders, for, in this narrow community as in wider circles of life, at times of restlessness and change, counsel that walks hand in hand with reason and restraint is out-footed by the Jezebel that jumps with fashion and the senses!

On a summer's evening at the Cross-roads, just where the Willtown road intersects the old King's

THE CAPTAIN

highway, half a dozen little black boys and girls, holding hands, had formed a ring while they slowly danced or shuffled around one of their number 'prisoned within. The members of the circle, in chorus, chanted the questions, one by one, and the shrill voice of the prisoner piped the answers.

"Who lick my chile?"

"Aaffy."

"Wuh you lick'um fuh?"

" 'E sassy."

"Who 'e sassy to?"

" 'E maamy."

The game was rudely interrupted by the sudden coming of a quick-stepping old black woman, at whose approach one of the girls, mumbling a frightened "grumma!" disengaged herself from the sportive ring and with lowered eyes awaited the scolding she knew was coming.

"Enty Uh tell you 'sponsubble fuh gone to de sto' en' tell you ma—da' 'ooman wuh you pa hab fuh wife—fuh come home quick ez 'e kin, en' fetch de med'sin Uh bin tell'um fuh fetch, 'cause you pa berry sick? En' 'stead'uh you tek de ansuh to de 'ooman lukkuh Uh tell you, Uh fin' you out yuh een de big-road duh play 'Who lick my chile? Aaffy!' Ef chile haffuh lick, de somebody wuh lick-'um ent haffuh name Aaffy! Wuh you got fuh say? Weh you ma?"

"Ma dey een de sto', muh. Uh tell'um de metsidge jis' lukkuh you sen'um, but him binnuh trade, en' 'e yent wan' nobody fuh bodduhr'um, so 'e

THE TIDE RUN LOW

tell me fuh run'way en' play 'tel him ready fuh gone home."

The old woman, accepting the child's statement, hurried into the big store, where she found her laggard daughter-in-law, the center of a group of men and young married women that presented as many triangles as a prism!

The obliging shopkeeper, in recognition of their liberal patronage, had surrendered for their use a section of the counter at the far end of the store, and here, with a watchful eye open for light fingers, he had allowed them to spread sardines, canned peaches, and crackers, upon which they feasted, while chattering as irresponsibly as a bunch of smart-set New Yorkers at a "protected" cabaret!

Into the "vicious circle" the old woman burst suddenly, and the fires of her wrath, long banked to keep them warm, now flared up furiously. "Come on home!" she shouted to her now frightened daughter-in-law. "Git you med'sin en' come on home! You lef' my po' son to 'e house sick 'tel 'e mos' dead, en' you en' all dese t'odduh 'ooman come yuh fuh mix'up wid dese debble'ub'uh no-'count he-Nigguh! Wunnuh ebb'ry drat one hab husbun', en' you ent sattify wid him, wunnuh haffuh hab conkywine too, enty? W'en man so ska'ce luk 'e yiz, one 'ooman fuh hab *two* man fuh feed'um, en' buy frock fuh pit 'pun 'e back, en' bodduh wid'um en' pledjuhr'um, enty? De po' husbun' wuh you got," she cried, turning to the other women, "dey dey to de phoskit bog'up to dem crotch een da' mud

THE CAPTAIN

en' blue clay, duh dig da' haa'd rock frum Monday mawnin' 'tel Sattyday night, en' haffuh nyam col' bittle w'en middleday come, en' hab chance fuh ketch de consumpshus en' de remonia, en' wuh dem got? Nutt'n'! Dem wu'k so haa'd fuh feed 'ooman wuh yent wu't'! En' dese conkywine wuh you 'ooman hab fuh sweeth'aa't!" with a wide sweep of her arm toward the men, "ef dem ent stop ramify 'roun' de neighbuhhood, razor fuh ride dem t'roat, sho' ez Gawd! 'Cause ef wunnuh husbun' tie een de pit all t'ru de week, him fuh yeddy 'bout de sweeth'aa't w'en 'e come home Sunday, enty? En' him fuh hab time, den, fuh shaa'p 'e razor, too!"

Stopping a moment for breath, the old woman's eye lit upon the heavy gold-washed brass earrings that hung from the ears of the errant wives before her, and, with the scorpion lash of her tongue, she scourged them again!

"Befo' de phoskit come to Pon-Pon all uh we black people binnuh git 'long berrywell. De man en' de 'ooman alltwo haffuh wu'k, en' ebb'rybody sattify, 'cause nobody got no time fuh idlin'. Wunnuh all git 'nuf fuh eat, en' de 'ooman hab frock, en' de man hab britchiz, en' alltwo got shoe. You nebbuh bin need nutt'n' mo'. You bin een Gawd' han', but you nebbuh hab sense 'nuf fuh know'um, 'cause de debble pull da' skin obuh you eye, sukkuh skin grow obuh rattlesnake' eye een Augus' munt', en' you nebbuh see Gawd' han'. Now, de debble got you, enty? Ebbuh sence dis rock come yuh, ebb'rybody tu'n fool! Wunnuh tu'n staa't

THE TIDE RUN LOW

fool! De man iz fool, 'cause dem wu'k so haa'd fuh de fool 'ooman; en' de 'ooman iz fool, 'cause dem t'row'way de man' money, en' pit t'ing 'puntop dem back en' t'ing, wuh mek'um look lukkuh de debble en' mongkey alltwo one time! Lookuh dem t'ing you got een you yez! Enty Uh tell you de debble got you? Dem ring duh him maa'k, en' him maa'k you yez sukkuh Buckruh cut swalluh-fawk en' popluh-leaf en' t'ing een cow yez fuh maa'k'um! Now, de debble pit you een him maa'k, en' tek you out'uh Gawd' pastuh weh you binnuh feed so peaceubble, en' you nebbuh fuh feed out'uh Gawd' han' no mo'! Tek you out? No, 'e nebbuh tek you out! 'E jis' t'row de rider off de stake, en' p'int to de gyap, en' wunnuh ebb'ry drat one jump da' fench wuh Gawd pit 'roun' Him pastuh, en' come out befo' de debble kin quile 'e tail! But 'e gott'um quile now, enty? Yaas, 'e yiz! 'E quile tight 'roun' all wunnuh nyung she-Nigguh, en' you conkywine, alltwo! Come on, 'ooman! Come 'long to you husbun'!"

"The least governed are the best governed" was wisely said a century ago; but, in respect to money that comes suddenly and easily into hands unaccustomed to its use, every thoughtful or observant man and woman must wish, every day, that some strong hand of restraint could be laid upon the expenditures of the wasters—for the wasters' good! And it is interesting to speculate upon what the economic effect of the Baring mines would have been on the Pon-Pon community could the stores within reach of the mines have been controlled by the mining company, and if stocks had been carried only of such staple commodities as the Negroes really needed—accustomed things, with which they were quite content until the Cross-roads shopkeepers, tempting them with fripperies, drew them away from plain living and the simple life. Without the temptations at their doors, some strong white man in whom they believed, perhaps one of their own race, might have induced them to put their surplus into betterments or to put by something for a rainy day; might even have led them toward higher standards of living!

But it was not to be. As in many another economic scheme, it worked out for the benefit of the few, to the ruin or the disadvantage of the many. The cupidity of the shopkeepers urged them to tempt the poor Negroes with things they didn't need and couldn't afford. Thro' their weakness, the women fell, and, falling, carried their men down with them. Now and then a man of rugged type would try to restrain the women of his household, and buck the tide of profligacy, upon whose current his compatriots rode so blithely; but fashion, like conscience, "doth make cowards of us all," and weaklings as well, so his protest was brief, for his women made his life miserable, and he was soon another chip, like his fellows, all going the same way.

And the wastefulness of the spendthrift Negroes enriched not only the shopkeepers, but the mine-owners as well, for the urge of their extravagances

THE TIDE RUN LOW

kept the workers at high pressure, and enabled the mine-operators, with abundant labor, to work at full capacity.

So much for the few. On the other hand, the plantations in the community suffered grievously through utter demoralization of their labor, but the greatest sufferers—the hopeless sufferers—were the poor Negroes, the highly paid wage-earners, who, according to the reasoning of gentlemen who discuss economic questions, should have been permanently uplifted; for, while the planters lost only the profits they might have made, the Negroes lost, presently, the simple plan of life they were accustomed to, under which they were making slow progress, and in time they lost far more, for the spirit of unrest was among them and would never be laid. While the women were the greater sinners in the moral decadence that had come upon them, the men were not without fault, for gambling was almost universal among the younger men, and bloodletting with knife and razor became common.

Nor were their moral and material losses all, for the hard work of the miners, often in the rain, almost always in damp pits, bore heavily upon the men, some of whom died quickly of pneumonia, others slowly of consumption, while the efficiency of many workers was seriously impaired by rheumatism. And the less wholesome food impaired the general vitality of men and women.

THE CAPTAIN

The birthrate declined. There was less time for children, and those that heaven wished upon them, "unbeknownst," were given less attention, as is the way in somewhat higher social circles, wherein, when life is so full, social duties press heavily upon population! So, infant mortality increased.

The Mitchell colony suffered more than any of the Pon-Pon plantations, for here the men lived in their own homes, were subject to no contracts, and were free to go as they pleased, and all who were strong enough elected to go, and by their going every household was weakened and gradually loosened from the land, which eventually fell from them, for the stronger men—those better fitted to hold on and establish themselves permanently —were, through their strength and their will to work, among the first to wreck themselves physically and pass from the scene of their labors, leaving wastrel widows to mate with weaker men, under whose ownership the cabins, in which their predecessors had such pride, soon tumbled down, and the land that had been loved and labored for was sold for taxes or to satisfy importunate creditors. And so it was with all of them, for at the end of a generation hardly an acre of the Mitchell land was held by the descendants of the hopeful colonists of 1874!

On a cold spring day, the Captain cantered down the long Oak Lawn avenue and entered the King's highway on his way to Willtown. He had been

THE TIDE RUN LOW

burning brush and briar-thickets in the morning, and, although the fires had now been beaten out, the wholesome smell of wood smoke was still in the air, while broad-winged "old-field" hawks hovered about, watching expectantly for such woodrats or rabbits as, forced by the fire to move house, might hazard a run across the open ground to seek new quarters.

Three hundred yards beyond the avenue, the Captain drew upon his left rein and turned into the Landing-road, but paused for a moment at the corner to look over his shoulder, across the antebellum orchard, at the beautiful avenue whose every tree he loved. Sturdy oaks and stalwart, these, under whose spreading boughs five generations of the Captain's people had found shelter from the sun; tough trees that, hacked and bruised by the vandal axes of 1865, were too hard for the wreak of the spiteful hands that sought to lay them low. Across these scars, which time had healed, the pitying ivy crept, and hid the wounds that man had wrought upon God's own handiwork!

The "orchard-field" had been plowed. The heavy land lay in long ridges, the furrows, thrown shoulder to shoulder, resting one upon another, awaiting the harrow that, in time, would crush the clods and crumble them into a friable seed-bed for the corn to be presently planted.

Brown field sparrows, uttering their plaintive little notes, drifted over the plowed land like flocks of wind-blown leaves, alighting for a moment,

THE CAPTAIN

hesitantly, then, as if caught up by a sudden gust, swirling on again; always drifting, drifting, as blackbirds drift over ricefield stubble.

The first of March. The month had blown in blusteringly. Storm-clouds, with flying manes, charged down the wind, as at a trumpet-blast—wild troops of pallid horsemen. And, as the leading squadrons plunged over the horizon's rim, and were swallowed up in the infinite, troop after troop rushed out of the west and followed fast, their boreal hoof-beats drumming! And from the moss-draped boughs of the avenue, a hundred far-flung pennons lay level in the wind. Gray troopers above, gray pennons below. . . . The old Confederate rode on.

Half a mile farther along the Landing-road the Captain turned into the pineland, and rode a few hundred yards across the ridge to look in on old Cassius, whom he liked and respected as one of the vanishing types of the old days. The cabin, built eight or nine years earlier and still in good repair, justified its builder's pride of craftsmanship, while fences and yard reflected the care of a painstaking and competent hand. The Captain's hail brought no response. The cabin door was closed, but the wisp of smoke that crept out of the clay chimney told that some one was within. Hitching his horse to the fence, the Captain passed through the gate and looked up for a moment at the three fine post-oaks that stood like sentinels at the old man's well.

In the March wind the last dead leaves of the

THE TIDE RUN LOW

fall rattled petulantly, as though loath to leave the trees upon which they had long since budded and blown in all their summer bravery, and turned, under the frosty fingers of autumn, into a glory of red and gold! Here on these limbs they had died, and clung in their russet robes all winter, chanting, like monks, their mournful songs of death and dissolution. Now, with the rising sap, each tender twig swelled with the promise of the resurrection, and buds of green and white tipped every twig and tendril, serving notice on the dead leaves that the dawn of a new day was at hand, and their time had come to go. So, one by one, they whirled complainingly to the earth, and, quiet at last, rested upon the bosom of the mother that gave them birth. So the old must pass, to make room for the young, that the promise of summer and winter, and seed-time and harvest may be fulfilled!

Lifting the latch of the cabin door, the Captain entered. The windows were shut, and the darkness was broken only by a handful of coals that glowed dully on the hearth. A sudden gust of wind, sweeping down the short chimney, fanned them for a moment almost into flame, and by the fitful light that crept into the shadows the Captain made out dimly the outlines of a bed, over which was spread a patch-work quilt, whose garish colors added a poignant touch to the tragedy before him. Above the quilt that reached up almost to her chin, lay the thin black face of an old woman, long dead, her eyes wide open, staring with the tragic intentness

THE CAPTAIN

of death! Her hands—poor gnarled and twisted hands—lay before her upon the quilt, whose putting together, bit by bit, had been a labor of love during the slow and heavy years. Brave, helpful hands that, shirking neither the enforced service of Slavery, nor the harder, self-imposed tasks of Freedom, were now pathetically still!

In a low rocking chair at the side of the bed, just at the chimney corner, sat old Cassius, crouched over the embers which he was trying to keep alive to warm the poor stark figure on the bed, while, as he thought, she slept.

Cassius looked up, as the Captain came near in the half-light and rested a kindly hand upon his shoulder, but his mind was wandering, and in the tall figure he saw his old master, now long dead.

"Mas' Edwu'd!—You come?—T'engk-g a w d! Maussuh?—*My* Maussuh!—Uh know you woulduh come w'en you ole saa'bunt pray Gawd fuh sen' you, 'cause Uh bring up een you han', Maussuh; en' me en' you blonx to one'nurruh, 'tel Gawd tek we een *Him* han', enty, Maussuh?—Yaas, suh, Uh know you woulduh say dat.—En' Phibby, Maussuh, Phibby will glad fuh see you, too, 'cause you ent bin to ole Cassius' house sence Uh mek'um, long time ago. Uh mek'um jis' like you l'aa'n me fuh mek'um een de ole time. Maussuh, no rain nebbuh fall 'pun Phibby een dis house! Ef you ax'um, him will tell you so, too.—Soon ez 'e wake.—Him duh sleep now, Maussuh. Shum dey, 'pun de bed! Phibby bin sleep long time. Seem ez ef him neb-

THE TIDE RUN LOW

buh fuh wake up 'gen, no mo'! But Uh bin yuh befo' de chimbley duh mek fiah all de time, so w'en Phibby wake, de house gwine be wawm fuhr'um. 'Cause 'e bin sick, Maussuh. De po' 'ooman bin so sick! En' Uh yent got no med'sin fuh g'em, nuh nutt'n'. None de black people bin 'bout me. Nobody come fuh see me. Uh nebbuh hab chance fuh sen' wu'd to de w'ite people. Uh yent bin strong 'nuf fuh go meself, Maussuh, 'cause Uh bin sick, too; but Uh yent bodduh 'bout dat, 'cause Phibby bin so sick, so sick. Ef ole Missis bin yuh, him woulduh fetch de po' 'ooman some tea frum de big house. Him woulduh fetch'um een 'e own han'. But ole Missis gone now. Ole Missis binnuh sleep een Gawd' han' long time—long time."

The effort of speech was too much for the poor, spent body, weakened by starvation, and, with closed eyes, old Cassius fell back in the chair. The Captain touched his pulse, and knew that but a raveled strand remained of the frayed cord that held him to life.

A flickering smile passed over the worn and wrinkled face. The eyelids slowly lifted. "Mas' Edwu'd!—Maussuh!—You 'membuh—de weddin', enty—Maussuh?—'Cause you—bin—dey. En' Missis, too. De—weddin', ent bin to de—big-house—'cause me en'—Phibby—nebbuh bin—house-saa'-bunt, fuh hab weddin' to—de big-house—we jis' bin po' fiel'-Nigguh—but Maussuh come—en' Missis—come. En' Missis sen'—Phibby—shishuh pooty frock.—'E bin w'ite—w'ite—lukkuh—shroud.—

THE CAPTAIN

En' Missis—fetch—de cake—een—'e own—han'—en'—"

The moments passed. Without, the wind-harps in the tops of a thousand pines droned a solemn requiem for those who die in love and faith, and, on the old post-oaks, the dead leaves shivered eerily. Within, as, one by one, the embers died, the shadows deepened, and bed and chair, with their dead and dying, were swallowed by the dark. Among the ashes on the hearth, a single ruby sparkled for an instant, and was gone!

Out of the darkness a whisper came.

"Mas' Edwu'd! — My — Maussuh! — P h i b b y! Phib—"

And old Phoebe's waiting was over!

Tiptoeing to the cabin door, the Captain closed it softly behind him. As he mounted his horse and rode away to summon the women of the neighborhood to their kindly offices for the dead, two brown leaves, torn from a single bough, fluttered down to earth, and lay side by side, at rest.

HUNTRESS AND THE BUCK

About four years after the close of the Confederate War, while the Captain was planting Sea-island cotton at Oak Lawn, he acquired a young hound to which, in view of her promise, he gave the hopeful name of Huntress. She came through adolescence to maturity in the Captain's hands, and the Captain trained her carefully. She was whelped "somewhere up-the-country," as the Pon-Pon people call upper Colleton, Orangeburg, and Barnwell, and was of alien stock to the Coast. Short-legged, thickset, powerful, with broad, rather short ears, and thick "feather-tail," she approximated in conformation the modern English type of fox-hound, but her color was her own—a solid, yellowish tan—a hazardous distinction, for on more than one occasion, while trailing silently through thick bushes, she was mistaken for a sneaking doe and narrowly missed a load of buckshot from a watchful "stander" nearby. And she resembled the modern English hound in character as well as in build, for she had great courage, great speed, and the "chopped-tongue"—the short yelp of the English dog.

For a long time Huntress was the Captain's only hunting dog. His nearest neighbor, Tom King, at the "Encampment" or "Blue House" plantation, as it was sometimes called, maintained a small tho' splendid pack, and to these, and the hounds of other neighbors, Huntress would be added whenever the

THE CAPTAIN

Captain joined a hunting party. As he often hunted alone, however, the tawny hound had been trained to meet the requirements of a solitary hunter, whose only chance was a "snap-shot" from horseback, as the deer "jumped," or sprang from his bed.

Huntress, silent on the trail, seldom gave tongue until the quarry was up and away, and the Captain had trained her to hunt cautiously, keeping only a few yards in advance of his horse as he slowly skirted the bays that intersected the pinelands, myrtle thickets at the edge of the old-fields, or other sheltered coverts where deer might lie. And, as the trail grew warm, the suppressed excitement of the hound and her quicker movements warned her master that the deer's bed—the spot where he had lain down when he came in at dawn from his night feeding—was not far away. There was always the chance that a deer, often hunted, would become apprehensive and, upon hearing horn or hound in the distance, would rise from his bed and "sneak" out of the drive, and this the hunter could never know until the bed was reached. But if Huntress raised her head, lifted her ears, and jumped up and down, like a rabbit-hunting bird-dog in a broom-grass field, the Captain knew the deer had not sneaked, but was still in his bed and almost within gunshot. If the covert were very near, he cocked both barrels of his Westly-Richards, steadied his horse and awaited the jump; but if time allowed he would ride ahead, skirting the thicket and hoping for a flank shot.

HUNTRESS AND THE BUCK

While the spoils of this sort of hunting were rather uncertain, the sport was always exciting, and by no other method could the solitary hunter, either on horseback or afoot, hope for success.

Sometimes, exploring a small drive whose outlets were controlled by only two or three passes or "stands," if Huntress developed a promising trail the Captain, leaving the hound to work it out for herself, would ride ahead, take up the best stand, conceal his horse, and await whatever the fortune of the forest had in store for him. If the deer jumped, the stander's chances were presently good for a shot. If the deer ran out by another pass, or had sneaked before the dog came to his bed, Huntress would come out of the drive on full cry, and the Captain would blow her off the trail, or ride her down and stop her.

Well suited as Huntress was for the Captain's solitary hunting adventures, and perfectly disciplined while under control of her master alone, she had two faults that made her sometimes an unacceptable member of a community hunting pack. To begin with, she often had the impudence to outrun Tom King's dogs—a venial offense in the eyes of all save Tom King. But a really serious fault which caused her to be left at home on many hunting days, was her habit of running silently ahead of a slowly trailing pack, to jump the deer prematurely before the passes had been taken up. A strange failing for a dog that hunted so cautiously when alone.

THE CAPTAIN

Old deer hunters know that deer are mortally afraid of a "silent" dog—one that gives tongue sparingly. During a certain hunting season, about ten years after the time of Huntress, all the deer were run out of the drives on and immediately around the Oak Lawn plantation, by the coming into the neighborhood of an undisciplined pointer, a powerful, splendid-looking brute. Tho' highly bred and properly trained in early life, he went back on both heredity and environment, scorned all feathered things, and insisted upon hunting deer! The slot of a deer meant no more to him than the "Mecklenburg Myth" means to Alex Salley—he couldn't have followed it ten feet—but if a hound opened on a trail anywhere within a mile and a half the Berserker pointer would join the hound, or the pack, in an incredibly short time. If the trail was cold, and the movement of the pack slow, he would keep in the vicinity, quartering the ground as desperately as if his life depended upon the number of intricate geometrical figures he could describe in the pineland.

And as the pack moved on the pointer kept along with them, apparently taking little interest in the game they were playing. Presently, as the trail grew warmer, he kept closer to the pack and, at last, when their lilting cry told him they were within, perhaps, a quarter of a mile of the "jump," he would rush ahead like the wind, flush the astonished deer out of his bed, and put him thro' the woods at top speed, running, a silent Nemesis, at

HUNTRESS AND THE BUCK

his heels. And as long as he could keep the deer in sight he kept running, his ears flapping wildly.

A few flights before this liver-and-white phantom of the woods were all a deer needed to force him to sanctuary many miles away, and until the pointer was sent out of the neighborhood the deer did not return to the Oak Lawn drives.

But, however unfitted for team work, the Captain would not have swapped Huntress for any pack in the Parish, and an exciting incident in one of his hunts kept her in grateful remembrance throughout his life.

On a sharp morning in November the Captain set out to try his luck on a solitary deer hunt. "Bill Arp," the beautiful stallion he bestrode, was one of those accomplished hunting horses of the Low-Country that always seemed more at ease among the hazards of the woods than in the open road.

As the Captain, leaving the open fields at "Cotton Hill," turned into the thick growth of "the Stackyard," his mount became more alert, his gait springier, and his restless ears were pricked to catch the sound of rustling bush or snapping twig telling of wild-life astir in the forest.

Frost had bitten and splashed with blood the foliage of gum and sourwood and, in spots in the open woods, in thick clumps along the margins of the backwaters, the fires of autumn burned redly, while on every knoll the spendthrift hickories scattered their golden leafage to the winds.

THE CAPTAIN

Skirting an ante-bellum canal, now dry and overgrown with briar-thickets and scrub, Huntress, trotting a few yards in advance of the horse, gave a savage yelp, and dashed into the canal with the hair bristling on her back, and the Captain knew he was in for a wild-cat hunt, for Huntress hated the bay-lynx intensely, and once on a hot trail 'twould be a waste of wind to try to blow her off.

While most fox-hounds follow indiscriminately the trails of deer, fox, and cat, and sometimes trail turkeys, to boot, certain Low-Country packs were trained to follow deer only and, under the discipline of frequent whippings, would raise their noses as scornfully while crossing the trails of cat or fox as if they had been rabbit tracks. Even among these cultured packs, however, there were one or two individuals, who, however loyal to pack-standards while hunting with the pack, would slip off upon occasion to pursue a private vendetta against the bob-tailed terror of the swamps.

Huntress, her master's only hunting dog, was hampered by no pack-standards and, tho' she never noticed foxes, she followed cats with savage energy, encouraged by her practical master who knew that however destructive to wild life—the fawns and turkeys of the woods—the depredations of the bay-lynx upon plantation farmyard and Negro hen-roost entailed a far greater economic loss, especially upon the Negroes, whose cabins were often at the edge of woods or swamps within whose fastnesses the four-footed spoilers lurked in perfect security,

HUNTRESS AND THE BUCK

for the Negro dogs were never able to cope with them.

But, for the present adventure, however beneficent its purpose, the Captain had little enthusiasm. He was intent upon venison, and for an hour he listened impatiently as Huntress followed the trail of the cat as he twisted and doubled through the thorny thickets of the old backwater, pursuer and pursued often passing and repassing within a few feet of each other, but separated by a wall of impenetrable briars. Whenever they came near together the hound's cry became an angry scream of disappointment that the hated quarry was so near and yet so far.

Meantime, the Captain, weary of the saddle, dismounted, hitched his horse, filled his pipe, and seated himself at the foot of a whiteoak commanding a full view of the path by which the wild creatures of the forest and the half-wild cattle and swine that roamed the woods with them crossed the overgrown canal in passing between the old backwater and the higher levels. By this path Huntress had followed the trail of the cat into the chaparral. By this path the cat would emerge whenever he thought the repeated doublings upon the back track had so perplexed his pursuer that the quarry could slip away to make confusing tracks in another thorny fastness. So these cunning creatures habitually throw off the hounds, doubling and twisting and worming their way along rabbit-paths through briars that, mak-

THE CAPTAIN

ing little impression upon their tough hides, would have torn a hound's skin into ribbons. If fallen trees lie among or near the briars the hound is more easily outwitted, for the cat, by running up and down the log a few times, leaping off as far as possible, first to one side and then to the other, and repeating the maneuver at intervals, can often so tangle his pursuers as to gain half an hour or more for a run to another retreat.

And the Captain knew that when the cat in the chaparral had woven his warp and woof of cross-trails into a pattern intricate enough to suit him, he would sneak out and make a dash for the high land, to re-enter the backwater, perhaps, at a point half a mile away. He knew, too, that the cat would almost certainly make his dash when Huntress, following the twisting trail, was at the farther edge of the chaparral; so, when the hound's halting cry told that she was puzzling over the trail at the other side of the backwater, the Captain knocked out his pipe, rose to his feet, and stood at attention in front of the whiteoak.

He hadn't long to wait. A slight rustling among the dead leaves in the old canal, the thump, thump of feet as of a rabbit slowly jumping, and a spotted thing topped the canal bank and leaped into the forest but forty yards away! One leap was all he took, for the gun was at the Captain's shoulder at the first warning from the dead leaves, and half the 16 low-mould buckshot met the moving target as it crossed the sights. At the boom

HUNTRESS AND THE BUCK

of the Westly-Richards—a full-throated report known throughout the hunting community—it rolled over, too dead to kick. A young cat, beautifully marked, its teeth and claws were yet formidable enough to have torn Huntress cruelly had she come to close quarters, and the Captain thanked the stars that watch over the fortunes of the chase as he tied the dappled killer behind his saddle.

At the sound of the gun Huntress went silent for a moment, and then gave tongue again, but in a half-hearted way as if expecting a recall. When it came, she was not slow to respond, and five minutes after the first blast of the horn she came out of the wilderness, and trotted up with mingled feelings of anger and delight, as expressed by hair and tail, as she saw the hated cat trussed up on Bill Arp's back.

Two hours of the precious winter's morning had slipped away, but they had not been wasted, the Captain thought, for cats were not killed every day, and he who put one away did something for the community, while he who killed a deer served only himself. Still, the Captain was out for venison, so, mounting his horse, he resumed his ride through the woods to the Cypress.

Traversing "Eight-acre," the Captain rode through the larger field beyond and entered the plantation road at the edge of the swamp. Crossing the bridges that spanned the "Cypress run," a sluggish tributary of Penny Creek, he passed into the farther "Cypress-field," a wide opening

THE CAPTAIN

lying between the "Elliott Big Drive" on the right and the thick coverts of the "Little Drive" on the left. Between these two drives the Captain hesitated. He leaned toward the left, for the myrtle thickets of the Little Drive almost certainly harbored deer, and its limited area made its exploration far easier for a single hunter than the wide spaces of the Big Drive; but, just as he drew upon his left rein to turn into the broomgrass, he came to a blind path crossing the road at right angles. Huntress, a few yards in advance, put her nose to earth and wagged her feather-tail with interest, and the Captain saw the slot of a large buck which had passed from the Little to the Big Drive, probably during the late hours of the preceding night, for the track was fresh. As a close examination showed no track going the other way, the buck had almost certainly made his bed among the canes and cattails of the Big Drive, for it was very unlikely that he would have re-entered the Little Drive by any other than the regular deer path.

The Captain quickly decided to follow the track, and he whistled Huntress on. The hound trailed slowly and, as always on a cold trail, silently, and the horse easily kept up at a running walk. Half a mile farther on they neared the first thick places in the drive where the deer might have found shelter, and the Captain rode nearer and watched the hound with keener interest, but her indifference puzzled him. If the buck had lain down in the covert just ahead he could hardly be a hundred yards away, and she should have been tense with excitement, yet she trailed as listlessly as tho' the quarry was at the other side of the parish.

In a moment the puzzle was solved, for the trail skirted the thicket, instead of leading directly into it, and passed to the higher ground on the left. Seeking a more luxurious bed farther on, the Captain thought, and one by one all the coverts of the Big Drive were passed by hunter and hound upon a trail that always skirted, never entered, them. At last they were through and, crossing the road leading from Adams Run village to Willtown, came into the high pineland stretching away toward Elliott's Wells to the right and Moss Hill to the left. "What the devil could the fellow be up to?" the Captain thought, and then the answer came; for, as the trail swerved sharply toward the left, an open spot in the pineland showed two sets of tracks, both going the same way, and going fast, as their widespread hoof-prints showed. The delicate slot of the young doe was but half the size of the big buck's, and the Captain knew that the burly Lothario, instead of going to bed like a Christian—giving Christians a chance to turn him into venison and say grace over him—had, under the magic of the November moon, been roaming the woods as ardently as the antlered Sir John Falstaff under the spreading oaks of Windsor Forest! And doubtless more successfully, for a mile beyond the start of the double trail the Captain found a broken twig from the low hanging bough of a

THE CAPTAIN

scrub oak across the way! And here the whitetails parted.

Huntress stuck to the trail of the now solitary buck, without a hint from the Captain, and the trail led toward Elliott's Wells, where he had doubtless taken shelter for the day. Approaching the swamp, the Captain noticed a sparse growth of cattails and broomgrass between the pineland and the thicket—an ideal place for deer to lie, if 'twere only to the south of the woods instead of the north, for an old buck loves a southern exposure on winter mornings, and a windbreak at his back. The Captain knew a thicker growth of cattails lay at the other side of the thick woods where, basking in the sun, he thought the big buck would be found.

But the old fellow, in a hurry to get to bed, had done the unexpected thing, for, when Huntress, a hundred yards from the nearest cover, suddenly threw up her head and gave tongue for the first time, there was a crash among the brittle reeds, and the great buck, carrying a splendid head of "basket" horns, broke cover and lumbered away, apparently in no particular hurry to bestir himself, with Huntress hot upon his trail.

Well out of gunshot, the Captain did not waste powder and, knowing the futility of pursuit, he determined upon a policy of masterly inactivity. The deer, following an almost invariable rule, made for the river; but the river was distant, the water was cold, and old bucks, master strategists—sometimes—oftenest when pursued by a single hound—

HUNTRESS AND THE BUCK

double upon their tracks or, making a long loop, run back along a parallel course and return to the cover from which they started. So the Captain waited and listened.

The day was still, and until the hound reached the Clifton place beyond the Willtown road, two miles away, her cry, though growing fainter and fainter, still came to the Captain's ears. At last it ceased. The minutes passed; five, ten, fifteen. Then came a raveled thread of sound from farther north. A moment, and it came again, stronger and more distinct. The buck had turned, the Captain knew, and, circling the Clifton gardens, was coming back through Marshall's Avenue to the Elliott Big Drive.

If he followed the usual run he would not pass within a quarter of a mile of the spot where the Captain waited; so putting spurs to his horse he dashed to intercept him at a stand he would have to pass. Concealing Bill Arp in a thicket behind him, the Captain had hardly taken position at the edge of a clump of dogwoods and young hickories, when the great buck burst into view a hundred yards away. He was running now. The hound was more than a mile behind him, but he had taken her measure and was showing her his heels to discourage the pursuit.

On he came in flying leaps, bounding over the bushes like a great rubber ball. Fifty, forty, thirty yards away! Then, for the first time, he saw the waiting stander and swerved suddenly to the right, but his turn only gave the Captain the flank shot

THE CAPTAIN

that he had hoped for, and he touched the hair-trigger of his left barrel, charged with extra heavy shot. At the crack of the gun the buck turned a somersault and lay still—as dead, apparently, as the 18th amendment in Philadelphia! But he wasn't. Laying down his gun, the Captain opened his clasp-knife and, seizing the buck's antlers with his left hand, stooped down to cut his throat, but, before he could use the knife, the buck rose suddenly to his feet, lunged forward, and knocked it out of his hand. Grasping the big horns with both hands, the Captain pressed the buck's head down as far as possible, to prevent him from striking with his fore feet, whose sharp hoofs could have cut like knives, but the plunging beast drove him back steadily, until, with his back against a clump of young dogwoods, he could be pushed no farther. And now the Captain thanked his stars for the "basket horns," with their incurving tines, for the big buck bore upon him with only their rounded outer surface. Had he carried open, spreading antlers the hunter would have been torn cruelly—perhaps killed.

The dogwood saplings, sprung from a single stump, grew close together, and a quick thought came to the Captain that, by putting them between the buck and himself, he could secure his own safety and hold the buck until the hound could come to his rescue. So, in a pause between lunges, he deftly released one hand from the antlers, slipped behind the saplings, reached through their slim trunks,

HUNTRESS AND THE BUCK

took hold again, and released the other hand to repeat the maneuver, holding the buck at last on the safe side of the clump with his skull pressed against its central sapling, while the Captain held the antlers firmly on each side. The buck who had been pressing forward so vigorously, now tried as ardently to go the other way; but 'twas useless, for whenever he pulled back, a twist of the curving antlers locked his horns against him, and the Captain held him fast.

But he was not idle. Infuriated by the bay of the hound, coming nearer and nearer, the buck struck savagely again and again, for his head, being now held higher allowed his feet more freedom. The intervening saplings saved the Captain, but the exciting tussle had exhausted his strength, and he was about to collapse, when Huntress, a yellow streak, dashed into the thicket and flew at the buck's throat. In time, she could, doubtless, have killed him, but the Captain, feeling both pity and respect for a brave antagonist, ran to his gun, and with a shot behind the shoulder ended his troubles. Then utterly worn out, he stretched himself on the ground to rest.

Fifteen minutes later he arose refreshed, and set about getting the heavy buck behind his horse —no easy task. Dragging the deer to a stout sapling, he bent down the top and tied it to the buck's horns. Then, bringing Bill Arp near—the sapling lifting half the load—he swung the deer behind his army saddle and made him fast, with the heavy

THE CAPTAIN

buckskin thongs that always hung at his cantle. An examination of the buck showed that the Captain had shot too high the first time, and, while the two or three shot that struck were enough to roll him over they did not touch a vital spot; and if, when he came to his senses, he had chosen to run instead of fight, he could have gone clean away.

The Captain rode home at sunset, Bill Arp laden with the spoils of an exciting and successful day.

Fidelity to her master's interests cost Huntress her life a year or two later. A savage watch-dog, she had bitten two or three Negroes who had prowled too near the Captain's barns and stables, and, word having gone around that she was a menace to the light-fingered brotherhood of the community, she was marked for poisoning at the first convenient opportunity. The regular yard dogs that stayed at home were far safer than watchful hunting dogs, for these, often abroad, were sometimes tempted while passing through Negro settlements to swallow food sprinkled with powdered glass—the lethal agent commonly employed along the Black Border for removing the too watchful dogs of "de Buckruh," or the too watchful husbands of domestic triangles!

On a hot summer's day, Huntress, having run a buck across the Toogoodoo, was returning home, spent and famished, along the Adams Run road, when a thievish Negro by the way, threw before her a piece of meat filled with the deadly dust. She never reached home, but died in agony by the road-

HUNTRESS AND THE BUCK

side, just across the "Run" beyond the village, on the way to the railway station. Here, when the birds of the air were through with her poor body, her scattered bones lay for a long time, whitening in the sun among the purple deer-grass, the partridge-peas, and the orchis of the pinelands, remembered still by those who value loyalty, fidelity, and courage, in dogs—or men!

THE RIVER AND THE SEA

A spring bubbling slowly up from among the roots of an old long-leaf pine, a tiny trickle of water feeling its way feebly down the little hollows in the sandy slopes, overcoming one by one the obstacles by the way—a dead leaf, a broken stick, a pebble in the path. First, swelling as though angered, the little rill mounts to the top of each pygmy barrier, tumbles petulantly over, and the murmur of an elfin waterfall mingles with the song of the wind among the pines.

Like little children learning to walk—stumbling, falling, up and going again—a thousand crystal threads creep down the rolling sand-hills of Lexington and, merging their waters into rill and rivulet, behold at last the branch, the creek, the river! Traversing the lower pine-belt through the stately forests and fertile fields of Orangeburg and Barnwell, the waters of the Edisto, still sweet tho' stained by the roots of millions of swamp trees, stoop to the coastal plain and flow majestically to the sea, laving on their way the banks of many once splendid rice plantations—dividing, beyond Willtown, into the North and the South Edisto, one branch turning toward Charleston, the other toward Savannah.

The North fork, taking the name of Dawhoo, washes the shores of Edisto Island on the south and the mainland plantations on the north, receiving along the way the waters of many muddy

THE CAPTAIN

tidal creeks and, like some of those whom God hath made in His image, losing in grace what is gained in volume!

Augmented at White Point by the inflow of Wadmalaw River and Toogoodoo, the strong tides of North Edisto Inlet sweep into the Atlantic, between Kiawah Island on the north, and Edisto Island on the south, as they reach the heaving bosom of the deep.

Kiawah (Keewaw) stretches toward Charleston long miles of smooth sandy beaches; at the back uprear the rounded ramparts of the dunes, their shifting sands held together by the tough roots of the sea-oats, whose graceful stalks bow to the winds with many whisperings of seed panicles.

Behind the dunes lie marshy flats, bisected by a bold tho' shallow creek, swelled to a lagoon at flood tide, and on the high ground beyond a dense chaparral of stunted liveoak and cassina scrub, thickly interspersed with young palmettoes, affords sanctuary to raccoon, deer, and lynx.

Forty or fifty years ago the planters along Pon-Pon and the Toogoodoo section of lower Colleton, now Charleston County, discovered the attractions of Kiawah Island as a camping and fishing ground, and thither for several successive seasons went parties during the summer or fall months, marooning in tents or palmetto thatched huts for ten days or a fortnight at a time, wearing little save their sunburned skins, and roughing it in the bracing sea air—fishing off-shore, or tramping along

THE RIVER AND THE SEA

the smooth beaches all day and sleeping, without dreams, in the strong seabreeze at night. Here they stored up strength and energy against the strain of the heavy atmosphere of their inland homes.

These parties, composed of six or eight congenial spirits, were usually organized a week or two in advance, and the days of preparation were full of interest, for boats had to be arranged for, a port of embarkation decided upon, servants engaged, and supplies and equipment assembled.

Campers who came to Kiawah fared well at all seasons for, save at periods of storm, there was seldom lack of fish or shrimp or crabs; but those who came in the early autumn months grew in girth, if not in grace, for then the shrimp had grown to the size of prawn, splendid channel bass were biting in the rollers on the outer beach, there were oysters in the lagoon, summer-ducks flew low at sunset, and the palmetto-cabbage, beloved of epicures, was ready for cutting in the chaparral! So much for material things. For others, the flames of the camp-fires flared more brilliantly in the frosty air, the breakers sobbed more poignantly at the passing of summer, and the sea-oats on the sand-dunes exchanged shivery confidences all through the night.

But autumn or summer, there was always life, always interest. Sea and sky and shining strand, the far horizons of distant forests, the vari-colored foliage of the nearer hummocks, the gray-green of the marshes, sandpipers running, and ghost-

THE CAPTAIN

crabs drifting along the beach. Low-flying gulls and loons and skimmers. Lofty eagles, moving in slow, wide circles, watching their handmaidens, the busy ospreys, below. Porpoises tumbling and romping outside the rollers, or driving the mullet up the creek; the slanting fin of a cruising shark. Far out at sea the trailing smoke of a coastwise steamer, the white sails of a bark beating to the southward. And always sea and sky—the infinite—fresh from the hand of God, unmarred by man! Sea and sky, in all their moods; of storm and calm, of smiles and tears, of peace and passion; the flying cloud-wrack of the tempest, the golden argosies that slowly float along the sunset skies. Sea and sky inseparable, and, as the sky, the sea, for the fair or frowning face of one was ever mirrored in the other!

On a July day a merry party assembled at a landing along the lower reaches of Toogoodoo Creek, here attaining almost the dignity of a river. Among those present were Dr. Osborn Barnwell from the village, Arthur Grimball and Roland Alston of the Oaks plantation, Wm. Henry Heyward, Jr., a rice planter of the neighborhood, and the Captain and a couple of young nephews from Oak Lawn. Of these but one or two survive, but forty-five years ago the names of Barnwell, Heyward, Grimball, Alston, and Elliott were household words throughout the Pon-Pon country.

For several days plans had been going forward, for the trip was to last a fortnight, and many details had to be arranged. The salt-water men,

THE RIVER AND THE SEA

those living on or near the coast, undertook to find suitable boats and competent boat-hands. Dr. Barnwell and the Captain, both epicures, collaborated in organizing the commissariat and selecting an expert cook. Axes and carpenter's tools, with liberal supplies of cordage, were provided, for it was planned to build a large Robinson Crusoe hut for sleeping quarters and a mess-tent, both to be thatched with palmetto leaves. A wall tent and a large canvas fly were also provided for emergencies.

Among the Negro personnel of the outfit the Captain included Henry, long an institution at Oak Lawn, where he had found sanctuary several years earlier.

One day there came to the Captain's nephew, then the youthful Railway Agent and telegrapher at Grahamville, an earnest Negro preacher who brought with him a wretched creature, pathetic in his rags and dirt. Henry, the Samaritan said, was an orphan, left at the coming of Freedom to the tender mercies of an uncle in whom there was no tenderness. Starved and maimed, he was the drudge of his uncle's family, so cruelly beaten at times that an arm and a leg had been broken, and allowed to heal as nature ordered, imposing upon the boy an awkward, shambling gait. Knots and scars upon his wasted body further attested the severity of the discipline under which the poor little slave had been driven to his daily tasks. Although about 14 years old he had been stunted to a twelve-year size. Dark tan in color, dirt and bruises had darkened him by several shades, and his plight would have softened harder hearts than those of Negro preacher or white youth. On one of his pastoral visits to the coast, fifteen or twenty miles below the railroad, the pitying preacher had found Henry and, having helped him to run away, now appealed to the railway man to send the boy away and protect him. So Henry, seeing a train for the first time, was sent fifty miles down the Railway to Oak Lawn, where he lived happily for many years, until, having reached manhood, he was lured away by the railroad hands to work on a section.

Henry responded marvelously to kindliness, good food, and soap and water. In a few months he had gained a normal year's growth and his sleek round face shone with happiness. He was a constant source of amusement to the family as well as a constant aggravation for, while at times almost half-witted in his ignorance, none could tell how much of his apparent simplicity was affectation, as a quizzical, raccoon-like expression sometimes crept over his laughing face, suggesting that he might be "playing" "de Buckruh."

Passionately fond of animals, Henry learned in time to drive up the cows and milk them, and to feed and rub down, even to saddle and bridle, the horses, but the art of harnessing these was only learned after many months of patient lessons at the Captain's hands, the learner's imagination meanwhile stimulated by many impatient and forceful objurgations from the Captain's lips. "Henry, you

THE RIVER AND THE SEA

imp of Satan, haven't I told you that the crupper goes under the horse's tail, not under his chin, and that the buggy saddle goes on his back, and not under his belly?"

"Yaas, suh, Mas' Rafe, suh!"

"Well, then. What did I tell you?"

"You tell me, suh, de crupper go onduh de hawss' belly, suh, Mas' Rafe, suh!"

"Henry!!!!!!!!"

"Yaas, suh, Mas' Rafe, suh."

Henry was a long time learning the colors by which horses are commonly known but, once acquired, he applied this equine nomenclature also to members of his own race, and he would sometimes report with much unction: "Mas' Rafe, suh, uh strange Nigguh bin yuh to see you dis mawnin', Mas' Rafe, suh."

"What did he look like, Henry?"

"Well, suh, Mas' Rafe, suh, he wuz uh sawt'uh bay Nigguh, suh."

"Red-bay, or pumpkin-bay?"

"Sawt'uh punkin-bay, suh, Mas' Rafe, suh"— and the visitor was identified.

But Henry never seemed sure of the chromatic scheme of his avuncular relative and sometime cruel task-master. Perhaps he thought it sacrilege to compare the lustrous coats of his beloved horses to the hide of an Okatee darky, and when asked his kinsman's color he was always hesitant.

"What color was your uncle, Henry?"

THE CAPTAIN

"Well, suh, Mas' Rafe, suh, he wuz uh sawt'uh bay, brown, black, ches'not kind'uh Nigguh, suh, Mas' Rafe, suh;" and further, Henry would not commit himself.

At last the voyageurs were all assembled. Because of the ever-present eleventh-hour men, the noon hour fixed for departure had long passed and the sun was well in the west before men and luggage were all at the landing. The laggards had lost them half the precious ebb-tide upon whose bosom even light winds would have borne them to the edge of the ocean before sunset, but now there was no hope of that, unless a strong and favoring wind should rise and the lost hours and the lost tide could not be recalled. Still, dark as would be the early hours of the night—for the moon would not rise until after midnight—the adventurers determined to sail, hoping to pass the shell-banks and cross-tides of White Point before nightfall.

The favorite boat along these sheltered waters was of the sharpie type—flat-bottomed, tho' shapely, the sides single planks 16 to 18 inches wide, bent to a long and graceful bow, and so drawn in that the width of the bottom was considerably less than that between the gunwales. The fineness of their lines and the centre-boards with which they were fitted combined to give these skiffs admirable sailing qualities, and it was surprising how close-hauled they could run. One with knowledge of the vagrant breezes that blow over the partially land-locked waters and familiar with the tides that meet and

THE RIVER AND THE SEA

mingle in the estuary of the North Edisto can flatten the sprit-sails and run "into the wind" marvelously well.

The sharpie in almost universal use was 16 feet long and 4 feet wide, fitted with a single mast, but the larger craft—20 to 28 feet long—were invariably schooner-rigged, carrying sprit-sails, and, sometimes, with a great deal of pride, a jib!

The present craft, 28 feet long and 6½ feet beam, was just from the hands of an expert Negro boat-builder, trained under slavery when plantation artisans, never hurried, used their masters' time lavishly and took pride in their work. Her cypress planks were copper-fastened, her cleats and oarlocks were of brass, her masts were scraped, and her sails were clean and white. Against her bright green hull the gray waters of Toogoodoo lapped petulantly, as though admonishing the loiterers that while tides "taken at the flood lead on to fortune," only tides taken at the ebb, lead down the estuary of the North Edisto! Still they loitered, for if not "many men" there were at least "many minds" and, lacking the wise guidance of woman, these masculine minds clashed as to the stowing of the cargo and the trim of the boat, and not until another three-quarters of an hour had passed did the graceful craft, loaded to her Plimsoll line, cast off and slip slowly down stream, her sails flapping falteringly in the errant breeze.

To the usual stores taken on a fishing party to supplement the spoils of their lines, the campers

THE CAPTAIN

had added a five gallon demijohn of old North Carolina corn whiskey and a hundred grains of quinine. Both were regarded as indispensable, for miasma lurked in the pestilential thickets beyond the creek at Kiawah, and within their fastnesses lay another creeping death, for here the dreaded "diamond-back" rattlesnake made his lair. Although "rattlers" had never been known to traverse the marsh, swim the creek, and sound their castanets along the outer beaches, such things were possible, and, as in those days of faith the good Dr. Evans had not robbed us of our belief in whiskey as a sovereign remedy for snakebite, every well-conditioned Southern gentleman who fared forth through summer swamp or forest learned to lean upon the generous flask that snuggled within his breast-pocket as "a very present help in time of trouble."

Sidney Lanier's beautiful "Marshes of Glynn" has been enshrined in thousands of Southern hearts for more than two generations, and the name Lanier has sung to their spirits with poignant sweetness. But the gentle Georgia poet was not the only Lanier whose name brought sweet memories and spiritual exaltation to South Carolinians, for, away off at Salisbury, Jim Lanier—"old man Lanier," as he was known affectionately to the multitudes that pledged him daily—made the best corn whiskey in a State which, until Lanier brought it distinction, was commonly regarded by Virginians and South Carolinians as an unpeeled foot-log lying between them, a something to be walked or "cooned" by those who

THE RIVER AND THE SEA

would cross from one to another of the two scornful aristocracies!

But Lanier's spirit changed all that, and as Lanier filled the jugs and the demijohns of Toogoodoo and of Wadmalaw, so he wrote their songs, and their songs were of Lanier, and for his sake they forgave the old North State her glorious climate, her purple mountains, the music of her falling waters. And only the mellowing influence of the yellow elixir could have warmed the South Carolina heart toward a commonwealth that lay cheek by jowl alongside East-Tennessee!

The five-gallon demijohn, securely boxed to withstand the bumping of the boat, was safely stowed at the bow where, under the watchful eyes of the entire party, its virtue might be held inviolate.

Under the impulse of the tide alone—"too full for sound or foam"—the sharpie moved steadily toward the distant bar, but as the sun slanted downward the breeze fell to a whisper, then died away. The useless sails were furled, four long oars were put out, one pair manned by the Negro boatmen, the others by two voyageurs, and the speed of the drifting boat was doubled. But the start was too late. The sun set, and night fell quickly, for with the dusk a heavy fog crept up that hid the stars and wrapped the marshes in a shadowy mantle whose murkiness was impenetrable, even to the eyes of the Negroes, who knew every dangerous oyster-shell bank and every eddy

THE CAPTAIN

at a point that a confluence of opposing tides made difficult to pass by day and hazardous by night.

The hours passed. The ebb-tide wasted away, and, having spent its life, was no more. The flood, coming into its own, sighed softly once then, almost imperceptibly, moved on. Those aboard the sharpie, shrouded in the fog, could not distinguish marsh from water, and believed they had now passed the dangers of White Point and were well down the open roadstead. Midnight passed. A gibbous moon crept from the Wadmalaw marshes and slowly climbed the sky, glowing weirdly through the fog, whose chill as dawn approached made even the lazy members of the party volunteer for a turn at the oars. The boat seemed to pull more heavily, but whether from the opposing flood or the prolonged labors of the oarsmen none could tell. The tide swept by unceasingly, but the tide was all they saw, for the ghostly, luminous mist shrouded marsh and land from the puzzled voyageurs, who by now should be nearing the mouth of the estuary. But the sharpie still swam on even keel. No heave of deep Atlantic swell, no crash of ocean surges on the sands, brought promise that they neared their journey's end. The silence of the fog was broken only by the soft lapping of the tide against the sharpie's bows as it hurried on its way.

At last the laggard morning came, and with the dawn a sudden breeze sprang up that swept away the fog, and in the pallid light, but a stone's throw away, lay the gray-green marsh of White Point,

THE RIVER AND THE SEA

upon whose dangerous shell-bank they had lain all night! Running full upon the bank at half-tide, the lowered centerboard had jammed tight and held fast, even against the later lift of the full tide. Here, trapped and immobile, they had strained through the long hours of darkness, buckling down manfully to pull upon futile oars that, at each stroke wedged them tighter and tighter in the sucking sands! The grouchy ones—the "I told you so" men—had a great deal to say, and said it; but there were philosophers aboard and a sense of humor, also a great deal of excellent corn whiskey, so the hardships of the night were soon forgotten.

The Captain took command. "Starn all!" he shouted. The oars were thrust through the shallow water at the bow, and jammed into the rotting shells. Willing backs bent to these pry-poles, and, heaving lustily, the centerboard was lifted and the boat swung clear. A few strokes of the long oars, and the point was rounded. The way lay fair to the open sea. The sharpie's spritted sails were spread. Close-hauled, she leaned to the fresh easterly breeze, "and southward aye we fled!" the little whitecaps dancing and water splashing over the lee rail. Henry, awaking from a troubled sleep, was just in time to receive the first splash full in the face. Wet, hungry, bedraggled, he was a pathetic picture of misery. "Henry," asked the Captain, "how did you sleep last night?"

"Mas' Rafe, suh," he replied. "Mas' Rafe, suh, Uh eenj'y uh berry oncomfuhtubble night' res', suh,

THE CAPTAIN

Mas' Rafe, suh!" And so did everybody else!

In two hours the sharpie had crossed the shifting bar of a bold creek leading into the tidal lagoon that divides the rolling sand dunes and the smooth outer beach from the palmetto thickets and the tangled chaparral of Kiawah. Driftwood fires were soon crackling, coffee and breakfast put into preparation, and the veterans spied out the land and selected a camp site.

Breakfast over, the Negro axemen took to the hummocks and cut quantities of palmetto thatch with which to cover the substantial framework of a shack left by campers of the previous year. Meanwhile, the Captain and Dr. Barnwell, the most expert fishermen of the outfit, had explored the lagoon in the skiff and, finding it teeming with shrimp, all doubts were allayed as to a supply of bait for hook and line fishing.

Before sunset the shack had been skilfully thatched, the evening's fires built and smudged with green marsh for the discomfiture of the sandflies and mosquitoes, and on the last of the ebb-tide the fishermen were hauling in whiting on the outer beach. Night fell. The campers drew closer to the smudged fires, with whose heavy smoke now mingled the fragrance of the smokers' pipes. From the sedgy marges of the lagoon the marshhens called the changing tide. Up aloft, a belated heron, hurrying homeward, croaked dismally. The ocean rollers drummed ceaselessly on the outer beach, and in the creek nearby the dancing stars were

THE RIVER AND THE SEA

mirrored in the slow-moving tide, now at the turn. But the figures around the fire were monosyllabic, or silent. The vigils of the night before, bore heavily upon the merriest among them. One by one, they stretched, and yawned, and slipped away to their blankets—awakening, with the morning light, to the incidents of another story.

THE TRENCHERMAN AND THE SHARK

Dr. Barnwell and the Captain, early risers all their days, aroused the camp cook at dawn as the morning star rode high and the barred-owls exchanged their last goodnights before turning in for their daylight slumbers—"taps" for the furred and feathered creatures of the night, but "reveille" for all who lived by day, for, in the far woods, away from the crowing herald of the farmyard, these last calls of the big owls often admonish campers that daylight is at hand.

To the south the smooth and silent sea, stretching away to the dim horizon, mirrored in the half-light the pallid moon and the swiftly fading stars that one by one, like lights burned low, faltered, and went out. As the light crept up and the stars went out, the glassy bosom of the deep took on the opal tints of dawn, and somber-gray was changed to pearl and mauve and green and blue. Then, as if blushing for her chameleon shift, a rosy seashell mist overspread the sea and warmed it into life. From the east long javelins of light shot up the sky and blazed the way for the triumphant sun, whose burning face in another moment topped the trees and looked upon his world of earth and sea and sky! And with the sun, the breeze sprang up and rumpled the waters with many laughing wrinkles. The tide was low. Just as it turned, and the pulses of the flood throbbed softly, the Doctor and the Captain threw their hand-lines

THE CAPTAIN

from the beach, and at once began to haul in whiting; a few casts of the net in the creek having provided the necessary shrimp-bait.

At the end of an hour, when the laggards roused themselves from their blankets, yawned and stretched, and called for coffee, the first of the catch were already in the pan, for the alert cook had gathered and prepared the fish almost as soon as they were thrown upon the beach. And as they were flipped from the pan into the tin plates the whilom laggards were waiting for them. No laggards now, for by the time the fishermen, answering the cook's hail, reported at the mess-tent for breakfast, there was little left of their finny spoils but the heads and tails the cook had saved to bait his crab nets! The Doctor's and the Captain's tongues were as sharp as the barbed points of their fish-hooks, and the Doctor and Captain, having the gift of expression, expressed themselves!

When they were through—as the most practical and experienced outdoor men in the outfit—they set about organizing the camp, allotting to each man the work he wished to do and could do best. The Negro servants were detailed to gather driftwood for camp-fires, marsh for smudge, and to "cast" with their nets for shrimp and mullet in the creek on "the last of the ebb and the first of the flood," of every tide between dawn and bedtime, and the Captain's boy Henry, now come to saltwater for the first time, was told to watch the baited crab-nets, set at the edge of the creek on

THE TRENCHERMAN AND THE SHARK

the young flood, and put his catch in a covered basket. And the Captain carefully coached the novice as to their handling so as to avoid the pinching claws.

"Now, Henry."

"Yaas, suh, Mas' Rafe, suh."

"You see this crab?"

"Uh shum, Mas' Rafe, suh."

"What is it?"

"Crab, Mas' Rafe, suh."

"Very well. Now, when you see a crab in your net, pull the net out of the water, turn it upside down, and shake the crab into the basket. If he holds on to the net with his claws, and won't shake out, then set the net on the sand, take this forked stick in your left hand, put the fork over the crab's back, and hold him down. Then, with the fingers of your right hand, catch the crab behind the claws, pull him loose from the net, and drop him in the basket. Now, do you understand?"

"Yaas, suh, Mas' Rafe, suh!"

"Well, then, what did I tell you?"

"You tell me fuh shake out de crab 'pun de san', Mas' Rafe, suh, en' tu'n'um upside down, suh."

"No, Henry! Turn the net upside down, and shake the crab into the basket."

"Oh, yaas, suh, Mas' Rafe, suh."

"Well, then, if the crab won't shake out, what do you do?"

"Tek de fawk stick een me han', suh, Mas' Rafe, suh."

THE CAPTAIN

"Which hand, your right or your left?"

"Me right han'—me lef' han', Mas' Rafe, suh."

"Your left hand. Now, when you take the stick in your left hand what do you do?"

"Jam de fawk down obuh de crab' neck, en' hol'um down, Mas' Rafe, suh."

"Crab's neck! The crab's back, Henry!"

"Yaas, suh, Mas' Rafe, suh. De crab' back, suh."

"Well, then, after you put the forked stick over his back and hold him down, what do you do then?"

"Grab'um behine 'e jaw, suh."

"Claws, Henry, not jaws!"

"Ketch'um behine 'e claw, Mas' Rafe, suh, en' t'row'um een de basket."

"Very well. You've got it right."

"Yaas, suh, Mas' Rafe, suh;" and the Captain left him, sure that before the rising tide had run its course Henry, inept as always, would prove by his own fingers that crabs really had the jaws he claimed for them—the deeply serrated claws of an old "rusty" bearing a rather close resemblance to the whitened skull of a small animal. And the Captain was right!

Another camping party, earlier in the summer, had left behind them in the creek an excellent 14-foot skiff, to which they had made the present campers welcome. An acceptable courtesy, for while the big sharpie could be used for fishing out in the channel or on the distant rocks a lighter and handier boat was needed for nearer off-shore work.

THE TRENCHERMAN AND THE SHARK

The skiff, anchored in the creek and chained, for greater security, to a drift-wood log on shore, was found in good condition save for a few leaks. To stop these, she was hauled out and turned over. The Doctor and the Captain had just begun to calk her seams when a wild yell came from the direction of the crab-nets, and Henry, poor wretch, was jumping an imaginary rope, in a violent St. Vitus's dance of agony, his left hand clasping his right by the wrist, while from its fingers dangled a huge rusty crab, both claws locked in a grip that would by no means be shaken loose.

When Henry had been extricated from the cruel pincers, he held his bruised fingers in the salt-water for relief, and told his story. By good luck he had contrived to shake all his crabs out of the net, one by one, without having recourse to the forked stick, for none of them had held very firmly to the woven cord, but when he netted the grandfather crab, he entangled a stubborn recalcitrant that clung to the restraining meshes as tenaciously as an Aberdeen Scot to a "saxpence!" Emboldened by his earlier successes, he shook the net until he saw that grandfather couldn't be loosened that way, when, seizing him by some of his hind legs, he pulled him off, but he must have tickled the crab in the wrong place for, before he could drop him into the basket, the creature twisted in his hands and clamped his claws upon his captor's fingers.

"Henry, didn't I tell you to grab him just behind his claws, so he couldn't twist them around and nab

THE CAPTAIN

you? Why did you catch him by his hind legs instead?"

"Mas' Rafe, suh, Uh t'aw't all dem foot bin claw, Mas' Rafe, suh. None dem claw nebbuh bodduh me, but da' t'ing reach 'roun' en' bite me wid 'e jaw, Mas' Rafe, suh, en' 'e jawbone full'up wid teet' sukkuh dog' skull, Mas' Rafe, suh, en' 'e bite me wid all dem teet', one time, Mas' Rafe, suh." And to the end of Henry's Kiawah days, crab claws were jaws —as Henry had good reason to know!

On the evening tide the Doctor, the Captain, and a boatman fished from the skiff, a few hundred yards off shore. Other fishermen, less energetic, threw their lines out from the beach, where whiting and other small fish usually bit freely. The campers who were too indolent to fish, afloat or ashore, slept or "rested" under the shade of the Palmetto-thatch, or lay on the open beach to "take the air." Then, when the evening shadows fell, the campers gathered around the fire after supper and talked and smoked.

There were no cigarettes in the Low-Country in those days, and men's lungs—and women's too— were strong and clean. Nor were there any cigars that a white man would smoke, unless Bacchus walked hand in hand with "my lady Nicotine!" Sometimes on Saturday nights a very tipsy Negro would light one of the horrible "twofers" of the country stores, stick it up in the corner of his mouth at a Joe-Cannon angle, and strut truculently

THE TRENCHERMAN AND THE SHARK

around the Cross-roads, inviting personal violence. Frequently the invitation was accepted!

But the campers on Kiawah, if they smoked at all, smoked pipes of clay, or cob, or briar-root; the clays fitted with long stems of cane-root or ti-ti. But these were for fireside smokers—men at rest. Those who smoked while on the move, carried cobs, with straight cane stems; short briars, with amber mouthpieces; or big-bowled briars, with long cherry stems. Now and then a smoker treated himself to a bag of "Bob-White," or other fine Virginia yellow-leaf, but the pipes of the Low-Country planters of forty or fifty years ago were almost invariably filled with Blackwell's Durham, heavily flavored with Tonka bean. And from the shelves of Cross-road stores and plantation commissaries, black-and-gold labels of every size, from the tiny ten-cent package to the impressive pound, set forth the merits of pure North Carolina leaf and blazoned the belligerency of the Durham bull!

So, if the South Carolina Low-Country couldn't use either the songs or the religion of the Tar-heel State, it could do very well with its whiskey and tobacco, and as our vices are often nearer our hearts than our culture or our religion, perhaps —just for that—the two Carolinas were stuck the closer together!

The incense rose from the smoker's pipes and, drawn by the strong draft, floated away to mingle with the heavy acrid smoke from the marsh-smudged campfire. With the party were some noted story-tellers, and these had many things to tell of sports by flood and field. The Doctor was an ardent fisherman, and sometimes hunted, but the Captain had tradition behind him—the background of "Carolina Sports"—and from a father, who had told him much as a boy, he had acquired and stored away rich lore of the hunting field and of the tidal waters that wash the coast from Stono to May River. Knew every deer stand on Pon-Pon, and Cheeha. Knew the very stand—in "White-Oak drive," on Social Hall—where his great-grandfather had killed a buck before the Revolutionary War; where, on the very spot, deer had since fallen to three generations of his descendants! He knew the black-drum drop by the fallen live-oak on the lower Ashepoo; and the famous spot at "Fishburne's Causeway" on the head-waters of the Cheeha, where, at certain times, monster rock-fish bit avidly! Knew how to find the famous "Hole-in-the-Wall" drumfish drop in Broad River by crossing certain "markers" on adjacent islands. Knew where sheepshead always bit alongside the pilings of the old wharf on Station Creek. Knew the very pond on Bay Point where, during the first year of the Confederate War, Captain—later General—Stephen Elliott, daring, as always, stripped and went down into an alligator hole with a looped plow-line, noosed the saurian and hauled him out. Knew that, whatever piscatorial idiosyncracies other wild-duck may indulge, the pin-tail widgeon is never fishy. Knew that Beaufort epicures esteemed

THE TRENCHERMAN AND THE SHARK

the golden-cavally as the finest fish that swims. Knew that a pea-field buck is at his best in August or early September, and in December a two-year old doe is "kidney-covered."

All these things, and many more, the Captain had learned by word of mouth, and along with them many stories of exciting incidents on land and water. These stories the Captain told with extreme deliberation, but fine dramatic effect. He never hurried, but savored each sentence as a connoisseur savors old wine. And he knew the value of the pause.

There were other tales by the campfire, too, told by others, and not all of sports, for the Confederate War was not very far away and Reconstruction was nearer still, and there was much to tell, many stirring scenes to re-enact. And as they talked, the black faces without the camp-fire circle watched intently, and every laugh around the fire was echoed from the outer circle, where the point of every joke was quickly caught and acknowledged with the keen humorous apprehension of most Low-Country Negroes. At last, the fires burned low, and one by one the drowsy campers crept to their blankets and "turned in."

For several successive days the campers pursued "the noiseless tenor of their way"—the usual routine of walking, swimming, fishing, and, now and then with a breeze that favored both ways, sailing a course parallel with the beach for miles toward Charleston, and back again, with the sharpie's sails

THE CAPTAIN

close-hauled and her lee rail awash. So passed the days, and if the nights were not "filled with music" there was always the voice of the sea, angry or subdued according to its mood, and if there was any breeze at all the sea-oats on the sand-dunes were stirred to sibilant whisperings—ten thousand gossips of the dark! And, nearer, around the fire, the pleasant voices of friendly men.

But on another day, toward the end of the trip, an exciting incident broke the placid spell and shook the camp with laughter.

Among the Island campers were several trench-ermen, whose wholesome out-door appetites brought pride to their possessors and reprobation from those who had to supply them with fish, for it has been observed that one's ability or willingness to eat fish is usually in inverse ratio to one's ability or willingness to catch fish.

Chief among these knights of the knife and fork was a gentleman who, then a rice planter, was sought for one August day by a waggish friend with an invitation to join a deer hunt on the following morning. As the master was not at his bachelor-quarters at the settlement, the visitor was advised to search for him in a distant field, and thither he rode. When he reached the spot indicated, there was no master in sight, but, among the weeds on the ricefield-bank, an old Negro mauma crouched over the dying embers of a brush-fire and an empty iron pot, from whose yawning mouth—

THE TRENCHERMAN AND THE SHARK

tragic in its emptiness—a long iron spoon protruded.

"Where's your Mas' Henry, mauma?" she was asked.

" 'E duh sleep, suh."

"Asleep out here in this sun!"

"Yaas, suh, 'e done eat, now 'e duh sleep."

"What did he have to eat?"

"Enty Uh cook fuhr'um? Uh b'ile piece'uh bakin, en' den Uh t'row two quawt uh peas en' two quawt uh rice een de pot, en', attuh 'e done cook, Mas' Henry nyam'um, en' w'en 'e gitt'ru, en' de pot done 'crape, him leddown een de sunhot 'pun de ricefiel' bank fuh tek 'e res'. Shum yonduh! You cyan' shum frum yuh, 'cause de weed so high, but him dey dey!"

Although nearly fifty years have passed, Mas' Henry, none the worse for his Gargantuan exploit, is doubtless still addicted to hoppin'-john and, on wintry days, still enjoys his "place in the sun."

And "Mas' Henry's" appetite accompanied Mas' Henry to Kiawah. When the horn was sounded at mealtimes to call the scattered members of the party from labor to refreshment, and the yellowtail and whiting, but now from the ocean, were almost "flapping in the pan," Mas' Henry's platter, like the North Carolina troops—"first at Manassas, last at Appomattox"—was both first and last on the gastronomic field! And when Mas' Henry's tin cup was passed 'round to the tapster, whose encircling arm clasped tight the wicker-covered demi-

THE CAPTAIN

john of yellow corn, the spirit seemed to gurgle more musically through the narrow neck of the Brobdinagian flagon, and the amber beads sparkled more brilliantly as they fell into the cup, for, like Haiti and the Philippines, they were sure, ultimately, of "benevolent assimilation!"

Dr. Barnwell, more gourmet than gourmand, was a devoted and an expert fisherman, sharing with the Captain the honor and responsibility of supplying the camp table with all the fish taken with hook and line; their catch being supplemented only by the shrimp and mullet that fell to the cast-nets of the Negroes, as they explored in the skiff, at low tide, the narrow tributaries of the lagoon. The Doctor, coming late to mess on several occasions, after a swim and a rub-down, found that the loiterers about the camp had left him little of the fish, for whose capture he had braved the blistering sun along the beach, or afloat and anchored in the channel of the inlet. The Doctor's temper was rather testy, and he expressed himself vehemently in respect to the "pressure of population upon subsistence"—a non-productive and insatiate population, whose pressure had left of subsistence but the heads and tails! But the Doctor's wrath only moved the full-fed men to laughter and, having safely stowed away his cavally and his sailor's-choice, they battened down their hatches and received philosophically, the teapot-tempest of the Doctor's tongue. The gust blew over, but the Doctor had a sardonic streak and a long memory, so he labeled his griev-

THE TRENCHERMAN AND THE SHARK

ance and pigeon-holed it for treatment at the proper time. And the time was at hand!

The waters roundabout were teeming with small sharks, and a six-foot fellow came one morning in front of the camp, and during the early hours of the flood cruised up and down just beyond the rollers, fishing, and picking up the scraps from the camp thrown out by the Negroes on the last of the ebb. The Doctor and the Captain at once began to lay plans for his capture. Among the other fishing-tackle, the campers had brought several hundred feet of shark-line and a "chain-hook," to insure against a shark's cutting himself loose if hooked.

In the early afternoon, at the turn of the tide, as the first rollers of the young flood broke upon the beach, the shark-hook, baited with the head of a large channel-bass, was thrown into the surf, with an empty powder-keg attached as a float. The shore end of the line was made fast to a drift-wood log lying on the beach at high-water mark, and the stage was set. The day had been hot, but as the sun declined a gentle breeze sprang up from the south, and brought to the drowsy campers the soothing solace of the sea. Mas' Henry, having dined to repletion, forsook the shelter of the palmetto-shack for the burning sands of the beach and, flat on his back, with his feet to the sea, he stretched his length, just above the high-water mark, pulled a battered hat over his eyes, and, full of "such stuff as dreams are made on," was soon

THE CAPTAIN

dreaming of fried whiting, curried shrimp, and deviled crabs!

The restless Doctor, his hands behind him, walked the beach, full of his thoughts—thoughts, perhaps, of his ricefields on the beautiful Edisto; perhaps of his student days in Paris; perhaps of his service as surgeon on the bloody fields of the Confederacy; but, whatever they were, they held him intently—so intently, indeed, that he had crossed and recrossed the outstretched shark-line two or three times before he noticed the powder-keg float, rising and falling with the gentle heave of the waves. From the float, the Doctor's eye followed the line up the shelving beach to the driftwood log at high-water mark, and near the log, wrapped in profound slumber, Mas' Henry lay, a ram ready for the sacrifice! The Doctor saw a great light, which quickly gave way to a dark purpose, and with a chuckle, he prepared, even as Abraham, to sacrifice the timely ram! Untying the line from the log, he carefully contrived a slip-knot which he stealthily slipped over the sleeper's feet, and, drawing the noose snugly around his ankles, the Doctor walked away, serene in the consciousness of a good deed well done.

The long afternoon wore on. Inch by inch, the slow rollers crept farther up the beach and broke into creamy foam. The campers drowsed or slept in the sensuous warmth—all save the restless Doctor, who, tense with nervous energy, paced the

THE TRENCHERMAN AND THE SHARK

smooth strand, just above the nearing tide, and watched by turns the lace-like patterns of the breaking surf at his feet, and the powder-keg slowly rising and falling with the rollers off-shore.

The swift rush of a slanting fin, the quick bobbing of the powder-keg buoy! and, as the shore-line tautened, Mas' Henry, flat on his back, moved with great dignity down the beach. The Doctor's war-whoop of delight roused the men in camp, and brought two or three on the run to Mas' Henry's assistance. They were just in time to check his enforced ablutions at the waist, for the shark had pulled him into the water up to the middle, when his rescuers, convulsed with laughter, seized the line, loosed the slipknot noose, and released the aristocratic feet of the most wrathful man that ever trod the sands of Kiawah! The code duello had not then been banned in South Carolina, and Mas' Henry was a ten-pace man! In fact, he intimated that only at a distance of ten paces, could he view the Doctor with equanimity! But, after much sound and foam, the troubled waters were quieted, and the terms of a truce poured from the demijohn!

Meanwhile the unhappy shark, released from his movable anchor on shore, made a dash for liberty, but the tackle held, and, after being played, by turns, for three-quarters of an hour by those who wanted exercise, and didn't mind bruised hands, he was hauled up on the beach and knocked in the head with an axe. The Negroes chopped him up for bait, and with the chain-hook tackle, caught other and smaller

THE CAPTAIN

sharks; but Mas' Henry's fish was, concededly, "the catch of the season."

At last, the day came to break camp. The sharpie —at once boat and bark—was "on the shore," and ready for sea. The surf was light, and two boat-hands, up to their knees in water, held the bow to the beach while the voyageurs drained "the last drop in the well"-beloved demijohn—the stirrup-cup.

There was a wicked twinkle in the Doctor's eye. "Henry," he said, "you will go down to posterity as the only man on this coast who ever caught a shark with his feet."

Mas' Henry glared menacingly. "See here, Osborn, a joke's a joke, but—Yes—Damn!—Yes!"

THE SHARPIE AND THE "TRUS'-ME-GAWD"

Another year, and another day. Another gathering of Pon-Pon planters at the landing on the lower Toogoodoo, ready to embark on another voyage to Kiawah. But with a difference, for the lessons of the preceding year had not been lost and the memory of the chilly night aground on the shell-bank at White Point had spurred them to punctuality, and this time they were all on hand and waiting for the turn of the tide, now almost at the crest of the flood.

The personnel of the party included the congenial spirits of earlier trips—among them Dr. Barnwell and the Captain—but two or three new members, younger men, had been added. And two boats swung at their moorings—the big sharpie, schooner-rigged, and a lighter craft of the same type but a "single-sticker," 16 feet long, carried as a fishing boat and for emergencies.

And the stores included, as usual, five gallons of Lanier's mellow old corn whiskey, and a hundred grains of quinine. These items, the Doctor and the Captain, as purchasing agents, had been directed to procure and bring, never mind what else they forgot. The Doctor and the Captain had not betrayed their trust, but, instead of a huge 5-gallon container, as on previous trips, the precious whiskey was carefully bestowed in two demijohns of two and three gallons, respectively, so that if

THE CAPTAIN

an accident befell one of them some consolation for desolate hearts could still be extracted from the other! Then, too, it was easier to gauge the outflow from the smaller receptacle, and know when to practice self-restraint as the tide ran low.

But the veterans had another reason—a reason of their own—for dividing the liquid treasure. The fishermen of the party, the Doctor and the Captain, were often absent from Camp for hours at a time, fishing in the breakers far up the beach, or off-shore, in the skiff; and while they were away the loungers about the camp, having little else to do, bore heavily upon food and drink. Food mattered little. The waters were full of fish, and a man shared out of his dinner needn't go hungry very long, but drink was another and a more serious matter, for even a five-gallon demijohn has a bottom, and he who would view that bottom before the day came to break camp must write himself down as one who loveth not his fellowman!

The Doctor and the Captain, having been demoted toward the end of the last trip—reduced from three fingers to one and a half—because of the excessive thirst of their friends, expressed themselves bitterly, for the Doctor and the Captain didn't like thimblefuls! But the reproaches of the shared-out men meant little to men mellow with the lion's share, and the bitter words were whistled down the wind.

But the Doctor and the Captain remembered, and when they were directed to buy five gallons

THE SHARPIE AND THE "TRUS'-ME-GAWD"

of corn whiskey and a hundred grains of quinine, they saw that the Lord, loving justice, had delivered those who had scorned and flouted them even into the hollow of their hand, for the quinine could be mixed with the whiskey!

There are men who can drink corn whiskey and quinine. It has been done, tho' it must be regarded as an acquired taste. The Doctor and the Captain took it often, medicinally, and said they liked it, but the Doctor was a stoic, and the Captain wore a beard! The facial contortions of any smooth-faced sober man who attempted a swallow in cold blood, without any preliminary warming up, would recall the writhing serpents of Laocoon, or the countenance of an adolescent Calvinist, bidden on an April Saturday morning, when fish were biting, to put away his rod and bait and memorize the Shorter Catechism against the Sabbath!

So the conspirators put the hundred grains of quinine into the two-gallon demijohn of old yellow corn whiskey, distilled by Jim Lanier, of Salisbury, North Carolina, thereby consecrating the elixir to their own use, as securely as, in the early days of the Mormon Church, the surplus Virgins of the congregation were "sealed" to the Prophet!

Having dosed the smaller demijohn, it was decided to save that for the last, and the members of the party were advised to start on the three-gallon package, and save the other for sickness. The conspirators were perfectly frank, for they knew that only "in case of sickness" would any

THE CAPTAIN

save the Doctor and the Captain have gone beyond the first swallow—a swallow that would have brought, not summer, but a very winter of discontent! And they knew that if the innocents drew the wrong cork and got but a taste of the bitter draft the expedition would have been halted and messengers sent hot-foot for a fresh supply. So the Captain took the smaller demijohn in the smaller boat, which he sailed himself, leaving the big sharpie in the competent hands of Dr. Barnwell, as sailing-master.

The tide was high at noon, and as it turned the boats cast off and drifted down the stream, catching, after awhile, a light breeze that, freshening gradually, held to the journey's end. Just as they rounded White Point, a big-bellied sharpie, schooner-rigged, came up from the sea, wallowing clumsily through the small, choppy waves of the inlet. "Ship ahoy! What ship is that?" the Captain sang out, as she came within hail. A blond giant rose from the stern-sheets, waved his hand impressively, and shouted: "Georgiana of the Wildwoods!" She looked it, for she was as green as the young leaves of a willow-oak! Her owner, a young Norseman who ran a large store on one of the nearby islands, had built and fitted her out for a pleasure craft, and he was returning with a party from a maroon on the Island. No one ever knew where he got the name. Perhaps from some blue-eyed, flaxen-haired girl, left behind in his land of icy winters and passionate sum-

THE SHARPIE AND THE "TRUS'-ME-GAWD"

mers. She may be waiting still, for his life was short. The blue fiords of some far Valhalla may yet float a shallop whose spirit crew will answer to the challenge: "Georgiana of the Wildwoods!"

Long before sunset the two boats landed the voyageurs on the Island, and camp was quickly made. But the mouth of the creek was changed as completely as that of a man who puts shears and razor to his bearded lips and comes forth clean shaven! The channel of last year was now a sandbank, and the strong tides had dredged a new and deeper channel where but now dry land had stood.

A week had passed, and at its end had also passed, as irrevocably, the contents of the three-gallon demijohn. The Doctor and the Captain drank with the rest, but admonished them that when it was empty, only the two-gallon reserve would be left and "something might happen to that." Something had already happened, but, having in good sportsmanship warned the wasters, the conspirators hugged the dread secret to their bosoms with consciences void of offense.

And on the very morning the yellow tide ran low another disaster threatened the camp. Two water-casks had been brought along, each with a week's supply of drinking water. The first had held out the allotted time, but when the second was tapped it was found that a slow leak had allowed all but two or three gallons to drain away into the thirsty sand. A serious matter, for while the brackish water of the island would do for

THE CAPTAIN

cooking, only a very thirsty or a very tipsy man would drink it. A fresh supply, therefore, was imperative, and the Captain volunteered to take a couple of hands in the smaller boat and refill the empty water-cask at Rockville or Little-Edisto. As a decision hung in the balance, Mingo Brown, an expert Negro fisherman and boat-hand who lived on Little-Edisto, persuaded the Captain to adventure there for water, telling him of a fine well near the landing, and offering, as a further inducement, to add to the fleet of the campers his dug-out canoe that could be towed back at the stern of the sharpie and would be serviceable for "casting" for shrimp and mullet in the creek; the skiff they had used on an earlier trip had disappeared.

Soon after breakfast, the boat was cleared, the Captain taking the empty cask, a young nephew as handy-man, and Mingo and his younger brother. The morning was sultry, and the Captain scanned apprehensively the "mackerel" sky, and the long "mare's-tails" that looked more like the tousled, wind-blown locks of the valkirs. "Rain before night," the prophet said. "But I think we can make it. Let's go!"

The tide was more than half-flood, and the breeze though light, should, with the help of the tide, put them at their destination by high water and give them the full strength of the ebb for the run back to camp.

THE SHARPIE AND THE "TRUS'-ME-GAWD"

The run up the inlet was without incident, for the breeze held and the flood-tide went all the way. When the plantation with the vaunted well was reached the sharpie's nose was run up on the shingle and the filling of the water butt was begun. It was not even necessary to remove the cask from its wedged-in position in the boat. The bung was taken out, and in fifteen minutes the Negroes, with a few turns of their buckets, had filled the cask. Then the bung was hammered home, and they were ready to start on the return voyage as soon as Mingo's dug-out could be secured. At the moment, it was serving as a feed trough for the plantation mules, who were eating their mid-day ear-corn under a live-oak fifty yards away from shore. Mingo looked somewhat abashed at the base use to which his coffin-like craft had been put, but he set out, nathless, to exalt its amphibian attributes.

"Cap'n, da' trus'-me-gawd, you shum stan' so, 'e oagly ez uh cross-eye' 'ooman, but him is uh nyuseful t'ing, sho' ez Gawd! You nebbuh haffuh do nutt'n' fuhr'um. 'E nebbuh need no paint, 'e nebbuh 'quire no pitch fuh calk 'e seam, 'cause 'e yent got no seam fuh calk! W'en you done wid'um een de watuh, you kin hice'um out, en' nyuze'um 'puntop de lan' fuh feed mule, en' ef you ent got no mule fuh feed, you kin tu'n'um upside-down 'pun de sho', en' de 'ooman en' t'ing kin seddown 'puntop'um fuh talk, jis' ez sattify ez dat, 'cause 'e yent got no taar 'pun 'e bottom fuh

THE CAPTAIN

spile de 'ooman' frock, en' 'e yent got no nail een'um fuh tayre de 'ooman' hanch. Him is uh cunweeyunt t'ing, Cap'n', but 'e cuntrady too, sukkuh 'ooman. Ef you ent watch'um close, wid you paddle een you han', him fuh tu'n obuh, en' t'row you een de sea!"

By the time Mingo had wound up his panegyric with the sting in its tail, the mules had finished eating, the corn-cobs were thrown out of the whilom trough, and the canoe was hauled down the slope by Mingo and his brother and slid into the water.

The "painter" at its clumsy bow was but a frayed and futile length of cotton plowline with which the Captain would not risk a tow, so three fathoms of half-inch manila rope were substituted, and the bow of the trus'-me-gawd was bound as tightly to the stern of the sharpie as was Mrs. Micawber to the inept bosom of her spouse—with no more prospect of desertion!

The sharpie's single sail was hoisted, the slender sprit slipped in, and, with the Captain at the tiller and the handy-man at the bow, boat and tow, with the impulse of the strong ebb-tide under their keels, moved slowly down the estuary toward the sea.

Fifty years ago flat-bottomed boats, or "sharpies," were in almost universal use along the tidal streams that flow into the North Edisto Inlet on their way to the ocean. In these waters round-bottomed, or keel boats, were seldom found.

THE SHARPIE AND THE "TRUS'-ME-GAWD"

Around Beaufort and in Charleston harbor fine, seaworthy boats of the "Whitehall" or similar type were common, but not on the Dawhoo or the turbid Toogoodoo. Nor, since the war, have the great cypress canoes been in evidence. The art must have passed with the ante-bellum artisans, for in the old days every plantation along the coast, from Georgetown on the east to Dawfuskie on the west, boasted its boat-builders skilled in fashioning out of the light and enduring cypress every craft from the graceful racing-boat, hollowed out of a single stick, to the great piraguas or periaguas—"pattiaugers" or "pettiaugers" in corrupted speech—plantation boats, sixty to seventy feet long and six or seven wide; commonly made of three planks, hewn out with broadaxe, and beautifully fitted together, and finished, with adze and drawing-knife. These piraguas, as long as the war-canoes of the South-Seas, were capable of carrying tons of supplies from plantation to plantation along the coast. And when a planter moved his family from one place of residence to another, the pettiauger took them all in, with servants and supplies—often, indeed, with bedding and furniture, sometimes with piano—or was it the harpsichord?—and, under the impulse of twelve lusty oarsmen, transported them safely and comfortably fifty to seventy-five miles in a day. These boats, made of "the wood everlasting," must have been long-lived, for in the early wills, of State and Colony, many a "pettiauger" was bequeathed to

THE CAPTAIN

"beloved son John" or "beloved daughter Jane."

But under Freedom the freedman swung his broadaxe only to hew the straight sides of "ranging-timber" and crossties, while the use of adze and drawing-knife were refinements in carpentry quite beyond him. So, the pettiauger disappeared from the bays and inlets of the Carolina coast full fifty years before the white-winged Yankee clipper vanished from the Seven Seas! The freedman still made dugout canoes but, freed from the white man's eye, his will was weak and his hand was slovenly, and the product of his labor was clumsy and unseaworthy—so unseaworthy, indeed, as to make singularly appropriate the common appellation of "trus'-me-gawd"—"I trust my God."

The dugout man achieves his trus'-me-gawd, as the caveman achieved his wife—by main strength. First, throwing a tupelo or cypress tree, he borrows, if possible, a cross-cut saw and a brother-in-black, and with their help saws off a twelve-or-fourteen-foot length. If saw and brother can not be borrowed his axe serves as well, for no obligation is imposed upon the trus'-me-gawd to be square at either end. Prying the embryo boat away from the dismembered tree, the axe-man, having an eye to utility rather than symmetry, proceeds to hew, or rather to chew, it away at stem and stern. Having gnawed it into the semblance of a sausage—for his craft is designed to be a double-ender—the artisan glows with pride, feeling that if the—

THE SHARPIE AND THE "TRUS'-ME-GAWD"

"Divinity that shapes our ends,
Rough-hew them as we will,"

should come along, he would find nothing more to do! Then the log is hewn flat on one side, and this, in the fulness of time, will be at once the deck or decks, the stern-sheets, and the fo'c's'le, to say nothing of the gunwales. And now, man having for the moment done his part, Nature, the great mother of us all, is allowed to intervene, for, instead of hollowing out the log by slow and arduous axework, he intends to invoke the aid of fire and burn it out! But the log is full of sap, and sap is water, and as water has always, in a manner of speaking, interfered with the self-determination of fire, the philosopher could only wait until nature dried some of the sap out of the log. Not that he minded waiting, for philosophers can always wait, and a delay of two or three months would make little difference for there were always boats to be borrowed from the neighbors, and the longer the delay in launching his own craft the longer could he postpone the evil day when he might be called upon to return the favor!

At last his log is dry enough to burn, and, having carefully wedged it in position with the hewn side uppermost, a few chops are made along the center and a shallow trench hollowed out, in which fire is kindled with lightwood and dry sticks, and here for hours on several successive days the fire-worshiper sits, watching the flames slowly eating the heart out of the log; the boat-builder helping out

THE CAPTAIN

from time to time with his axe, chipping away the high spots that the fire had touched but lightly, until, between fire and axe, the log, fairly smooth on the inside, is at last a dugout and ready for launching.

If fresh-water run or salt-water creek be near, three or four short round logs are cut, and upon these rollers the canoe is "snaked" through the forest; but if water be distant, horse, mule, or ox, with the running gear of a one-horse wagon, may provide transport. Once at the water's edge the trus'-me-gawd takes to it with as little ceremony as a frog! After the splash the builder watches critically to see if his "coonoo" be down by head or staa'n; or if she list to starboard or port, for the achievement of an even keel at the first launching is beyond the hope of any save a master-builder, the haphazard axe of the plantation artisan aspiring only to an approximation. If the boat be too badly out of trim, she is hauled out of the water, turned upside down, and hacked or hewed into rectitude, as, by the same methods, the early martyrs were brought into line with the true faith!

Once in trim, short pieces of plank are fitted at bow and stern, a couple of thwarts nailed down, a staple driven in the bow for the "painter," an anchor assembled—composite of the rusty shards of broken pots and old plow-points or moldboards—and the trus'-me-gawd is ready to hazard the perils of creek or river or open bay. And the hazard is sometimes great, for in rough water there is no

THE SHARPIE AND THE "TRUS'-ME-GAWD"

clumsier craft—none so prone to turn turtle—yet the coastwise darky will adventure forth in bad weather, loaded to the gunwales with women, shell-oysters, seed-cotton, and anything else he can stow away—but always women, whatever other home-grown commodities may be out of season—her blunt nose bumping the whitecaps under the impulse of the paddler at the stern, while the women bailed as they prayed. Strange that these Negroes and the whites, who should have known and told them, never adopted the simple outriggers in universal use in the South-Seas on similar cranky craft. These primitive devices would have saved the lives of many venturesome freedmen who, caught in sudden squalls in open waters, were swamped, with their faith, in the "trus'-me-gawd!"

For two hours the boats moved down the inlet by grace of the tide alone, for the wind was but a breath, and that breath from the south, against them. The Captain looked up anxiously. He was weather-wise enough to feel the coming squall and knew that 'twould catch them in open water long before they could make camp.

"We're in for a squall, boys," he said. "Can you swim, Mingo?"

"No, suh, Cap'n. Me en' me bredduh, needuh one kin swim," he replied with a laugh, "but Uh yent bodduh 'bout dat, 'cause Gawd nebbuh mek we fuh drowndid."

THE CAPTAIN

"Well, if we are swamped or capsized, you'd better swing to the ropes, and hold on to the gunwales if she fills, or to the centerboard if she turns turtle."

"Cap'n, you needn't fuh bodduh 'bout we, en' we yent haffuh bodduh 'bout ketch no rope en' t'ing fuh sabe we, long ez da' trus'-me-gawd dey dey, 'cause him *haffuh* float. 'E cyan' sink no mo'nuh log, en', ef Gawd choose fuh spill we out'uh Him han' een dis ribbuh teday, me en' me bredduh fuh climb 'puntop de coonoo, Uh dunkyuh w'edduh 'e duh stan' 'puntop 'e top, uh 'puntop 'e bottom, en' we fuh hol' we holt 'tel Gawd drif' we een da' Rockwille maa'sh!" But notwithstanding Mingo's faith, the Captain, looking doubtfully at the clumsy thing wallowing in his wake, thought more than once that when the squall struck it might be necessary to cut the painter and cast the tow adrift, to allow the sharpie greater freedom of action. And the squall was about to strike!

To the south, towering thunderheads, big with the promise of rain that the wispy mare's-tails of the morning had foretold, piled Pelion upon Ossa above the heavy dun cloud-bank that rested upon the gray waters at the horizon's rim. Slowly they reared their fleecy crests toward the zenith, like cobras about to strike!

A filmy sheet of cloud veiled the brazen face of the sun for a moment, then the nearest cobra struck, and the thunderhead swallowed the burning disk! The clouds turned black, and the world grew dark! The wind died suddenly, and not a ripple ruffled

THE SHARPIE AND THE "TRUS'-ME-GAWD"

the glassy surface of the lazy swells. Suddenly, a crooked kris of flame flashed athwart the dark cloud-bank, and there came the sullen thump of thunder! The sharpie's sail hung from the sprit like the broken wing of a wounded gull, while her hull and that of her clumsy tow rolled sluggishly on the oily tide.

A sudden flash of flame that seemed to disembowel the heavy cloud, and the quick crash of thunder followed! Out of the west hurried a witch-like wind-cloud, black locks disheveled and ragged skirts trailing just above the horizon, while under the ominous shadow the waters rumpled and blackened in the squall!

A quick command from the Captain, and the sharpie's spritted sail was deftly furled and lashed. The oars were manned, and the two Negroes bent their backs and pulled with all their might to meet the white-caps rushing toward them like packs of hungry wolves. The pygmy waves looked like towering seas above the low freeboard of the skiff, and as they came tumbling aboard she was half-swamped and driven back, against the utmost efforts of the powerful oarsmen. As her stern bumped against the clumsy, snub-nosed bow of the heavy dug-out—filled at the first break of the squall, and now wallowing awash, too low to feel the impact of the wind, which was driving the lighter craft rapidly out of her course—the Captain had an inspiration and, quickly loosing the tow-rope from the stern, sent the handy-man splashing up to

THE CAPTAIN

the bow to rive it thro' the iron ring, and, shoving the canoe away with a push of the paddle, the two boats quickly changed positions, and the ponderous waterlogged trus'-me-gawd became, by her "masterly inactivity," her inertia, as serviceable a sea-anchor as one could wish for! And this very present help came none too soon! Now, as the rope grew taut and held the sharpie's bow steadily to the wind, all hands commenced to bail and soon lightened her so that she rode the racing waves as buoyantly as a cork, tho' with many a flat-bottomed spank of protest!

Slowly the skiff and her phlegmatic consort drove down the wind, with the lee shore, a point of marsh at the entrance to Bohicket Creek, less than a mile away, while the lightning flashed spitefully, and the almost instant response of the thunder showed that they were near the storm-center.

Then came the rain! Level, stinging rain, that drove through the thin cotton clothing, and lashed like whips! It chilled to the bone, and half-filled the boat with water, but its impact beat the crests off the white-caps and smoothed the seas somewhat.

Altho' the sea-anchor pulled back as stubbornly as a balky mule, yet, under the impulse of wind and rain, the sharpie drove steadily down toward the lee shore; but her head was held to the wind, and the water she took in over the bow was bailed out as quickly as it came in. At last, with the marsh but a hundred yards away, the wind fell to a strong breeze. The sometime angry cloud lifted her rag-

THE SHARPIE AND THE "TRUS'-ME-GAWD"

ged skirts and moved on, as if ashamed of her passionate tempest of tears, and on a rain-washed world the sun looked down and smiled, for the thunder-squall had passed as suddenly as it came.

The tow-line of the trus'-me-gawd was shifted from the sharpie's bow to her stern; the oars were manned, and the boatmen pulled away for an offing. Three hundred yards off shore, the wet sail was unfurled and spread, the sharpie curtseyed to the wind and sped away over the dancing white-caps, her crew drenched, tho' happy and exhilarated over their exciting experience. The heavy tow retarded their progress, for she was full of water and awash, but there was no way to bail her out in the choppy sea and they were quite willing to pull, under sunny skies, a load whose inertia had served them so well when lowering clouds hung over them! Mingo was jubilant. "Cap'n, enty Uh tell you 'bout da' trus'-me-gawd? Ef 'e had'n' bin fuh him, Uh woulduh wet een da' sea!"

The Captain reminded him that he was wet enough, as it was.

"Yaas, suh. Dat so. But Gawd wet we wid Him rain. Him nebbuh t'row de sea 'puntop we."

Just before sunset the water-carriers reached camp with more water than they went for. While they were unloading the water-cask the Doctor came down to the boat.

"Well," he said cheerfully, "we thought you were drowned in the squall, so we stretched the tent-fly and caught rain-water enough to fill half

THE CAPTAIN

the buckets in camp. You need a snifter. Have a drink?" The Captain would, and as he followed the Doctor to the shack and saw that the two-gallon demijohn had been broached, he didn't need the Doctor's wink to account for the coldness of the camp or the dour visages of those who, having swallowed their evening dram, now sat around waiting for supper.

The Captain seated himself on an empty box, and the Doctor poured for him generously, while the others watched and listened. The friendly "glug-glug" of the flagon fell upon their ears, and the amber beads—the rosary of Bacchus—sparkled in the chalice! The Captain bowed with accustomed courtesy, raised the tin cup slowly to his bearded lips and, as they gazed, round-eyed, he sipped! Sipped and smiled, and sipped again, as one who savors sherris-sack or malmsey!

"Rafe," said the Doctor solicitously, "you're wet; you ought to take some quinine, you know. If I can find where I put it, I'll give you a dose."

"Thank you, Osborn," said the Captain sweetly.

HOW THE DEVIL LOST HIS TAIL

The Captain, fond of quizzing Negroes and "feeling" them out, discovered in the early days of the camp that Mingo was full of superstition, from the horny sole of his foot to the kinky crown of his head. And he was a capital story-teller, having on several occasions, when drawn out by "de Buckruh," enlivened the camp-fire by humorous and philosophic reflections upon his fellow-blacks, set forth with the fine sense of dramatic effect that seems inherent in most Negroes. Tragedy, comedy, melodrama were expressed by quickly shifting changes of voice, gesture, and facial expression. And the earnestness with which he would swear to the truth of a fantastic fairy-tale would have convinced any jury that his intentions toward chickens were honorable, even if he were caught in the coop with both hands full of feathers!

But Mingo was at his best when dilating upon "hants," "sperrits," and other mysterious phantoms of the night, without whose occasional manifestations the poor Negro would be deprived of the dearest terrors of his life. So, on the last night of the camp, the Captain laid his plans to give Mingo a shivery thrill, whose echoes and elaborations would keep Little-Edisto in a state of jumpiness for many a month to come!

The Captain had a night-shirt. Men who wore night-gear at all wore night-shirts in those days, for there was nothing else to wear, until, a genera-

THE CAPTAIN

tion later, Billie Burke put pajamas on—the map!

The Captain's night-shirt was home-made, of snowy long-cloth, and fashioned after the pattern of "the Fathers." It was long and straight, and uncompromising as to gores or any deviations whatsoever from the straight line of its fall from the Captain's chin to his ankles; and it fell far, for the Captain was well over six feet!

And it was rough-dried. Men on the plantations —bachelors, at least—seldom bothered with ironed things fifty years ago. The fragrance—the sun-dried sweetness of sheets and pillowslips, thrown over jessamine-trellis or rose-bush to dry, can never be forgotten—and these are the sweetest memories of the days of Reconstruction!

During seven or eight months of the year the community heard little of the Captain's night-shirt, but in summer, when the ladies of the family went away to the mountains, and bachelor-quarters were established on the plantation, it was the Captain's custom, for coolness and comfort, to don the night-shirt at dusk, tilt back his rocking-chair in a corner of the piazza, rest his feet and the bowl of his Powhattan clay pipe on the banister rail, and slowly puff the cool smoke drawn thro' a five foot cane-root stem. Often, as the night wore on, he would draw on his boots, for the little arrow-headed ground-rattlesnakes—the "watch-path" of the Negroes—often lay in wait for frogs in the open places on summer nights. Then, booted and night-shirted, and with a shorter pipe, the Captain would slowly

HOW THE DEVIL LOST HIS TAIL

walk up and down under the overarching oaks of the long avenue, cooling off in the air; alone with his thoughts and the voices of the night. His thoughts were his own—perhaps of the work in hand, always pressing, insistent; perhaps of long-past happier days in his own life, as boy and man; perhaps of the long generations behind him, now mingled with the dust! Brave, kindly, cultured people—men and women—who built houses, planted oaks, and turned the wilderness into a rose-garden; who held spiritual above material things, and by their lives left the world better than they found it. Somewhere, between the gray moss and the stars, their spirits must be abroad, the Captain thought, in the stillness of the summer night!

Not always still, for from far plantation and Negro settlement—Encampment, Battlefield, Mitchell's, even from little homesteads near the Village—came, on quiet moonlight nights, the faint barking of dogs. The rolling, deep-mouthed bay of a hound as he challenged a passer-by; the gruff, assertive bark of the professional watch-dog, conscious of responsibility and authority; the nervous, querulous yelp of a lowly cur, willing to do his duty, but scared to death, and hoping the intruder would go away!

From near at hand, the mournful, quavering cry of the screech-owl. From the deep recesses of a distant swamp, the low muttering of his giant congener, the horned terror of the dark! And, near and far, the forests echoed the whoops, the shouts, the laughter of the barred-owl; from a distance,

THE CAPTAIN

the far-flung "who-o-wah!" full, and round, and sweet, like a trumpet call; nearby, a sudden terrifying scream, and cackling, maniacal laughter! The cry of a bittern from the backwater. The bellowing of great frogs in canal and lagoon. The chirps of crickets and the shrilling of cicadas, the bumping of clumsy beetles through the dark. The whispering hum of other flying things on gauzy wings. The croaking, smothered scream of a frog in the jaws of a snake. The voices of the night!

Sometimes the Captain would pass out of the avenue, cross "the Big-Road" and seat himself on one of the great roots that buttressed a fine live-oak by the roadside, whence he commanded the King's Highway, and the railway running almost parallel forty yards away. The Negroes traveled both roads in passing between the depot and the Cross-roads and intermediate settlements, and on nights when the white-robed Captain was abroad they seldom passed without a thrill!

Lucky the wayfarers if the Captain walked in the avenue when he first came within their view, for, tho' the shadows were deep under the oaks on dark nights and the moss-draped boughs wrought ghostly patterns in the moonlight, there was still a fence between, and the railway and the Big-Road were open at both ends!

Sometimes those who passed saw at the far end of the dim aisle, against the somber background of the ivied ruin, a tall white thing that moved slowly and with precision, as one would step ten paces

HOW THE DEVIL LOST HIS TAIL

where disputants face death, or as the great white crane, with dagger poised, stalks through the shallows! And above the shrouded figure hung a wisp of smoke, as vapors veil the bosom of a lake at night! That wisp of smoke was sometimes all that kept black feet upon the ground, for not even the most superstitious among them believed that wraiths and plat-eyes could puff Bull Durham!

"Lookuh da' t'ing! Lookuh da' t'ing! Shum! Shum!"

"Yaas, Uh shum, but Uh yent 'f'aid'um, 'cause Uh see da' smoke, enty? W'en Uh shum, Uh know 'e duh Mas' Rafe, een 'e shu't-tail, duh walk ab'nue duh night-time, same lukkuh Gawd walk een Him gyaa'd'n een de cool uh de day."

But all of them didn't know the Captain's habit of taking the night air, and if a chattering group containing women chanced to come along while the Captain rested under the buttressed oak by the roadside, the "Spirit of the Time" would teach them such speed, as only a scared darky with his "foot in his hand" could attain. If the Captain heard them coming, in time, he would step behind the oak and wait until his victims came within range—near enough to get the full effect of the white robe, yet not near enough to make out the long chestnut beard—beards being regarded as not necessarily appurtenant to those who walk in the spirit. Then, from behind the oak, an apparition as pallid as the pale horse of the Apocalypse, would step slowly

THE CAPTAIN

forth, and wave long arms, as if in warning to those who would be saved!

One look was enough. "Oh, Gawd! Wudduh dat? Wudduh dat?"

"Oh, me Jedus! Uh dunno wuh 'e yiz, en' Uh yent got time fuh ax'um. Uh *gwine!*"

"Hukkuh you git home so fas'? Uh t'aw't you bin gone to de praise meet'n' to Pa Lestuh' chu'ch, en' now you come back befo' you gone half way! Wuh you do wid dem t'ree t'odduh 'ooman wuh staa't out wid you fuh gone to de chu'ch? Dem come back, too?"

"Bubbuh! Don' ax me nutt'n' 'bout no 'ooman. Da' t'ing maybe ketch'um en' cya'um 'way een de element fuh all me know 'bout de 'ooman."

"T'ing! Wuh t'ing dat?"

"Lemme tell you. We fo' 'ooman binnuh gwine 'long de big-road, en' all binnuh talk one time. Sookey Wineglass him bin een de lead, 'cause 'e hab hebby shoe 'pun 'e foot, en' ef somebody haffuh step 'puntop'uh snake een de road, 'e mo' bettuh fuh Sookey fuh do'um, enty? Berrywell. So Sookey bin walk fus', en' me bin jis' behin'um, en' me en' him bin hab uh hebby 'spute 'bout sperrit. Sookey say ef him ebbuh meet one dem t'ing duh paat', him gwine quizzit'um sho' ez Ebe got Adam' rib! 'E say him gwine ax'um wuh 'e name, en' weh 'e come frum, en' w'edduh de ainjul sen'um down yuh fuh watch Nigguh en' see wuh dem duh do. But Uh tell'um, 'No, man! Dem t'ing ent fuh 'tarrygate! Le'm'lone! Ef Uh ebbuh chance fuh

HOW THE DEVIL LOST HIS TAIL

come 'cross'um, Uh gwine g'em de road! Him tek him road, en' me tek my'own! En' ef da' sperrit ent tu'n 'roun' berry swif', me fuh tek my'own fus'!'

"W'en Uh tell'um dat, Sookey suck 'e teet' at me, en' 'e say 'Shuh!' *him* ent 'f'aid da' t'ing none'tall. Jis' ez 'e say dat, 'e holluh, 'Oh, Gawd!' en' Uh shum 'toop down, but Uh nebbuh stop fuh see w'edduh 'e duh tek off 'e shoe, uh hice 'e 'coat, 'cause w'en Uh look, me eyeball' pop! De sperrit walk frum behine de tree! 'E stan' nine foot high! 'E shroud reach down to 'e foot! Fire duh bu'n een 'e mout', en' smoke come out'um, en' rise een de ele*ment* lukkuh you duh bu'n trash! W'en Uh shum stan' so, bubbuh! Uh reach down, Uh graff me sku't by 'e bottom, Uh hice'um up to me crotch, Uh loose me two foot, Uh tu'n 'roun' 'pun me backtrack, en' Uh *gone!* Uh see de fiah-fly duh fly 'bout een de daa'k, ez Uh pass'um by, Uh yeddy me foot beat de du't, en' da' duh all! Me foot 'tretch'out wide, sukkuh rokkoon' foot 'tretch'out w'en you nail 'e skin 'pun de do' fuh dry, en', fus' t'ing Uh know, Uh git home!"

But after a while, the more sophisticated Negroes enlightened their brothers and sisters as to the man in white who walked abroad on summer nights, and the avenue gradually lost its terrors!

The Captain enjoyed another distinction in the possession of the most distinguished rooster in the community, a present—with a couple of companions of the opposite sex—from a clerical kinsman in Charleston.

The huge fowl, a "Light Brahma" of high Orien-

THE CAPTAIN

tal ancestry, was as tall as a turkey gobbler, and weighed 14 pounds. He was feathered to his feet, and when he ran the rustling of feathered legs against each other was as the *frou-frou* of Mid-Victorian starched pantalettes, when the poor little girls that wore them—yearning to be tomboys—tried to run! And when the rooster crowed he reared back as impressively as a certain professor in Columbia, "learned in the law," when about to make a speech!

His style, his weight, and his plumage made the Captain's rooster the envy of all the dusky sisters that came about the place, and, one by one, with many a simpering smile, with many a conciliatory curtsey, they besought the Captain to lend the tall fowl, if only for a day, that his majestic proportions might be gazed upon by the feathered proletariat of their humble hen-roosts. "Do, Mas' Rafe! Do, please, suh, len' me da' roostuh, ef only fuh one day, my Maussuh, so Uh kin ketch de breed. Uh yent got nutt'n' fuh gi' you, but ef you do'um, Uh do you uh fabuh sometime, sho' ez Gawd!"

But the Captain was wary, and resisted all their pleadings—not because they had no "Exchange Professor" to offer in return, but he knew that if once they "caught the breed," the presence of Light-Brahma feathers in their yards would be justified ever after.

"Old Bo'sun" summed it up succinctly: "Go 'way gal! You cyan' git da' roostuh! Buckruh fedduh blonx een Buckruh yaa'd, en' Nigguh fedduh blonx

HOW THE DEVIL LOST HIS TAIL

een Nigguh yaa'd; en' ef Buckruh fedduh chance fuh grow 'puntop Nigguh fowl, ebb'rybody gwine s'pishun you t'ief'um, eb'n ef da' fowl blonx to you, en' you c'arricktuh gwine spile. Go 'long 'bout you bidness. Go 'long! Go 'long!"

The tall rooster had long since been called to roost among those that, living worthily, have been summoned to higher places—the worthiness of his life attested by the number of his descendants that, for many generations thereafter, peeped and squawked and crowed and clucked and cackled about the Oak Lawn farmyard, moving with their progenitor's awkward goose-like gait, and sporting on hackle and tail the distinctive white feathers tipped with black!

But the long night-shirt went with the Captain to Kiawah, and the recollection of the havoc it had wrought upon the nerves of the Pon-Pon people, tempted him to try its supernatural suggestiveness upon the imaginative Mingo. So, taking the other members of the party into his confidence, he set the stage and laid the plot to lead up to a dramatic climax.

The last evening at Camp was a merry one. Resentment at the Doctor's prank had worn off somewhat, for they had learned how to gulp down the bitter stuff, with scant consideration for the palate. After all, the effect was what they wanted, and, as none would admit that he really liked the taste of corn whiskey, even when unmixed with quinine, why worry about a bitterness that could at least

THE CAPTAIN

be made aromatic by chewing a bit of dried calamus root after each snifter! So the hours passed in friendly intercourse, until the time came to set the trap for the event of the evening.

Now and then a Low-Country gentleman, having occasion for forceful speech yet mindful of the scriptural injunction, "swear not at all," will, in a spirit of compromise, express determination "By the Ghost of Lignum-Vitae!"—a mouth-filling oath, pleasing to the ear and, withal, without reproach to the conscience! So the Captain, clearing his throat impressively, began to improvise, for Mingo's benefit, the tragic story of the Ghost!

"Men said Lignum-Vitae's heart was hard. It was. No harder heart was known in all the pathless forests of Guiana where, as the years rolled on, Lignum-Vitae grew from a tiny sprout to a giant of the woods, to fall at last, because his heart was hard, under the axe of a tawny savage. He fell, gentlemen, but not to die! His body, cruelly dismembered, yet lives to justify his name! In the crude clubs of jungle savages near at hand, Lignum-Vitae—hard and ruthless always—crushes the skulls or breaks the joints of other savages at war! In the far-flung forums of peaceful peoples, gavels, cut from Lignum-Vitae's heart, call lords and commoners, senators and deputies to order, as the centuries march by! Men live their lives, for good or ill, and return to dust; dynasties rise, crumble, and fall; parties form, live their day, and make way for those who sometime have opposed them;

HOW THE DEVIL LOST HIS TAIL

but the body of Lignum-Vitae lives on, for 'the whirligig of time brings in his revenges,' and the gavel that raps down Conservatives today may discipline Liberals tomorrow!

"So much for his body, gentlemen," said the Captain, with vibrant voice, looking through the inner circle toward Mingo, who, crouched on the outside, hung upon every word with tense interest. "So much for his deathless body, but what of his soul! that restless spirit that walks the earth on dark or stormy nights?—"

The Captain paused eloquently, and scanned the sky, now overcast. The wind from the east, tho' light, was rising, and the sea-oats rattled creepily. The Captain's signal was understood, and a tall member of the party quietly withdrew from the circle around the fire and passed behind the mess-tent where, earlier in the evening, the ghostly night-shirt had been carefully concealed.

The Captain's voice rose, and became tremulous! "What of the spirit, gentlemen, the dreadful spirit that prowls through the dark on nights when moon and stars are hid, seeking another body to replace his own, that men have cut to pieces? Lignum-Vitae was black, or nearly so, and his spirit can never rest until it finds a man whose body is as black as the body that was lost. Then the ghost will throw away the black man's spirit and enter into his body. That is why, on cloudy nights, all black men's spirits are in danger, and the most fearful oath that men can swear is *'By the Ghost of Lignum-Vitae!'* "

THE CAPTAIN

As the Captain reached his climax he rose suddenly and looked toward the creek. The Doctor, beside him, sprang to his feet and, pointing in the same direction, shouted in an agonized voice: "My God! What's that?" Mingo, already pop-eyed with fright, jumped up to "view with alarm" a tall, shrouded figure advancing slowly thro' the darkness. 'Twas only a tall camper in the Captain's nightshirt with a towel tied over his head, but Mingo saw a disembodied spirit seeking a dark person of just about Mingo's size and color, whose spirit he would presently evict, and take over the tenancy of his body!

As the apparition met his eye-balls, Mingo almost turned in the air and bolted for the sand-dunes, crashing thro' the sea-oats like a Cape-buffalo in the Papyrus, tho' uttering such yells as no buffalo could ever have managed! And the other Negroes were close at his heels.

The camp rocked with laughter. When it had subsided, the Campers shouted, in turn, for the recall of the runaways. But no answering voice came back, and, after half an hour, members of the party walked up the beach, blowing the horn and at intervals calling the Negroes by name. At last, after they had gone a mile, their hail was answered, and the frightened fugitives came out of the reeds and returned with them to camp.

Mingo's teeth were still chattering. The Captain poured him out a stiff drink of the bitter whiskey.

HOW THE DEVIL LOST HIS TAIL

When it had warmed him up, he was asked: "Why did you run, Mingo? That was only a gentleman walking in his night-shirt to keep cool."

"Yaas, suh, Cap'n, Uh know dat. But w'en Uh yeddy suh da' Ghosh duh hunt fuh Nigguh wuh stan' black lukkuh me, en', w'en 'e ketch'um, him fuh t'row'way de Nigguh' sperrit, en' tek de Nigguh' body fuh walk 'bout een, no, suh! Uh cyan' tek chance fuh 'low da' t'ing fuh creep up on me, long ez Uh got me two foot! No, suh! Uh got nyuse fuh me own meat! Da' Ghosh cyan' tek *my* meat en' mek cunweenyunce out'um fuh peruse 'bout een'um same ez ef de meat bin britchiz, eeduhso shu't! Uh got black-snake skin, fuh true, but duh my'own, enty, suh? Leh da' Ghosh gone to dem sabbidge wuh chop'um up een da' wood, en' tek *dem* meat, ef 'e shame fuh walk duh paat' een 'e shu't-tail!" An argument that none could dispute.

The Captain, in high spirits over the outcome of his ghost-story, was moved, in a spirit of generosity, to give Mingo a turn at the role of Sheherezade, and at the same time satisfy his curiosity as to a remark Mingo had made the day they were caught in the thunder-squall. "Mingo," said he, "the other day when I told you those mare's-tails in the sky meant rain, what the devil did you mean by calling them 'devil's-tails' or 'shift-tails'?"

"Cap'n, dem t'ing iz shif'-tail fuh true, en debble-tail, too, alltwo one time. Ef you please, suh, gimme anodduh leetle tetch, Uh tell you 'bout'um."

The "leetle tetch"—a generous dram—was poured

THE CAPTAIN

out and gulped down, and Mingo, now as mellow as a medieval monk at the vintage, began.

"One time, Debble meet 'Ooman duh paat'. Debble is uh berry mannussuble man wid 'Ooman, so, w'en 'e shum 'e t'row 'e tail obuh 'e aa'm, same lukkuh 'e bin cloak, en' mek'um uh berry stylish bow. De 'Ooman toss 'e head, 'e grin, 'e ketch 'e frock by de bottom wid alltwo 'e han', 'e hice'um up to 'e knee, en' 'e drap'um uh low cutchy, 'cause him en' Debble git'long berry well, *berry* well!

"Attuh de time uh day done pass, de Debble ax de 'Ooman how 'e mek'out 'long de man; w'edduh 'e done l'aa'n how fuh manage de man, en' fetch'um to 'e han'. De 'Ooman laugh. 'Budduh,' 'e say. 'Hukkuh you kin ax me dat? Enty you l'aa'n me how fuh 'ceitful? Enty you show me how fuh do'um? Enty Uh folluh yo' exwice? Uh got de man gwine! 'E dunno w'ich way 'e duh gwine—but 'e gwine my way, enty?'

" 'Tell me how you do'um,' de Debble say.

" 'Uh got good ecknowledge how fuh fool de man. Uh got 'tring tie 'pun de man, en' w'en we git to de fawk uh de road, weh one de road lean one side, en' t'odduh road lean t'odduh side—w'en Uh git to da' place, ef Uh gwine one road, Uh pull de 'tring fuh lead de man een de t'odduh road. W'ichebbuh road Uh want, Uh pull de man een de road wuh Uh *yent* want, 'cause de stubbunt creetuh so cuntrady en' haa'dhead, ef him see me foot lean fuh one road, him foot fuh lean to de t'odduh one, 'cause him t'ink man fuh hab 'e own way. Him eegnunt to dat! So

HOW THE DEVIL LOST HIS TAIL

dat how Uh gitt'um fuh trabble my road, en' de man nebbuh know weh 'e duh gwine, but 'e ben' 'e neck en' pull de load, jis' ez sattify ez ox wuh done bruk!'

"De Debble mek 'e mannus to de 'Ooman. 'Paa'dnuh,' 'e say. 'You do berry well. You smaa't, fuh true! How you do 'bout money? You tek all de man got? You s'aa'ch 'e pocket?'

"'Uh s'aa'ch 'e pocket, yaas,' de 'Ooman say, 'but Uh too smaa't fuh tek all 'e mek. Ef Uh do dat, him will stop wu'k, enty? Uh cyan' 'low'um fuh do dat! No, budduh! So, ebb'ry night Uh s'aa'ch de man' pocket attuh 'e drap 'sleep. Uh yent tek all 'e money one time. Uh yent bite'um hebby; Uh jis' pinch'um light. Den, nex' mawnin', Uh watch-'um close, w'en 'e pit on 'e britchiz. Sometime 'e run 'e han' een 'e pocket en' pull out 'e money. "Eh, eh!" 'e say. "Uh t'aw't Uh bin hab mo'nuh dis!" Uh ax'um ef 'e bin count'um befo' 'e gone 'sleep. "No," 'e say, "Uh nebbuh count'um, but Uh t'aw't Uh bin hab mo'nuh dis." W'en 'e say dat, Uh know 'e duh git s'pishus, en' 'e gwine count 'e money befo' 'e tek off da' britchiz da' same berry night. So, soon ez 'e gone 'sleep, Uh creep easy to da' pocket, en', 'stead'uh tek some de money out, Uh pit some mo' money een de man' pocket. W'en 'e gitt'up duh mawnin' soon, Uh watch'um, en' Uh shum sneak off een de cawnuh fuh count 'e money. De mo' 'e count'um, de mo' 'e 'cratch 'e head, 'cause 'e got mo' money duh mawnin' den 'e bin hab w'en 'e gone 'sleep duh night. Uh ax'um wuffuh 'e duh 'cratch 'e head. 'E say 'e money ent come out right. Uh

THE CAPTAIN

ax'um hummuch 'e loss. 'E say 'e yent loss none, dat w'at bodduhr'um. De nex' night, en' two-t'ree mo' night, Uh do de same t'ing. Uh pit leetle bit uh money een de man' pocket wid him'own, en' ebb'ry mawnin' de man 'cratch 'e head fuh try fuh 'splain'um, but 'e cyan' do'um. Den, Uh watch me chance, en' de fus' night de pocket stan' fat, Uh bite-'um! En' Uh bite'um deep! W'en de man gone een 'e pocket nex' mawnin' en' see how 'e stan', 'e holluh, en' 'e holluh loud! Uh ax'um wuh 'e duh groan 'bout, en' Uh tell'um him nebbuh bin loss no money 'cause 'e count ent wu't'! En' Uh 'membuhr'um 'bout dem time 'e count bin run obuh. Attuh Uh do dat, 'e nebbuh crack 'e teet' no mo'! De man' pocket duh my'own en' me han' fuh dey een'um long ez Uh lib! Ebb'ryt'ing wuh de man got duh my'own, en' Uh nyuze'um ez Uh please. Uh 'low'um fuh hab 'e han' en' 'e foot 'cause him haffuh wu'k fuh me, enty? Uh mek 'e yeyeball see puhzac'ly wuh Uh wan'um fuh see. Uh mek 'e yez yeddy puhzac'ly wuh Uh wan'um fuh yeddy, en' ef de man' eye en' 'e yez cyan' see en' yeddy fuh suit, Uh tell'um 'e yez en' t'ing ent wu't'. En' him *b'leebe* me! Budduh! De po' creetuh *b'leebe* me, 'cause him is nutt'n' but Man, en' me en' you duh de 'Ooman, enty? Berry well.'

"De Debble grin. 'Tittuh,' 'e say. 'You *done* fuh schemy! Ef dishyuh britchiz wuh Uh got on bin hab pocket, Uh wouduh 'f'aid fuh come close you! You done fuh schemy!'

"De Debble quile 'e tail, 'e t'row'um obuh 'e aa'm.

HOW THE DEVIL LOST HIS TAIL

'E tell de 'Ooman, 'So long, tittuh! Uh fuh see you 'gen, bumbye, enty?' en' 'e gone!

"De 'Ooman suck 'e teet'. 'Uh bin fool,' 'e say. 'Uh hab bidness fuh tek da' tail off'um w'ile Uh had'um een me han'. Uh coulduh do'um easy. Now, 'e git'way en' gone, en' Uh dunno w'en Uh gwine git chance fuh ketch'um 'gen. Da' Satan iz uh 'ceitful t'ing, sho's you bawn! Him ent hab uh Gawd' nyuse fuh 'e tail, 'cep' fuh switch'um 'roun' fuh bresh fly off'um, en' Uh yeddy suh da' place weh him lib stan' too hot fuh fly. None ent fuh dey dey. En' ef Uh bin hab dat tail Uh coulduh nyuze'um berry well, 'cause 'e long sukkuh plow line, en' Uh coulduh 'tretch'um 'twix' two tree en' heng me shimmy en' t'ing 'puntop'um fuh dry.'

"De mo' de 'Ooman study 'bout da' Debble' tail de mo' 'e hankuh attuhr'um, en' 'e mek up 'e min' suh da' tail haffuh git! 'E lub da' tail 'tel 'e dream 'bout'um. Him know 'e fuh shum 'gen, 'cause de Debble him ent fuh gone fudduh frum 'Ooman' sku't! So 'e wait 'e chance en' watch fuhr'um, en' ez 'e watch 'e scheme.

"De 'Ooman know suh de Debble kin fly, 'cause 'e got wing sukkuh le'dduh-wing bat, en' him know de way 'bout 'mong de cloud, 'cause him bin lib een de element one time, 'tel 'e git mischeebus, en' Gawd t'row'um out. En' de 'Ooman know suh lightnin' berry lub fuh 'trike i'un, en' 'e t'ink ef him kin git chance fuh tie wire 'puntop de Debble' tail, en' 'suade'um fuh fly een de cloud w'en t'unduh duh roll, de lightnin' will hab chance fuh cutt'um off. Berrywellden.

THE CAPTAIN

"Jis' ez de 'Ooman done mek 'e plan de Lawd t'row de Debble een de 'Ooman' han'! Yuh 'e come! 'E prance 'long wid 'e tail quile obuh 'e aa'm, 'tel de 'Ooman haffuh clap 'e han'! 'Ki!' de 'Ooman say. 'Uh nebbuh see shishuh stylish tail lukkuh you got! En' shishuh wing! Ef Uh bin hab wing lukkuh dat, Uh woulduh climb da' t'unduh-cloud, en' look down 'puntop de buzzut' back.' De 'Ooman sweetmout' de Debble summuch, en' nice'um up, 'tel, fus' t'ing you know, de 'Ooman wrop de wire 'roun' de Debble' tail close to 'e hanch. 'E tell'um fuh hice 'e tail up stiff, sukkuh lightnin'-rod, en' gone!

"Ki! De Debble do lukkuh de 'Ooman tell'um, same ez ef him bin man! 'E 'tretch 'e wing, en' 'e shoot up een de sky. T'unduh duh wait fuhr'um! Soon ez 'e come close, lightnin' flash 'e shaa'p knife out de cloud, same lukkuh snake lick out 'e tongue, 'e ketch de wire, en' 'e cut off da' tail clean ez ef you bin chop'um off wid axe!

"De Debble clap 'e two han' to 'e hanch. Nutt'n' dey dey! 'Eh, eh!' 'e say. 'Da' debble'ub'uh 'Ooman fool me out me tail, fuh true!'

"Ebbuh sence da' time, de Debble ent got no tail, 'cause da' tail dey een de sky, 'tretch' out; en', w'en 'e gwine we'dduh, de tail kibbuh wid de 'Ooman shimmy en' t'ing, heng out fuh dry. En' dem shif'tail flap 'bout de sky de day befo' de rain come, but w'en de rain git close, you nebbuh shum, 'cause de 'Ooman tek dem shimmy off de line so 'e yent fuh wet."